ANGEL

ANGELS *of the* FLOOD

Also by Joanna Hines
from Simon & Schuster/Pocket Books

Improvising Carla
Surface Tension

ANGELS
of the
FLOOD

Joanna Hines

SIMON &
SCHUSTER

LONDON · SYDNEY · NEW YORK · TORONTO

First published in Great Britain by Simon & Schuster UK Ltd, 2004
A Viacom company

Copyright © Joanna Hines, 2004

1 3 5 7 9 10 8 6 4 2

Simon & Schuster UK Ltd
Africa House
64–78 Kingsway
London WC2B 6AH

www.simonsays.co.uk

Simon & Schuster Australia
Sydney

A CIP catalogue record for this book
is available from the British Library

Hardback ISBN 0-7432-4017-0
Trade paperback ISBN 0-7432-4799-X

Typeset by SX Composing DTP, Rayleigh, Essex
Printed and bound in Great Britain by
Mackays of Chatham plc, Chatham, Kent

For Caroline V and Caroline M
both links with Italy and best of housemates
with love and gratitude
and for all the *Angeli del Fango* who shared those
strange months in Florence in 1967

PART I

Chapter 1

Marsyas

David Clay was wondering what it was like to be skinned alive. The most excruciating pain, surely. Unimaginable terror. Strange, then, that the figure he was looking at radiated serenity, as though the people round him had sharpened their blades simply to shave his stubble or lance a boil. Not to remove, inch by agonizing inch, the entire burden of his skin.

The victim was suspended upside-down from a branch by a heavy cord tied round his ankles – neat, hairy ankles topped off with cloven feet. There was another rope around his wrists, which were hanging down below his head. Considering the agony of his position and the torture about to begin, he looked grotesquely relaxed.

'Marsyas is about to be flayed,' Kate said. 'That's flayed as in "skinned alive". It was his punishment for presuming to compete with the gods – a lesson for us all, you might think.'

David nearly hadn't bothered to come but this was turning out more interesting than he'd expected. A casual invitation from an old friend he'd not seen in years wasn't usually enough to persuade him to spend his afternoon in a lecture hall, but at the last moment curiosity triumphed. It was Kate Holland who was speaking, after all – not just any old aquaintance. So he'd hurried through the midsummer rain to join the audience at the National Gallery and found a seat in the packed lecture theatre between a stern-faced woman with white hair and a couple of foreign students who sat with pencils poised over their pads, ready to jot down every word.

Kate had kept her audience spellbound for over forty minutes. She spoke well and clearly and her material was fascinating. David found it hard to believe she could have ever suffered from public-speaking phobia, as she'd claimed when they bumped into each other a few days earlier. 'I don't know why I'm inviting you,' she'd said with a laugh. 'I get nervous enough without old friends peering up at me from the audience.'

No sign of nerves now. She looked good, every inch the confident public speaker. Middle age had been kind to her. Kate had the kind of attractiveness that lasts, good bones, a strong, intelligent face and expressive brown eyes. She'd kept her figure too and knew how to show it to advantage. An ebony jacket in some kind of silky material was stretched to shining tension by her full breasts and her skirt fell in an uneven swoop from her hips. It was an outfit which indicated both authority and style, while her high-heeled sandals, in sizzling blood-red, warned against too easy pigeonholing. Clothes to match her performance: highly professional but not for one moment predictable or dull.

Now David came to think of it, she looked a hell of a lot better than she had done the last time he saw her, which, if you didn't count their chance meeting at the South Bank earlier in the week, was over twenty-five years ago. Back then she'd been drugged against the pain, lying in an iron bed in an Italian hospital ward with a helmet of bandages clamped to her head. Back then Francesca's recent death had cast an impossible shadow between them. 'I want to forget,' she told him, or words to that effect. 'I don't want to see you again, not ever.' Thus breaking his youthful heart, probably. Those first rejections are always the worst, he reflected, before you've learned that even the sharpest pain dulls with time.

Kate was explaining that the painting on the screen was a copy of the famous Titian that hangs in Prague. 'In Titian's far greater original,' she told them, 'the first cut has already been made into Marsyas's flesh and a small dog laps the blood as it falls. Here, however, all is anticipation.' She paused and hooked a strand of dark hair over her ear before adding quietly, 'All the horror lies ahead.'

A memory stirred at the back of David's mind. *All the horror lies ahead.* Where had he heard those words before? A line of poetry, perhaps, or a phrase from a film? No, it was more personal than that. Whatever its origins, the sentence came freighted with an aura of menace. He was in a strange house, the kind of house you visit in dreams, a remote place detached from the everyday world. It was a house of breathtaking beauty, but sinister in some kind of way he couldn't explain, which made him keep glancing over his shoulder. And now he realized it was a woman's voice echoing in his mind – *all the horror lies ahead* – a voice associated with cool morning light, which was somehow eerie, as though filtered through mist. There was the scent of woodsmoke in empty rooms. For a moment, the intensity of the memory made him almost forget where he was.

Frowning, he focused on Kate again. She had paused, glanced down at him and caught his eye. He got the feeling something was bothering her too. Was it possible the words had triggered a similar memory for her?

She cleared her throat and looked back at her notes. 'So,' she resumed briskly, 'since my subject is Conservator as Detective, where is the mystery in this painting? We've looked at how X-ray helps us to unravel the artist's journey, and now this painting of the unfortunate Marsyas illustrates another kind of puzzle, that of the Amateur Vandal. Let me show you what I mean.'

It was her voice that was doing it to him. Voices are always so evocative; no wonder it was the singing of the sirens rather than their beauty that drove mariners to destruction. Kate's was cool and musical, a flute in the orchestra of voices, with just a lingering trace of the old-fashioned army vowels of her childhood. The sound, forgotten for so many years, was coaxing him away from the present. Fragments of his long-buried youth were breaking free and drifting back into his memory, disjointed fragments he'd never expected to encounter again: those strange weeks in his nineteenth year, a time out of time, when he'd been hardly more than a cauldron of teenage hormones cobbled together in a young man's body, and he and Kate had worked together in the mud and dust of Florence after the catastrophic flood of 1966 – how could he have forgotten those most intense weeks of his life?

He was all attention now as she showed her audience details from the Marsyas painting: a snake emerging from its discarded skin, a luminous husk portrayed by a few deft brushstrokes of pearly paint. 'We might feel the symbolism is somewhat heavy-handed,' she said, with a smile that made her audience complicit in the judgement. 'The snake sheds its skin in order to renew itself, whereas for Marsyas its loss means torment and death. So far so good – unless, of course, you're Marsyas. But what are we to make of these two characters?'

She clicked forward to the next image and a small rat-like creature with an insect between its jaws filled the screen. 'Here we have what looks like a rat eating a tasty bee.' Her tone was relaxed, almost conversational, indicating that she was launching into a light-hearted appendix to the main body of her argument. 'An art historian who tried to figure out the symbolism here would be wasting their time: this detail has been added within the last twelve months.'

Kate paused to look intently at the screen. When she next spoke David had the impression she'd departed from her prepared notes and was speaking the thoughts just as they came to her. 'We have no idea why this curious detail was added or by whom, since the painting was sent to my studio by an owner who insists on remaining anonymous. Why? A rat eats a bee . . . maybe its purpose is to depict a small act of violence in contrast to the monstrous crime being inflicted on poor Marsyas, but then again . . .'

She hesitated for a second time. David wondered why she was spending so long on this picture, since the example it contained was hardly central to her argument. She frowned at the image on the screen, almost as though seeing it for the first time. The two students next to him ceased their diligent scribbling and looked up, waiting for her to continue.

'So *that's* the secret, I knew I'd seen it before.' And now Kate let the words fall so quietly that in spite of the microphone clipped to her lapel David had to strain his ears to catch what she was saying. 'But why send it to me? And who—?'

This time, when she stopped talking, it was obvious the
break was unscripted, no longer a pause for dramatic effect but
a silence that was spinning out into unbearable tension.

Get on with it, Kate, just get on with the bloody lecture,
David was willing her to continue. Behind him, the audience
had begun to fidget and murmur their complaint. Prestigious
lecturers weren't supposed to lose the plot. David's armpits grew
damp with anxiety. Was this what she'd meant when she talked
about public-speaking phobia? Don't screw up now, Kate, for
God's sake. You had them eating out of your hand a minute
ago. Whatever's distracting you, forget about it till this is over.
Just get on with it and finish the damn lecture.

But Kate seemed to have forgotten where she was. She stared
at the screen. Oblivious to the ripples of unease in her audience,
she raised her left hand to her mouth and bit the edge of her
thumbnail thoughtfully. David felt suddenly winded by the
gesture. The first time he'd seen her, or the first time he'd
noticed her, or maybe it was the first time he'd singled her out
as the girl he wanted, the one he was going to fall in love with,
she'd been in some kind of bar or café – it must have been
Florence, but the background was a blur, and so were the faces
round her. A young Kate, fresh out of school, with her dark hair
slanting over her shoulders and her eyes glowing with that
particular Kate-enthusiasm that people were drawn to. She'd
been laughing at a joke, no doubt obscene – most of the group's
jokes were obscene back then – and then something had been
said, maybe the joke was deflected on to her. The laughter had
died in her eyes, she'd withdrawn, sat back from the group and
raised her hand to her mouth and thoughtfully she'd bitten the
edge of her thumbnail. David had wanted to take her hand in
his and kiss her right there, in front of everyone. And now . . .

Now, he just wanted her to speak again. Say something, anything that would show she was back in control of her lecture. He was sitting forward in his seat: just finish, Kate. You're nearly there. Just finish the goddamn lecture.

Kate shuddered, like someone coming out of a trance. Blinking, she turned back to her audience: she looked almost startled to see there were still other people in the room.

'Conservation as detective work. Yes.' Frowning, she checked her notes. 'I guess I surprised myself with that one,' she said ruefully. 'It's more of a puzzle than I'd bargained for.' Then she looked up at her audience, and smiled, just a whisker of a smile, but enough for David to sink back in his seat with a grin of relief. It was okay, she was back on track. Their star speaker hadn't come adrift after all. Kate had regained her firm, impersonal lecturer's manner and everyone relaxed. 'My next example, you'll be pleased to know, is more straightforward.'

David almost cheered. He was amazed by the strength of his reaction. It had been a long time since he'd wanted anything as much as he'd wanted Kate's lecture to finish as successfully as it had begun. Amazingly, he'd actually forgotten about himself for nearly an hour. Kate's magic was as potent as it had ever been.

She clicked the remote and the troublesome little rat, teeth bared cruelly as it gripped the insect in its mouth, vanished from the screen. David almost believed that, before its image was wiped out, the rat closed a single eye in a conspiratorial wink, just for him.

Chapter 2

Summer Rain

Trafalgar Square glittered with sunshine after rain; even the pigeons were transformed, their wings gold-tipped against a pewter sky as the storm clouds rolled back. Tourists were shucking off their plastic macs and drifting about with infuriating slowness, getting in the way. Kate bristled with impatience. Always after a lecture there was an excess of energy, but today that energy felt uncomfortably close to panic: an urge to run, to escape back home – the only problem was, she didn't know what the hell she'd be running from.

She was aware of David, an oh-so solid presence at her side. Having surprised her by turning up at the lecture, he seemed to have assumed some kind of proprietorial rights over the rest of her day.

He told her how interesting the lecture had been, repeated one or two flattering comments he'd heard from the audience as they'd shuffled out, then asked casually, 'So how come you almost lost it back there?'

'Was it that obvious?'

'Only to me.'

Kate knew he was lying to spare her feelings. She said, 'I don't know. It was weird . . . I felt . . . as if . . . it was like I was . . .' She gave up. There was no way to explain her shock when that detail from the Marsyas picture had suddenly loomed up on the screen, a monster rat chomping on an enormous bee. It wasn't as though it was the first time she'd seen it, but still . . . one moment she'd been progressing smoothly with the lecture, aware that she was drawing to the end of her performance, aware that it had gone well, and the next moment she'd felt herself plunging through the surface of the present into an inky black crevasse. Her audience receded to an irrelevance and all that mattered was that crudely sketched image, that evil little rodent with the helpless insect gripped in its jaws.

An act of vandalism, she'd called the alteration of the painting during her lecture, a random act of vandalism, but it wasn't random at all. Random, she could have coped with.

'You look like you could use a drink.'

For the second time that afternoon, Kate clawed her way back to reality to find David Clay close at hand, intrigued and concerned.

'Yes,' she said, and then, 'No. Look, David, I have to go back to the studio. There's something I want to check .'

'Is it to do with that picture?'

'Sort of.'

'Mind if I come too? I've never seen a conservation workshop before.'

'Okay.' She didn't particularly want him along, but it seemed simpler not to argue. He gave the impression of a man who was not easily deterred.

It was odd sitting next to him in the cab that took them to the street off Primrose Hill where she had her studio and home. If someone had asked her a month before what David Clay had looked like, she'd have been hard put to describe him, and yet she'd known who it was the moment she set eyes on him on the concourse at the South Bank. In spite of the grey hair and heavy jaw, he was unmistakably the person she'd once walked with beside the Arno during those strange weeks when the air was clogged with dust and the streets were slippery with muck. They'd cleaned mud from cellars and thrown talcum powder at the walls of the Baptistery and, so far as she could remember, almost but not quite fallen in love. He had retained the broad shoulders and easy movement of the sportsman; his face, no longer handsome, was stamped with a shrewd intelligence, and his eyebrows, always his strongest feature, had remained dark while his hair grew pepper and salt. And at his core she sensed the stillness, the certainty, that had always been so much a part of him, and which she'd forgotten entirely. It should have made him a reassuring person to have around, especially now, when she felt haunted by the enigma of that weirdly altered picture. The only trouble was, she couldn't help wondering if David might himself be contributing to the problem. If she hadn't caught sight of him sitting in the third row of the lecture theatre, a man who'd been so much a part of those unforgettable weeks, would the Marsyas detail have had the power to sabotage her well-planned lecture?

She was still considering this while she unlocked the door to her studio, a large, airy, north-facing space which took up the entire first floor of the house and a generous extension into the garden as well. He seemed fascinated by the tools of her trade. While she tidied away the slides and her notes, he prowled round, examining everything, from the high-tech magnifier to the maulstick, a small piece of cloth wrapped tightly round the end of a piece of wood that artists have used to rest their painting hand on for centuries.

'Isn't there a Rembrandt self-portrait that shows him holding one of these?' he asked. 'At least you're in good company, Kate.' When she didn't answer, he sniffed the air, then said, 'I know what's strange. I expected this place to smell of turps and oils, but it doesn't. Why's that?'

'We use acrylic paints when we have to retouch paintings,' she told him. 'It's easier for future conservators to remove and it's the only way to get a permanent match since oils darken over time.'

He considered this. 'Presumably you want to restore the picture as nearly as possible to its original state.'

'There's a lot of debate about that,' she told him. 'Some conservators think the retouching should be easily distinguishable from the original. The most famous example of that school of thought is the Cimabue crucifixion in Florence which was so badly damaged by the flood. Do you remember that? It was almost destroyed, and they decided not to try to retouch it at all, just coloured the damaged bits in a kind of neutral cross-hatching as a memorial to the destruction. Now a lot of people think that was too extreme. There's no one right way of doing this job.'

'Oh look,' said David. 'Here's Marsyas.' He'd found the painting on an easel to one side of the studio. Kate didn't look up. She was searching through a box of slides. 'Are you going to remove the animal graffiti?' he asked.

'We're waiting for instructions from the owners.'

'I thought you said they were anonymous.'

'Yes, but we can communicate via the dealer who's acting as go-between.'

'You recognized the painting, didn't you?'

Kate froze. Something was squeezing her ribs, making it hard to breathe. She said, 'I – don't know.'

'We both recognized it,' David said firmly. He'd moved quietly across and was standing right in front of her. His bulk seemed to be sucking the air out of the room. He said, 'It was at the—'

'I really don't remember where I saw it before,' she interrupted him quickly.

'The Villa Beatrice.' He pronounced the words in the Italian way – Bay-ah-tree-chay. Kate recoiled. *The Villa Beatrice.* Extraordinary how just hearing the name of that place had the power to take her breath away even after all these years.

'Maybe,' she said. There was some kind of constriction in her throat.

'You know it was.'

'Maybe,' she said again. Her fingers had been flicking through the slides. Now they stopped. She'd reached the ones she was looking for, but found she was reluctant to touch them, as though these particular slides were coated with poison. And, in a way, they were.

'What's that?' asked David.

'Just another picture.'

'So?'

She hesitated, then, 'This one was altered as well.'

'And then sent to you?'

Kate nodded.

'By the same person?'

'I don't know.'

'But you think it is?'

'Yes, probably.'

'Can I see it?'

'It's not—'

'I'd really like to have a look.'

Gingerly, Kate took a slide from its cover and set it in the viewer, before passing it to David. He looked at it for a few moments, then said, 'Explain, please.'

She moved a little distance away and began picking the dry leaves off a geranium plant. They released their cool aromatic scent against her palms, astringent and calming, but her heart was still pounding. She said, 'This is a canvas which was sent to my studio towards the end of last year. It's anonymous, probably Italian. It's an allegory entitled "Truth is the Daughter of Time" – *Veritas Filia Temporis* – you can see the inscription on the bottom right. The theme was a popular one at in those days. Basically the libidinous couple romping in the foreground are about to be exposed by Father Time – the old gentleman behind them. Highly moral and not all that subtle. Your crimes catch up with you in the end, is the obvious author's message.'

'So who's Miss Furry Boots?'

'The figure watching them on the right? That's Deception. She has the face of a beautiful young woman but the body and soul of a monster.'

'Ah yes, I know the type well,' said David with a smile. 'And this painting was changed too? How?'

Kate hesitated. 'It's probably just a coincidence.'

David looked up at her and raised his dark eyebrows, clearly not believing her statement for a minute. Kate sighed and pulled out another slide, replacing the one in the viewer without a word. He peered at the small screen and Kate saw him stiffen. 'Oh my God,' he said. He shifted his stance to get a better look. 'It was like this when it was sent to you?'

'Yes.' She remembered the shock of opening the painting when it arrived in its wooden packaging that cool October morning. The image itself was horrific enough, but when she'd realized which detail had been added recently, she'd been tempted to send it straight back to Signor Barzini and refuse the commission. But at the same time there'd been a fascination, a ghoulish fascination perhaps, which persuaded her to see the job through.

'So much blood,' said David. 'It's grotesque – like a scene from a horror film.'

'Yes.' It had taken Kate weeks of patient work to clean away the blood. No wonder the owner wanted to remain anonymous. Some brainless vandal had overpainted Deception's neck with gore, as though her throat had been cut. There was blood pouring over her shoulders, saturating her gown and making scarlet pools on the ground. And still Deception's beautiful face bore that sweet, untroubled smile, so disconnected from her ravaged flesh. Kate had worked obsessively on the picture, refusing to allow any of her assistants to help. Returning the image to its original state had become a labour of love, almost an act of penance, as though by restoring it she might somehow restore the life that had been destroyed.

David straightened up and looked at her very directly. 'Remind me again how Francesca died,' he said quietly.

Kate winced. *Francesca.* It was years since she'd heard the name spoken out loud. She said, as briefly as she could, 'It was a car crash.'

'Yes, but . . . I remember now. Wasn't she on one of those

scooter things? A Vespa? And she was in a collision with a little Fiat? And the way she fell—'

'That's right,' Kate intervened quickly. 'The way she fell – on the windscreen or the car mirror – it went through her neck and – and . . .' She stopped. *And she was almost decapitated.* Even now Kate found herself choking on the words.

'I'm sorry, Kate. That was insensitive of me. I'd forgotten you were there.'

She shrugged. 'I don't remember any of it. I was knocked out by the collision.'

'And you weren't driving.'

'No.'

'Kate, are you okay?'

'I could use some air.'

'Fine. We'll go out for a bit and talk about something else.' He smiled grimly. 'We'll stick to neutral topics like the situation in the Middle East or euthanasia or fox hunting. Good idea?'

She nodded. Anything to get away from those hideous images.

And it was a good idea, at least to begin with. They walked up onto Primrose Hill and looked out over London. Huge patches of the city were sparkling in the sunshine while other parts were shrouded by grey veils of rain. While they wandered the paths they stuck to the normal births, marriages and deaths topics two people talk about who haven't seen each other in years. Kate told him briefly about her first marriage, to Martin, who was an architecture student. That had broken up soon after the birth of their son, Luke. 'Martin couldn't really deal with being a father,' she told him, 'though he and Luke have got closer recently.' Her second marriage, to a civil servant called Ben Lumins, had ended three years ago. Tara, the daughter from that marriage, was currently at art school.

'And since then?'

'Since then I've rather enjoyed being single. How about you?'

David stared out over the city. 'Three kids, married twenty-five years, divorced eighteen months. But I'd rather not talk about it.'

'I'm sorry.'

'No, Kate. You misunderstand me. Recently the whole subject has become pretty much of an obsession. I've lived and breathed and probably talked about my chaotic private life non-stop. I expect I qualified for great bores of today ten times over. But since your lecture this afternoon I haven't thought about it at all. And that's a relief, believe me.'

Kate looked at him to see if he was teasing her. She'd never known the topic of Conservator as Detective have such a profound impact on any member of an audience before. But so far as she could tell, he meant what he said. She wondered briefly if he had expectations of more than a bottle of wine and a meal when they went back to her house. She hoped not. Distracting someone who was still raw and bruised from a recent divorce was not part of her plans for the evening. Especially not when the recently divorced someone kept reminding her of a time and place she'd long ago made it her business to forget.

She was about to concoct a story about a previous engagement for that evening when the first large drop of rain landed on her wrist. And then half a dozen more. All about them people were scattering to the edges of the park. Within seconds those first raindrops had turned into a deluge. Kate's jacket was soaked almost before she'd hooked the collar over her head.

David was only wearing a shirt and it was plastered to his shoulders and upper arms by the time they reached the gates.

The streets were deserted. Pedestrians huddled for shelter in doorways and peered out as water cascaded off awnings onto the pavement. The rain was so fierce it bounced up again, each drop a vigorous tick of water. The gutters were streaming. Cars swished by, their headlights sparkling in the sudden dark.

Kate and David stopped and looked at each other. 'Do we take shelter too?' he asked. His face was shining with wet.

She shook a halo of water from her hair. 'What's the point?'

They were both laughing as they hurried back to her house, then stood in the hallway and dripped generous puddles onto the mat.

'Don't move!' said Kate. 'I'll throw you down a towel.'

She hurried up the stairs, found a couple of towels for David, then peeled off her jacket and skirt and roughly dried her hair. She pulled on a pair of loose trousers and a zippered top that were draped over the back of a chair in her bedroom. When she went back downstairs it was obvious that David's towels weren't having much impact on the rain damage. He followed her to the second bedroom where she found him a tracksuit of her son's, which was too small, but dry at least, and he retired to the bathroom to change.

By the time he reappeared in her kitchen she'd poured two glasses of wine and was hunting through the fridge for the makings of a meal. 'You're in luck,' she told him. 'I can do you smoked salmon pasta and salad.'

'Sounds good to me.'

The drama over the rain had caused a shift between them. Kate forgot she'd been planning to invent another engagement for the evening. Now that David was standing in her kitchen doorway wearing a pale blue tracksuit that was loose on her lanky son but stretched tight over his shoulders and chest, he was an altogether different proposition from the almost-stranger who'd been part of her audience a few hours before. It was weird seeing Luke's clothes on a man who'd known her in the time before she was ever a mother, a man who knew nothing about the person she'd become. A man who, if he remembered her at all, knew a side to her that no one in her present life was aware of.

She nicked the skin of four tomatoes, put them into a small pan of boiling water, waited half a minute, then took them out with a slotted spoon and set them on the chopping board. David had moved silently on bare feet across the room: standing behind her he put one hand on her waist and rested his chin lightly on her shoulder. 'Anything I can do?' he asked.

Kate felt that tightness round her ribs again. She flexed her shoulders just enough to shrug him off and said without turning round, 'You could try telling me what the hell's going on.'

'Hm.' David went to the window and looked down at the garden. 'It's stopped raining,' he said.

She began pulling the skins off the tomatoes even though they were still hot and their flesh scalded the tips of her fingers. 'Why?' she asked angrily. 'That's what I don't understand. What's the point of messing around with those pictures and then sending them to me? Who's doing it? What do they want?'

She was chopping the tomatoes ferociously. She hadn't meant to bring up the topic of the paintings again. 'The Daughter of Time' had been sent back to Florence three months ago. 'Marsyas' had sat for weeks in her studio; she'd hardly ever talked about them with her colleagues. But David was different: he'd been there. You couldn't just pretend the whole thing was a long-forgotten nightmare when one of the actors in that particular nightmare was standing in bare feet in your kitchen wearing your son's too-small pale blue tracksuit.

'Which question first?' asked David, pulling a metal chair away from the table and sitting down.

'It's like being stalked,' said Kate, finally identifying the sensation that had been haunting her for months. 'That's what it is. Just knowing that someone is out there, some warped, obsessive crackpot, has got me in their sights. Someone's looking at me and I can't see them.' She shuddered. 'It's . . . it's horrible.'

David was silent for a few moments, considering. 'You're sure the pictures were sent to you deliberately? Not just to your workshop?'

'My name was on the consignment note. The dealer said he was under strict instructions not to give out any information at all.'

'Isn't that unusual?'

'Yes, but not unprecedented. Owners of valuable works of art often don't want their identity made public for fear of burglary.'

'Valuable paintings? I thought you said the Marsyas was a copy.'

'Yes, but that doesn't stop it from being valuable. Titian made copies of his own work – or his assistants did. We don't know for sure. You have to think back to a time when there was no other way of recording images. And plenty of other artists made copies of work that impressed them. Any painting by Rubens, say, or Sir Joshua Reynolds, is going to be extremely valuable, even if it is, technically speaking, a copy.' She frowned. 'I don't know who painted those two pictures, but I'm sure they're worth a hell of a lot more than the insurance price.'

David seemed intrigued. 'Let me get this straight. You've been sent two paintings by an anonymous owner and both are undervalued?'

'Yes.'

'And they've both been altered in a way that could relate to Francesca's death.'

'That's right.'

'And where is the dealer?'

'Florence.'

The dark eyebrows shot up. 'So that implies . . .?'

'Well, obviously, it was someone who knew . . . how she died.' Kate was melting butter in a shallow pan. She crushed two cloves of garlic into a smear of salt with the flat of her knife, then chopped it quickly into a paste. She was working faster, more intensely than her usual leisured style of cooking, all her nervous energy funnelled into the task.

'There was an inquest, wasn't there?' asked David. 'So the details would have been public knowledge.'

'Then why drag it all up now?' Kate tipped the garlic and tomatoes into the pan and pushed them around in the melted butter. She ground some black pepper over them, then crumbled in some feta cheese. 'Why go to all the trouble of altering those pictures and then send them to me, just so I get to put them back how they were?'

'Maybe it's two different people,' said David. He inhaled deeply. 'Mm, that smells fantastic. Look, just suppose there's one person who changes the paintings, and another person who doesn't want them changed. That's the person who sends them to you to have them put back how they were.'

'Maybe.' The tomatoes were melting into the butter and garlic, their delicate coral flesh marbled white with the feta. Kate remembered how Deception's pale throat had been necklaced with acrylic blood. But it was the other picture, those two little creatures, superficially as innocent as characters from a cartoon, which haunted her most. What was their significance? Because there was a significance, she knew. The answer was inside her skull, hidden deep in her memory, but she didn't know how to access it. More to the point, she wasn't convinced she *wanted* to access it.

'Once you know who's been sending the paintings, my guess is you'll have the answer to "why".'

'Maybe it's best not to know.' Kate emptied half a packet of penne into a pot of boiling water and stirred vigorously.

'Do Francesca's family still live at the Villa Beatrice?'

'It's been turned into some kind of foundation for the arts, apparently. The Bertoni family are connected with it, I think.'

'Sounds like that would be the place to start asking questions, then.'

Kate turned to him, appalled. 'You mean go back to the Villa Beatrice?'

'Why not?'

She shook her head in disbelief, then went back to her cooking, tearing the smoked salmon into strips and mixing it with the tomatoes and feta. David made it sound like such a simple task: *why don't you just go back to the Villa Beatrice and find out what's going on?* Did he have any idea what he was suggesting? 'I won't go because I don't like being manipulated,' she said, 'Just because some freak's got nothing better to do with her time than stick graffiti on perfectly good paintings, then send them off to me, doesn't mean I have to go charging halfway across Europe. Why should it bother me anyway? All I have to do is clean it up and send my bill.'

'You said, *her* time.'

'Did I? It could be his.'

'But you think it's a her. Which implies you've got a hunch who's doing it.'

Kate didn't answer. She poured some cream onto the sauce, then got salad out of the fridge and put it in a bowl. 'We can eat,' she said.

'Here, let me.' David intercepted her, hefted the saucepan off the stove and began pouring the pasta into the colander in the sink. Thick steam rose up to fill the air between them. 'So who do you think might be sending you the paintings?' he asked.

Kate didn't speak. David had stretched out his arms stiffly and drawn back his head to avoid the steam as the boiling water sloshed from the pan. For a moment his upper body almost disappeared behind dense vapour. Kate was seized with a plummeting sense of dread, a memory of figures seen through glass but obscured by a veil of – of what? Mist? Spray? Dust? There was a sense of movement, and the half-seen figures were scurrying about in panic, the way ants do when their nest is disturbed. And all the time the terror was growing. *All the horror lies ahead.* But what horror? What was it that lay ahead?

She forced herself back into the present. There must be some way to empty her mind of these half-remembered fragments.

'Let's eat, shall we?' she said. 'I don't want to talk about it any more.'

Chapter 3

Mousetrap

Kate couldn't say she hadn't been warned.

Denied the chance to talk about the altered paintings, David fell back on the topic that he'd already admitted was his current obsession. Kate tried to give him her full attention as he told her his story, the tale of a clever young man who, on his return from Florence at the age of nineteen, had taken the easy route and slipped into a job with the family firm. This happened to be a chain of dry cleaners, but could just as easily have been car dealers or food shops or whatever: the money was good and the work was undemanding. The young man had thought he could play the game and take the money and live comfortably while he waited to discover what he really wanted to do with his life, until gradually he'd realized it wasn't a game any more and hadn't been for years. He was head of the firm, people depended on him, he had a wife and three children, and it was far, far too late to change direction.

So the no-longer young man had softened the edges of

boredom with drink and meaningless affairs, waiting for the moment when he'd make a break for freedom and kick-start his real life. Then suddenly, a couple of years ago, the decision had been taken out of his hands. The family firm was swallowed up by a national conglomerate, his wife turned into a walking cliché and ran off with her fitness coach, and he found himself middle-aged and marooned, looking across the empty half of their bed at a photograph of a laughing young couple he no longer even recognized.

Kate tried to listen to his story, but her mind kept skittering away. She was irritated at the way the Marsyas picture had almost derailed her talk that afternoon, and some of her irritation was spilling over to include David. She tugged a grape from the bunch heaped up on the celadon plate in the centre of the table and examined the delicate grey bloom on its ruby skin, the way it absorbed the light. Her mind kept returning to the questions that nagged at her: who had sent those pictures and why?

'Kate? Am I boring you?'

'What? Of course not . . . I . . . well, it's been a long day.' With any luck, he'd take the hint and go. Maybe if she was left alone, she could forget about the whole business.

'Not that long,' said David tersely. And then, 'You're still thinking about it, aren't you?'

'Of course not.' Kate stood up suddenly and began clearing away the plates. She yawned ostentatiously. 'Coffee before you go?'

'Not for me.' His black eyebrows slewed towards each other in a frown. 'There has to be some way to figure out what the pictures mean.' He just wouldn't let the problem alone. 'After all, there can't be that many people who know how you and

Francesca were connected. Try to think, Kate. If you don't get to the bottom of it, you're just going to be sitting here waiting for the next one to come and that's—'

'Oh, for God's sake, stop going on about it!' Suddenly Kate was shaking with anger. 'I'm sick of thinking about the bloody pictures. Why don't you just go! They don't matter, can't you understand that?'

'Kate, I'm sorry, but—'

'And it's got nothing to do with you! You only make it worse. Just because you were there, you think you've got some kind of inside track, but you couldn't be more wrong. You know nothing about it, absolutely nothing!'

'Okay, okay.' David stood up and picked up the bowl of grapes.

'Keep out of this!' said Kate furiously, reaching to snatch the bowl from his hands, but it slipped from her grasp just as he released his hold on it and fell to the floor with a crash. Pale green shards of china and red grapes lay scattered on the floor between them. 'Oh, no!' As Kate stared down at the wreckage, a sob rose to her throat, all the tension of the day releasing in a wail of dismay. 'Damn, damn, *damn*!' She dropped to her knees, frantically gathering up the jagged fragments. An edge sliced her finger and a pearl of blood appeared just below the tip.

'Kate, stop it.' David crouched down beside her. 'There's no point, I'll clear it up for you.'

'No! I'll fix it!' Frantically she scrabbled in the mess.

'You can't, Kate. Not even you. It's broken into a million pieces.' He reached out to put his arms round her but she pushed him away angrily. He drew back. 'I'm sorry, Kate.'

'That was my favourite bowl.' She picked up a handful of bits and a single tear splashed down on the back of her hand.

He stood up. 'I'll buy you another just like it,' he said.

'No. Ben and I bought it in Palermo,' she said with a sigh, sitting back on her heels. 'David, you don't know what it's like.'

'It was my fault.'

'No, it's not the bowl.' She wiped her eyes, then stood up. 'It's the pictures. I don't know why they've upset me so much but . . . it's like someone's trying to get inside my brain. Why bring it all up again after so long? What do they want me to do?'

'Who, Kate?'

'Francesca.'

'Francesca's dead.'

'I know. It doesn't make any sense. And I can't stop bloody thinking about it.' She sniffed, then patted her pockets and smiled ruefully. 'And I haven't even got a sodding tissue.' She reached onto the counter and tore off a square of kitchen paper, then blew her nose. David waited quietly. He was very close to her.

'Kate?'

'Yes?'

She stood immobile, swayed forward just a fraction, as he leaned towards her and touched her lips with his. A shudder ran through her body, a letting go. Maybe this was the solution; maybe this was the only way to escape the tension that was tearing her apart.

'Don't stop.' She moved closer, put her arms around his neck and kissed him full on the mouth, then slipped her hands under the waist of his sweatshirt and touched the soft skin beneath. She smiled. 'I've never made love to a man dressed all in pale blue before.'

'You don't know what you've been missing,' said David huskily.

'We can go upstairs if you like.'

But David was happy where they were. They kissed some more, then he cupped her buttocks in his hands, supporting her even as he pushed her back against the fridge. For a moment, Kate was confused by the speed at which the change had taken place between them. Was this the distraction she wanted? There was a brief fumbling, her fingers brushing against his as they struggled with zips and elastic, then his erection was hot against her hand and suddenly Kate found she was as aroused as David was. Outside, the rain had begun again, fierce summer rain, its drumming merging with the pulse beating in her ears, David's quickened breathing and her gasp of pleasure as she allowed her mind to disengage, surrendering to the demands of touch and sensation. He began to move inside her, a flush of pleasure was spreading through her body, even while she registered the discomfort in her feet which were raised on tiptoe to match his height, and the unyielding surface of the fridge against her back and calves. And then, just at the moment when she felt herself sliding into that deep sea of sensation where words no longer have any meaning, a connection sparked in her brain, a flash of understanding, and she cried out in triumph, while waves of exultation radiated from her core to the tips of her fingers.

She held him a little longer until he came, her cheek resting against his shoulder. A new kind of energy was coursing through her.

She knew the answer to the puzzle.

She understood.

Kate flung her bedroom window wide. The rain had stopped but the air was still heavy with moisture. There was a smell of damp earth and vegetation, her little garden briefly transformed into a tropical jungle as it soaked up the wet. Traffic hummed in the distance. Somewhere, a siren whined: those distant, unknown tragedies that punctuate the London night.

'My trousers haven't dried yet.' David appeared in the doorway.

'You can stay the night,' said Kate. 'I'd offer you the spare room, but it's a bit late for that. You're a fast worker, Mr Clay.'

'Fast?' He grinned. 'I've only waited more than twenty-five years. Must be the slowest courtship in history.'

'Well, if you put it like that.'

'It's like something out of one of those endless South American sagas.'

She smiled. Then: 'No, don't put on the light.'

'Okay.' David moved through the darkened room to stand beside her. Kate was filled with excitement. She was longing to tell him the revelation that had come to her while they were making love, had been wanting to tell him ever since, but she had a hunch his masculine ego would not appreciate discovering the main reason for her cry of triumph.

'It's strange, isn't it,' she said. 'After so long.'

'I suppose so.'

'David.' She couldn't hold back any more. 'I know why those details were added.'

'You do? The rat and the bee?'

'Not a rat and a bee.'

'But —'

'It's a mouse and a wasp.'

'How do you know that?'

'Because Francesca was riding a Vespa when she was killed. And *vespa* in Italian means . . .'

'What?'

'A wasp.'

'And the mouse?'

'The car I was in, one of those little Fiats. They're called Topolinos.'

'Jesus. A *topolino* is little mouse.'

'The little mouse eats the wasp. The Topolino destroys the Vespa.'

'That's sick. Ingenious, but still sick.'

'Yes. Like they think Francesca's death was some kind of a joke.' She shivered. 'It's creepy.' They stood for a few moments without speaking. Outside, as night filled the garden, the last blackbird abruptly stopped its song.

Eventually David said, 'You'll have to find out, you know.'

'How?'

'Visit the dealer?'

'He'll never tell me.'

'Then go to the Villa Beatrice.'

'I can't.'

'Why not?'

Kate turned to face him. In the semi-darkness it was easy to imagine David had hardly changed from the boy who'd been her companion during those far-off weeks in Florence. It was years since she'd been with anyone who'd known Francesca. Years since she'd trodden those particular walks of memory.

She said quietly, 'I've never told anyone this before but . . . her mother blamed me for what happened.'

'What? But that's ridiculous. It was an accident, wasn't it? And you weren't even driving the car.'

'Of course, it's crazy. But her family *were* crazy, don't you remember?'

'I didn't spend time with them like you did.'

'And even Francesca was . . . well, different.'

'Was she?'

'But . . . I loved her, David. I really loved her. I've never told anyone that before, either, because no one knew her, no one would have known what I was talking about, but you did. I guess you always feel that way about people who die young, but Francesca was . . . well, special. And I owe her so much. Everything, really. I'd never have done any of this if it hadn't been for Francesca. I'd probably have stayed a secretary and been miserable all my life. She made it seem possible. I feel I owe her.'

'But she died, Kate. In an accident. And it wasn't your fault.'

'I know that. But . . . it's so weird. A couple of nights ago I dreamed someone was locked in a dark room. They were trapped and frightened, and they were calling out to me, trying to get me to help them, but I ignored them. And when I woke up I was shattered; it felt as if I was turning my back on someone in trouble. I felt so . . . guilty, but I knew it was all connected with the pictures.'

'What are you suggesting, Kate? You think those alterations are some kind of cry for help?'

'It could be that.'

'Or a trap. Some mad psycho who's still obsesssing about Francesca's death.'

'Yes, I know.'

David sighed. 'Kate, I know you don't want to go back there, but supposing I came with you? Wait, hear me out. My youngest daughter's studying in Rome. I've been meaning to visit her for months. We could combine the two. And I'm nearly as curious as you are now. What do you think?'

Kate didn't answer for a long time. Eventually she said, 'I

haven't thought about it in years. And now I don't seem to be able to stop. Do you remember the night we met Francesca? We'd been to that restaurant.'

'No, we'd been to the consul's party.'

'Oh my God, I'd forgotten about those.'

'It was on the way back.'

'That's right. She was on the bridge.'

'Do you think she would have tried to kill herself?'

'You never could tell with Francesca, could you?'

David slipped his arm round her waist and they looked out into the darkness in silence. Starting to remember.

Chapter 4

Lungarno Corsini Due

Florence was a city of strange magic. The air was hazed with grey and there was a smell of damp plaster, sewage and mud – every kind of mud, mud everywhere. Mud ruled their lives: they worked in it by day and in the evenings they had to slither and slip through streets slicked with mud, coated with mud, treacherous with mud. Only a few cars ventured into the areas that had been worst affected by the flood and even pedestrians had to pick their way with care. There were potholes where the river had ripped up the cobbles, larger holes where pipes were in the process of being mended, rubble and muck heaped up and left in stinking piles on street corners. In some places beside the Arno whole chunks of river bank had been gouged away by the deluge and were still awaiting repair.

The city famous throughout the world as the cradle of western civilization had been brought to its knees by the bombardment of muck and filth, and in January 1967, two months after the devastation, its recovery remained uncertain. Florence, during those precarious winter months, was a city out of time.

In the evenings, its strangeness was intensified. The haze caused by evaporating mud seemed thicker at night and the street lights – those that were still working – bloomed fuzzy haloes against the dark. The pollution was so severe that nearly all the Florentines who'd been unable to escape from the city suffered from bronchial problems, but for the flood volunteers it was all part of the romance of the situation. Anna, who wrote poetry, described the streetlights as 'dandelion clocks gone out of focus'.

It was Friday night, the second Friday since Kate had come to the city. She emerged from the hostel and she and half a dozen of her friends linked arms; together they laughed and skidded through the muddy streets towards the British Consulate. They'd worked hard in mud-filled cellars all week and now it was time to party. In honour of the occasion Kate had put on a clean pair of jeans and an embroidered peasant blouse, her favourite dangly earrings, lashings of mascara and ghostly pale lipstick. She felt good, really good, especially when she thought how horrified her parents would have been if they could glimpse her now. Mr and Mrs Holland's plans for their seventeen-year-old daughter had gone no further than a safe secretarial job to keep her occupied until she got married. Universities were for clever boys, in their opinion; too much education for a girl put men off and only led to future unhappiness.

They would have been especially horrified if they'd known that Aiden, the young man with the long custard-coloured hair and the black cape who'd linked arms with Kate on her right, claimed to have worked as a pimp when he first arrived in London, or that the poetic Anna was rumoured to be a nymphomaniac, or that Don's arms were pocked with scars from his heroin habit, or that handsome Gordon and gnome-like Mike had eyes only for each other. Kate wasn't sure how much she believed of what anyone told her, but she did know that the sedate world she'd grown up in seemed wonderfully far away. In spite of the filth and the hard work and their primitive living conditions in the hostel, she was glowing with happiness. Ever since she could remember, the word 'grown-up' had been synonymous with responsibility and seriousness, yet here she was, fresh out of school and without a care in the world. She was free. Life was an adventure.

'Look, there's that girl again.'

Kate had noticed the stranger earlier, when she was walking back to the hostel after work. There was something about the solitary figure that drew the attention, even in this city of misfits and foreigners.

Tall and well-groomed, she was much too elegant to be one of the flood volunteers. Her tumble of light brown hair was caught up in a pair of tortoiseshell combs and the velvet collar of her coat was turned up against the raw night air. She wore black leather gloves and her black patent-leather bag matched her shoes. But one of the combs was slipping, a mass of hair drooped over the side of her face, and her shoes were caked with mud, dismal grey mud that spattered her stockinged legs. She was walking slowly towards them. Eyes to the ground, the unknown young woman was in a world of her own – and it didn't look like a happy world either.

Instinctively, the gaggle of volunteers slowed down, breaking the chain to let her through.

Kate's happiness that evening was the kind that wants even strangers to share her good fortune. '*Buona notte*,' she said, but the girl didn't acknowledge the greeting and stepped between them like a sleepwalker.

'Stuck-up cow,' said Don.

'Good legs, though,' said Aiden.

A faint aroma of expensive perfume lingered after she'd passed. Kate turned and watched her as she walked away. At the end of the street the stranger hesitated, as though uncertain whether to go towards the Piazza Signoria or over the bridge. Kate had a sudden urge to invite her to join them, but didn't want to risk a second rejection.

Don suggested a speedy remedy for such prissy-looking solitary females, and everyone laughed. Aiden linked his arm through Kate's again and they continued on their way to the party and forgot all about the elegant stranger.

Lungarno Corsini Due, the building which housed the British Consulate, fronted onto the Arno and had therefore borne the full brunt of the flood's impact. The road outside was still impassable to cars. In fact, it looked as though a large bite had been taken out of it by the river, and the wrecked section was roped off.

But once they climbed the stairs to the first floor the volunteers entered another world. There was an awesome array of drinks, canapés on huge platters borne round by uniformed staff and three sorts of cigarettes in silver cases scattered around the room. And on top of that, the other guests seem to have been invited for the sole purpose of telling the volunteers how heroic they were.

'Stand in front of me, will you, Kate,' said Don, who was already emptying the contents of one cigarette case into his pocket.

'Shouldn't you leave one or two?' she asked. 'It's a bit obvious taking the whole lot.'

'Too late now.' Don was cheerfully helping himself to a glass of wine from a passing tray.

Across the room, Kate could see Aiden sliding a half bottle of vodka into his inside pocket; his large cape had many advantages. She only hoped the British Consul didn't realize how his hospitality was being abused.

'Kate, you look fantastic!'

She spun round. 'David, when did you get here?'

'About half an hour ago. I thought I'd better get here early before it all got pilfered.'

Kate liked David – but at that stage she liked all her fellow volunteers. He was a couple of years older, and possessed an engaging mixture of naiveté and sophistication. He'd arrived in Florence right after the New Year, same as her, and thrown himself wholeheartedly into the life of the mud angels. He had heavy black eyebrows and a determined jaw. His clean-cut good looks had seemed a bit too clean-cut to begin with, but already his hair was straggling over his collar and his voice was gravelly with pollution and cigarette smoke.

'Who's that man Anna's making up to?' asked Kate. She was looking across the room to where Anna was doing her sex-kitten impersonation for the benefit of an odd-looking middle-aged man with a goatee beard who looked as if he'd be more at home wearing a pair of lederhosen and scrambling up the side of a mountain than at a consulate party. 'I wouldn't have thought he was her type.'

David laughed. 'It's the casting couch, Florence style. Apparently he's been sent over by the V and A to organize some of the work at the Uffizi. So far as Anna's concerned, he's the ticket to an easier life than muck shovelling.'

'Really?' Kate looked at the London expert with a new interest. 'What's his name?'

'Professor Fuller. Want me to introduce you?'

'You bet.' Kate refilled her glass and prepared to be charming. Working with real works of art was what she had been hoping to do in Florence all along.

Promotion turned out to be surprisingly easy to arrange: Professor Fuller was more than happy to add another good-looking girl to his team. He even agreed to take David on as well, just to show he wasn't only employing pretty women. Three glasses of wine and half a dozen sausage rolls later, she emerged into the night with David, both of them bubbling with excitement at their good fortune.

'Let's celebrate,' said David. 'I'll buy you dinner.'

'Shall we wait for the others?'

'No, just the two of us, for once.'

He draped his arm across her shoulder. Kate realized he'd reached that stage of drunkenness where the protective male arm becomes surprisingly heavy, but she was not exactly sober herself and in no mood to criticize. David was attractive and good company and she was happy to spend the rest of the evening with him, flirting and maybe kissing a bit if it turned out that way. She hadn't kissed David yet. She'd kissed Aiden because everyone seemed to have kissed Aiden; it was as though he expected it, felt he'd let you down if you didn't. And she'd kissed Hugo, who'd been drafted in by the consulate to help with the extra work, because he'd expressed serious interest the night she arrived and she couldn't think of any reason not to. But that was as far as it had gone. The volunteers talked about sex almost all the time but, so far as she could tell and apart from vague rumours about Anna, not much actual sex was taking place. A fair amount of kissing and heavy-duty petting, but no real sex. Their communal living conditions were a handicap, but also there seemed to be a general reluctance to break up the group by forming serious pairs. For the time being, this suited Kate fine. She'd made love five times with Matt, her serious boyfriend in England, and though she'd have died rather than admit the truth, her main impression had been of discomfort and embarrassment. Escaping Matt and his speedy, unsatisfying grapplings had been one of her unspoken reasons for coming to Florence.

'Where shall we go?' asked Kate.

David stumbled on a loose cobble and the arm across her shoulder got even heavier. 'Let's go to the other side of the river.'

'Is there anywhere to eat over there?'

'Must be,' said David.

They crossed over on the Pont'alla Carraia. Above the river, the air was even colder, chill damp rising from the black waters. Kate always found the Arno sinister at night. By day it seemed placid enough; in fact, it was often hard to imagine how it had turned into the savage tide that had bounced cars and even lorries through the streets. But after dark it was different, a silent, indifferent force flowing through the centre of the city, elemental and dangerous. She was glad, even in David's company, when they reached the other side.

They walked a little way, almost to the Ponte S. Trinita, then drifted to a halt near one of the few streetlamps that was still working on this side of the river. There were no cars here and the street was deserted. David was smiling blurrily as he leaned forward and kissed her. His lips were cold and tasted of cigarettes and Scotch whisky. Kate closed her eyes and kissed him back, letting her lips part to receive his tongue, moving her own in response. The proper kissing technique had been much discussed in the previous two weeks, and anyway, she was enjoying herself. By the time they both came up for air, their lips were no longer cold.

'Oh look,' said Kate suddenly. 'There's that girl again.'

'What girl?' David mumbled indistinctly into the collar of her coat. His nose bumped against hers as he moved to kiss her again, but Kate turned her head and pulled back. Something in the way the girl was standing near the middle of the *ponte* alerted her to danger, clearing the wine- and kissing-induced fuzziness from her head.

'The one I saw earlier. Look. What's she doing?' David sighed, but turned to follow the direction of her gaze. Kate was thoroughly alarmed by now. 'She looks like she wants to jump in,' she said.

'Do you think?' He seemed to be having trouble switching his attention from Kate to this unknown female. 'Best not to interfere.'

'But we can't do *nothing*,' said Kate. The girl was leaning over the parapet, leaning too far. She looked fascinated by the dark water. Then, as they watched, she straightened up, put both her hands firmly on the parapet and hoisted herself up, so she was sitting there, her body twisted round, at an angle over the water, so that if she just shifted her balance a fraction . . .

Kate was gripped with a cold fear. She took a couple of steps in the direction of the bridge, then turned to David. 'We have to act as if we haven't noticed her,' she whispered, 'or she might get scared and – and jump. Maybe if we carry on kissing . . .' She put her arm round his waist, turning to kiss him as they walked. Every now and then she broke off to glance at the elegant woman sitting on the parapet, who was leaning ever closer towards that murderous, ink-black water. As they drew near, Kate saw her put her hand to her mouth and tug off a single glove with her teeth. Then, very slowly, she stretched out her arm and let the glove fall. It vanished into the darkness long before it hit the water. An odd little smile appeared on her face. She reached out her arm again, but this time it was her bag she was holding. Then she let that go too . . .

By the time they drew level with her, Kate was so tense she'd forgotten to breathe. She tried to make her voice sound light, casual even, as she said, 'Hi, it's Louise, isn't it?'

Startled, the stranger looked round. In that moment Kate noticed that she had the most incredible eyes, not beautiful exactly, but compelling. She stared at them, but didn't answer.

'Didn't we meet this afternoon? No? I could have sworn . . .' David, she was glad to see, had moved a little further ahead, so that he was on the other side of the girl, while Kate talked on. 'Oh, well, sorry. Must be my mistake. My name's Kate by the way. I've just been to the party at the consulate and was on my way for a meal. Maybe you'd like to come too?'

By now, Kate was standing right beside the girl. If she made a move, there was a chance Kate could catch her by the sleeve of her coat.

'Are you English?' asked Kate. Eyes fixed soberly on her face, the girl shook her head slowly. 'Oh well, at least you understand English. I'd hate to think I'd been babbling on if you only spoke Italian. I'd feel like a proper fool. It's beautiful here, isn't it?'

Maybe the girl just lost her balance. She seemed to lean

away from Kate, as though she meant to roll silently over the edge of the parapet and into the swirling dark of the river below. Kate lunged forward and caught hold of her coat, David grabbed her round the waist and pulled, and the next moment the stranger was standing between them on the hard surface of the bridge.

'You nearly lost your balance there,' said David.

'Had me scared for a moment.' Kate smiled encouragingly.

The woman blinked. Those incredible eyes again. Then she glanced back over her shoulder at the river and shuddered. She looked down at the one glove remaining in her hand and said, 'I lost my bag.'

'Yes,' said Kate.

A tiny smile flickered at the corners of the woman's mouth. 'You thought I was going to jump,' she said. A slight inflection at the end of the sentence made it almost a question. Kate couldn't place her accent. Not English, certainly, but not Italian either.

'No, of course we didn't,' they both blustered.

The stranger hugged her arms across her chest. 'It's so damn cold at night,' she said. 'Sometimes it gets hard to think straight.'

'Doesn't it just,' said David. 'Look, why don't we all go to a bar and have a drink? Get warmed up a bit.'

Her eyes were sparkling with tears. 'All my money was in the bag. And my left luggage ticket.'

'That's okay. It's my treat tonight,' said David.

'Really? But . . .' She hesitated, and Kate got the feeling the woman was uncomfortable with his generosity. She was fascinated by the girl's eyes. They were long and mysterious, like the eyes you see sometimes in Renaissance paintings. Unforgettable eyes.

Kate said, 'Let's go somewhere warm. You'll feel better then.'

'Okay.' But warily. Again that suspicion of their kindness. She must have realized right then that she didn't have many choices. The stranger held out her hand. 'Thank you,' she said. 'My name is Francesca.'

Chapter 5

La Valletta

It should have been idyllic. First there was the leisurely drive in the taxi from Florence in the September sunshine through a landscape that was familiar from countless paintings, with its little hill towns and winding valleys, olive groves and cypresses, and the verges scattered with late summer flowers of dusty blue and faded yellow, the vibrant pink stars of cyclamen glowing under the trees. It was a landscape that grew wilder as her taxi approached the Villa Beatrice so that Kate had looked out over a vista hardly altered since Renaissance times: a panorama of rolling hills and secret river valleys and blue-shadowed woodland. The air was filled with the scent of aromatic leaves drying in the sun, and that deep silence of the countryside, a silence that is only intensified by the insistent pulse of the cicadas.

It should have been idyllic. But it wasn't. She had to keep fighting the urge to turn round and escape, back to Florence, back to Rome where David was visiting his daughter, back to London and her own safe world.

As the taxi turned off the country road and began the slow, winding ascent to the villa, Kate knew that she was now on Bertoni land, entering a space she'd never expected to see again – that she'd never wanted to see again. A world she'd filed away in the deepest recesses of her memory. She'd been so successful that until a few months ago she thought she'd finished with it for ever. That feeling of having entered another world, utterly remote from the traffic and hubbub of modern life, was exactly how the Villa Beatrice had struck her on her first visit, all those years ago. But what was she doing here anyway? Only the picture carefully wrapped and in a case of its own on the seat beside her kept her focused on the task ahead. All she had to do find out who'd sent it, persuade them to use a more orthodox way of contacting her in future, preferably one that didn't involve vandalizing old masters, and then leave. All perfectly straightforward.

Except she knew that where the Bertoni family was concerned, nothing was ever straightforward.

She'd decided to begin her search at the Villa Beatrice. Francesca's parents, if they were still alive, must be in their seventies or eighties. But there had been a younger sister. What was her name? Sylvie? Sandra? Something like that. It made sense to start with her.

Kate kept trying to steady her nerves with phrases like 'It makes sense' and 'It's all perfectly simple' but her heart was pounding. The place the taxi brought her to was familiar, and at the same time totally different from the way she remembered it that final, terrible weekend. For one thing, she'd forgotten how beautiful the Villa Beatrice was, how it worked its magic right from that first glimpse halfway up the driveway when you saw it soaring pale and perfect high above you, like an exquisite stone bird that has just that moment come to roost on the curve of the hill. The house, in that setting, possessed the kind of beauty that catches at your throat, a seductive beauty blinding you to danger.

Close to, the Villa Beatrice's beauty was almost overwhelming. When she'd seen it as a teenager Kate had known only that it was the loveliest building she'd ever been in. Now she was able to recognize it as a near-perfect example of early-eighteenth-century Palladian style, its white colonnades spreading like welcoming arms on either side of the classical facade. The massive blocks of stone had been cut with such skill they seemed almost weightless, mere columns of light, yet as natural as if they'd grown from the soil on which they were planted. Kate got out of the taxi and lifted out the painting. She told the driver to wait; she wouldn't be long. And all the time, she had to shake off a ridiculous notion that she was stepping onto enchanted ground. Get a grip, she told herself sternly; you saw the sign back there. This isn't Bluebeard's Castle – it's a centre for young people and the arts. Now, just how prosaic is that?

She went up the wide, shallow steps and paused to glance up at the words carved in the white marble above the doorway. A simple inscription read: IN MEMORIAM FRANCESCA BERTONI 1946–67. That was all. Just her name and the dates. She was still standing there, staring at the letters, when a red-haired woman appeared and asked what she wanted. Kate told her she was looking for Signora Bertoni, the sister of Francesca. Ah yes, said the woman, she's at the Valletta where the theatre is. Simona is at the theatre.

Kate tried to look as if that was what she'd been expecting to hear.

Simona. That was the name of the little sister.

Simona.

Kate's nerves tightened. So, the Bertonis were still here after all. She had been half hoping strangers had taken over the Villa Beatrice, half hoping that the picture had been sent from somewhere else and she'd have to admit defeat and return it to the dealer in Florence through whom it had come. But Simona was here: Simona, whom she'd last seen through a cloud of dust, running in panic and distress just before Francesca was killed . . .

'*Signora*, do you want to see her?'

'Yes.' The woman's question returned Kate abruptly to the present. 'When are you expecting her back?'

The redhead smiled. 'The theatre is here, *signora*, at Villa Beatrice. I will take you.'

Kate followed her round the side of the villa and down a long gravel walk that led from the formal gardens near the house through some sparse trees to an area of open ground. La Valletta, it turned out, was an open-air theatre formed from a wide basin in the side of the hill.

'Shall I tell Signora Simona you are here?' asked her guide.

'No, thank you, I'll wait.'

Kate stood on the rim of the amphitheatre and looked down on the scene below. She assumed some kind of dramatic exercise was taking place, though it looked more like a weird initiation rite. About twenty people were crawling around on the grassy floor of the theatre, but there was no way of telling which was Simona since they were all wearing rigid white masks. Kate had always been uncomfortable around masks. It was something to do with the frozen face and the eyes that didn't belong, a lack of context for the character, everything hidden from sight. Those rigid masks meant that in theory any one of those figures could have been Francesca's little sister.

She reached into her bag and pulled out her mobile phone, then scrolled down to David's number.

'Are you there yet?' He answered almost at once. 'What's it like?'

'Weird,' said Kate. 'I'm watching some kind of outdoor drama group.'

'Have you found the sister yet?'

'I think I'm looking at her, but I can't be sure.'

'Are you okay?'

'Yes, but I wish you were here too.'

'I can drive up tomorrow if you want.'

'Why? Aren't things going too well with Lucy?'

'It's okay. But, well, to be honest, it could be better.'

'We can meet up tomorrow, but not here. I'm only staying for an hour or so. My taxi's on hold. David . . .'

'What is it?'

'I was just thinking . . . it's so weird being back here. I recognize bits, and yet it's completely different, like it's some kind of a facsimile of the Villa Beatrice we knew. The same, but not the same at all. And my memories of the place are such a jumble. It feels as if they've been stored away in some damp dark cupboard and they've been nibbled by woodworm and mice. There ought to be a new profession: memory conservators. People who do what I do with pictures, but with memories.' She laughed awkwardly. 'What do you think? Then you'd be able to call someone up to repair the damage.'

Her tone of voice must have betrayed her unease. There was a brief silence at the other end, then David said thoughtfully, 'Kate, just find out who's been sending the paintings and get them to stop. Then leave. That's all you have to do. We'll meet up tomorrow.'

'But . . . ' Kate lowered her voice. 'Okay, someone's coming. I'll call you later.'

While she'd been talking on the phone, one of the ghostly, white-clad figures – a female one – had looked up at her, pale mask gleaming where it caught the sunlight, then detached herself from the others. There was tension in the shoulders and the slightly outstretched arms. So much could be detected when the face was rubbed out. Now she was walking up the steep slope to the ridge where Kate was standing. Long, easy strides. Purposeful. Kate slid her phone back into her bag and gripped the case that held the painting against her side. Like a shield.

Halfway up the hillside, the figure paused and tugged off the mask, releasing a tumble of grey-brown hair. Kate stepped half a pace back in shock.

She'd not reckoned on Simona reminding her so strongly of Francesca. Sure, the two girls had been similar. They'd both had those strange, wide-spaced green eyes, the thick brown hair and that sudden, disarming, toothpaste smile. But next to her glamorous older sister, Simona had been the ugly duckling. When Kate knew her she'd been lumpish and awkward, shoulders curved with teenage embarrassment at her woman's budding figure, buck teeth and braces to make her shy of smiling.

Well, it had been a long time, so it was hardly surprising if the little sister had done what ugly ducklings do best and transformed herself – with the help, obviously, of the best orthodontist money could buy – into a beautiful swan. For there was no doubt that the woman, tall and slim and strong, who was approaching now, was strikingly attractive.

'Simona Bertoni?'

'Yes?'

'I am Kate Holland.'

But the woman had known that without being told. There'd been a moment of recognition, a flash of understanding in those strange green eyes before her guard snapped in place, like a visor.

'What are you doing here?'

Her voice was familiar too. That accent that was part American, part Italian, part English, an accent, like her sister's, that seemed to belong everywhere and nowhere.

Kate didn't answer. If Simona was the person who had sent the altered paintings, then it was up to her to make the first move. Kate certainly didn't intend to give her any clues.

The other woman held her gaze for a few moments, then glanced down at the package under Kate's arm. 'You brought the painting?'

'You know it?'

An almost imperceptible nod of the head. 'Marsyas.'

'Did you know it had been altered?'

Simona stared at her. 'Why didn't you tell me you were coming?' she asked. No doubt about it, Simona was definitely nervous.

Kate said, 'I thought perhaps you were expecting me.'

'I had hoped . . .' Simona's voice trailed away.

For the moment, surprise had given Kate the upper hand. She said, 'This painting will have to be returned to Signor Barzini in Florence, since it came to me from him. But I thought you might be able to tell me who has been altering the pictures. This is the second one I've received. It's extremely irresponsible to allow valuable paintings to be vandalized in this way, as I'm sure you realize.'

'Kate, stop. Please.' Simona ventured a smile, though her

expression was still haunted. 'You've taken me by surprise and there is so much . . . Don't be angry. It was so important that you come.'

'Then it *was* you who had those details added? But why?'

'Oh, so many reasons. But . . . you should have warned me you were coming.'

'I don't understand, Simona. If you wanted me to visit, why not just get in touch in the normal way?'

'Would you have come?'

'Maybe, but . . .'

Kate's moment of hesitation seemed to give Simona the opportunity she needed. 'Come up to the house, Kate. How did you get here? You must be thirsty after your long journey. Do you have any luggage?' She had stepped into the role of hostess, filling those awkward first moments with the kind of conversation that would have done for any visitor. As they walked along the path through the trees towards the house, she pointed out the changes and improvements that had been made to the Villa Beatrice, gave a brief account of the work of the Fondazione.

'We run courses all through the summer. This is the last day of the season. Tomorrow we have our closing ceremony – it's quite an event. You'll enjoy it. Luckily I have no guests at La Rocca so there's plenty of room.'

'La Rocca?'

'You remember the tower house. Where my uncle lived.'

Kate shivered as another memory struggled up into the light. 'I'm not staying,' she said firmly. 'I have a taxi waiting.'

'A taxi? But of course you will stay. We have such a lot to talk about. So much catching up to do.' And when Kate was about to protest again Simona said firmly, 'You can't go now, you've only just got here. And if you want to go later on then my driver will take you. Please, Kate, just stay a little while.'

Kate couldn't think of any logical reason to refuse. It was the sensible thing to do, after all. She needed to get to the bottom of this business with the altered paintings; she had no other plans for the rest of that day and David wouldn't be able to join her till tomorrow; it was an invitation to spend time in one of the most beautiful estates in Italy; she was interested in the work of the Fondazione . . . all perfectly logical reasons for accepting Simona's invitation. On the opposing side there was nothing but the fact that her gut was twisted with anxiety at being here again – and that instinctive urge to flee.

Simona dealt with the taxi, laughing incredulously when she saw how much it cost Kate. 'If you'd phoned me from Florence,' she said. 'I would have sent my driver to pick you up.' She picked up Kate's suitcase and put it into the back of an open-top car. 'It's lucky I drove down this morning,' she said. 'La Rocca's so close, I usually walk. Maybe it was a premonition.'

Kate hesitated, her hand on the top of the car door. 'How did you know where to find me?' she asked.

Simona pretended to search her memory for the answer, though Kate had an idea she knew perfectly well. She said, 'I think it must have been seeing your name in a magazine – that's right, it was *International Conservation* a couple of years back. Didn't you write a piece about the Goya forgery that was sent to you? There was a photograph beside your name – of course, it helped that you kept your maiden name.'

'But I still don't understand why you couldn't just write . . .'

Simona laughed, though her eyes remained wary. 'Well, you know what they always say: a picture's worth a thousand words.' She got in, and reached over to open the passenger door.

Kate felt annoyed. She was impatient to discover what Simona was up to, but she sensed that the more she pushed, the longer it would take to find out. Somehow, Simona had gained the initiative and she wasn't comfortable with that but, just for now, she didn't know what she could do about it. A group of young people, laughing and talking, appeared round the corner of the villa.

'Quick,' said Simona. 'Before I get waylaid with some problem.'

Kate got into the car and Simona started the engine.

'It's the reason I moved up to La Rocca,' said Simona, following the drive that led further up the hill. 'It became impossible to carry on living at the villa. The kids were all right, but the staff never left me alone. I'm incredibly lucky to have such a dedicated team, but if I'm within shouting distance, they come to me with every little problem. Even though La Rocca is only half a mile away, the fact that I'm out of sight means they're somehow miraculously able to cope on their own. Which is better for everyone.'

Kate didn't answer. The road wound between spacious trees. When she'd been here before it had been winter. Now there was a scent of dust and warm pine needles. She was aware of the hard edge of the case that held the painting pressed against her thigh, a trickle of sweat edging down between her shoulder blades.

La Rocca appeared briefly through the trees, then vanished again, and then they drove round a final bend into sunlight and the house was before them. A square, medieval tower, it had been built just below the summit of the hill, with only a bare triangle of rock rising up behind. In winter, it had been grim and imposing. Now, with the late afternoon sun warm on its walls, festoons of creeper round the windows just starting to take on autumn colours, it looked mellow, almost welcoming.

Simona turned to Kate with a smile. 'Remember this? My uncle used to live here. And La Rocca is a better size for just two people.'

Kate assumed she must be talking about her partner. 'You're married?'

Simona turned away to get out of the car. 'No,' she said. 'I was married years ago but it didn't work out. I live here with my mother.'

In spite of the afternoon warmth, Kate felt a chill pass through her. Simona's mother. Signora Bertoni. The woman who'd made Kate the target of her grief-crazed hatred. Now Kate had an even better reason for making this visit as brief as possible. She had to force herself to get out of the car and say, 'And your father?'

'He died six years ago. Mamma carried on living in Verona for a while, but recently she's gotten confused a lot, so she came here. We thought it was best.'

Kate wondered who the 'we' referred to. She said, 'I'm sorry about your father.' She could play the game of polite platitudes just as well as Simona.

'It was cancer,' said Simona simply and then, 'Leave your things,' as Kate lifted the picture out of the car, 'Dino can bring them in later.'

'But I must keep this with me until I return it to Signor Barzini.'

Simona looked shocked. 'It's *my* painting,' she said, and then, quickly, 'We'll phone Barzini straight away and tell him what's happened. Will that make it okay?'

'I suppose so. But you'll have to check it first.'

'It's okay, I trust you.'

'For God's sake, that's not the point.' Kate's was annoyed. It was bad enough that Simona had made her a player in some elaborate secret game, but the way she'd abused valuable works of art was unforgivable. She said, 'Both those paintings you sent me are worth a small fortune. God only knows why you put such a ridiculously low figure on them for insurance.'

'But they're only copies,' protested Simona.

'Yes, but extremely valuable copies all the same. I didn't investigate them at all, but my hunch is the Marsyas is late-sixteenth century, maybe even a replica from Titian's own workshop. And the other is no later than mid-seventeenth century.'

Simona seemed puzzled. 'Are you sure? The last person who looked at them insisted they were just nineteenth-century copies.'

'Who was that?'

'Oh . . . just a dealer.'

'Barzini?'

'No. It doesn't matter.'

'Yes it does, Simona. It matters about a million pounds worth.'

Her eyes widened with shock. 'As much as that?'

'I did some research for you,' said Kate, wondering how Simona could have been so ill-informed about one of her pictures. 'A painting a little bigger but done at about the same time was auctioned recently for £480,000. Yours would fetch at least a quarter of a million.'

Simona's shock was genuine enough, though she tried hard to hide her feelings. 'Well, fancy that,' she said with phoney brightness. 'What about the first one you got? The Daughter of Time? That was undervalued too?'

'Sure it was. By about £400,000 at least.'

'Holy saints . . . ' For a moment or two her gaze was distant, then she forced herself to say lightly, 'Lucky for me you came, eh?'

'Why? Who's been giving you bum advice, Simona?'

'Oh . . . It must have been a mix up. But . . . ' She and Kate had been moving slowly towards the door. Suddenly Simona gripped Kate by the arm and stared intently into her eyes. 'Kate, I need to ask you a favour. It's important. You mustn't tell anyone about this. Not about the details I added in, and not about the value of the paintings. Promise?'

'Maybe – if I had some idea what this was about.'

'You will. But right now, you have to promise. So far as anyone else is concerned, you just happened to be passing this way and thought you'd drop by and . . . don't mention the paintings. I didn't tell anyone I sent them to you. Please, Kate, you have to promise me. It's important.'

If Kate had needed a reminder of what it was like to enter the Bertoni world, she had it now: that looking-glass world of secrets and deceits, that giddy sensation of taking part in a drama where none of the other players could spare a moment to tell her the script.

They were inside the hall now. It was cool and dark, with stone floors and patterned rugs and a huge vase of white lilies. It smelled the way old houses smell when there's an army of servants to polish and dust and clean, where every surface glows. An old dog, large and pale as a polar bear but much friendlier, had padded over to investigate, its nails clacking on the stone floor.

Kate told herself that if she went along with Simona's demands, she'd discover the reason behind all this sooner. 'All right,' she said.

'You promise?'

'I said all right, didn't I?'

'It's just that it's so important. Remember, you just happened to be passing and dropped in. Nothing to do with the picture. I do have reasons, Kate. I don't want the staff, or my mother or . . . or . . . or Mario . . .' she added the name to her list with studied casualness, 'or anyone else to know.'

Kate reached out and gripped the edge of an old oak table. 'Mario?'

'Yes.' Simona looked away, reaching down to fondle the dog's ears. 'I know, Rollo, it's hot, isn't it?'

'Mario Bassano?'

'That's right.' And then, with deceptive sweetness. 'Do you remember him?'

Kate felt as though someone had just kicked her in the stomach, but she was getting the hang of the Bertoni conversational style. 'I – I suppose so. He was a doctor, wasn't he?' She forced her fingers to release the edge of the table and returned Simona's smile with one just as artless. Just as phoney.

Mario Bassano. *Il dottore.*

Surely it wasn't possible for a name to have such an impact after all these years – was it? But yes, obviously it was: the answer was there in the sudden rush of adrenaline, her quickened heartbeat.

'That's right,' said Simona. 'He still works as a psychiatrist two days a week.'

'And you see him?'

'Most days. I could never have set up the Fondazione

without him. He's been wonderful, just like he always was.' Her praise came out sugared and false.

Kate was still having trouble getting her head round this. Mario was someone who belonged so deep in her past, his memory was so tangled up in those forgotten young girl's dreams of happy-ever-after and first love and infinite possibility, that the person she'd become was finding it hard to imagine a world in which Mario Bassano still walked and breathed.

She was aware that Simona was studying her reaction closely, but she was at a loss for words.

Simona said smoothly, 'I'm expecting him any time now. He usually joins me and my mother on a Friday evening. So you'll be able to see him again.'

This was altogether more than Kate had bargained for. She said, 'I don't know how long I can stay.'

Simona smiled, the smile of someone who's just played their trump card so the game has fallen out exactly as intended. An old woman had emerged from a room at the back of the house. Simona spoke to her in Italian, then turned back to Kate. 'I told Angelica to put your case in the blue bedroom. We'll phone Signor Barzini now and tell him about the painting and then we can go on the terrace and have a drink.' Her long eyes shone with triumph. 'You must be tired after your journey. Now you can relax.'

Relax? It was a long time since Kate had been so strung out, every nerve humming with tension. All this was Simona's fault. She reminded Kate so powerfully of the friend she had loved and lost. For a moment Kate was overwhelmed with an unreasoning hatred of Simona for having survived and aged when Francesca's life had been cut so brutally short. It wasn't fair, it wasn't right. If only Francesca had survived – the two of them could have been talking now, instead of this infuriating younger sister with her mysteries and her neatly booby-trapped surprises.

Simona's smile faded. 'Kate, are you all right?'

'Yes, I suppose . . . it must be the way you remind me of Francesca. I wasn't prepared for that. It's the family resemblance, perfectly natural, but still—'

'I remind you of Francesca?'

'Yes.'

'Thank you, Kate. Thank you so much.' Ridiculously, Simona's eyes filled with tears. 'You've no idea what it means to me to hear you say that.'

Kate's irrational dislike had subsided as quickly as it arose, but she remained annoyed with her hostess. The Fondazione might be an admirable achievement, but Simona was clearly neurotic and Kate could think of many ways she'd rather spend an evening . . . but then she thought of Mario, and her curiosity about him was reason enough to stay a little while longer.

Chapter 6

Mario

Mario Bassano had travelled a long way in his life. As everyone knows, the first necessity for a long journey is comfortable footwear, and, like many people who've grown up in poverty, Mario had a weakness for fine shoes. Each spring and autumn he had two pairs hand-made for him in Milan from supplest calf leather that whispered onto his feet. As soon as they were scuffed or beginning to wear at the heel he gave them away. That glue smell of the cobbler's evoked all the misery of his childhood: cast-offs that never fitted, cramped and painful feet. In addition to his twice-yearly order at Salvini's, he found it hard to resist impulse buys. The more expensive the shop, the more tempting the purchase. That was how he'd been seduced that afternoon, when his work at the centre was finished, by a pair of tan loafers, exquisitely topstitched and outrageously priced.

Shoes were his only real indulgence. His domestic arrangements since his separation from his wife were simple, some might say austere. His clothes were expensive but not ostentatious. The car he was driving now, as he turned off the *autostrada* and began the slow climb into the hills, was a two-year-old Audi, satisfying in its performance and speed, but hardly an extravagance considering his position.

As the road narrowed he changed down from top gear, good driver and good car making the transition smooth as silk. Mario derived sensual pleasure from the action. It therefore troubled him, as he pressed his left foot on the clutch, that the rim of his tan shoe rubbed slightly against his heel.

He was irritated. Unless the shoes were perfect from the start, he'd get rid of them. He pressed a button and the car filled with the cool, mathematical perfection of Bach. After a week of listening to troubled voices – anguished, angry, suicidal, psychotic – he slipped gratefully into a sphere of luminous harmonies and order. He couldn't analyse why the music was such a reliable palliative: it was one of his many regrets that his early years had been too crammed to allow more than a cursory knowledge of musical theory.

Dr Bassano's patients would have been surprised to know the extent of his anxieties and regrets. He knew they regarded him as a paragon of wisdom and calm. Nowadays, that went with the job. Doctors, especially psychiatrists, had replaced priests as idealized male figures. When the psychiatrist in question was, like Mario, good-looking, courteous and kind, then it was hardly surprising if most of his patients, and a good number of his co-workers, fell in love with him at one time or another.

He was aware of the devotion. Sometimes it was irksome; more often he felt humbled by the gulf between what people saw in him and the truth he knew about himself. He did his best to live up to their expectations. No doctor more conscientious or hard-working than he. Or more self-effacing. He was at pains to keep secret the fact that for the past twenty years he had worked without remuneration at the Mission for Santa Cecilia. Let the spoiled contessas and the bored wives of industrialists subsidize the human flotsam that washed up daily at the doors of the good sisters.

About ten minutes from the motorway he saw the side road that led to his apartment in Montombroso. More than anything he wanted to go home, shower and change and have a long cool drink. It had been a demanding week and the heel of his new shoe was definitely rubbing.

He drove straight on. For him, duty did not finish with the end of the working week. There were his two daughters to consider and his estranged wife. There was the Fondazione, now reaching the end of its tenth season. There was Simona.

Recently, he'd been more than usually concerned about Simona. Most probably she was unsettled by having her mother come to live at La Rocca – after all, the two women had never had an easy relationship. He'd lost count of the times Simona had vented her rage over her mother to him. 'That bitch! I hate her! Why doesn't she die?' But Mario knew that hate between parents and children is never a simple thing: love damned up, polluted, driven off course, turned back on itself – but always some remnant of love. Even if, as Simona's for her mother, it felt poisonous as hate.

Whatever the reasons, he'd been anxious about her. She'd done so well since she got the idea for the Fondazione. It had turned her life around and she had found a serenity that had been missing before. He'd been pleased for her, and proud. This past ten years, busy and productive, had lulled him into a false sense of security. Even now it was hard to put his finger on the problem – it wasn't like the violence of the past. He'd become aware of her lack of attention, a sense of distance, a hint of secretiveness. If anything, he found this more worrying than the problems she'd had before. Her present behaviour, elusive and private, was a mystery. And Dr Bassano did not like mysteries.

He crossed over the narrow bridge and followed the road that ran along beside the river until the turn-off by the abandoned lodge. This approach to Bertoni land was always a kind of pleasure. From far off there was the first sight of the bare dog's tooth of the summit, the ancient tower of La Rocca just visible below. Then, as you got closer, the high point was obscured by trees as the countryside became deeply wooded and mysterious. It wasn't until halfway up the drive that the Villa Beatrice came into view, pale and serene, like a light shining from the edge of the mountain. And always as he drew closer, there were two sensations coexisting inside him: a sense of homecoming, but also the feeling that prison gates were closing behind him.

Five thirty on a Friday: Simona was usually still busy at the Villa Beatrice. Mario pulled over, but there was no sign of her. He learned from Magda, one of the administrators, that an Englishwoman had arrived earlier and that she and Simona had gone up to La Rocca. Simona had left orders she wasn't to be interrupted unless there was a real emergency. He tried to remember if Simona had said anything about friends coming at the weekend, but he was fairly sure there'd been no such plans. Tomorrow the Villa Beatrice would fill with all the visiting dignitaries who were joining them to celebrate the end of the tenth season. Simona usually tried to keep her diary clear for a few days beforehand.

He drove thoughtfully the last half mile to La Rocca. After the public elegance of the Villa Beatrice, every bush clipped, every terrace swept in honour of the ceremony the following day, La Rocca was private and remote. By the time he got there, the sun was casting long shadows across the forecourt. A noisy swarm of swifts, like a hail of black arrows, was circling the tower, making that high-pitched excitable noise that was so much a part of summer evenings at La Rocca. He got out of the car, stooping briefly to pat Rollo's pale back. Now that the sun was less hot the old dog had moved from the cool hall into the fresh air. He checked the cars on the forecourt; they were all familiar. The visitor must have left hers at the Villa Beatrice. Mario walked round the outside of the house to the terrace under the vine where Simona usually entertained guests at this time of day.

He was right. The two women were seated in a pair of enormous wicker loungers, champagne flutes in their hands. He heard their laughter before he saw them, and recognized the sharpened gaiety of two people who are striving to appear friendly.

Simona saw him first. The Englishwoman, whoever she was, had her back to him and all he could see was the top of her dark head above the high wicker rim of the chair.

'Mario!' said Simona. 'Punctual as always!' She looked up at him, her eyes shining with amusement and what looked to him like triumph. 'I told Kate you'd be here on time. You remember Kate Holland, don't you?'

A cold-water shock of recognition. Yes, he remembered Kate

Holland all right. How could he forget? He was furious at Simona for not having warned him in advance. He didn't like surprises at the best of times, especially not one like this when he was already exhausted from his long week. He walked casually across the terrace and found himself staring down into a face that was instantly recognizable. Her dark hair was untouched by grey – which could have been thanks to a good colourist – but her brown eyes still had that unnerving direct-ness, a kind of transparent honesty which he'd once found so attractive, but alarming also. He realized with annoyance that she'd observed his discomfort, though he struggled to suppress it as soon as he could. This unspoken communication was an intimacy too soon. How long had Simona been planning this little reunion, and what the hell was Kate Holland doing here anyway?

'Kate!' Years of dealing with difficult patients had given him remarkable powers of recovery. 'What a surprise! As lovely as ever.'

She smiled up at him, entering the game. 'Don't tell me, Mario – I haven't changed a bit!'

'Only to grow more beautiful. Welcome to La Rocca.' He went to the side table and poured himself a large scotch with a small squirt of soda. He was in no mood to celebrate with champagne. He turned and said smoothly, 'Simona never told me she'd invited you here. I would have come earlier if I'd known.'

'Well . . .' Kate looked down into her glass.

Simona stepped in. 'Isn't it extraordinary, Mario? Kate just happened to be passing this way and thought she'd drop by. Just to have a look at the place. Of course, I recognized her at once. I've persuaded her to stay the night.'

'Excellent,' said Mario. 'Did you leave your car at the villa, Kate?'

'No. I haven't got a car.'

'But I thought you said —'

'I came by taxi.'

'You're staying at Montombroso?' Mario's question was casual.

'No. I came up from Florence this afternoon.'

'In a taxi?' He was unable to keep the incredulity from his voice. 'You just happened to be passing in a taxi?'

Kate laughed. She'd always had an attractive laugh, rich and bubbling and infectious. Only right now, Mario did not feel like laughing along with her. Kate's cheeks were slightly flushed with champagne as she said, 'The last of the extravagant travellers, that's me. And I never drive when I'm abroad. It's just—' Suddenly the laughter died in her eyes. 'It's just something I never do,' she muttered. She leaned forward and set her glass down on the low table. She was frowning.

Mario had learned enough to be on his guard. He decided to change the subject. 'How is your mother?' he asked Simona. 'Will she be joining us this evening?'

'I expect so. She had a bad morning, but she was asleep all afternoon and now they say she's fit as a flea. But she may change her mind. You never can tell with my mother. She's so unpredictable.'

Mario sat down and leaned his head back and closed his eyes. The scotch was releasing some of the tension in the back of his neck, but he dared not let his guard slip, not for a moment.

Simona's mother was unpredictable. You could call it that.

But then the whole family was unpredictable, Simona more than anyone. He sighed. Where the Bertoni family was concerned, unpredictability was the only thing you could be certain of.

Chapter 7

Fogbound

Annette Bertoni wasn't exactly sure where she was. The fog had been bad bad bad all day. It came down for long periods, blocking out light and sense. Some days, the clouds bunched up at the sides and she was able to find her way through the tunnel they made – though where in darnation the tunnel was leading, she didn't know. Sometimes, rare as hen's teeth, there was a shaft of bright light round her, like the sunshine that poured down like a waterfall in the big spaces between the trees where she used to play in the woods behind Grampy's house in Maine. In the brightness, which should have been an improvement but never was, she saw clearly – and she didn't like what she saw.

Right now, all she could see through the engulfing mist was that darn spot on the sleeve of her blouse. A grey blemish, shaped like a slug. She shook at it, to make sure it wasn't just a scrap of fluff, then rubbed it with the tip of her bony index finger. It stayed put.

'Nancy!'

'I'm here, *signora*. It's Giulia—'

'Don't cheek me, girl. See here, this shirt is dirty. Get me another.'

'That's just a fleck in the linen, *signora*.'

'Look – don't argue – look – a mark – there – see it!'

'Yes, *signora*. Right away.'

Annette Bertoni's arms and shoulders were stiff with outrage as the girl's broad hands removed the offending linen, then slid the pale silk on her body. She felt so mad and frustrated and helpless it was a wonder she didn't spit sparks like a Catherine wheel and burn up with the rage. Ha, that would be the way to go. A shower of burning colours and then, phut, nothing at all. If only.

'She's ready now.' That wretched girl was talking about her. Did they think she couldn't hear?

'I'm not ready! Don't tell me I'm ready!'

That patient sigh. Those huge brown eyes. It was like lashing out at some dumb cow. 'What do you need, *signora?*'

The question flummoxed her. What did she need? There must be something she needed, but just for the moment, she couldn't think what it was. When she first came to Italy as a bride, there'd been strict rules about what young ladies should and should not have with them. Gloves at all times. Tissue paper for packing undergarments. And . . . Right before she set off travelling with a friend, just before a short journey from Verona to the south, there'd been that conversation with her mother in law. *A young lady must always carry* . . . what was it? What in darnation had been so important that . . . ?

She nailed the thought and smiled, remembering the reassuring feel of hard metal through embroidered silk. She struggled to get out of her chair. When the bovine young maid tried to help her, she shook her off. 'I can manage!' she said angrily, then gripped the back of her chair and reached out across the empty space to her dressing table. Two tottery steps and she was there. She hunched over the drawers, trying to make herself wider, so cow-eyes wouldn't see what she was doing. Pulled open the third drawer on the right. A couple of chiffon scarves, smelling of lavender and stale face powder, then her fingertips touched heavy silk embroidery, pressed down to feel the smooth outline of the pistol inside. Did it still work? She must try it out some time. But not now. For now, it was enough to know it was there.

She pushed the drawer closed and turned round, leaning back against the dressing table for support. 'I'm ready now,' she said. 'Tell Dino I'm ready.'

'Here, *signora*.' He must have been waiting just outside the door. He crossed the room and took her by the arm. A lady must always go in to dinner on the arm of a gentleman.

Ha! Not that Dino was any kind of gentleman.

But he was reliable. A reliable peasant. That was the best that could be said about *him*.

He didn't smell right, though. His head was smooth and shiny as a billiard ball, and he was common as dirt. But he was good and strong. As was his smell.

'Dino, don't you ever take a bath? You stink like a barnyard.'

He merely grinned. That Humpty Dumpty face of his was just made for grinning. Like a big round plate with a smile in the middle. Mind you, it was always possible he didn't understand a word of what she was saying. She might have spoken to him in English. Sometimes she had a job to keep track of which language was which.

It was hard work going down the stairs. She had to concentrate, but it was easier once she reached the flat and was headed into the dining room. Ah yes, there was company, and they were waiting for her. Let them wait. Mario – it must be the weekend again already – and Simona and . . . looked like a visitor. Good, an extra person might liven things up a bit round here. About time.

For the next little while the mist settled round her again, blocking out the others in the room. All her attention was on the food, and the wine in her glass. Nothing seemed to have much flavour these days, but she enjoyed putting it in her mouth. You had to concentrate though. Food didn't act like it used to. It slid off the fork and skittered across the plate and sometimes even escaped out of the corner of her mouth right in the middle of chewing it. The wine brightened her up. Even if it did bounce around in her glass like a storm at sea. She got it down, slurping a bit but she got it down.

That was better. The mist was thinning and she could hear voices. She looked round the table. The newcomer was seated right across from her. A woman with dark hair, who, now she looked at her more closely, seemed familiar, somehow. Reminded her of someone, though darned if she could remember who. An uneasy feeling was spreading through her body, up from her gut. It was kind of like fear, only Annette Bertoni had never been frightened of anyone, so it couldn't be that. Darker than fear. Felt like hate. A sense of black wings flapping across her mind, that plunging terror of sudden loss. She didn't want this woman here, whoever she was. She ought to go.

'Who the hell are you anyway?'

Her question punched a hole in the conversation. Three heads swivelled to stare at her.

'I introduced you already, Mamma. This is Kate Holland, a friend from England. You met her years ago, but you probably don't remember.'

'I remember just fine. Don't you go telling me I have a problem with my memory.'

'Sure, Mamma, anything you say. Just that I already told you who Kate was ten minutes ago and you've forgotten already.'

Annette Bertoni stared. That smart-alec woman speaking was definitely her daughter. Only problem was, she couldn't figure out which one. Sounded a bit like Francesca when she was getting fresh, but come to think of it, Simona had been pretty hard to handle recently and anyway Francesca was . . . Francesca was . . .

It was like someone dropped a dark red curtain down inside her brain. That agony of loss, pitching her into endless darkness. Where was her baby? 'What have you done with her?' she asked plaintively, but no one answered, they just carried on talking as if she wasn't there.

She had to get their attention, before the blackness swallowed her up. 'I know you,' she said loudly to the strange woman. 'You've been here before.'

'That's right,' said the newcomer. 'I'm surprised you remember.'

'Oh, I remember all right. How would I forget? You were here when my baby girl died. You were—'

'Mamma, please.' That was Simona, trying to sound like a dutiful daughter. As if. 'You'll only upset yourself.'

'I'll say what I want and don't you try to stop me. What did you say your name was?'

'Kate. Kate Holland.'

'That's right. You wanted to take them away from me, didn't you? You thought you could interfere in my family and then you tried to run away and . . . and—'

'Mamma, stop this right now!'

But she was on a roller coaster, couldn't stop if she wanted to. 'You killed my baby! It was all your fault! All of it!'

That shook them. That made them sit up and pay attention. That set the goddamn cat among the goddamn pigeons. Oh yes it did! It made her laugh to see how they all spluttered and gawped. Even Dr Nothing-ever-bothers-me-because-I'm-perfect bloody Mario.

The woman they said was called Kate was open-mouthed and shaking, like she'd just wet herself – ha! And that po-faced daughter of hers – which one did she say she was? – looked like she wanted to wallop her one. But she'd never dare.

Shuffle, shuffle. Everybody flap around and fluster.

'Mamma, why don't you keep your foul mouth shut?'

'Signora Bertoni, you've got it wrong.'

'Annette.' Only Mario ever called her Annette now. 'You mustn't excite yourself.'

'Why not?' She turned to him. 'That woman killed my baby girl. She deserves to pay the price, just like I did.'

'Mamma, that's enough.'

More kerfuffle and bother. It was good to be the centre of attention again. She always enjoyed that, but suddenly Signora Bertoni felt hugely tired. As though she wanted to lie down and sleep for a week. That was the trouble when the fog cleared. The view was always of something hateful, something that upset her and made her so goddamn-tired she wouldn't mind curling up and sleeping right here. Still, at least she'd shown them. They'd know not to underestimate her in future.

'Where's Dino? I want to go back to my room.' It was always better to quit before they threw you out.

Her daughter – it must have been Simona – muttered

something about small mercies and rang for Dino. He came at once. He helped her from her chair and it felt good. Like being a child again. A satisfied and naughty child.

A very naughty child indeed. But that was all right. Naughty little girls can get away with anything.

Chapter 8

La Guardia

'Why did you come back here, Kate?'

A stranger might have thought it a casual question. Kate knew better. She didn't answer right away – La Rocca was no place for off-the-cuff answers.

She and Mario were alone together in the dining room. Signora Bertoni had retired to her room, much to Kate's relief, on the arm of the silently smiling Dino. She still felt shaken by the old woman's outburst. A little later Simona had been called away to the phone. It was apparently some problem to do with the Fondazione and they could hear her voice clearly. Long gaps where she said only, '*Si . . . si . . . si . . .*' followed by a torrent of rapid Italian.

Kate sipped her wine. 'No particular reason.' The meal had been excellent, several courses in Italian fashion: delicious *raviolini in brodo*, with the ambrosial scent that only Italian home cooking can achieve, followed by succulent little steaks, then salad. Now a huge plate of cheeses and two plates with fresh figs and white fleshed peaches had been placed on the table. The whole meal was perfect in its simplicity. Which made it all the more of a shame that Signora Bertoni's attack had robbed her of her appetite. She went on quietly, 'David wanted to spend a couple of days in Rome . . . do you remember David Clay? He was in Florence in '67.'

Mario shook his head. 'I do not remember.'

Kate wasn't sure that she believed him. And anyway, was it just David he had chosen to forget, or was it . . . much more? She said, 'David's daughter is studying in Rome and I thought I'd like to see this place again.'

'Why didn't you tell Simona you were coming?'

'I didn't think the family would still be here.'

'It's a long way to travel without an invitation.'

'What's the matter, Mario? Anyone would think you didn't like me being here.'

'Yes.' He held her gaze. 'They might think that.'

Kate felt a prickle of discomfort burning her skin. Long-buried questions were rising to the surface. She had been intrigued at the prospect of rediscovering the man she'd once thought was the love of her life, the man whose loss had affected her far more deeply than the end of her first marriage had done, but this was turning out to be more than intriguing. It was disturbing.

Superficially he had not changed all that much. His thin face and quick intelligent eyes had always given him more appeal than many flashier men. His command of English was much improved. She seemed to remember that when she'd known him he'd had a quirky grasp of the language that was especially engaging. Now, all the wrinkles had been smoothed out. He spoke with grammatical perfection and only a slight trace of an accent. It was a polished performance, just like the rest of him. In the past, he'd been almost as much at sea in the Bertonis' complex world as she had been. Now he gave the impression of a smooth operator, sleek and well fed, a man who knows how to enjoy the small comforts of life and not ask for too much else.

She said, 'Does Signora Bertoni often freak out like that?'

He shook his head. 'You brought back bad memories for her.'

'The woman's crazy.'

'Maybe so. She never really recovered from Francesca's death and now that she is old . . . well, sometimes the memories get too strong for her. You must not take it personally.'

'Don't worry, I won't.'

He smiled. 'Still so determined?'

Kate didn't answer. How strange that he remembered her as being determined.

Mario picked out a peach and began removing its skin. He did so carefully, his short, workmanlike fingers a contrast to the elegance of his clothes, his glossy, well-groomed exterior. He said easily, 'So, tell me about yourself, Kate. Are you married? Do you work?'

'Divorced. And yes, I do work.'

He was cutting the peach carefully into quarters with a little ivory-handled fruit knife. 'And what is it you do?'

'I work with pictures. I'm a conservator.'

'How very interesting. Unfortunately much of the Bertoni collection has been sold off to finance the Fondazione. But there are still several which might interest you. You must ask Simona to show you. If there's time. When did you say you had to leave?'

'I didn't.'

'Ah.' He shot her a questioning glance.

Kate couldn't resist saying, 'I thought I might stay a few days, actually,' and noted with interest the quick frown that shadowed his face. No doubt about it, Mario was not relishing this opportunity to stroll down memory lane. She said, 'Is it a problem for you, Mario, me being here?'

'For myself, no, of course not. I am delighted to see you again.' The impersonal professionalism was in place again. 'But for others . . .'

'Because of the way Simona's mother reacted?'

'No. She is old and confused.' Kate heard the ruthlessness in his voice. 'She does not signify any more.'

'Then what's the problem?'

Mario glanced towards the half-open door of the dining room. Simona's voice could be heard quite clearly. He sighed, then said quietly, 'Simona. Our dear Simona is the problem. She should not have asked you to stay.'

'This is her house, Mario. Surely she can invite who she wants?'

He pounced on her words. 'Simona invited you? I thought you told me she didn't know you were coming.'

'She didn't, but once I showed up, she said why didn't I stay. That's all.' Anyone would think, thought Kate, he was trying to catch her out. Why? Simona had been very insistent that Mario musn't be told about the value of the paintings. Was he involved in some kind of scam to defraud her? 'Any particular reason why she shouldn't?' she asked.

'It is difficult to explain.'

'Try, anyway.'

He sighed again, then leaned back in his chair, staring thoughtfully at the four quarters of peach arranged on his plate. 'Simona has a sensitive nature.' He was choosing his words carefully, as if calculating how much information it was safe to give away. 'She reacts differently than other people would. Especially when it's anything to do with her sister.'

His words brought back another conversation, long ago. Where? Kate had a vague memory of a bar, a place without comforts, just simple tables and in the background a jukebox playing. Hadn't Mario offered similar veiled warnings about Francesca? Was she supposed to believe that both sisters were so sensitive that exposure to someone like her would threaten their mental stability? And what exactly were the ties that bound him and Simona together? Already the questions were piling up. This had always been a place with more questions than answers. 'So why do you think she wants me to stay?'

'That's what—' He broke off as Simona returned to the dining room.

'Sorry about that,' she said, looking questioningly from Kate to Mario. 'Last-minute glitches in the arrangements for the gala day tomorrow. You'll be able to see the Fondazione congratulating itself, Kate. Now that we are successful everyone wants a piece of the action. They're even sending some big shot from the department of culture in Rome.'

'Kate may not be able to stay another day,' said Mario.

'Oh, but she must. She's only just got here.'

'Did you know Kate works with pictures? She's a conservator?'

'Is that true, Kate?' Simona simulated surprise. 'How fascinating. We'll have to have a proper tour in the morning, so you can see what we have left. Not so much as my uncle had, but still not bad for a private collection.'

'You could show them to her now,' said Mario.

'No, daylight is best. So, Kate, how would you like to be entertained this evening?'

'Kate is no doubt tired after that long taxi ride,' said Mario, the slight emphasis on the last three words betraying his suspicion.

'Oh, don't be so boring, Mario. It's still early. You go home if you want to, but these last evenings of summer are so special it's a crime to waste them. I know!' She clapped her hands together in a theatrical gesture, as though the idea had just that moment occurred to her. 'Let's walk up to La Guardia. It's nearly a full moon. We may even hear the nightingales.'

'La Guardia?' Kate asked. 'Isn't that an airport?'

'It means The Lookout. It's the highest point of our land you can reach without mountaineering equipment.' She laughed, but her enthusiasm for their evening walk sounded forced. Kate thought perhaps she was trying to get some time with her away from Mario. 'From there you can see halfway to Florence. It's wonderful at night.'

'Sounds good to me,' said Kate. 'I'll get my jacket.'

'And some sensible shoes,' warned Mario. He turned to Simona, 'Don't forget to tell Dino.'

'Oh, he'll be safely tucked up in the kitchen drinking grappa till midnight.'

'Best tell him anyway,' said Mario. 'To be on the safe side.'

'What does Dino have to do with it?' asked Kate. The notion that Signora Bertoni's round-faced escort needed to be told of their plans made her uncomfortable.

'It is his job to patrol the grounds at night,' explained Mario. 'A remote place like this attracts all kinds of undesirables. You cannot be too careful.'

'Are you coming, Mario?' Simona asked him casually. 'Or do you want to get home?'

'Oh yes, I'll come,' said Mario. He smiled. 'I haven't been to the Lookout at night for months.' If Simona was disappointed by his decision, she was careful not to show it.

They assembled at the back of the house. Simona had brought a torch, but didn't use it. The moon, a few days away from full, had risen some time before and, once their eyes had adjusted to the outdoors, the path was clearly defined as it wound between boulders and outcrops of rock on the way to the summit. The cool air was still sweet with the fragrance of dry leaves. Far off, beyond distant hills, thunder rumbled, a harmless reminder of the coming winter storms.

They walked in single file, Simona leading the way and Mario bringing up the rear. After the warmth of the day, Kate was surprised how quickly the temperature had dropped. The air was chill against her cheeks. It was refreshing, clearing her head which was muzzy from the champagne and the wine they had drunk with dinner.

The path climbed steeply. Soon they were looking down on the lights of La Rocca and, half a mile further down the hillside, the glow in the trees that showed the location of the Villa Beatrice. From this angle and in the darkness La Rocca's origins as a medieval stronghold were sharply outlined. Already the view was stupendous. They were only an hour's drive from Florence, but they could have been in a different world. On all sides were steep wooded hills, and in the valley below lay the river like a curve of silver rope. Kate had been in cities so long she'd forgotten how spectacular the night sky is away from the pollution caused by urban lights. She paused for a moment to catch her breath and marvelled at the sheer bigness of sky and landscape.

'It's good, isn't it?' said Mario, coming up behind her in

the darkness. For the first time, his voice sounded almost friendly.

'Wonderful.'

She had lost sight of Simona, striding ahead of them, confident and at home on the uneven mountain path. While she and Mario were gazing up at the stars, Simona vanished behind an outcrop of rock a little way ahead, so they never saw exactly what happened next.

There was a piercing scream and the rattle of small stones. Then silence.

'Simona!' Kate called out. 'Are you all right?'

'Simona!' Mario's voice behind her was ragged with fear.

Kate began running up the path but Mario was faster, pushing past her in his urgency.

They rounded the corner. A pale shape beside the path a little way ahead moved slightly. Then Simona struggled to her feet. 'It's okay,' she said, brushing grit from her trousers. 'No bones broken.'

'Are you sure?' asked Mario. 'My God, Simona, you could have been . . . You must be more careful. You know how dangerous that corner is.' He was helping Simona to her feet, fussing and scolding. There was nothing phoney about his concern this time. To Kate's ears it sounded very much like the panic you only really feel for those you love. She would have given a lot, right then, to know the precise nature of their relationship.

Alerted by the anxiety in his voice, Kate looked down beyond the small patch of rough ground where Simona had fallen. A few stunted bushes, a small boulder . . . and after that the ground plunged dizzyingly down. A sheer drop of hundreds of metres. A small stone, loosened by her foot,

bounced down and down and then vanished into the void.
She never heard it hit the bottom. Kate stepped back,
suddenly feeling sick.

You could have been killed was the meaning behind Mario's
words, but all he said was, 'You should have worn proper
shoes.'

'Don't fuss,' said Simona. 'We're nearly there.'

But she was limping badly as they made their way, cautiously
now, along the final fifty metres of track to the Lookout. Kate
found herself on a small oval of ground just below the summit.
It was well worth the climb. Up here you got that top-of-the-
world sensation; Kate felt that if she stretched out her arms she
could almost brush her hands against the stars.

They stood in silence for a while. La Rocca and Villa Beatrice
lay on the far side of the mountain. From here, though the view
stretched for miles, few lights were visible. Kate, whose image
of Italy was all of cities and paintings and cultivated land, was
taken aback by the wildness of the scene.

'How do you like it?' Simona had hobbled over to a seat
carved into the rock.

'It's fantastic,' said Kate. 'I can't think why Francesca never
showed me this.'

'The path didn't exist back then,' Simona explained. 'We did
once clamber up here but there was hell to pay when the adults
found out what we'd been doing. I got the men to make this
route a few years back.'

Mario emerged from the shadow of the rock where he'd been
standing in silence and crouched down beside Simona, cradling
her foot in his hands. 'You're bleeding,' he said.

'Am I?' Simona peered curiously at her leg. A thread of blood
was trickling over her ankle.

'Look.' His voice was full of angry concern. Still holding her foot, Mario rolled her trouser leg back to reveal a deep gash. Kate felt a sudden gust of sexual attraction, a deep tug of memory. One night, long ago, a young doctor had taken her foot in his hands, just so, and rubbed her flesh to warm it. And then . . . was it present attraction she was experiencing now, or was it just the echo of remembered desire?

'Damn,' said Simona. 'These shoes will be ruined.'

'Never mind the shoes,' said Mario. 'Flex your toes. That's right. And does it hurt when I—?' Simona's yelp of pain was all the answer he needed. 'This needs a dressing. We're going back to the house.'

'But we only just got here.'

'And now we're leaving.'

'But Kate—'

'Kate can stay if she wants to but I'm taking you back to La Rocca.'

Simona protested some more but Mario was adamant.

'I'll follow in a few minutes,' said Kate as Mario helped Simona to stand. Perhaps it was the effect of the moonlight, but her face did look very pale.

'Have my torch,' said Simona. 'There's only one way down, so . . . are you sure you'll be okay?'

'I'll be fine.'

'Just follow the path.'

'Don't worry about me.'

Mario put his arm round Simona's waist and they walked away slowly, still muttering with intimate crossness to each other, like some long-married couple. Kate's curiosity was growing. Simona had mentioned that Mario had a wife, but that was all Kate knew.

She heard their voices fade as they vanished behind an outcrop of rock, Mario gently fussing while Simona protested that she was fine. Then silence. Kate settled back to enjoy herself. It was years since she'd been alone in such a beautiful and lonely spot.

But as soon as their voices vanished, the darkness sprang alive with tiny sounds. There was a dry rustling in the bushes below where she was sitting, then a small movement over gravel that might have been a slithering . . . Kate had no idea what creatures lived on a hilltop such as this. Were there snakes? Wild boar? Were there wolves?

The hair on the back of her neck was moving, as though someone's hand was hovering just inches away, or as though a breeze was passing, but even at this height the night air was utterly still. From far below in the valley came a sharp scream: something weak falling prey to a stronger foe.

Kate reminded herself she was here to listen out for nightingales. She looked up at the stars and tried to recognize the constellations. Something scuffled in the rocks behind her head.

Every nerve was strained, but even so, she didn't hear it coming. An awareness of movement made her turn suddenly, just in time to see the owl swoop past, a glimmer of pale feathers and speed only yards from her place on the hillside. Kate caught her breath. The silent predator was beautiful and deadly and utterly regardless of her presence.

Kate had never felt like such an interloper. This mountaintop belonged to wild creatures. She had no right to be there, trespassing on their world.

A crack of thunder decided her. The elusive nightingales would have to wait for another time.

As she stood up she heard a louder noise in the scrubby bushes that clung to the hillside just below the Lookout. Something big was moving around down there. She hated to imagine what size of animal would cause such a disturbance. She told herself that noises are amplified at night. Perhaps it wasn't as large as it sounded – a hedgehog, or something. But did they have hedgehogs in Italy?

She clicked on the torch and began to walk back down the path. No need to hurry, she told herself. No reason to panic. She resisted the temptation to quicken her pace and break into a run. That could be dangerous. She was easing her way carefully along the narrow stretch of path where Simona had fallen. Coming to the place from above, the drop which Simona had so narrowly avoided seemed even more terrifying than before. Her heart was thumping and she cursed herself for not having gone back with Mario and Simona. No view is that good, she told herself, and as for nightingales . . .

Another crash in the bushes below. From up here whatever was making that noise sounded large as a cow. Or a person. Kate slowed up just enough to turn and look down. When she shone her torch into the blackness its beam flickered with the shaking of her hand. Something was moving through the stunted trees and scrub. It looked horribly like the figure of a man, but that didn't make sense. Surely Simona had told her there was only one path between La Rocca and the summit, and anyway, why would anyone else want to go clambering over the mountain this late at night?

Her ears were straining to hear the smallest noise above the rasping of her breath and the slip and scuffle of her feet on the path, so the explosion when it came was deafening. There was a whistling noise as the air was cut by the bullet's path, then a shattering crack, like cymbals clashing between her ears, when it struck the rock.

'Hey, stop!' Kate's reflex was instant. 'I'm here!' It had flashed through her mind that whoever was out hunting this late at night thought they had the mountain to themselves.

The second shot disabused her. This one connected with the rock even closer to her head. *Jesus.* Some maniac down there was aiming at her! Kate didn't shout again. She crouched down behind the shelter of a boulder, clicked off the torch, then took off towards the house. Never mind that it was an impossibly awkward position for running, never mind that her shoe came off and her trousers ripped on a branch of thorn . . . Kate was transformed into a concentrated arrow of flight, hurtling down towards the lights of the house. She was running faster than she'd run in years but still it wasn't fast enough. Her body felt slow and cumbersome, as though she was trying to force herself to move through thick, clinging mud. Her lungs screamed with pain, her legs were heavy, like lead weights. And all the time she felt so huge and unmissable she could have been surrounded by white light and visible for miles around, waiting for the shot and whistle of the gun. Next time . . .

The path dipped down. Kate stumbled, her knees fell on jagged stones and there were thorns in her palm. She righted herself, plunged on . . . and there was the house ahead. The back door open. All she had to do was reach it, get over the threshold, escape the darkness.

Blood was pounding in her ears. She was gasping. Terror was playing tricks with her hearing. As she flung herself into the pool of light from the back door, she could have sworn she heard harsh laughter, high above her head.

*

'Kate, what is it?' Simona was sitting quietly in the drawing room, a white bandage round her ankle.

'Someone –' she could hardly speak, 'someone – shooting.'

'Shooting?' Simona stood up in alarm.

'At – me.'

'*What?*'

'Someone – just tried – to shoot me.'

Appalled, Simona was at her side in an instant. It occurred to Kate, in spite of everything, that Mario's bandage must be very effective: Simona was hardly limping at all.

Then Kate's legs gave up the strain of holding her upright and she slumped down on a chair. 'Some fucking maniac out there was shooting at me,' she gasped. She heard her voice saying the words. In here, in firelight and candlelight and surrounded by Simona's beautiful things, the statement sounded ludicrous. Preposterous. It couldn't be true. Hysterical laughter bubbled up close to the surface.

Simona had crouched down, her arm round Kate's shoulder. 'Tell me what happened.'

'Christ, I wish I knew. I was coming back down from the Lookout. There was someone below me, in the scrub. Then they shot at me, twice.'

'I'd better warn Dino.' Simona stood up swiftly. Then, suddenly, she clapped her hand to her forehead in a theatrical gesture. 'Oh my God! Dino!'

'Dino?'

'It must have been him.'

'But why on earth—? Why would Dino want to shoot me?'

'He didn't know it was you, Kate. I told him we were going

up to the Lookout, but when he saw me and Mario coming back to the house, he must have assumed you were back too. Oh, my God, I don't believe it! That man is so *stupid*!'

'But why was he shooting?'

'He's our nightwatchman. This place is a prime target for burglars, everyone for miles around is convinced it's still full of priceless treasures. Oh, Kate, I'm so sorry this happened. But don't worry, you weren't in any real danger. Dino is so blind he couldn't shoot straight to save his life and he only ever fires blanks.'

'What? Simona, those were bullets.'

'Impossible.'

'Believe me, I heard them hit the rock.'

'You must have imagined it.'

'Jesus, Simona. I was almost *killed* out there and now you're telling me I'm imagining it!' Kate was shaking.

'Oh, Kate, I'm sorry. I didn't mean . . . Let me pour you some brandy. Here, have my shawl.'

Simona was all concern. Kate was still shivering, as though with immense cold, but the brandy and the shawl helped.

'I'll go and find Dino,' said Simona. 'And work out what's going on.' She looked worried.

Kate didn't like the idea of being left alone. Her city-dweller's relish for solitude had deserted her. 'Is Mario still around?'

'Oh, I don't think so.' Simona was vague. 'I think he just left. Stay here, Kate. I'll be back in a minute.'

She hurried from the room. Only a slight limp, Kate noticed. She could hear raised voices from the back of the house. She stood up and began to pace restlessly up and down the room. From time to time she sipped her brandy and felt the warm glow spread from her throat to the pit of her stomach. Logs crackled in the grate. Slowly, slowly, her heart rate returned to normal, her breathing eased.

But that sense of being a moving target, huge and unmissable as she raced down the stony path – that feeling was harder to shake off.

Chapter 9

Sweet Dreams

'Will you come to bed, now, *signora*?' Giulia stifled a yawn.

The old woman was pretending she hadn't heard. She knew more tricks than a circus monkey. She stayed at the window, holding onto the ledge and leaning out as she had done for nearly half an hour. Giulia had tried to get her away from the window, but without success. 'Did you see that?' the *signora* called out, to no one in particular. 'Did you see how she ran? Ha!'

'It's late, *signora*.' Giulia was pleading. 'I've been up since six. Why won't you let me put you to bed?'

No answer, of course.

It was no joke looking after the *signora*. Giulia's friends thought she had it easy, but she'd rather be working in a café or a shop. At least then you could go home at the end of the day. You'd have time off to spend with your mates. Sometimes Giulia thought she was little better than a slave. The old woman looked so fragile and refined, like one of those dignified old ladies in the films, but she was a nightmare to handle. Like a child, but more cunning, more devious. Like a monster, sometimes. She'd never admit it to anyone, but Giulia was frightened of the *signora*. It was hard to know what she was thinking about – and when you did know, well, that was even worse. Giulia had never known anyone so eaten up with spite and bitterness as the older Signora Bertoni – and Giulia had mixed with some pretty rough characters in her short life.

Even when the old witch was being nice, you had to watch your back. Like last month, when she'd given Giulia a little brooch from the box on her dressing table. 'Take it, take it,' she'd said. 'It's worthless anyway and I never liked it. Go on, have it, it's yours.' But the first time Giulia wore it, the next Sunday, the *signora* screeched like a boar in a trap. 'My brooch! How dare you steal my precious brooch! Give it back right now!' It was no use explaining; the crazy old fool was all set to call the police. Giulia got quite scared in the end. Even if the stupid woman didn't call the police, she was working herself up to have a fit right there and die of apoplexy. Giulia couldn't think of a more suitable end – but she knew there'd be hell to pay if anyone discovered her lack of care had contributed to the old woman's death.

'*Signora*,' she said dully, not expecting Annette to pay any attention. 'Come away from the window. It's cold. You'll catch your death.'

'Stupid girl, it's not *my* death you need to worry about.' Her old voice was harsh and ugly as a crow's. 'Did you see how she ran? Ha! Fell down, too. Good! Serves her damn right.'

Giulia didn't have a clue what the *signora* was talking about. And she didn't want to know either. All that bothered her was that her charge had been standing by the window for ages now, peering out into the darkness as though she was looking for something. Then there were those shots, two shots, and the old woman almost fell over with excitement. Crazy, that was her trouble. Most likely the men were frightening off some kids from the village. Giulia didn't like the way they used guns round here. One day someone was going to get hurt. She remembered when Mollina's son had been peppered with shot a few years back. The Bertonis had to pay the family money to keep that one quiet, though the boy wasn't badly hurt. Just flesh wounds. She'd seen him boasting about it in town. All the local kids liked to trespass: it was a game for them, seeing how far they could go before someone saw them.

If she could, Giulia would have chucked the job in months ago. She'd begged her dad to let her work somewhere else, anywhere else. She didn't mind where. But he wouldn't hear of it. 'Keep it in the family,' he said. Well, it was all right for him to say, he didn't have to put up with the old bitch all day long.

'*Signora* . . .'

To Giulia's amazement, Signora Bertoni turned away from the window. She was grinning, as though someone had just given her a treat. 'What?' she said. 'You still here? Then you might as well put me to bed.'

Giulia couldn't believe her luck. The *signora* leaned on her arm and tottered slowly to the bed. She allowed herself to be put between the sheets and lay back against the pillows with none of the usual fuss and struggle.

'What a good girl you are,' said the *signora*, her harsh voice sounding almost mellow. 'Just like your father. He's a good man, Dino. I can always rely on him.'

The *signora* was still smiling when Giulia bid her goodnight and put out the light.

Chapter 10

Night

Each time Kate closed her eyes she saw the uneven path in the moonlight, felt terror pumping through her body as she ran . . .

Shreds of panic still clung to her, driving off sleep. She sat up and switched on the light, told herself not to be such a drama queen. Look on the bright side, her sensible voice told her. If she was fated to spend a sleepless night, then she couldn't have chosen a better room. Five-star insomnia was guaranteed at La Rocca.

Like all the rooms in the house, this one was high-ceilinged, with lofty beams and tall windows shuttered against the chill night air. There was not much furniture, but the few pieces were exquisite: a huge half-canopy antique bed, an eighteenth-century painted wardrobe complete with dancing nymphs and swags of fruit and leaves, a couple of chairs and a writing table and thick rugs underfoot. Three of the paintings, a fifteenth-century annunciation, a landscape by Claude and an orchard scene by Sisley, were well worth staying awake for. No wonder Simona employed someone to patrol the grounds at night.

There had been no satisfactory explanation for the shooting. Dino was nowhere to be found, and though she didn't say so, it was obvious that Simona still believed he only ever fired blanks. His eyesight had deteriorated recently and he'd stopped going hunting last year. Kate must have imagined the impact of the bullets against the rocks.

Kate knew that wasn't true; she was angry at not being believed. They parted coolly.

Now, Kate told herself it must have been Dino. Maybe he'd been scaring off predators. Maybe he just liked frightening the Bertonis' guests. She'd thought he was creepy when she'd seen him walking down the stairs with Simona's mother on his arm, the fragile old lady and the oafish-looking man with the bulbous head, like a parody of a devoted old couple. And it was creepy the way he never stopped smiling. Maybe he'd been smiling as he raised his ancient gun to his shoulder, looked down the sights with his blurry, imperfect eyes, and took aim . . .

Kate pulled her dressing gown on and padded to the window.

For the first and, she sincerely hoped, the last time in her life Kate had been a moving target in the moonlight – and now she was told it had been an accident. A terrible mistake, so Simona had said. The danger was past and she was safe.

So why did she still feel frightened? Was it just that her nerves were raw and jagged or was there another reason? Why did every creak and whisper of the old house cause her to shiver with apprehension? She had spoken to David in Rome and he was driving up to join her tomorrow. He might stay here with her for a day or two or they might leave right away for Florence. All perfectly safe and normal.

Wasn't it?

Small, niggling doubts remained. Like the way the second shot had been fired after she called out. And Simona's limp that came and went. The way Mario had apparently left as soon as Simona was bandaged up, not waiting for Kate to reappear. The fact that none of it quite added up.

What was she saying? That Dino had been out there on the mountain taking pot shots at her on purpose? Why? Unless he took a psychotic delight in using house guests for target practice, he had no possible motive. But maybe it hadn't been Dino. After all, Mario had made no secret of his belief that she ought not to have come to the Villa Beatrice in the first place. Why? Because of his guilty conscience about the undervalued paintings? He'd claimed her presence made him anxious for Simona, but there'd been no chance to find out what exactly he meant by that. Still, whatever his concerns for Simona's well-being, it was unlikely they extended as far as trying to shoot anyone threatening her peace of mind. Talk about taking a sledgehammer to crack a nut . . .

Her mind was racing with possibilities. Mario need not have even fired the shots himself. All that was required were a few words to Dino as he helped (the still limping?) Simona into the house. 'By the way, Dino, I think I saw that wolf up by La Guardia just now. If you want to get a shot at it, this would be a good chance.' And the dutiful, half-blind and not-too-bright Dino obligingly set off with his gun.

But why stop at Mario? Looking back, it struck Kate as highly suspicious that Simona just happened to fall on that particular corner of the path. She must have walked that way hundreds of times before. How convenient that Mario and she went back to the house early, leaving Kate to follow on her own.

Of course, they couldn't have been sure she'd choose to stay up there alone, but there had to be a sporting chance.

Kate went to the bathroom – her huge and beautifully appointed black marble bathroom – and splashed cold water on her face. This was crazy. What was she thinking? That Mario and Simona had planned this whole episode?

'For Christ's sake, Kate,' she told herself angrily. 'It's not like you to be paranoid.'

Yes, well. She'd never been shot at before either. Remember what they say: just because you're paranoid, doesn't mean no one's trying to kill you.

Kill? It was bad enough if someone had been trying to frighten her off – but *murder*?

And why suspect Simona? Mario might be hostile, but Simona had been welcoming – she'd even sent her those pictures to get her to visit the place. And what motive might Simona have?

Kate couldn't think of one. But she remembered Signora Bertoni's chilling outburst at the dinner table. '*You killed my daughter*!'

Kate groaned. Maybe Simona shared her mother's crazy logic and held her responsible for Francesca's death. How had she ever imagined that the years would be sufficient to wash away the horror of that tragedy? It was crazy to hold her responsible, but maybe it was enough that she'd been a part of it. She could understand how Signora Bertoni, in the confusion of old age, had turned on her.

Kate had been a player in the tragedy. She'd been there.

Suddenly she found herself sitting on the edge of the bed, her face wet with tears. The panic was washed away and in its place was an ache of loss . . . she knew now why she'd come back to the Villa Beatrice after all this time. Partly, yes, it was curiosity about the altered paintings, who was sending them, and why.

And partly it was the chance to travel with David and find out if their relationship had any mileage in it, or if it was to be just a summer affair. This journey had been his idea. 'I'll spend a couple of days with Lucy in Rome. You can stay with your friends in Siena and then we'll go to the villa together.' But at the last minute she'd decided to come on ahead. It was better that she go alone to this place that had had such an impact on her life.

Because most of all she'd come back to the Villa Beatrice for herself. She'd reached the age when she was starting to glance back over her shoulder, to wonder which had been the key moments when she chose one path instead of another.

Florence in 1967 had been one such moment. Florence and the friends she had made when working there after the flood. And one friend in particular: Francesca Bertoni. They had been mud angels together and they had explored what it was to be grown-ups and free. And then Francesca had brought her here, to the Villa Beatrice estate. For one brief and glorious and terrible weekend Kate had become a part of the Bertonis' lives, and had fallen in love, that desperate illusion of first love when anything is possible. And yes, she'd been a player in the sequence of events that culminated in the outrage of Francesca's death.

For years she had thought she could close the door on the past. Carry on. Make a life. And so she had. A good life. But now she was back and the nightmare was closing in on her again.

All Kate's instincts told her to escape. Get out while she still could. Even now, at four o'clock in the morning, she must be able to call a taxi. She could even be in Rome for a late breakfast.

Yet still the tears flowed – old, old tears – and she did not move. Her heart ached for Francesca. She'd never imagined it was possible to miss someone after so long.

She tried to think clearly, but she was numb. The more she struggled to work out what she should do now, the more her thoughts drifted back to those weeks she'd shared with Francesca in Florence and the person she'd been, so gloriously and stupidly certain that the present was theirs to enjoy. And so innocently sure that their futures would be filled with endless opportunity.

PART II

Chapter 11

Flood

November 1966

In Italy it had been a wet autumn. The rivers were full and the ground saturated. At the beginning of November, swollen mountain streams in the north-east of the country caused landslides and destroyed bridges, cutting road and rail links. Rough seas burst through the dykes and large areas of the Po river valley were flooded. Venice was badly hit, the islands of Pellestrina and Sant'Erasmo being completely inundated. In Venice itself large famished rats were reported to have emerged from the sewers and attacked a group of children.

Italy was cut in half by the storms that raged from Sicily to the Brenner Pass. A pilot who flew across the centre of the country said it resembled a storm-tossed sea with only the tops of bell towers and tall trees breaking its surface.

On the afternoon of the third of November, while Prince Philip and his five companions were bagging nearly two hundred and fifty pheasants during the first shoot of the season at Sandringham, a series of torrential downpours fell on Florence and the surrounding hills. As night fell the rain became continuous and it did not let up till late the following day. By then over eighteen centimetres of rain had fallen.

A peculiar meteorological situation, much discussed on Italian radio in subsequent days, meant the rain and high winds were prevented from moving away. The Arno rose twenty feet in as many hours and finally burst its banks. The force of the flood was devastating. An unstoppable sea of chocolate-coloured water, mud mixed with oil from burst central heating systems, surged through the streets at up to forty miles an hour, hurling cars and even lorries into piles. In some areas the flood water was over six metres deep. On the Ponte Vecchio, the age-old jewellers' shops were smashed. Cars, tree trunks and even bloated cattle plugged the gaping holes.

For twenty-four hours the city was virtually unreachable; it was without piped water, electricity and phones. The archives in the National Library were swamped with the toxic mix of mud and naphtha. On that first terrible night, volunteers formed human chains to hand the sodden books and documents to safety. For many of the city's treasures, it was already too late.

On the evening of the fourth of November, as the rain eased and the flood waters subsided, a man was seen walking knee deep in mud; he was weeping. In his arms he carried the remains of an enormous wooden crucifix; he was followed by a sombre line of workmen, students and friars. Professor Ugo Procacci, superintendent of the Uffizi gallery, was carrying all that remained of the Crucifixion by Cimabue, the greatest artist of the thirteenth century. This irreplaceable masterpiece, ruined beyond repair, was to become the symbol of Florence's tragedy.

The flood waters left in their wake a residue of slime and mud, cars and lorries stacked on top of each other, shops and houses in ruins. Ten days later, in the New Market piles of decomposing fish and vegetables had turned sections of the piazza into a giant compost heap, while behind the church of Santa Croce dead animals were still rotting where they lay.

Young people responded at once and gave what they could. School children, students and foreign visitors worked tirelessly in cold and wretched conditions. Over the following weeks their example was followed by youngsters from further afield in Italy, from Britain and Scandinavia, Canada and the States. They stayed to help with the clean-up for a few days or for months. In time these bands of youthful volunteers came to be known affectionately as Mud Angels. Or, occasionally, as Angels of the Flood.

Chapter 12

Uffizi

Kate had never been on such intimate terms with anyone's head before. She reckoned the boy was about fifteen years old, a good-looking youth with a straight nose and intricate curls covering his scalp. As the days passed, each detail was becoming as familiar as her own body, the dimple on his chin, the hollow at the base of his throat, his nostrils. Luckily he was attractive enough to make the attention worthwhile.

The sixteenth-century bust of an unknown youth had been stored in the basement of the Uffizi when the flood struck. Large dark patches, where oil and gloop had penetrated deep into the stone, gave his face a piebald appearance. Kate's task was to apply a poultice of absorbent paste, making sure every smallest crevice was filled, and then, after a period of about forty-eight hours, during which some of the muck had been drawn out into the paste, to remove it again using toothpicks and fine brushes. The whole business was then repeated. When the process was explained to her, Kate expected the work to be tedious, though obviously a doddle compared to cleaning cellars. She was in for a surprise. As her fingers moved over the delicate curls, the firm lips and the gently rounded cheeks, she experienced profound intimacy, not just with the stone, but with the hands and mind of the anonymous artist who had carved it over four hundred years before her birth. Experiencing art through her fingers was proving to be a revelation.

Their studio workshop on the ground floor of the Uffizi was a long, cold room sparsely furnished with trestle tables and benches. Like everywhere in Florence during that extraordinary winter, it smelled of wet stone and decay, and the little heaters were inadequate against the cold.

At a nearby worktable, Francesca was busy cleaning an enormous eighteenth-century gilded frame, a task requiring delicacy and patience and an inexhaustible supply of cotton buds. 'Treat it like a butterfly's wing,' the professor had instructed her. 'The gold leaf was blown on in the first place, so it's just as fragile.'

Kate realized that Francesca was the sort of person who always got assigned the most delicate jobs. After she and David had taken her back to the hostel after the consul's party, she'd had the weekend to settle in during which she mysteriously collected her belongings from Left Luggage. Unlike most of the volunteers, Francesca seemed to have access to plenty of money, but she never let on where it came from. There was no problem about getting her work with the English team at the Uffizi. Two days working in the cellars was all it took to demonstrate that she had no familiarity even with the humble dustpan and brush, let alone with spades and shovels. Besides, the London expert was happy to employ attractive young women – and Francesca was as attractive as they come.

Of all the mud angels, Francesca was the only one to look remotely angelic. With her long, expressive eyes, fine bone structure and tumble of light brown hair, she might have stepped down from a fourteenth-century fresco.

'Have you noticed,' Professor Fuller commented one afternoon, 'that no invented angel is ever more beautiful than an attractive young man or woman?' Anna, who was pretty, with long hair which she hadn't cut since someone had told her it made her look Pre-Raphaelite, assumed he was referring to her, but Kate realized he was looking at Francesca. A shaft of light was falling on her hair, causing it to shine with iridescent colours. Head bowed over her work, she remained unaware of the attention.

None of the group *had* ever noticed the human quality of angels, as it happened, so he went on thoughtfully, still gazing at Francesca, 'Our mortal imaginations cannot conjure up an image of any creature more perfect than what we know. I suppose that's why God had to take human form. Greater beauty may well exist in some other realm, but it's beyond the grasp of our feeble perception.'

Something in his tone caused Francesca to look up and catch his eye. Maybe she realized she'd been the trigger for his angelic musings, because she coloured, then looked away and asked in a strained voice, 'Is it normal for angels to have black hearts?'

There was a tense silence. No one had the faintest idea why she had reacted so strangely, and even Professor Fuller was nonplussed by her question. Kate had already observed Francesca's tendency to go off at a tangent to everyone else. To lighten the mood she started singing, 'Teen Angel', which Anna followed with 'Venus in Blue Jeans'. The others all groaned and told them to shut up and the tension eased.

The professor had been intrigued by Francesca from the start. 'Are you by any chance related to Signor Bertoni?' he asked when she told him her name.

'Who's he?' She looked blank.

'The art collector, Umberto Bertoni. He lives at the Villa Beatrice about fifty miles from Florence. They say the paintings no one has seen are far more valuable than those on display. I thought perhaps you might—'

'Never heard of him,' said Francesca flatly. 'Besides, I'm American.'

She was being evasive, Kate thought. If Umberto Bertoni had been really unknown to her, then surely she'd have been curious about her famous namesake. And the way she'd stared unblinking at the professor when she denied even having heard of him reminded Kate of the time she and some friends had tried to brazen it out with their headmistress when they'd been spotted in a coffee bar with a group of boys instead of doing a cross-country run.

Still, if Francesca was being dishonest about her background, then so were many of the volunteers. Quite apart from the girl who said she was having an affair with the Aga Khan, no one could be quite sure that Jenny the dancer really had worked in West End musicals, or that Dido's father was a cabinet minister, or that Aiden, with his black cloak and his yellow hair, had once worked as a runner for a Jamaican drug baron the way he claimed. Since the city of Florence was so different from its normal self, it seemed as though everyone there could experiment with different pictures of themselves: like skinny Larry with his squeaky voice who claimed to be a brilliant intellectual, in spite of working in a tax office, or like Hugo, doing floodwork at the consulate, who described himself as 'to all intents and purposes a virgin' – a phrase which was endlessly dissected but which he never precisely explained. Then there were the people who were just pretending to be young and rootless, men who'd taken time off from wives and jobs in England, but were simply too old to be working for nothing and talking endlessly about sex with a bunch of kids fresh out of school or university. Even Kate, who told no overt lies, was pretending to be a sophisticated woman of the world, whereas she'd only left school six months before.

Francesca was unusual simply because she alone was trying hard to be just like everyone else. She gave the impression, right from day one, that she wanted to be ordinary, but she lacked the reference points the others shared. Conversation in the studio at the Uffizi while Kate and Francesca and half a dozen others worked together on the damaged sculptures was not all highbrow. It was soon obvious Francesca had never heard of *Top of the Pops* or the *Avengers*, nor even of American imports like *The Lone Ranger* or *Bonanza*, and her curiosity about what she'd missed only made it more obvious.

'Where did you grow up?' asked Jenny one day when Francesca had been asking about family relationships in *Peyton Place*. 'On a desert island?'

'Of course I didn't!' she snapped. 'That's a stupid thing to say!' And she sank into hurt silence for the rest of the afternoon.

'They don't like me,' she said to Kate later that evening when they were back in their digs and changing to go out. Now they were officially employed by the Uffizi they had moved out of the hostel and were sharing a room with Anna. Dido and Jenny had the room across the corridor. The *signora* who owned the flat was so far uncomplaining about the number of 'friends' who often shared their rooms with them. Francesca peered into the mirror to apply some of Kate's white eyegloss. 'Everyone thinks I'm odd, but I'm not!'

Kate was still young enough to be flattered by confidences. 'We're all odd,' she reassured her, 'so I don't see why you should be any different. But it might help if you didn't try so hard. Sometimes that puts people off.'

'You're criticizing me!'

'No, I'm not. Honestly. It's just that you make life hard for yourself sometimes. People like you the way you are. However that is. Even if you did grow up on a desert island.'

Francesca stared at her. For one moment Kate thought she was going to be angry. Then, suddenly, her eyes filled with tears. 'Do you mean that, Kate?'

'Which bit? About people liking you how you are? Yes, it's true.'

Francesca turned away quickly. 'You are so strange, all of you.' Her voice came out a bit growly. 'I don't understand it.'

'It *is* puzzling,' teased Kate. 'Why would anyone like you how you are?'

Francesca regarded her warily before asking in an uncertain voice, 'That's a joke?'

'It's called irony, Francesca. Sarcasm's grown-up sister.'

Francesca sighed. She seemed baffled by the joking and the approval. But it was true that she was popular, even though she could be difficult sometimes. Ever since she joined the group, she'd become a kind of unofficial mascot. The story of her maybe-suicide had spread quickly and her transition from doom to cheerfulness made everyone feel happier about themselves. In the ten days since joining them, she had blossomed.

'Do you want to borrow my earrings?' she asked suddenly.

Yes, Kate would. Francesca's earrings were the most beautiful items of jewellery she'd ever seen, strange and delicate birds made of silver and enamel.

'What are they?' asked Kate as the two birds lay in the palm of her hand.

'Phoenixes,' said Francesca. 'It's kind of crazy to have two of them, because the poor things never have partners. They live for a bit and then they just burn up.'

'So where does the next generation come from?'

'Each one is reborn out of its own ashes.' She smiled her odd little smile. 'My kind of birds.'

'What a way to carry on,' said Kate, clipping the phoenixes on her ears. 'Imagine, never having any sex.' She slid a glance at Francesca, to see if she'd offer some information about herself. Alone among the group, she never talked about boyfriends. Aiden said it was obvious she was a virgin and she neither agreed nor disagreed with him.

'They're more than two hundred years old,' she said.

'They must be valuable.'

'I suppose so.'

'Then you'd better wear them. I'd hate to lose one.'

'It's just jewellery,' said Francesca as Kate admired her reflection in the mirror. She'd never worn anything so beautiful. 'They suit you. You should keep them.'

'Don't be daft,' said Kate with a laugh. 'But I'll wear them tonight, for Jenny's birthday.'

They were going that evening to a slightly more expensive restaurant than their usual cellar taverna serving cheap pasta. Jenny had received money for an advertisement she'd done in the summer and wanted to spend it taking her friends out for supper to celebrate her birthday. No one objected to being treated.

For Kate's first couple of weeks in Florence money had played almost no part in their lives. She and the other volunteers lived for free at the hostel and were fed three times a day. The only cash they needed was for cigarettes and drinks. Once they got work with the Uffizi team, this prelapsarian state of affairs came to an end. They were now waged, so they'd moved into lodgings and had to start buying their own food. However, thanks to the Uffizi's eccentric payment methods, they never had any cash: they received their wages on a Friday afternoon but the man who paid them left for the weekend at Friday lunchtime, so as often as not they returned with nothing. An elaborate system of debts and loans and counter-debts had grown up to deal with this situation. Many of these revolved around Hugo, who was paid regularly by the British Consul. He looked like an untidy choir boy, brimming with enthusiasm but horribly accident-prone. Also he was so generous that on pay day he invariably took someone out for a blow-out, then lent what remained of his wage packet and ended up with less than anyone. The prospect of a meal where only one person was going to be responsible for the bill was nearly as attractive as the food. Jenny's birthday dinner was going to be a special occasion.

Jenny was a dancer, now 'resting' between jobs. She had shaggy dark hair and moved with an almost feral grace and exuded languorous sexuality. Hugo confided to Kate that she terrified him, but Aiden and Larry were obviously attracted from the start. For her part, Jenny looked on her weeks in Florence as a kind of working holiday, and was clear that she wanted to avoid any emotional involvement. She was fascinated by the Florentines, mostly poor, who had remained in the city, and took endless photographs of their suffering, but as she sent the films straight back to London to be developed, no one ever saw them.

By the time Kate and Francesca arrived at the restaurant, Jenny was already looking overwhelmed. 'I never realized how many friends I had here,' she commented, looking round the room at the twenty-odd people who'd shown up on the rumour of a free meal.

But after the first few carafes of cheap red wine had been consumed, even she stopped worrying about the bill. Between courses Aiden played a heartfelt version of 'I'm a man of constant sorrows' on the guitar, gazing meaningfully at her through his floppy yellow hair. Kate and David re-enacted the spaghetti-eating scene from *Lady and the Tramp*. Ross, a New Zealander who hadn't been able to take his eyes off Francesca since she arrived, wanted to sing 'Waltzing Matilda', but no one would let him. Dido and Jenny had a whispered conversation on penis size and whether bigger was always best. The few diners in the restaurant who weren't mud angels were soon looking as if they wished they'd gone somewhere else.

But when it came to paying the bill, there was a problem. Jenny's money wasn't enough. Hugo instantly emptied his pockets and produced two banknotes of gigantic size; Jenny took one and made him put the other back. Kate, Dido and Ross each contributed some coins, as did a few of the people who'd turned up on the offchance of a free meal. Aiden had no money at all and looked depressed. Several others who had no money didn't seem bothered at all. The restaurant owner, who had been all smiles at their arrival, now looked stern.

Kate and David offered to wash up. The restaurant owner changed from stern to contemptuous.

Francesca fidgeted, then spoke to the patron in rapid Italian. Kate caught a few words, but her grasp of the language wasn't yet up to following complicated negotiations. Whatever Francesca had said, it worked like magic. His face was wreathed in smiles in an instant and he went away to get liqueurs.

'How did you manage that?' asked Jenny.

'Did you offer him your body?' asked Hugo wistfully.

'I told him I'd pay the whole lot,' said Francesca with a smile. 'It's my pleasure, Jenny. After all, it's your birthday.' She pulled a fistful of notes from her bag and there was a general sigh of relief.

Jenny frowned and pushed the notes away. 'Thanks, Francesca, but no thanks.'

'What?' Francesca was bewildered.

'This is my party and I said I'd pay.'

'But you don't have enough money and I do.'

'I'll pay it somehow.'

'Let me pay half, then. That way it's still your party.'

Larry and Aiden, agreeing for once, said that sounded fair.

'No,' said Jenny.

Francesca appealed to Kate. 'Why's she being so difficult? Make her see sense, Kate.'

Kate was on the verge of doing so, but she held back. The little silver phoenixes were brushing against her cheeks and she had the uncomfortable feeling that her support was expected, not because Francesca was in the right, necessarily, but because Kate owed her. She said, 'It's up to Jenny to decide,' and avoided Francesca's horrified expression by rolling herself a cigarette.

Francesca shoved the heap of money across the table. 'Take it,' she said.

Jenny shoved it back. 'No.'

'Why not?'

'I don't want your money.'

Francesca looked stumped. She shook a cigarette out of a packet lying on the table, clicked her lighter once, but let the flame die down before the cigarette was lit. Removing it from her mouth, she ground it to shreds on the table in front of her. She glanced warily at Jenny, then at the pile of unwanted money on the table. A flush spread across her face.

'You really don't want it? You're sure?'

Jenny nodded.

'I'll have it,' said Ross, but Francesca didn't seem to have heard.

She picked a note from the pile, then twisted the control of her lighter, and this time when she clicked the trigger, the flame shot up like a blow torch. The corner of the banknote floated into the edge of the flame.

Kate reached across the table. 'Francesca, don't be such an idiot,' she said, trying to pull the banknote out of her hands, but Francesca whisked it out of reach, holding it aloft until the flames were about to touch her fingers, then she released it to fall in a curve of ash. No one moved. She picked up another, let it catch the flame, then another, until all her money had been reduced to a drifting pile of ash. Without another word, she stood up and stalked out.

Jenny lit up a cigarette.

'Wow,' said Aiden. 'Heavy trip.' He began strumming his guitar. 'Nobody loves you when you're down and out.' Singularly inappropriate, Kate thought.

'She's crazy,' said Dido. Her mother, the wife of the cabinet minister, had been in analysis for years, so Dido was an expert on crazy.

'Yeah,' said Ross, 'and I reckon we were pretty crazy to let her do it.'

'Why didn't you want her to pay?' asked David.

Jenny looked baffled. 'I don't know, exactly. Just something about Francesca and money – I didn't feel comfortable with it.'

'You didn't want to owe her?'

'Maybe.' Jenny gave up the attempt to explain and went to negotiate with the patron about owing him the balance of the bill for a few days.

The evening continued as before, but Kate was no longer enjoying herself and decided not to wait for the others. She'd been feeling bad about Francesca ever since she stalked out of the restaurant and now she wanted to be on her own. She promised Jenny to help with the bill as soon as she got paid, and left.

She walked slowly, savouring the solitude and the strangeness of the Florentine night: its rich smell of damp and dirt, wet plaster and sewage. Battered and forlorn, the city possessed a quality she knew it would never have again.

This is my city, she thought, stepping carefully to avoid yet another hole in the ground, yet another heap of rubbish and muck. If she ever came back, the place would be buzzing with tourists and traffic; it would be bright and confident again, but now it was deserted. This wounded, suffering city felt as if it belonged, just for a little while, to her and the others who had come to help save it.

That evening the only people still on the streets were two or three prostitutes, each one immaculately turned out even on a chilly January night, and surrounded by acres of mud. There was one in particular they'd come to recognize who usually stood with her little dog two streets away from their lodgings.

They'd dubbed her the duchess because she had especially aristocratic bearing, even for a Florentine prostitute. There'd been some thought of clubbing together and giving Hugo an hour with her as an early nineteenth-birthday present, but he admitted to Kate that the prospect alarmed him as much as it excited him. Kate smiled at her as she passed. '*Buona notte.*' But the woman ignored her.

On the corner of the next street, under one of Anna's fuzzy dandelion lights, stood a prostitute who seemed to be having trouble with a punter. It looked like they were arguing. Kate saw the woman gesture, as though turning him down, and start to walk away, but he moved quickly after her, out of the circle of light, and grabbed her by the arm. She spun round and struggled to shake herself free, but he was too strong for her. She was yelling at him, but still he didn't let go.

Kate wavered. Her instinct was to run and help, but the world of the Florentines was foreign to her, especially the world of the prostitutes.

And then she gasped. Not a prostitute. Not even a stranger. Francesca.

Kate broke into a run. She was furious. Italian men could be a nuisance sometimes, but she'd never come across one as persistent as this. How dare he! Her feet skidded on the slippery surface of the street. She was trying to remember the Italian for 'Go away!' but her mind was dulled with anger, so she yelled, 'Leave her alone!'

Startled, the man released Francesca's arm.

'Leave her alone!' she shouted again. 'Go away!'

Francesca and the stranger turned, their faces blank with surprise. Then the man asked Francesca a question in Italian. She answered in English, 'Kate is my friend.' He nodded, and peered at Kate curiously. On closer inspection he looked much more studious and good-looking than the kind of youth who usually hassled them.

It occurred to Kate that the situation might not be as straightforward as she'd imagined. She asked, 'Are you okay, Francesca?'

'Yes, I think so.'

The man started to talk to Francesca rapidly, but Kate said firmly, 'I'll walk home with you.'

'Okay. Thanks.'

Kate put her arm round Francesca's waist, but the stranger had not given up entirely. He caught Francesca's wrist and forced her to face him. That was when Kate remembered her limited Italian. '*Va via!*' she shouted at him. '*Bastardo!*'

She was totally unprepared for his reaction. He broke off in mid-sentence and stared at her, then turned questioningly to Francesca. Suddenly the two of them burst out laughing. Kate felt like a fool.

'What's going on, Francesca? What's the big joke?'

'Oh, Kate, my dear Kate. You are wonderful. I love you, truly I do.'

As explanations go, it wasn't much help.

'Who is this man?' she asked.

'I'll tell you later.' Francesca turned to the stranger and spoke to him in Italian. It sounded like they were making some kind of deal. He looked serious, checked one or two points with her, but this time when she and Kate started to walk away, he made no attempt to stop her.

'Who was he?' asked Kate again.

'Just a friend of my family's,' she said. 'My parents aren't too happy about what I'm doing so they got him to make me come home. But I won't. Florence is my home now, with you. Do you realize, Kate, this is the second time you've rescued me? You must be my guardian angel.'

When they reached the end of the street, Kate turned. The stranger was still standing where they had left him, under the fuzzy cone of light, like a single figure in a spotlight on the stage. Even at this distance, his whole way of standing spoke of utter desolation.

But Francesca offered no further explanations. Kate knew better than to question her. No one could clam up faster than Francesca when the questions got personal. But when they got back to the room they shared with Anna, she found one of Francesca's phoenix earrings was missing.

'It must have fallen off while I was running to help you,' said Kate. 'I'll go back and hunt for it.'

Francesca smiled. 'Don't worry, Kate, it's a phoenix. It will rise from its own ashes, you'll see.'

'What's that supposed to mean?'

'I can always have it copied,' said Francesca.

Chapter 13

The Doctor

One good thing about the flood, the roads round Florence were still much emptier than usual. As he drove away, Mario Bassano tried not to worry about what would happen if his little Fiat broke down. He'd only had it six months, almost the first thing he'd purchased for himself since he qualified as a doctor, but it was elderly and temperamental. Money was in short supply, even though he'd qualified: he had his younger brothers to support as well as a pile of debts to pay back. It would be years before he'd be in a position not to worry about repair bills, let alone afford to buy a car that was new.

But his mind was too full for him to worry about his little car for long. He was thinking back, as he so often did after seeing Francesca, to the first time they'd met. If she hadn't been crying, he would probably never have plucked up the courage to introduce himself. Four years ago he'd been in his final year of medical school, more at ease with cadavers than with attractive young women. His natural reticence was compounded by his poverty: with no spare cash even to invite someone for a cup of coffee, he'd learned to make do without female company, most of the time. Until he saw Francesca.

She'd been seated on a bench in the sunshine in a little park the middle of Padua, not far from the medical school. It was a warm afternoon, sprinklers were turned on in the flower beds and the air was sweet with the scent of freshly clipped box. People were criss-crossing the park on the gravel walks, casting curious glances at the girl seated on the bench, tears streaming down her cheeks. She was completely still in her grief. Mario recognized the relaxation of utter despair.

He was not the only man to have spotted her. Like sharks scenting blood, half a dozen off-duty *Alpini* from the nearby barracks were circling her bench at a slight distance, tossing vacuous remarks in her direction to see if she was interested. She didn't notice them at first, but when two passed within a couple of feet, leaned in her direction and both said, '*Ciao, bella*,' she jerked back her head, appalled at the invasion of her privacy.

Mario went straight over and sat down beside her. 'Pretend you are pleased to see me,' he said. 'If they think we are friends, they will leave you alone.' Then he added simply, 'You are unhappy.'

His voice must have reassured her. Without turning to look at him, she said, 'I don't have a handkerchief.'

He fished one out of his pocket and handed it to her, then stretched his legs in the sunshine, leaning back as though he'd just joined an old friend. Or a girlfriend. He tried to look relaxed, but his heart was thumping. She dabbed at her tears, then turned to thank him. That was when he first noticed her amazing eyes. It felt like a revelation, though what was being revealed, he had no idea. Later, he often wondered if he'd known in that moment, when she'd handed back his threadbare, much washed and ironed handkerchief, that his life had been changed irrevocably. Maybe it was simpler than that. Maybe he simply recognized great beauty when he saw it.

He couldn't remember what they talked about. She was obviously confused and vulnerable, so he spoke calmly as if she were a child facing painful treatment or a relative bracing themselves to hear bad news: those situations he knew how to deal with. He learned she'd left her home in Verona the day before, after a row with her parents. She told him she was twenty-one, though later he discovered she was only seventeen. He told her he was from a village in the south, which was true, and that he was twenty-four, which was not, but he wanted to make their ages seem closer. In fact he was twenty-seven.

When Francesca finally stood up, she swayed like someone about to faint.

'Are you ill?' This was something he could deal with.

'No, just hungry, I think.'

Apparently she'd spent the previous night wandering near the bus station and hadn't eaten for over twenty-four hours. She'd left her Verona home in a hurry and without any money, so he took her to a nearby restaurant and watched while she ate pasta followed by steak and green beans.

'Why aren't you eating?' she asked, when he ordered her single meal.

'My landlady will have food waiting for me,' he said.

She accepted his explanation, never guessing his landlady was a fiction and that her meal was taking up all the money he had for the entire week. But for once being prudent, which normally absorbed so much of his energy, was no longer important. He'd have happily starved for a month just to see the way her lips curved into a smile when she thanked him. By the time they stood up to leave the restaurant, Mario Bassano was in love for the first time in his life.

He persuaded her to go back to her parents by promising to meet her again on his afternoon off the following week. Through that summer they met twice every week. As Mario slowly came to understand what had driven her to run away from home in the first place, he was appalled: it had never occurred to him that wealth and misery might be such close bedfellows. He planned a future in which they might be together always. But Francesca was not prepared to wait. One afternoon she turned up at the house where he was renting a small room. She had a suitcase.

'I'm never going back to my parents,' she told him. 'From now on I want to be with you.' He took her in his arms, then made the hardest decision of his life and told her she must go home.

'What's the matter? Don't you love me?' she demanded.

'You know I love you. I will always love you, but this is impossible. You must go back to your parents.'

'I'd rather die.'

He pleaded with her, but she was adamant. 'I want to live with you always,' she told him. 'Isn't that what you want too?'

'But we can't live together until we marry.'

'Then let's marry.'

'I can't support you.' But Francesca, as he knew already, had no idea what having no money meant. Her parents claimed to be poor but lived like lords. She accused him of being mercenary, then she took a heap of jewellery from her bag and said they could sell it and live on the proceeds. Mario knew even less about jewellery than Francesca did about being poor, but he guessed that what she had was worth more than he could make in a year. Eventually, worn out by arguing and misery, they fell asleep in each other's arms on his narrow bed. They had never yet made love and that was the only night they spent together. Mario was traditional enough to want his wife to be a virgin when they married and one day, when he was a qualified doctor and his debts were paid off, he intended to marry Francesca. Until then, he had no alternative but to wait.

Her father, hammering on the door at four o'clock in the morning, had his own interpretation of events. Seeing the rumpled sheets, his precious daughter and a stranger both in their underclothes, he was not inclined to be charitable. He called Mario every vile name he could think of, and then, when it became obvious that Mario was unlikely to hit back, he punched him on the jaw and dragged his daughter, still protesting violently, outside to the car.

Mario did not see Francesca again for three years. At first he wrote to her every day, but then, getting no reply, he went to her home and waylaid one of the maids as she went shopping. He was desperate for news. Where he came from in the south, unmarried girls who brought dishonour to their family were treated harshly, sometimes even killed. And he'd heard enough from Francesca about her parents to know that in their own way they were quite as ruthless as the most primitive village family. At first the maid was too frightened to speak at all, but eventually he won her over. She told him Francesca had been sent away to America. To college, she thought it was. Or some kind of school. At first Francesca had refused to go, but then she'd fallen ill. She was shipped off while she was too weak to put up any resistance.

Mario was frantic. He refused to lose Francesca without a fight. It must be possible to persuade her family they'd misjudged him. After the way Signor Bertoni had insulted him, Mario decided to concentrate on Francesca's mother. From what Francesca had told him before she vanished, her father's bravado that night had been quite out of character: the real power in the family lay with her mother.

Mario happened to meet Signora Bertoni at a fund-raising function. She knew who he was at once, but was less hostile than he'd expected. She was gracious, even welcoming after a while, but far too wily to let him know where Francesca was. Quite by chance, one afternoon when he was visiting and she was called out of the room, he happened to notice a letter concerning Francesca written by the director of a place called Maple Grove in Connecticut. Not a finishing school at all, as her mother had implied, but a psychiatric clinic. He was horrified: he'd thought the days when daughters who disobeyed their parents were diagnosed as mentally ill were long gone. He memorized the address and, as soon as he got home, he wrote to her there. Two months later, he received his reply. He also made discreet professional enquiries which eventually led to the director of the clinic reluctantly agreeing to let her come home.

When Francesca finally returned to Italy, in December 1966, just over a month after the flood, it was Mario, now a fully qualified but still very junior psychiatrist, who met her at the airport. He drove her home, but refused to come in and meet up with her family again. He loved her as much as ever, but he was realistic enough to recognize it was going to take time for them to get to know each other again. Just as she had changed during her years in the States, so he'd changed from the diffident young medical student who had first found her on the park bench in Padua. While she'd been away, he'd learned that a good-looking young doctor is particularly attractive to middle-aged women with neglectful husbands and too much time on their hands.

He was more confident now; his debts were starting to be paid off and he was at last in a position to propose. But after her restricted life in the clinic she was desperate to spread her wings for a while, and, though it cost him dear, he knew he had to bide his time. He visited Francesca once or twice in Verona and they talked frequently on the phone. Always, so far as he was concerned, there was the unspoken understanding that in time they would be together. Then, in the middle of January, Francesca disappeared. After all the work he'd put into convincing her family he was a suitable prospect as a son-in-law, she ran out on him. He believed she loved him as much as he did her, but he was afraid that the clinic might have made her phobic about being tied down. He felt himself caught in an impossible situation: if he put pressure on her, he could drive her away. If he kept his distance, she would think he no longer cared. But first, he had to find out where she was.

It took him less than two weeks to track her down. He was disturbed when he saw that she'd joined the international flood volunteers. Francesca, always so elegant and well groomed, was wearing filthy jeans and a man's shirt. Already the young foreigners were getting a reputation for wildness and loose living. Mario might be prepared to wait while Francesca had some fun before they settled down together as man and wife, but hanging out with a bohemian group of foreigners was more than he'd bargained for. And a situation without clear boundaries was, in his professional opinion, precisely the sort Francesca was least equipped to cope with.

He'd tried to make her see reason, but reason and Francesca were not always the best of friends. As Mario drove away from Florence that night, it occurred to him that just as he'd had to make friends with her family in order to stay close to her in the past, he might now do well to get to know her foreign friends.

He could start with the dark-haired girl who'd flown at him in the street, her eyes blazing with rage as she thought she was coming to her friend's rescue.

He laughed at the irony of the situation. If she'd only known how wrong she was.

Chapter 14

Bar Donatello

Kate had got used to being followed. Italian youths seemed to regard it as a question of national pride not to let an attractive foreigner pass them on the street without some attempt at a pick-up. Sometimes it was tiresome, but so long as both sides understood the rules of the game it was not a problem, and she certainly didn't feel threatened by it. But this time it was different. This time she had that being-looked-at feeling which made the back of her neck tingle, but there was no '*Ciao, bella,*' or ''Ello, I am your Latin loverrrrr,' to identify who precisely was doing the looking.

For once she was alone on the streets of Florence in the middle of the morning. Her period had arrived two days early, catching her unprepared. Usually one of the other girls could help out, but not today. She had to go back to her lodgings near Santa Croce.

It was a sunny morning. Almost for the first time since she'd arrived there was a scent of spring in the air, a fledgling hope

that the trauma of the flood would one day have an end. There
were a few more Florentines out and about than there had been
a week before, people going about their business, trying to do
normal things like shopping for food and talking to neighbours
in the street.

But Kate couldn't shake off the feeling that she was being
followed. It made her uneasy. Instead of their usual short cut,
she kept to larger roads. Only when the front door had closed
behind her and she was going up the narrow stairs to the flat
where she shared a room, did she breathe easy.

By the time she emerged back into the sunshine, ten minutes
later, she'd forgotten all about being followed. She pulled the
door closed behind her, turned to go down the street, and
found her way blocked.

'*Signorina, momento.*'

Shock made her angry. 'Leave me alone!' Then she recognized the thin, serious face of the man who was standing in
front of her. The last time she'd seen him, he'd been standing
under the hazy glow from a street light and watching as she
took Francesca away from him. Away from danger.

'*Mi scusi, signorina,*' he said. 'I must talk with you.'

'I don't want to talk. You're the man who was hassling
Francesca, aren't you?'

''Assling?' He looked perplexed at the word. 'Sorry?'

'You and she – the other night.'

'Francesca and I talk, yes.'

'Didn't look to me like she wanted to talk to *you.*' But even
as she said it, Kate remembered how they'd both joined in
laughing at her, when she'd leaped to Francesca's defence.
Surprise was replaced with curiosity. She said, 'Why are you
following me?'

'You are friend for Francesca.'

'So?'

'I am friend for Francesca too.' He spoke quietly.

Kate had the feeling that he might be a more subtle adversary than she'd first thought. She said, 'Bully for her, having so many friends.'

'Bully?' He looked even more perplexed than before. The expression suited him. With his dark eyes and round, thin-rimmed glasses, he was unlike the Italian men Kate had encountered so far. If he'd been wearing a greatcoat, she thought, he could have passed for one of those idealistic Russian revolutionaries circa 1913, the kind who spends all his money on books and forgets to eat.

She said, 'Francesca's family have sent you, haven't they?'

He looked shocked. 'Francesca – she want to be secret from her family. I do not – hm – betray my friend.'

Kate told herself to be on her guard. In daylight, he did not look the least bit threatening. In fact he looked surprisingly attractive. And Kate hadn't talked to a man wearing a suit, apart from the British Consul, in a long time. 'If you're not here to spy on Francesca, what are you doing?' she asked.

He looked serious. 'Francesca, yes. Hm. She is reason I yam worry.'

'You are worry?'

'Yes, I yam very worry.'

In different circumstances, Kate realized she could easily have been won over by the way he spoke – 'I yam worry,' and the little 'hm' that went with his search for the correct English phrase. As it was, she was merely curious.

'I've got to get back to work,' she said. 'You can walk back with me, if you want.' He fell into step beside her. Before he had a chance to say anything, she said, 'Francesca doesn't give the impression that she wants to be *your* friend right now. Is that what the two of you were arguing about the other night?'

Kate wasn't sure how much he had understood. He said, 'I yam friend also to her family. Hm. They do not know where is she. She make me – hm – *la promessa* . . .'

'The promise?'

'*Si, la promessa* – that I not speak them where is she. But they are – hm – very concern for her.'

Kate was enjoying herself. Obviously, he was on the side of Francesca's parents, and therefore fair game. She said teasingly, 'So, not only are you very worry but also very concern.' He nodded his agreement, and his sincerity made her feel bad about the teasing. 'Look,' she said, as if to make it up, 'it's time for my mid-morning break. We can talk about this over a coffee if you like.'

'Yes, I like,' he agreed happily.

Don't be taken in, Kate told herself firmly. Find out what you can, then report back to Francesca. Maybe you can learn something that will help her. He stopped outside a small bar and stood aside to let her go in before him. Among the volunteers, only Hugo had old-fashioned manners, and was frequently teased for them. Kate decided that espionage, while it involved Francesca's mysterious friend, might have unexpected bonuses.

The Bar Donatello was on the corner of the next street. Two old men were having one of those shouted conversations with the bartender that sound like matters of life and death, but are probably to do with the weather.

When Francesca's worried friend had ordered them two tiny cups of espresso coffee, he pulled out a chair for Kate at one of the little zinc-topped tables and then held out his hand. It was a remarkably clean and scrubbed-looking hand compared with everyone Kate knew these days, each nail clipped tidily short. Kate shook hands with him quickly, then put her hands out of sight, on her lap.

'Mario Bassano,' he said, with a formality that made Kate half expect to see him click his heels together.

'Kate Holland.' She smiled.

He remained serious as he sat down. 'Kay-teh 'Ollander?' Despite dropping the 'H' he seemed to have added a couple of extra syllables to her name. She decided it sounded better with an Italian lilt, less fixed and aggressive.

'Kate is short for Katherine,' she explained. 'Caterina in Italian.'

'Yes. Of course.' With the emphasis on the 'of'. 'You are American?'

'English. We're mostly English working in the Uffizi team.'

'Hm.' He looked puzzled. Kate wondered if it was the word 'team' that had defeated him.

'Group,' she said. 'It's an English group.' And then, hazarding a guess she said, 'Gruppa.'

'*Gruppo*, yes,' he said. 'I yunderstand – hm – even though I speak not good. When I study many books are from English. But I yam not good to talk.'

'You talk just fine.'

'Thank you. You are very kind. I yam 'appy Francesca has good friend for you.'

No doubt about it, Mario Bassano was an unusual charmer. He had none of the usual flash and dazzle of the Italian male on the offensive, but a kind of integrity and lightness of touch. All the same, despite his protestations, he must be allied with the family Francesca was trying to get away from. She said firmly, 'Francesca and I have become very close. She's a lovely person.'

His expression cleared. From behind the round glasses his eyes looked directly into hers for the first time. It was a distinctly unsettling experience.

He said simply, 'Francesca is beautiful – hm – like the morning.'

Kate was at a loss. She didn't know how to respond. Either this man was the most pretentious she'd ever met, or . . .

'Well,' she said eventually, and the 'well' came out rather croaky. 'She's very pretty. But there's no reason for you to worry about her, Mario. We might look like a bunch of scruffs but we've all got hearts of gold really. She's just having a good time like everyone else.'

'Yes, but Francesca is not same like other people.'

'Well, yes, not everyone is beautiful like the morning, obviously, but apart from that . . .'

'*Signorina*, you do not understand the worry. Francesca is special person, very different – fragile.' He said it the Italian way, stretching it over three syllables: fra – gee – lay.

Kate checked, 'Fragile?'

'Yes, sometimes in her mind she is fragile. Then – hm – she need the care of the family and the friends.'

'The friends like you?'

'Yes. I yam medical dottore. I have the psychology specialism.' The way he said it, a lot of extra syllables seemed to have crept into the last two words, making them sound wonderfully exotic.

Kate pondered what he was saying. She remembered Francesca's face behind the glow from the cigarette lighter in the restaurant that night when Jenny wouldn't let her pay for the meal, that strange intentness which, now she thought about it, went beyond the normal. She said lightly, 'Are you implying Francesca's unbalanced? A nutter? A fruitcake?'

'Excuse me?'

'You think she's not right in the head?'

He frowned. 'She is sometimes too much sensitive. She 'ave the big and generous 'eart and she is very serious. Sometimes for her the simple things they are complicated. Life it is 'ard. Then she need the support.'

'So she's not mad?'

He looked shocked. '*Certo, non.*'

'That's a relief then.'

'But sometimes she do the crazy thing.'

'Not so good. Like what, for instance?'

Mario hesitated, then said, '*E difficile per me.* Is difficult. I yam in the middle. I respect Francesca – hm – her want to be free with new life and also I know her parents how worry they are.'

'And you're worried about her too, right?'

'No. Because now I 'ave talk with you. You are trust. I give you telephone from my 'ouse and work and ask that you will telephone to me when any worries.'

Kate had never been told she was 'trust' before. She quite liked it. Then she remembered that this man was not 'trust' yet. She said, 'I'll tell Francesca we've talked.'

'*Signorina*, no.' He looked anguished. 'I do not like to 'ave the secrets, but it is not good for Francesca she know. She maybe do crazy thing. Like run away or – or . . .'

Or throw herself off a bridge. Kate found herself finishing the sentence he'd left in mid-air. She felt trapped. She wasn't at all happy about keeping her meeting with Mario secret from Francesca, but in the circumstances she didn't feel she had much choice. He was a psychiatrist, after all, and had clearly known Francesca for longer, and better, than she did.

'Okay, then,' she agreed reluctantly. 'I won't say anything right away.' The deception felt uncomfortable, all the same.

'Is good.' His face relaxed into a smile. 'Now I give you my telephone numbers.' He took a notebook out of his jacket pocket, wrote down some numbers in neat black writing and tore the sheet out. "Ere is 'ouse and 'ere is work. You must promise you telephone to me if you are worry.'

'I promise.' Kate felt obscurely pleased to have merited his smile of approval. She wondered if perhaps she'd given too much ground without finding out anything that could be of help to Francesca. Perhaps when she talked to Mario again, she'd be better prepared to get something from him. She said, 'Maybe we should talk again quite soon. You know, if Francesca starts acting strangely or I'm worried about anything.'

'You will telephone to me,' he said firmly.

They parted just outside the café. Mario said he had to get back to Lucca for patients at two o'clock. He shook her hand with the same formality as when he'd introduced himself, then walked quickly away down the street to where he had left his car.

Kate wandered slowly back to the Uffizi. When she went into the studio Jeremy was telling David and Aiden about his musical epiphany listening to Mahler's Fifth in a booth in a record shop in Edinburgh. Dido and Jenny were giggling helplessly over the sexual applications of Mars bars, while Francesca struggled to make sense of both conversations. 'Is that like a Hershey bar?' and 'Why didn't you just buy the record?'

Kate didn't feel like joining in with either group. Her friends seemed to manage to be silly and pretentious at the same time. She concentrated on the curls of her young boy's head and at one o'clock she made an excuse to go off on her own and eat her sandwich looking across the Arno. Not that she fancied him or anything ridiculous like that, but she couldn't help wondering what it would be like if a good-looking young doctor – maybe one of Mario's friends, for instance – ever told her she was beautiful like the morning.

That afternoon she watched Francesca as she worked on the enormous gilt frame, now almost completely restored to its pre-flood state, and wondered what exactly Dr Mario Bassano had meant when he described her as fragile.

Chapter 15

Flood

Writing to his superiors when the waters had receded, the British Consul reported that the flood of November 1966 had brought out both the best and the worst in the Italian character. When faced with an immediate problem in their workplace or home, no one worked harder or with more enthusiasm than the Italians, and during the days right after the flood students and schoolchildren made a crucial contribution to the clean-up. But there appeared to be no mechanism to extend these qualities to the level of local or national government. In many cases it was the very safeguards put in place to stop embezzlement which prevented effective action of any kind being taken.

The Italian Red Cross was criticized for its failure to act decisively. The inertia at local level made it politically impossible for the International Red Cross to launch an appeal over their heads. The central government in Rome, well aware it was being accused of not doing enough to help, responded by playing down the gravity of the situation. The Municipality of

Florence did likewise, since they were anxious not to scare off the tourists whose money they needed in order to put the city back to rights.

Wealthy Italians were suspicious of their own organizations and preferred to channel their donations through the committees set up by the British and Americans. In England a fund was organized under the leadership of Sir Ashley Clark and money poured in. The London team based at the Uffizi thus found they were needed in several places at once. There was work to be done in the Bargello and in Santa Croce. A group was also sent to work in the Baptistery.

This octagonal building, clad in green and white marble like the next-door cathedral of Santa Maria del Fiore, was probably the oldest building in Florence, parts dating back to the fourth century. Dante, like many other famous Florentines, had been baptized in its font. Like the rest of Florence it had been devastated on the night of the fourth of November 1966. Water had poured in and filled the interior to a height of about twenty feet. The force of the flood was so powerful that several panels from the priceless Ghiberti bronze doors were dislodged and damaged. They were taken away for repair. Meanwhile a team of volunteers set to work cleaning the walls.

Chapter 16

Baptistery

During their first weeks in Florence, the lives of the volunteers were dominated by mud; once they began working at the Baptistery, mud was replaced with talcum powder.

This talcum powder was a revelation. It bore no resemblance to the sickly smelling stuff that came in little tins with violets on the outside which David gave his aunts at Christmas. This was serious talcum powder, which arrived at the Baptistery in industrial-sized sacks, had no odour at all and was always cool when you plunged your hand in, no matter what the temperature outside. The idea was to cover a section of wall with talcum powder, which would then draw out the mud and muck that had saturated the stone on the night of the flood. After a couple of days the talcum powder was swept away with an ordinary household broom and the process repeated. The trick was getting the talcum powder to remain on the wall in the first place.

Various methods were tried, patting and smearing and

pressing, but the powder only stuck to the walls when applied with some force. The best way of doing this was to throw it. Francesca worked out the technique first. She positioned herself about six feet away, dipped her right hand into a bucket of talcum powder and pulled out a handful, then hurled it with all her strength at the wall. When she got it right, the powder covered the wall in a circle a couple of feet in diameter. 'The trick,' she explained, 'is opening your fist at exactly the right moment.'

The others tried with varying degrees of success. For the first two days sections of the walls were randomly spattered with white polka dots, but gradually they got the hang of it and the gaps between the dots got smaller, coverage more even. In the early mornings, when it was still cold in the Baptistery, they did proper bowlers' run-ups before elaborate overarm throws to get warm. Jenny preferred to stand on a chair and throw underarm, while Aiden perfected a wide-arm throw, as though skipping stones.

It wasn't long before they discovered that the walls, once they'd been evenly coated with white powder, made a perfect surface for pictures and slogans. After the inevitable large-nosed character peering over a wall – 'Kilroy woz here' – they tried out various Lichtenstein-inspired epithets: 'KPOW!' and 'BAM!', which surprised the occasional tourists who looked in to see how the heroic rescue effort was progressing. Mostly, they settled for noughts and crosses.

Inevitably, a good deal of the talcum powder ended up all over the throwers and sweepers. Their hair, faces and clothes all turned a ghostly pale by mid-morning, but no one cared. Especially not Francesca. The well-groomed young woman Kate had first encountered on the bridge was now indistinguishable from the scruffiest of the mud angels, and she obviously loved her new persona. One night, after it had been raining all day and the dirt in the streets had turned back to mud, a group of them were taking a short cut back from the cantina to their lodgings when Kate slipped on a particularly treacherous corner. She fell flat on her back in a puddle. For a moment she was too stunned to move and, when she did try, a sharp pain shot through her upper leg and into her hip. She cursed.

The others contemplated her predicament.

'*Nostalgie de la boue*,' said Dido. It was one of her favourite phrases. 'I've never known anyone take it literally before.'

' "All of us are in the gutter but some of us are looking at the stars," ' said Larry helpfully. His fellow volunteers were beginning to notice that his intellectual pretensions involved endlessly quoting other people. He was less good when an original observation was required.

'Stendhal,' said Anna.

'Oscar Wilde,' corrected Larry.

'Isn't anyone going to help me up?' demanded Kate.

'You look kind of sexy lying there,' said David.

'If female mud-wrestling is what turns you on,' said Aiden. 'Personally—'

Suddenly Francesca flopped down in the road beside Kate. Lying on her back she began to swoop her arms up and down through the mud. Kate thought for a moment she'd gone completely mad and she'd have to get in touch with Mario straight away.

'Like this, with your arms,' said Francesca, a bit breathlessly. 'Flap them as if you're trying to fly. In the States we used to make snow angels this way. When you stand up, you'll see. Look.'

Kate was touched. It must be a true definition of friendship, stretching out in the mud beside your companion. She took her hand and gripped it.

Laughing, Francesca struggled to her feet and helped Kate to stand as well. The pain had miraculously gone away.

'Look,' said Francesca again. 'The shape in the mud.'

Kate looked. For a moment, in the glutinous surface of the road, the outline of two angels was faintly visible. But mud was a less stable medium than snow, and as they looked, the images melted away.

The bar was crowded with Italians, mostly men in their working clothes. Kate fended off the attentions of a boy with down on his lip who wanted to brush up his amorous English before the hoped-for influx of tourists at Easter. No sooner had she got rid of him than she had to seek his help to use the public phone.

'Like so,' he said. 'I 'elp you. You want see picture of me on 'orse?'

'Later,' said Kate. 'First I must talk to my friend.'

'Is very fine picture.'

'I bet it is. Not now. Oh, hello?' She read from the scrap of paper on which she'd written down the Italian for 'I want to speak to –'. '*Voglio parlare con Mario Bassano.*'

'*Pronto.*'

'*Mi scusi. Mario Bassano per favore.*'

'*Pronto.*'

Kate was getting desperate. What the hell did '*pronto*' mean? Since her entire time in Florence had been spent with English speakers, her grasp of Italian did not get beyond ordering coffee or meals, or simple directions in the street. Her carefully rehearsed phrases didn't mean she was able to make sense of the replies. She said, '*Non parlo molto italiano.* Is Mario Bassano there please?'

'This is Mario Bassano.'

'Oh. I see.' Now she felt foolish. *Pronto* must be the Italian for 'speaking'. 'This is Kate Holland.'

'I know. Is there problem for Francesca?'

'I'm not sure exactly.' Since her meeting with Mario in the Bar Donatello, Kate had found herself thinking about him several times. It felt quite grand to have an Italian acquaintance. Now the volunteers had become such a close-knit bunch, they had very little to do with any of the locals. And she was curious to know what Mario's interest was in Francesca. Obviously it was more than just professional – but what? She said, 'She's been acting kind of weird lately.' Kate frowned. The boy who had helped her operate the phone had been searching through his wallet and now drew out a dog-eared photograph which he thrust in front of Kate's nose.

'See,' he said. 'I am on 'orse. Very sexy, no?'

'No,' said Kate, turning away. 'Not sexy at all, actually.'

'*Mi scusi?*' came Mario's voice over the phone.

'Sorry. Just a bit of local interference. The thing is, Francesca's okay, there's nothing major for you to worry about. Just one or two things I wanted to check with you.'

'I am listen.'

'Yes, but it's difficult to talk on the phone. I thought if you were coming to Florence again soon we could discuss it properly. I mean, I have been sort of concerned about her. It's probably not significant but . . . better safe than sorry, eh?'

'Tomorrow is not possible.'

'The next day, then? Ouch.' Turning her back on the equestrian youth had been a tactical mistake, Kate realized, as soon as his hand descended on her rump. She spun round and glared at him so fiercely that he retreated a couple of steps, but she remembered to put her hand over the speaker before saying, 'Get lost! Can't you see I'm talking to someone?'

'Yes. That is Thursday.'

'Great. I'm about to run out of money. Bar Donatello like before?'

'Okay. Five o'clock?'

'Yes. See you then. *Ciao*, Mario.'

'*Ciao*, Kate.'

She put down the phone.

Her helpmeet was waiting. 'Now you see very fine picture me on 'orse?'

'Actually, I'd rather see a picture of you being roasted over a slow fire,' Kate said, and though he didn't understand the words, her tone was unmistakable, and it did the trick.

Kate left the Baptistery early on Thursday afternoon and went home to have a bath and wash her hair. The bathroom in their lodgings was shared by the other girls staying there who all worked odd hours at unspecified jobs, so Kate was relieved to find the bathroom empty. There was no shower, but then Kate had always washed her hair in the bath or basin at home; only Francesca lamented the lack of a shower. The bath water was soon opaque with talc and soap.

She had washed out a shirt the previous evening. Now she borrowed their landlady's iron and put on a pair of tight-fitting jeans that were almost clean. She was tempted to dig her only miniskirt out of the suitcase under her bed, but decided not to as it would only arouse the curiosity of her friends and she had promised Mario to keep this meeting secret.

When she was finished she stood on the bed, then crouched down in front of the mirror to see the effect – it was only possible to view a section of her reflection at a time. She had mixed feelings about the results. In common with practically every eighteen-year-old she'd ever met she worried that her bottom was too big, but from there up matters improved. She cinched a belt around her waist, making it smaller, and undid the second button of her shirt so the generous swell of her breasts was revealed. Encouraged, she experimented with undoing the third button too, but even her best bra was too old and grey to risk revelation, so she did it up again.

After all, it wasn't as if she was trying to seduce him or anything. She only wanted to look reasonably smart so he'd think well of the mud angels. It was important that he realize Francesca's new friends were people she could be proud of, even if they did look a bit peculiar. Mario had been courteous when they first met, but his courtesy had been the kind that men like him extend to everyone, even his most bedraggled and un-attractive patients. Kate had been suddenly aware of how scruffy she looked. This time, she wanted to make a more favourable impression.

Mario must have arrived early because he was already at the café when Kate arrived punctually at five. Kate made a mental adjustment: he looked younger than she remembered. Maybe it was because she'd been thinking of him as Francesca's doctor, and doctors were the same age as her parents. But Mario was still young, not much older than the oldest of the volunteers. Compared to all her friends he looked extraordinarily well-groomed and straight, but in spite of that she could see that others might find his narrow, serious face extremely attractive.

He rose to his feet as she approached and pulled out a chair for her. No one had ever pulled out a chair for her in her life and Kate almost went to sit on another one, thinking it was for himself, before she realized. She sat down quickly.

'How are you?' he asked politely.

'I'm well. And you?'

'Very well, thank you. You would like some coffee? A drink?'

What Kate really felt like was a cup of hot chocolate, but she said airily, 'A Campari soda, please.' She loved ordering Campari, a drink she'd never encountered in England and which had become fused in her imagination with Florence. Mario came back with her Campari soda and a cup of hot chocolate for himself. He looked as though he wanted to say something more, some compliment, perhaps, some natural consequence of the surprised admiration she'd seen in his face ever since she stepped into the café, but then he frowned and said, 'It is kind for you make time see me.'

'Oh no, I like to . . . I mean, for Francesca.'

'You think there is problem?'

'That all depends. Sometimes she acts a bit strangely. I thought I might be able to be more help if I had a better idea of the background, what exactly it is you're worried about.'

'I understand. She – hm – is acting strangely how?'

Kate hesitated. She had thought of telling him about the night she and David had found her on the bridge, but was afraid that might worry him too much. And Francesca had changed a lot since that meeting. 'Well, for instance, the other night she set fire to some money.' Mario's eyes widened in surprise. Kate leaned forward, feeling the stretch of her breasts against the cotton shirt. Mario glanced down rapidly, then wrenched his gaze back to her face. She said, 'Quite a lot of money, actually.'

'She fires money? Why?'

'She was overreacting. A friend had taken us all out to dinner and then at the end she didn't have enough money to pay. Francesca offered to pay the lot but Jenny didn't want her to. So Francesca burned the money. It was pretty dramatic.'

Mario didn't respond right away. Kate was aware she'd given the impression the incident had taken place since their last meeting, not before it.

She said, 'You see, if I had a better idea what exactly you were worried about – you know, what sort of fragile she is – then I'd know what to look out for.'

'She burns money one time?'

'I've only seen her do it once.'

Mario sighed. 'Is not so good.' He thought for a bit, before saying, 'Her family it is – hm – complicated. Once or twice in the past there have been – hm – episodes.'

'Episodes?'

'Yes.'

'Like burning money?'

He shook his head. 'More serious.'

'Like what?'

'Is not possible to say now. But if she burn money then it is not – hm – good sign. Francesca have always the problem with money.'

'Me too,' said Kate, who was getting tired of talking about Francesca. 'Never enough of the stuff where I come from.'

He smiled. 'Francesca likes to live in a world of – hm – dreams, where money it have no importance. Sometimes she is like a child. A spoil child.'

Kate looked deep into his eyes and sighed, as though she too had been saddened and perplexed by Francesca's lack of worldly sagacity. She said, 'I wonder if Francesca knows how lucky she is to have a friend who worries about her like you do.'

His cheeks were faintly tinged with pink, as though he was blushing. Kate was filled with a sense of her own power. She guessed that Mario was a young man who had been serious for too long and had missed out on the kind of irresponsible fun that she and the other volunteers took for granted. Even though he must be at least ten years older than her, she felt in some ways more sophisticated than he was.

She said, 'It must be wonderful to be a doctor. I mean, lots of work, I'm sure, but brilliant to know you're helping people. Even saving their lives.'

'Sometimes, yes, it is good. But so often there is nothing we can do. Or we are too late. Yesterday I saw a girl from a poor family. She was only fourteen, like a beautiful child, but she was pregnant. She use a stick – hm . . .' He paused and made criss-cross gestures with his hands.

'A knitting needle?'

'Yes, exactly. A k-nitting needle – and when she arrive to *ospedale* is too late. So many times it is the – hm – ignorance that kill. Is very tragic.'

'That's so terrible.'

'Yes,' he said simply. 'Is not always easy to be a doctor.'

Kate was moved by his sincerity. She could imagine him moving up and down the crowded wards, a bit like an Italian Dr Kildare. He'd give an encouraging word here, a sympathetic hand on the brow there, sometimes just suffering shared in silence. Throwing talcum powder at walls, even walls as venerable and steeped in culture and history as the walls of the Baptistery, seemed hopelessly trivial by comparison.

She said fiercely, 'I want to do something useful with my life too.' The thought had only just occurred to her, but as soon as the words were out, she knew they were true.

Mario looked surprised. 'You?' he said.

'Yes. I don't think I want to be a doctor. I wouldn't want to be surrounded by all that ugliness and suffering. I like having beautiful things around me.' Mario was smiling. Kate warmed to her theme. 'I love the work I'm doing here. Not just throwing powder at the walls, but working with beautiful objects. I love restoring them to how they once looked. It's like a kind of healing too, you know. I'd love to work in conservation or galleries or something like that.'

'That is – hm – fine ambition. And you will get it, I am sure. You are – hm – very strong person. I think you will always get what you want.'

'You do?' Kate sat back in her chair. No one had ever expressed such confidence in her before. She felt winded by the possibilities opening up in front of her.

Chapter 17

Viareggio

Florence was getting tidier. As the raw winter cold gave way to softer days, signs of recovery were appearing like the first green shoots of spring. In the city's historic centre most of the main streets were cleared of muck and rubble, a few shops had reopened for business, everywhere cement mixers churned and desperate repairs were made – desperate because the city was depending for its financial recovery on income from tourists at Easter.

As the city grew more civilized, most of the volunteers were headed in the opposite direction. By the beginning of February, they had turned into a semi-feral band, at least by Florentine standards. Weeks of living and working in close proximity had forged strong bonds between them and all outsiders were regarded with scorn. Even Hugo at the consulate had long hair now. Scruffy and bedraggled, they strode around Florence as if they owned it, and, for those few weeks, they almost felt as though they did.

Florentines were less quick to call them 'angels' these days. They were getting a reputation for immorality and loose living which did not endear them to the locals – the sexual revolution had not penetrated very deeply into Italy by then. Sometimes people shouted '*Capelloni!*' at them in the street – which they knew meant beatnik – and once, when Kate and David were tramping away from the Uffizi for their lunch break an old woman hissed '*Disgrazia!*' at them.

They were quite proud at being called disgraceful. Despite their louche appearance, their wildness was more talk than action. There were occasional rumours about the elfin-faced Anna who had a tendency to vanish for ten minutes or quarter of an hour at restaurants where a good-looking waiter had caught her eye. And it looked as if it would only be a matter of time before Aiden and Jenny got together, though she spent hours listening to Larry when he held forth on Nietzsche. She had told Kate she was in love with Larry's brain but was sexually attracted to Aiden, a state of affairs that left both men fighting for her sole attention. Like most of the girls in the group Kate had spent some time fumbling with Aiden under his black cloak, but though he claimed to have used it once as a cover for intercourse on the top deck of a 73 bus, no one admitted to having gone the whole way with him in Florence.

So far as David was concerned, the volunteers weren't wild enough. His sexual experience to date had been limited to a one-night stand when he was seventeen with a girl who worked in their local chip shop and a brief affair the previous summer with Sarah Pringle, who'd been his sister Susan's greatest rival in their Pony Club days. Sarah was sporting about sex, as she was about most things, but he always found her hearty enjoyment a bit dispiriting. For one thing, he'd never been able to discover what she got out of it. She grinned and made helpful noises and afterwards said it had been fab, but he'd imagined real passion would add up to more than that.

Aiden, who remained the self-appointed expert in all things sexual, turned out to have a surprisingly romantic view of the whole business. One evening in the cantina after a good deal of red wine, he'd reflected sadly that he'd had sex too often and made love too seldom. David thought perhaps that was the problem with Sarah Pringle. They'd been having sex, not making love. In that case, he was keen to progress to the next stage: making love. Until a couple of weeks ago, that would have meant Kate. But now he wasn't so sure. He was still in love with Kate, obviously, but he seemed to have fallen in love with Francesca as well. Partly this was because Francesca was being very friendly towards him these days, whereas Kate appeared to have cooled, but partly it was because Francesca was beautiful and mysterious and never talked about herself. No one even knew if she was still a virgin. Or even how old she was. Dido said she was twenty-two, which made it unlikely that she was still a virgin, but you couldn't be sure.

When not talking about sex with the others, David spent most of his time thinking about it.

He was thinking about it on the bright Saturday morning when about ten of them clambered on the bus to Viareggio. The previous afternoon had been one of those miraculous Fridays when the man who paid them was actually to be found in his office at the Uffizi, and handed them each a wad of ochre-coloured banknotes. There followed a long session in a nearby bar where everybody put aside what was owed to landladies and bars, then handed money round to everybody else – to and from Hugo most of all – until all the complicated debts were settled. To their amazement there was enough left over for a day trip to the sea.

As soon as they tumbled off the bus at Viareggio, the pungent breeze off the Adriatic brought home just how polluted the Florentine air was that they'd been breathing all this time. They went down on the beach and ran in circles, then took off their shoes and socks, rolled up their trousers and paddled. The water was so cold their feet and ankles were numb within minutes. David was fascinated by the sight of Francesca's long, pale feet as the icy water rippled over them. He ran up behind her and pushed her, making her lose her balance. She shrieked and fell backwards into his arms – which had been his intention. She lay in his arms, smiling up at him with those incredible long eyes and, without thinking about it at all, he leaned forward and kissed her. The smile vanished from her face, but apart from that she didn't respond at all, and remained quite still in the crook of his arm. Her eyes were wide, their expression unreadable.

'Atta boy, David,' said Ross, who was standing not far away and trying to skip stones.

Kate was watching from a little distance. She looked surprised.

Suddenly David felt uncomfortable. He stood Francesca back up and said with an awkward grin, 'We should try that again some time.' She looked at him intently for a moment, but said nothing, only turned and began walking up the beach, kicking up the sand with her bare toes. Kate, with a single backward glance at David, followed slowly.

Ross skipped another stone. 'So, what's it like kissing the virgin goddess?' he asked casually.

'All right,' said David. In fact he was feeling slightly breathless.

'I tried it a few nights ago,' said Ross. 'Just the same reaction. I reckon she's frigid.'

'Maybe she just doesn't fancy us.'

'Then why doesn't she say so, like any ordinary girl? Instead of going all passive and giving you the big freeze. Nah – ' Ross tossed another stone into the sea and this time it managed three skips before hitting a wave – 'definitely frigid.'

David picked up a stone and hurled it as far out to sea as he could. Then another, larger stone. It didn't go so far, but smashed into the waves. He felt savage. He wondered if it was possible for this degree of sexual frustration to make you seriously ill, or mad, or just raging out of control.

The girls went off and came back with bread and cheese and salami, and a paper bag full of wizened yellow apples that tasted delicious. They sat in the cold sun at the top of the beach and washed the meal down with bottles of wine. Francesca was sitting across the circle from David, while Kate, to his surprise, was sitting next to him. She fed him small pieces of salami and swigged red wine. Her cheeks were flushed from sun and wine and David forgot about Francesca. Kate had been his first choice all along.

Later, as their shadows lengthened across the sand, Jenny listened to Larry with admiration as he leaned back on his elbows and declaimed Keats and Auden. When he came to a temporary halt, Aiden, who had been watching with a hangdog look through his curtain of yellow hair, took his guitar and sang a couple of songs, 'Nobody Loves You When You're Down and Out' and 'I Am a Man of Constant Sorrows'. By now everyone knew most of Aiden's songs by heart, especially those two, and either sang along or continued talking – even Larry and Jenny. When he'd finished, Aiden was looking less loved and more constantly sorrowful than ever. Larry, ignoring him completely, was reciting a poem about hymens and gasometers which he turned out to have written himself. Jenny said it was so beautiful it should form the basis for a short modern ballet: a choreographer friend of hers would love it. Aiden suggested without much hope that he might write the music.

The sun was sinking towards the horizon, but no one wanted to finish the day just yet. It got colder and their circle drew close round the empty bottles and the remains of the picnic. Kate and David sat a little apart from the others. He touched the fine hair at the top of her neck and she inclined her head towards his. He was so full of desire, he knew this must be real love. He bowed his head slightly and murmured, 'Kate, I love you,' to the woolly neck of her sweater.

'Mm,' she said. They nuzzled each other, not kissing exactly, but letting the sexual tension build. David could feel her heart, or maybe both their hearts, beating fiercely under the layers of clothing. He wondered if sex was possible on an Italian bus.

He said, 'I love you,' again.

'Really?' She drew back slightly to look at him. 'Do you think I'm beautiful like the morning?'

To be honest, the idea had never occurred to David, but he wasn't to be put off. 'More beautiful than any morning I've ever seen,' he said. She sighed and settled back close to him.

In the circle, they were talking about the difference between male and female attitudes to sex. 'A girl has to be in love to enjoy it properly,' was Jeremy's opinion. His father was an antique dealer and he wanted to work in an auction house. Anna, whose delicate face was peering out from the shelter of his jacket, nodded her head in agreement. 'But a man,' Jeremy continued, 'he just enjoys the sex, no matter who it's with. Within reason, of course.'

'I think a woman can enjoy sex without being in love,' said Dido.

'But not in the same way,' said Jeremy.

'In a different way. But just as much.'

Aiden was watching Jenny. Larry had his hand on her jeans near the top of her thigh. Jenny was leaning back in his arms, her lips parted a little and her eyes fuzzy from wine and desire. Aiden sighed, then said, 'I saw a woman once making love to a boxer. I was walking home across our local golf course after a party just as it was getting light and I nearly tripped over them. They were in the rough grass. She certainly looked as though she was enjoying herself.'

'A boxer?' asked Francesca. 'There was a wrestler on television I really fancied when I was about sixteen, but I can't remember his name.'

Aiden smiled. 'Not that kind of boxer. This was a dog.'

An image came into David's mind, a picture of Francesca and a large dog, having sex. He was shocked by the erotic power of the idea.

'No,' said Francesca. 'That's impossible. A woman and a dog, you're making it up.'

'No, I saw it. Some women get off on that kind of thing.'

There was a ripple of embarrassed laughter. Francesca did not join in. Larry said airily, 'A donkey was executed for bestiality in the seventeenth century. Some poor frustrated git had buggered it and the donkey was held criminally responsible, so both partners were hanged at the same time. The defence tried for a plea of duress but—'

'Stop making this up,' Francesca interrupted him. 'It's disgusting.'

'No, honestly, Francesca. People do those kind of things,' said Ross. 'When I was in Greece I was woken up every morning by this goat complaining while the landlord—'

'I don't believe you,' said Francesca.

David and Kate leaned back into circle. It was almost dark now, the lights of Viareggio coming on all along the esplanade. David said, 'It's not just animals, Francesca. Some men really have a thing about corpses. Some kind of 'philia, but I can't remember which.'

'Coprophilia?' suggested Dido.

'No, necrophilia,' said Larry with authority. 'The urge to make love to corpses. Luckily it's not very common, but—'

'Shut up!' Francesca was scrambling to her feet. 'Shut up, shut up, SHUT UP! You're disgusting, all of you. You're lying! It's not true, none of it, not the animals, not the corpses, none of it! So stop with these lies, do you hear me? Just stop!'

She was stamping furiously, spraying them with sand.

'Hey, steady on, Francesca,' said Dido. 'We were just talking—'

'Shut up!' She was panting with rage, spiralling out of control. 'It's filth. You're making it up. You're disgusting, all of you.'

'Oh, sorry, your ladyship,' said Ross icily. 'We'll check with you before we speak in future.'

But Aiden had been watching her closely. He stood up and went over to where she was standing. She raised her arms as if to defend herself against him, but he made a gentling noise, the kind of hissing that soothes frightened horses. 'It's okay, Francesca,' he said. 'We won't talk about it any more. It's okay. It's all okay.' He put his arm around her shoulders, folding her into the shelter of his cloak. She stiffened, then suddenly something shifted, and she allowed him to pull her close. He smoothed her hair.

'Nice one, Aiden,' said Ross sardonically.

'Have a good time under the cloak, Francesca,' said Anna.

Aiden looked at them all with something close to contempt. 'You're such babies, all of you,' he said. 'Can't you understand when someone's serious?'

Chapter 18

Now

It all seemed like such a long time ago.

Kate woke shivering from a bad dream. She had finally dropped off, but her sleep was not restful. She got out of bed and pulled a dressing gown round her shoulders, padded to the window and looked out into the smooth darkness that was quilting La Rocca and the whole Beatrice mountainside. From far below – it must have been from one of the bunkhouses at the villa – came the sound of a Verdi chorus being struck out on the piano, voices singing along in harmony. It was the last night of the summer season at the Fondazione and the young musicians were carousing the night away. With grand opera, no less – the chorus of the Hebrew slaves from *Nabucco*. Youth nowadays, thought Kate wryly. Much more cultured than we were. Had I even heard of Verdi, back then?

She pulled the gown tighter round her shoulders. She was shivering, but not with the cold. Somewhere out there in the darkness, not long ago, someone had taken a shot at her. Two shots. She could have been killed. And in the dream which had just now woken her, Francesca had been walking towards her, smiling and stretching out her hands. Just below the smile, her throat had been cut so deeply that her neck was ringed with a scarlet ruff of blood and her head was almost entirely severed from her body. Kate felt nauseous. Poor, poor Francesca. She had been so much more vulnerable than they ever realized. How could they have been so blind?

Impulsively, Kate picked up her linen trousers and a jacket. She must go down to the *giovani* at the Villa Beatrice and warn them at once. Tell them how fragile life was, and how precious. They mustn't make the same mistakes as she had done. There had to be some way to avoid the horror. She could tell them and they'd be safe . . .

Impossible. She flung her clothes down on the end of the bed and slumped onto a low chair. They'd think she was a crazy woman if she burst in on them in the middle of the night and told them to be careful, warning them like some middle-aged English Cassandra, all streaming hair and wailing hysteria. Don't take it all for granted! Cherish every moment and remember – but remember what? How could they have done it differently back then? What different action would have saved Francesca's life? If Kate could only put her finger on the precise moment, the single decision which had made it all start to go wrong . . . but it was like trying to follow a strand of thread back into a mass of tangled lines. She'd never learn how to unravel it and make sense of the story. Never.

She leaned forward, her chin on her fists, and stared at the floor. Seeing Simona again after all these years had stirred up so many memories, so many thoughts of Francesca and the people they had been during those brief weeks in Florence. They had thought they were so worldly-wise, striding round the city in their ragged clothes as if they owned the place. But they hadn't been wise at all – quite the contrary, in fact. They'd been like sleepwalkers. Their whole existence in Florence had been a kind of game: as though the most beautiful city on earth had been turned into a playground just for their entertainment. They had been innocents on the edge of a larger game they never even began to understand. And they thought they knew it all.

Such a strange time it was. That much they knew. A time without responsibilities of any kind. David had been more aware of that than most. He'd often said he was 'making hay while the sun shines'. Maybe it was because he knew he would soon have to go back and take his place in his father's company. There'd be no more freedom for him once that life started.

Kate no longer knew what her own future held. She knew she couldn't go back to the life her parents expected her to live: a string of secretarial jobs 'for experience' before getting married to a man who was as much like her own father as possible. But that wasn't enough any more. For her, those few weeks without responsibilities of any kind gave her something more valuable by far: they gave her ambition. She knew, before that final, fatal weekend, that she wanted to spend her life repairing beauty. In among the filth and the destruction, Kate's aesthetic appreciation had been born.

The November flood had stripped Florence of its surface gloss, but the bones of the place, its real beauty, was untouched. There had been an illusion that the Florence the mud angels knew was somehow more 'real' than the restored Florence that would be open to tourists again once the clean-up was completed. In the same way, they had thought that their present lives, scruffy and intense and disconnected from family and their everyday world, were somehow more 'real' than the 'normal' lives they had left behind. They maintained this pretence even though it was rumoured that Anna's brother had been diagnosed with leukemia, Dido's parents were heading towards a messy divorce, Jenny had a back injury that might make it hard for her to return to her career as a dancer, and Larry was not the free-floating intellectual he pretended to be: Hugo had heard from someone that he had a wife and baby in Enfield. Such inconveneint details had no place in their angelic world. They were leading a charmed life.

What an illusion that had been. It made them feel infallible, as though nothing bad could happen to them while they were still living in their magic city.

They were free and they were safe.

Kate sat alone in the darkened room. She didn't know what had happened to any of the others, apart from David, and she'd only caught up with him in the last few months. After Francesca's death she'd broken off all contact with the others. After Francesca's death, those lazy illusions had had no place in her life. After Francesca's death, everything had changed.

Chapter 19

Ghosts

Kate finished brushing talc off one section of wall and looked around her in the twilight gloom of the Baptistery. It was over half an hour since Francesca had slipped out for a cigarette and she still hadn't returned. Kate decided to go and look for her. She pulled off the scarf that was supposed to protect her hair, releasing a cloud of white powder, and went through the wide doors into the sunshine. Even though it was nearly March, there still weren't that many people in the square so she was able to spot Francesca right away. She was sitting at a little table outside a café and she wasn't alone.

When she saw who Francesca's companion was, Kate felt unreasoning fury: how dare she skive off without telling anyone! How dare she meet up with Mario without including her! How dare Mario show up in Florence and not tell her first! Kate was supposed to be keeping an eye on Francesca for him, so why hadn't he told her he was coming to Florence today? What the hell was going on?

She was so angry, so eaten up with unexpected jealousy, that she acted without thought. Circling round the outside of the square, she approached the café from behind them, then hovered, trying to make out what they were talking about so intensely. If only she'd learned more Italian during her weeks in the country! She heard Mario use the word 'game' – he was calling something a 'stupid game'. Then Francesca tilted back her head and said defiantly that it wasn't a game, it was her new life. Kate saw Mario gesture his annoyance, a downward movement of the hand. Clearly, he was running out of patience. Good, thought Kate. He probably wanted to see her really, not Francesca.

'Hi, Francesca!' She came round into their line of vision, smiling, as if she just happened to have noticed them there. 'I thought it was you.'

Francesca seemed relieved to see her, but Mario caught her eye and frowned, a small, instinctive frown of warning that Francesca did not see. Of course, thought Kate. We're not supposed to know each other. Their shared secret, something Francesca didn't know, was a small glow, deep inside her. She pulled a chair from one of the other tables and said brightly, 'Mind if I join you?'

'Of course not,' said Francesca. Mario looked away. He was tapping his foot lightly as he always did when something displeased him. He pulled a crumpled pack of cigarettes from his pocket, shook one free and lit it quickly.

'I hope I'm not interrupting,' said Kate.

'Not at all,' said Francesca. Mario slid her a sideways glance, but remained silent.

'Isn't this the man who was hassling you that night?' asked Kate. 'I thought you might need rescuing again.'

Francesca raised a single white eyebrow. 'Do I need to be rescued, Mario?' she asked in English.

He shrugged, then said coolly, 'You will introduce me for your friend, Francesca?'

'Sure. Kate, this is Mario Bassano. I've known him for a long time and – well, I've known him for a long time, that's all. Mario, this is Kate Holland. She's . . .' Francesca hesitated. She caught Kate's eye and Kate smiled encouragingly. 'Kate is my very good friend,' she finished firmly.

Mario put out his hand, as if to a total stranger. 'Good day, Kate 'Ollande.'

'Pleased to meet you,' said Kate. A small cloud of white powder rose from her hand as Mario gripped it in his. But that couldn't have been the reason for the jolt of electricity that seemed to pass between them as their palms met. Mario must have felt it too, because he withdrew his hand quickly, as though he'd been stung. Kate laughed, her laugh just a little too sharp and too loud. 'Sorry. Now you've got talc all over your sleeve.'

'Talc?' asked Mario.

'It's what we use to clean the walls,' explained Francesca.

'Did you realize,' said Kate, 'that you've just shaken hands with one of the six professional talcum-powder throwers in the world? I can't believe we exist anywhere but here.'

'Is it our tea break?' asked Francesca. Behind Kate, a handful of pale figures were emerging from the Baptistery into the sunlight.

'Yes. A chance to refresh our battered lungs with a cigarette.'

Mario offered her one. 'Tell me, Kate,' he said. 'How long you are in Italia?'

She hesitated. He knew precisely how long it was since she

came to Florence. 'Nearly eight weeks,' she said, entering the game. 'I arrived just after Christmas.'

'And 'ow you like our city of Firenze?'

'Oh, I love it. Even with all the mud and problems, I think it's the most beautiful city in the world.'

He smiled. 'Firenze is fortunate to have the *angeli dell'alluvione* to work for her.' Kate felt the compliment was more for her acting skills than her work as a mud angel. She was enjoying herself. There was something unexpectedly sexy in this game of let's-pretend-we've-never-met-before.

'And how about you, Mario? Do you live here in Florence?'

'No. My 'ome it is in Lucca. I work at the *ospedale*.'

'Oh really?' Kate feigned surprise. 'You are a doctor, then?'

'Yes, I qualify as *dottore* since one year.'

'Are you an ordinary doctor or are you some kind of specialist?'

It was a trick question. 'I am working with the neurology specialism. In two years I will be – hm – the psychiatrist.' As well Kate knew. Only three days ago, when they'd last met, she'd made him say the word 'psychiatrist' several times, just to hear the way his pronunciation teased the word out into its separate consonants.

Francesca was watching them closely. She said, 'Mario will make a great psychiatrist. He's got a real weakness for crazies.'

'Is my job.'

'It must be why he's so devoted to my family.' She turned to Kate. 'Mario has been trying to persuade me to visit my relatives.'

'Ugh.' Kate pulled a face. 'Don't do it.'

'You do not understand, Kate,' said Mario earnestly. 'Is most important that Francesca she make visit to her uncle 'ouse next weekend. Her parents are go. He is very ill man. The *ospedale* can do nothing for him more. The cancer it has spread to his bones. Francesca must make the visit before he die.'

'Oh, I'm so sorry, Francesca.'

'Why? I want him to die,' said Francesca. 'Slowly and painfully. He deserves to suffer.'

Even Kate was shocked. Mario said, 'Francesca, you must not talk that way about your uncle.'

'But it's the truth, Mario. I've had enough of all the hypocrisy, all the lies and pretence. I can't do it any more. I won't do it. I hate Zio Toni and I'm not ashamed to admit it. He's a wicked old man and—'

'Enough. If you will not make the visit for your uncle, then make it for your parents. They go at the weekend, too. Is big occasion for them. Very important.'

'I'm not going, I tell you,' said Francesca. She looked around restlessly. 'Isn't there any service in this place? I'm going to the bathroom. If a waiter ever does appear, you can order me an espresso.' She stood up swiftly and disappeared inside.

Kate let out a sigh of relief. '*Ciao*, Mario.' She leaned towards him. 'How am I doing?'

'You're doing good,' he said. He was regarding her thoughtfully.

'This is fun, isn't it?'

He said, 'Kate, I think maybe you can 'elp me.'

'How?' Kate liked the way Mario's eyes were studying her face and she had to remind herself that Francesca was her friend. She knew almost nothing about Mario, except that he had the kind of attractiveness that grew on you.

He said, 'It is most important that Francesca she make visit with her family this weekend. *Molto importante* – for her, most of all.'

'But if she doesn't want to go?'

'In her heart she want to. And is one day only. Maybe two day. Make big difference for the rest of her life.'

'Why's it so important?'

'She will tell you, if she want.'

'So what do you want me to do?'

'Make her be sense. Persuade her to go to the Villa Beatrice at the weekend.'

'The Villa Beatrice?' A memory was stirring in Kate's brain. When Francesca first joined the team, Professor Fuller had mentioned someone with the same surname as her who lived at the Villa Beatrice, but Francesca had denied the connection.

'Is where her uncle live,' said Mario.

'And his name is . . . ?'

'Signor Bertoni.'

'Does he have a private art collection?'

'*Certo.* Is famous art collection.'

'Why won't Francesca visit him?'

'They have big fight, before she go to America—'

'America?'

But before Mario had a chance to answer, Francesca was coming back, an apologetic waiter in tow. When he had taken their orders, Kate asked casually, 'What's the Villa Beatrice like, Francesca?'

'Nothing special,' said Francesca swiftly.

But Mario answered at the same time, 'Is like no other place. The situation is most beautiful. Kate, you should make visit at same time as Francesca.'

'Kate wouldn't be interested,' said Francesca scornfully.

'But it sounds like magic.'

'Black magic,' Francesca corrected her.

'Besides, I've never really seen the Italian countryside, apart from that trip to Viareggio.'

'Near the Villa Beatrice is very different,' said Mario. 'Many mountains and woods and rivers. You will like it.'

'She's not going.'

'And La Rocca,' said Mario, 'where the uncle live, is very old tower 'ouse.'

'So who lives at the Villa Beatrice?' asked Kate. She liked the way the Italian pronunciation sounded on her tongue.

'It's empty,' said Francesca. 'My family get to use it for visits.'

'An empty house . . . ' Kate was thoughtful.

Mario said, 'Simona will be there too.'

'Simona?' Francesca's white-fringed eyes were suddenly huge.

Mario nodded. 'She come back from England this week. She will be happy for see you.'

'Who's Simona?' asked Kate.

'My sister. Maybe she can visit me here?' She was appealing to Mario.

He shook his head. Francesca slumped.

Kate said, 'Do you think your uncle would let us use his house for a party? I mean, this villa place sounds ideal for a visit. Maybe we should all go. Make it a day trip like the visit to Viareggio. Everyone's getting restless here. Jenny and Dido will be leaving in ten days – we ought to have one real party before it all stops.'

Mario frowned. Kate had overstepped her usefulness. 'Party is not good idea,' he said firmly.

Francesca had cheered up. She grinned. 'Sounds okay to me. Do you think anyone would come?'

'Are you kidding? They'd all jump at the chance.'

'No,' said Mario.

'Kate, that's a brilliant idea. We'll all go, liven the place up a bit, have a happening.' Francesca's eyes were bright with the prospect of scuppering Mario's plans.

'But your parents,' he said.

'We'll go on Friday. They only ever visit for the day on Sundays. We can have a great time for a couple of nights and clear out before they ever get there. Do you really think it will work, Kate?'

'Sure it will.'

'But your uncle—' protested Mario.

'Oh, I'll go and see him too, don't worry about that. I'll do the dutiful family thing and have fun at the same time. This way everyone gets what they want. Kate, you're a genius.'

Francesca sat back in her chair and sipped her coffee. Under its coating of white powder, her face was shining with anticipation.

Mario, on the road out of Florence, did not share Francesca's belief that Kate was a genius. Far from it. He was angry that the two girls had conspired to make the situation even more complicated than it was already. He worried all through the drive back to Lucca. The consequences if she turned up at the Villa Beatrice with her disreputable friends in tow might well be worse than if she didn't show up at all. He gripped the steering wheel and cursed.

How could Francesca be so wrong-headed? It was because of her parents' crazy world of show and no substance that she was so naive about money. Her whole future depended on whether her uncle left his estate to her and her sister or to a cousin. All she had to do was go along with the family plans for a few more weeks, otherwise . . . He loved Francesca and wanted the best for her. Why did she have to make it so difficult?

On the journey back to Lucca his little Fiat was caught behind a huge oil tanker which belched black exhaust at him. He rolled up his window in a vain attempt to keep the toxic fumes out of the car. The trouble with these little Topolinos was that they were not much bigger than the wheel of a large lorry, so his head was at the worst height. Already his lungs were raw from the pollution of the Florentine air. He glanced down and noticed the white smudge on his jacket where the talc had fallen from Kate's hand. Again, that jolt of sexual energy. Well, so what? He wasn't going to do anything about it, and if she was attracted to him, he might be able to use that . . .

Mario was well aware that most of his contemporaries, unless they were actually training for the priesthood, regarded the annual influx of nubile young foreign girls as a gift straight from heaven. Italian girls were still strictly watched by their families, but these Swedes and Americans and English girls seemed to have no brothers or fathers to watch out for them. They wore shorts and halter tops in the street and tried to gain entry to churches dressed for the beach. They were fair game. Some of them, it was rumoured, came south because they were looking for adventures, their own northern menfolk lacking the sexual prowess of Italians. Like fishermen watching out for seasonal shoals, Mario's schoolfriends had hung round the stations and the main tourist attractions waiting for the first tourists of the spring. It was a sport, like football. Everybody played.

Mario had never had much time for these games. In his teens all his energies were focused on his single aim of getting away from his home town and becoming a doctor. All he knew was work. It seemed cruel timing that now he should find himself attracted to a foreign girl for the first time in his life. Now, when more than ever before he needed to keep his mind on the target.

Kate stood next to Francesca while she dialled the number on the public phone. Behind them, the bar was noisy with the dubbed voices of an American soap chattering on the television, Gilbert Becaud on the jukebox. Francesca pushed the money in. Her shoulders were hunched and, when she spoke, it was in a voice quite unlike the one she used with her friends. It was breathless, like a little girl's. Kate picked out the words 'my friends' and 'maybe three or four'. She smiled. If Francesca's weekend party was anything like Jenny's birthday supper, there'd be more than three or four of them turning up at the Villa Beatrice this weekend.

'*Grazie*,' said Francesca several times in her little girl voice. Then, '*Arrivederci.*'

She hung up. 'All settled,' she turned to Kate with a grin. 'We can go on Friday night.'

'Fantastic,' said Kate. 'A real party in a real stately home. Let's go and tell the others.'

At precisely the same time, Mario was also using a public phone.

'Signor Bertoni?' he said in Italian. 'Mario Bassano here. I've been talking to Francesca. Yes, she's well. No, I promised her I wouldn't say where she was, but . . . I know, I know it's difficult for you. Listen, I've persuaded her to visit the Villa Beatrice at the weekend . . . yes . . . the only problem is, she's planning to go down on the Friday night and take some of her friends . . . yes, she has new friends now. The thing is, she may not stay till

Sunday, you know how unpredictable she is. Of course, she's eager to see Simona . . . how is Simona? Good, excellent. I was just thinking, if you were to go to the villa a day early, on Saturday, maybe, instead of Sunday. You'd be sure to see her. Yes, I thought you'd see it that way. No. No, it's no trouble at all. I'm glad to be able to help. I know how important it is for you right now. Okay. I'll see you then.'

Mario put down the phone. There was a queasy feeling at the pit of his stomach. Sometimes, when you did the right thing, it felt uncomfortably close to betrayal. All he wanted was what was best for Francesca, but would she see it that way? He had to be wise for both of them.

He sighed. He'd been intending to go straight home, but instead he went to the bar and ordered a grappa. The fiery liquid burned his throat. He hoped Francesca never discovered what he'd just done.

Still half asleep, Kate padded along the corridor to the bathroom. She had no idea what time it was – maybe around two or three in the morning. The door was open about an inch, with light shining through. Someone must have left the light on by mistake.

'Hello? Is anybody in there?'

No reply. Kate put her hand against the door, then stopped. There was a faint groaning noise, then the unmistakable sound of retching.

'Are you okay?' she asked the unseen sufferer.

'Kate?'

Faint, but it was Francesca's voice. Kate pushed open the door and saw Francesca crouched by the lavatory. In the harsh light from the single overhead bulb, she looked grim, her face a sickly greenish-grey, strands of hair plastered across her forehead.

Kate knelt down beside her and put an arm across her shoulders. 'Is it something you ate?'

Francesca shook her head. 'I couldn't sleep. I started worrying . . . about . . . tomorrow.'

'What? Going to your uncle's place?'

'Yes.'

'You don't need to worry about that,' said Kate, relieved that Francesca's problems were so straightforward. She knew what it was like to suffer nerves before giving a party. 'Everyone will have a great time,' she said reassuringly. 'You won't have to do anything except be there and—'

'No. You don't understand. It's not that. It's . . . the place. And my uncle. Him most of all.'

'Why? He can't be that bad. And the villa sounds fabulous.'

Francesca turned away. 'You don't understand,' she said again.

This was obviously true. Kate decided to concentrate on practicalities. 'Are you finished being sick? I'll get you a towel. You'll feel better when you're cleaned up.' Kate went back to the room they shared with Anna and returned a couple of minutes later with towel, flannel and cologne. Francesca was passive while Kate gently cleaned her face and hands, then sprinkled cologne on the towel and patted her dry.

'Mm, that feels good. Thank you, Kate.'

Kate yawned. 'Let's go back to bed. You'll feel okay in the morning.'

'No. Wait, I still feel . . . so ill, I . . .' Francesca gripped Kate's hand as she turned towards the lavatory bowl. A dry retching was all she achieved: her stomach was empty.

'What's the problem, Francesca? How can your uncle be so terrible? Or the house? I don't get it.'

Francesca grabbed the towel and wiped her mouth, then leaned her head back against the bathroom wall. Her eyes were closed. She opened them slowly. 'Believe me, Kate. He's bad.'

'Did he mistreat you?'

'Oh, no. I was always his favourite. He always made a fuss of me, gave me anything I wanted. My mother used to tell me what to ask for. But I never liked being with him. Even when I was a little kid I knew there was something creepy about him.'

Kate could guess what was coming. When the silence had gone on too long she prompted, 'What was it?'

'It was . . .' Francesca hesitated. Then she said, 'Oh, it was nothing. I just didn't get along with him, that's all. I guess we were incompatible or something.'

Clearly there was a lot Francesca wasn't saying. Kate debated whether to prompt her further, but she was feeling cold and stiff and longing to return to her warm bed. There'd be plenty of time for confidences another day. She said, 'Anyway, its not as if you'll have to see him much. And there'll be a whole crowd of us there with you.'

'Yes, you will be there. I wouldn't go if it wasn't for you, Kate. I'm okay when I'm with you.'

Kate smiled. She was flattered. 'That's right. We'll have a great time, you'll see.'

'Do you think so?'

'I'm sure of it.'

'You saved my life that night on the bridge, you know that.'

'Well, maybe. Let's go back to bed, shall we? I'm pooped.'

'Okay.' Francesca allowed herself to be helped to her feet. She leaned against Kate as they shuffled out of the bathroom and started down the corridor. 'I trust you, Kate,' she said, sniffling slightly. 'No one has ever—'

But suddenly Kate didn't want to hear the end of Francesca's sentence. It was flattering, yes, but their intimacy was becoming burdensome, like a responsibility that was too heavy to bear. She wasn't ready for the weight Francesca was shifting onto her shoulders. 'Oh, nonsense. Anyone would have done the same,' she said briskly. 'It wasn't that special, you know.'

Francesca was not to be deterred. 'It was to me,' she said firmly. 'It changed my whole life.'

Kate didn't know what to say. Why did Francesca always have to spoil things by being melodramatic, she thought as she got into bed and wriggled down under the bedclothes. All they were doing was going to her uncle's house for a party. It wasn't such a big deal.

Chapter 20

A Bird in the Hand

Crouched in the ditch, out of sight of oncoming cars, David observed the two girls' technique. Kate bent over to hook up the cuff of her jeans in a parody of the provocative hitch-hiker, then turned into the wind, so her dark hair blew off her face. Francesca stuck out her thumb and wiggled her hips at every passing car. Even though they were now on a quiet road David estimated it wouldn't be long before they got a lift since either of them was guaranteed to stop any male motorist at a hundred yards.

David was hopeful that this weekend would see some progress with either Kate or Francesca. This villa they were going to sounded like the ideal place for things to get serious. He must be in love with both of them, because he didn't care which one he ended up with, so long as he made it with one of them. A bird in the hand . . . as his granny used to say. He had an idea Francesca might spell trouble if they were to embark on a serious relationship, but what the hell, he was going back to

England in a week or two, he'd probably never even see her again, and she was the most fascinating woman he'd met so far. And the way she'd been acting since they left Florence after lunch, well, it certainly didn't fit with Ross's verdict that she was frigid. Kate might be a better long-term prospect, since they had a lot in common and he could see her again when they got back to England, but right now, long-term prospects were not what was bothering him. Sexual frustration was. He wanted to get laid this weekend. He wanted it badly.

A car not much bigger than a garden wheelbarrow was trundling down the road towards them. Kate flaunted her ankle and Francesca whirled an imaginary hula hoop round her waist and the little car puttered to a halt. David remained crouched in the ditch while Francesca leaned over and talked to the driver, then, as she pulled open the door, he stood up and walked towards the car. The driver's face, which was pink with lust at the prospect of two such good-looking women sharing his car with him, fell at the sight of David, five foot eleven and built like a centre forward, but he accepted him with good grace, only insisting that Kate sit beside him in the front.

David obligingly clambered into the back beside Francesca. The car had obviously been designed for pygmies and the rear seat was about the size of the average bathroom shelf. It meant he had to sit practically on top of Francesca, but she was giving the impression she liked being this close. Unfortunately he was too contorted to take advantage of the situation. His knees were grazing his chin. Still, it could have been worse. Their last lift had been in a pickup truck: while Kate and Francesca sat in the front with the driver, he'd been put in the back with two dogs and a can of kerosene, and a pile of logs that rolled onto his legs at every sharp corner.

'What an amazing car,' said Kate. 'Makes a Morris Minor seem like a Rolls Royce.'

'It's a Fiat 500,' said David. 'A Topolino.'

The driver grinned and nodded.

'It means "little mouse",' said Francesca.

Kate was delighted with the idea. 'A little mouse of a car,' she said. 'Isn't that brilliant? Do you think it gets put away in a matchbox at night? And if cars are phallic symbols, what does this one say about our driver?'

Francesca giggled. 'Mario has one.'

'Who's Mario?' asked David.

'I like little mouse cars,' said Kate.

'Try sitting in the back, then,' said David. Already he was so stiff he thought they might have to take the car apart around him, just to let him out.

'Now what?'

'We'll never get a lift here.'

At Francesca's instructions, the driver of the Topolino had deposited them on an empty stretch of road in the most sparsely inhabited countryside they'd yet seen. They had just driven over a small stone bridge which looked as though no one had used it for about two hundred years. Behind them a river flowed peaceably. Wooded hillsides rose steeply on either side. Not a house to be seen anywhere and no sound of cars or people. Somewhere far off, a donkey brayed.

Kate was bowled over by the scene. 'I didn't know they made bits of Italy like this,' she said.

'We're here,' said Francesca, hoisting up her rucksack.

'Here? Where?'

'You'll see. Come on.'

Francesca started walking briskly down the road. Kate looked across at David and raised her eyebrows. He grinned back at her: like him, she must be feeling as if she'd been snatched up from their familiar world and plonked down in the middle of nowhere. With any luck it might bring them closer together. He looped his arm over her shoulders and together they followed Francesca along the road beside the river. After about a hundred yards, she turned off to the right, where a cement track led up the hillside at right angles to the road. She strode ahead for about a quarter of a mile, then waited for them to catch up where the track forked.

'We'll take this route,' she said, indicating the left-hand path. 'It's slightly longer but you get the best view of the villa.'

Kate looked wistfully at the right-hand route. 'Maybe we can do the view thing later?'

Francesca walked resolutely on. They followed. After about five minutes Kate said, 'Why didn't you get our mouse driver to bring us up here? He offered to take us to the door.'

'It's better to walk,' said Francesca. 'And my uncle doesn't like strange cars on his land.'

Kate stopped in the middle of the road. 'You mean all this is his?'

Francesca nodded. 'It's all part of the estate.'

'The whole mountain?'

'Sure. It's not a proper mountain, though. More a big hill. Well, several hills, actually.'

'Bloody hell.' Kate and David exchanged glances once more, then walked on in silence. Their footsteps crunched on the dry surface of the road. The air was country-sweet after the pollution of Florence. David tensed with anticipation. He'd been expecting a party in an empty house, that was all, but this place was special: he was entering a new and unknown world. A few birds were singing on the slopes of the hill. Now and then a turn in the road revealed a flash of the river ever further below them, then it was just trees again. Trees and stillness.

'It's like a whole different world,' Kate said to David, echoing his thoughts.

Francesca had stopped at the sharpest point of a hairpin bend. 'Now look,' she told them.

David and Kate separated and went to stand on either side of her. Tilting back their heads, they saw a perfect white villa perched on top of a waterfall of rock. Above it were more trees, fingers of dark cypress and the shimmering grey-green leaves of holm oaks, and above those, a bare tooth of rock against the sky marked the summit.

'Wow, it's beautiful,' said Kate.

'Too much,' said David. 'Eighteenth century?'

Francesca didn't answer. She was looking up at the villa with a strange expression, almost as though she was reluctant to go on. She moved towards David and slipped her arm through his. He noticed that her hand was shaking. 'I never expected to come back,' she said in a quiet voice.

Kate was staring up at the pale villa and hadn't registered Francesca's change. 'Christ, if I had a house like this in my family I'd never leave!'

The pressure of Francesca's hand on David's arm increased. It was strange, but she seemed scared. He put his arm round her waist and said as reassuringly as he could, 'This is a great place for a party.'

She looked at him. She really did have the most incredible eyes. And mouth, too, why hadn't he noticed it before? 'Maybe this wasn't such a good idea,' she said. 'Maybe we should go back to Florence.'

'Francesca!' Kate exclaimed. 'You can't rat out on us now. Everyone's coming.'

'They might change their minds.'

'Are you kidding? They've been looking forward to it all week!'

'Oh well . . . So long as the others make it.' Francesca still sounded doubtful. 'And it's only for one night, isn't it?'

'Sure.'

She turned to Kate and linked arms with her on her left. 'That's better,' she said, and burst into exaggerated laughter. It sounded almost like the prelude to hysteria. 'What do I have to worry about anyway? You two are my bodyguards, aren't you? You can take care of me.'

'Why do you need taking care of?' asked Kate.

But David liked the idea. Two beautiful women and a weekend of freedom ahead. With luck, he mght end up being able to make a choice. Suddenly he felt enormously strong, as if he could protect Francesca from whatever fears this house inspired. He wanted to wrap her in his arms and look after her for ever. 'Don't worry, Francesca, Kate and I will keep you safe.'

'They thought we were lesbians!' Anna shook her long hair off her face. 'Three guys in an Alfa Romeo picked us up and wanted to take us for a drink, but Dido started stroking my knee and told them we were "special friends" – *amiche speciali* – so they left us alone.'

Dido grinned with satisfaction. Tall and short-haired, her neat face free of make-up, it was easy to see how the men had been fooled.

'So what's the problem now?'

Francesca and the others had arrived to find the two girls sitting beside each other with their packs on the steps of the villa, the front door locked shut.

'They won't let us in,' said Dido. 'Maybe they already heard about us being special friends.'

'Huh,' said Anna petulantly. 'Some stupid cow who acts as if she owns the place refuses to unlock the door. We told her you were coming but she wouldn't listen. What's going on?'

Francesca showed no surprise. Detaching herself from David and Kate, she walked briskly up to the front door and knocked loudly, then shouted in fluent Italian. The door opened so quickly Kate guessed the woman must have been standing right behind it. Still issuing orders, Francesca turned to beckon the others to follow, then swept in. Kate watched fascinated. On the phone to her uncle, Francesca had adopted a little girl voice, but now, faced with an obstreperous servant, she was ordering her about to the manner born.

She followed Francesca up the steps and entered the cool darkness of the hall. A heated argument was taking place between Francesca and a short stout woman in a shapeless black dress. She had only five visible teeth, but those five were works of art, huge and separate and flashing quantities of gold. The old woman's protests continued while the unwelcome guests trooped past her into the hall, but Francesca was adamant and was clearly getting the upper hand. Kate guessed the toothy housekeeper would fight a continuous verbal rearguard action, but would do as she was told.

Anna's disappointment had turned to raptures the moment she saw the grandeur of the interior. 'Wow, just wait till the others see this place! It's incredible. Look at those pictures, and all the statues! I can't believe it. This is the kind of villa Byron must have stayed in, or George Sand. Can't you just imagine them? It's the most fantastic place for a party I've ever seen.'

'Do you want to see round?' asked Francesca, as they dumped their packs in the hall. She still seemed to be finding it hard to realize that her uncle's house was of interest to anyone.

They responded eagerly and she gave them a tour of the main rooms on the ground floor. 'Wow!' 'Too much!' 'This place is fantastic!' Her tour was punctuated with shouts of amazement. But in spite of their enthusiasm, there was something about the house that made it less than ideal as a party venue. It was too big, too imposing, too impersonal. All the rooms had titles that derived from their style rather than their function: the fresco room, the gilt room, the panelled room. The bedrooms were off-limits; on this point the housekeeper wouldn't budge. If Francesca wanted her to open up the first floor, then she'd have to get authority from her uncle. Francesca looked surly, and told them they'd have to use the downstairs rooms.

As the others arrived in dribs and drabs through the late afternoon, the villa seemed to swallow the numbers up. Jenny had hitched with Larry, who'd tried to engage an elderly banker who gave them a lift in a discussion about Pirandello and Marcuse. Aiden was hitching alone and still hadn't turned up. Maybe when he arrived with his guitar the atmosphere would improve. Kate was feeling almost homesick for their crowded Florentine existence. This was a house that needed a hundred guests to make it festive, not the dozen or so who managed to hitch there from Florence. It was chilly, with that chill deep in the walls of a house that hasn't been lived in for some time; the lighting was wrong and they hadn't brought enough music. They set up the record player in a room where the walls were covered with frescoes of robust goddesses tossing garlands and silk scarves at each other. Francesca prised some bottles of wine from the clutches of the housekeeper, the inappropriately named Angelica, but there wasn't much food around and no one had thought to bring any.

'I can walk to the nearest village and get some bread and stuff,' said David. But Francesca said the nearest village was five miles away and the shops would all be shut by now.

'Why don't you go and get something from your uncle?' asked Anna. She'd already told Kate that she'd fallen in love with the place and wanted to see everything. 'I'll come with you if you like.'

'No,' said Francesca flatly.

'Aren't you going to see him at all?' asked Kate. She remembered how anxious Mario had been that she pay a last visit to her dying uncle. She felt uneasy. Being the guest of an unknown host made her feel like a trespasser.

'I might go up there tomorrow.' Francesca was sounding like a surly little girl again. 'It depends how I feel.'

'How far is it to his place?' asked Kate.

'La Rocca? About ten minutes' walk, further up the mountain.'

Anna was in raptures. 'Imagine having a house like this and not even living in it.'

'He used to.' Francesca spoke dismissively, as if everybody's uncle had two houses to choose from. 'But it got too cold for him in the winter so he did up La Rocca as a place to hibernate.

Then one spring he didn't bother to move back. And now he's dying. He won't come here again.' She looked thoughtful, before adding, 'We're safe now.'

What an odd way to talk about your uncle, thought Kate. She tried to catch David's eye, but he was asking Francesca if she wanted to dance. He put his arm round her shoulder. Bob Dylan was croaking away on the turntable, not the best of music to dance to, but Francesca moved into his arms and he curled his body round her protectively. Kate felt obscurely annoyed.

An antique clanging through the whole house alerted them to a new arrival. 'Oh good,' said Francesca, breaking off from her dance. 'That must be Aiden or Hugo.'

They were the only two who hadn't arrived yet. Aiden looked so strange he was probably having a hard time getting lifts, and Hugo had been unable to get the day off from his work at the consulate so had to leave later than the others.

It wasn't either Aiden or Hugo.

Kate felt a rush of pleasure when Mario stepped into the room. He was wearing jeans and a dark sweater: for the first time she realized he was really quite handsome.

'What are you doing here?' asked Francesca.

'You invited me,' he said with a smile. 'Have you forgotten?'

'Who is this?' David asked Kate.

'Oh, just a friend of Francesca's.'

'Do you know him?'

Kate hesitated. 'Not really,' she said. And thought to herself, but I wouldn't mind getting to know him better.

'You can tell he's never shovelled muck out of cellars or lobbed talcum powder at ancient walls,' said David grouchily.

Kate was surprised. David normally liked people unless there was a good reason not to. 'Are you jealous, by any chance?' she asked.

'What the hell would I be jealous of?' he asked.

Why has he come, wondered Kate. Was it to keep an eye on Francesca? Or was it Kate herself he really wanted to see?

Chapter 21

Stranded

Kate was enjoying herself. The party was turning out to be a
success after all, and mainly thanks to Mario. Not only had he
brought several large bottles of wine, he'd also brought bread
and cheese, an obscene-looking salami which gave rise to much
joking, and, most important of all, about two dozen records,
mostly Beatles and the Everly Brothers, but by this stage in the
evening no one was complaining. He also acted like a human
tranquillizer on Angelica who grinned so broadly that two more
gold teeth came into view on each side of her mouth and she
entrusted him with olives and cheeses that had previously been
hidden away.

Angelica wasn't the only woman to be impressed by Mario.

Dido said appreciatively, 'There's nothing more attractive
than a beautiful man who's *shy*. Most of them are so full of
themselves.'

Kate had never thought of Mario as beautiful before. She
examined him with new interest. Larry was treating him to a

squeaky lecture on the Laingian theory of schizophrenia. Mario listened politely, but it was obvious that he knew far more about the topic than Larry ever would and he soon excused himself and went to help Anna set out the food.

'Why's Francesca kept him hidden away for so long?' Jenny wanted to know. 'Do they have a thing going?'

'They used to, but now they're just friends,' said Kate.

'More fool her,' said Dido. 'Still, it's nice to know he's free.' And she moved across the room to help him change the record on the little portable gramophone. At once, to Kate's annoyance, Mario joined her in an animated debate about the comparative merits of the Rolling Stones and the Beatles. Kate wandered over.

'I didn't know you liked pop music,' she said to him.

He smiled at her. 'I like all music that is good,' he said.

'In that case,' Dido asserted firmly, 'you *must* prefer the Rolling Stones.'

Mario disagreed, but with such charm that Dido, always so dogmatic in her views, seemed on the verge of capitulating. Kate felt obscurely annoyed that he was as warm towards Dido, whom he had only met half an hour ago, as he was to her.

Aiden arrived just as it was getting dark. Larry and Jenny had been dancing together. Jenny was in her element on the dance floor, with an individual style of movement that was sinuous and deeply erotic. Larry was obviously excited by her dancing, but arousal only made him talk all the more and his dance movements were little more than jerky gestures to emphasize his words. When the song ended, Jenny went to say hello to Aiden and within a couple of minutes she was dancing with him while Larry watched with irritation. Aiden hardly moved at all when he was dancing, just enough to frame Jenny's moves.

Mario was watching the dancers, a glass of wine in his hand. Kate wanted him to dance with her, but felt unexpectedly shy. Why didn't he ask her?

She felt restless. The air was full of sexual tension.

'Do you want to dance?' Kate turned to David, who was nursing his glass of wine.

'Sure.'

They went and joined Aiden and Jenny on the dance floor. As soon as the music started Kate realized it had been a mistake. She was a good dancer, by normal standards, but next to Jenny, even a good dancer looked awkward. Mario, like everyone else, had his eyes on Jenny's gyrating hips. When he happened to catch Kate's eye and smiled encouragingly, that somehow only made it all worse.

Their dancing was interrupted by a loud clanging that rang through the house, which turned out to be the telephone. The housekeeper, whom Dido had already nicknamed the Tooth Fairy, summoned Francesca to the hall. Kate, seeing Mario go after her, decided to follow as well. David was not far behind.

'It's Hugo,' said Francesca, putting her hand over the mouth-piece. 'He's got as far as Dorabo but he had a bad experience with his last lift – apparently the guy tried to make him have sex or something and he wants to know if we can get him a taxi. I'll send Dino.'

'No, I forbid,' said Mario. 'Dino's drive is more bad than dog.'

'Who's Dino?' asked Kate.

'He's got a licence,' said Francesca.

'Licence to kill someone,' said Mario. 'I will pick up your friend.'

'Have it your way,' said Francesca. She turned her attention back to the phone. 'Where exactly are you? Okay, I know the café you mean. Mario will be with you in about twenty minutes.'

Suddenly Kate saw her chance to get Mario on his own. She wasn't quite sure why that was so important, only that it was. 'I'll come and keep you company,' she said.

'I'll come too,' said David quickly, prowling round the hall like an angry bear.

'You don't have to,' Kate told him.

Francesca put down the phone. 'We'll all go,' she said.

'Is small car,' said Mario superfluously once they were outside and he was towering above his little Topolino. It was identical to the one they'd travelled in that afternoon.

To Kate's relief, David backed away. 'No thanks,' he said. 'I've had enough Chinese torture for one day. Stay here, Kate. You don't know what it's like in the back of one of those things.'

He reached out to take her arm but she took avoiding action and climbed into the back.

'I'll drive,' said Francesca, holding out her hand for the keys.

'You have drink already,' said Mario.

'Not as much as you have drink,' said Francesca, grinning. 'And anyway, you're tired from driving and being up all last night.'

'Why were you up all last night?' asked Kate.

'He was on duty at the hospital,' said Francesca as Mario handed over the keys. Kate was annoyed that Francesca seemed to know so much more about Mario's life than she did. And then, as she climbed into the driver's seat, Francesca said, 'Great, I love these little cars. Just like dodgems.'

She switched on the ignition, Mario got into the passenger seat and they set off at a brisk pace down the long drive.

Leaning forward she peered into the darkness and complained, 'I don't think much of the lights on this thing.'

'Is night-time,' said Mario wearily. 'You need big lights also.' He showed her how to flick onto high beam.

'That's better,' said Francesca, changing up into third as the little car whizzed round a sharp corner.

'Why are you going this way?' asked Mario. Kate found she could understand the language when he spoke it.

'It's quicker,' said Francesca, in English.

'But other way is better for night-time. Go more slow, Francesca,' said Mario. 'Is dangerous road.'

But Francesca ignored him. 'It only seems fast because this is such a little car.' Kate was giggling . This was just a toy car, after all, and accidents never happen to toy cars, everyone knew that. As they swerved round another hairpin turn, Mario spoke sharply to Francesca. 'What did he say?' asked Kate.

'He says it's a steep drop and we might be killed if I don't slow down.'

Kate grinned. Mario was fussing. They were on the Villa Beatrice estate, a private road in a private world, and nothing could possibly go wrong. Besides, one of the advantages of a Topolino was that you were never more than a couple of inches from all the other occupants of the car. From her perch in the middle of the back seat, her nose was almost touching the back of Mario's head. She resisted the urge to plunge her hand into his thick dark hair which, now she came to think of it, had grown quite a bit since she'd first met him. She made do with breathing in the smell of him, a potent mix of his own masculine aroma, a hint of aftershave and something else as well, something sharp and antiseptic – maybe the soap they used at the hospital.

The Topolino dropped into a pothole and bounced out again. Kate was thrown forward so that her mouth banged against the back of Mario's head. He leaned away from her and turned. 'You okay, Kate?' And then to Francesca, 'This is main road coming, now you slow down.'

'There's never anyone on this road at night,' said Francesca as the Topolino shot off the Villa Beatrice road like an electric hare. They passed the spot where they'd been dropped that afternoon and crossed the narrow bridge. Kate caught a glimpse of the darkly moving river and then they were climbing on the other side. Now there was no need for Mario's injunctions to go more slowly: the gradient of the hill was too much for the 500cc engine and Francesca was obliged to change down into second, then first. Kate bobbed up and down on the back seat, urging the car to go faster.

When they were close to the top of the hill the car suddenly filled with light.

'What's happening?' asked Francesca.

'It's an alien space ship,' said Kate, glancing behind her into two brilliant lights. 'He's landed just behind us.'

'Why's he so close?' Francesca put her hand over the mirror. 'His lights are dazzling me.'

Mario turned so his face was almost touching Kate's. She beamed at him. He turned back to Francesca. 'Is just a big car.'

'Make him pull back. He's making me nervous.'

'Is foolish driver. I expect – hm – he leave the road soon.'

But as they reached the top of the hill the driver stayed only inches from their rear bumper. 'Why doesn't the bastard dip his lights? I can't see a thing.'

'Pull over,' said Mario. 'He has powerful car and he want to go past you.'

'Why should I have to change? He's no right to drive that way.' Francesca was getting increasingly agitated.

Kate felt a twinge of anxiety. It was no fun riding in a toy car if real cars didn't know the rules of the game. 'Careful, Francesca. After all, I'm the one in the back. He'll hit me first if he rams us.'

'What does he look like, Kate? Wave at him, make him pull back. Those lights are giving me a headache.'

Kate twisted round but all she could see was a blaze of lights, very close.

'Slow down, Francesca.' Mario gave the command in a voice Kate had never heard before and Francesca did as she was told.

'Go on, then,' she muttered into the rear-view mirror. 'Overtake if that's what you're so keen on.' But the lights remained only inches away from the back window. 'Damn him,' said Francesca. 'What's he playing at?' She was screwing up her eyes against the dazzle.

They had reached the top of the long hill. Lights and valleys and more hills lay ahead of them.

'Is some crazy peasant,' said Mario. 'Stop the car and I drive now.'

'No,' said Francesca, suddenly decisive as she pressed her foot down on the accelerator. 'It's time that jerk learned a lesson.'

'What you doing?'

Francesca didn't bother to answer. Kate imagined she could almost hear the Topolino heave a sigh of relief as it crested the top of the hill and set off gaily down the winding road the other side. Francesca changed quickly through the gears to top. Mario shouted at her in Italian. Francesca ignored him. She kept glancing in the rear-view mirror. Kate wondered if she was trying to throw their pursuer off: if so, it was a futile effort. The

Topolino was zooming along at full tilt while the car behind was just cruising. Kate didn't find it funny any more.

She said, 'Francesca, slow down for Christ's sake!'

'You want me to slow down?'

'Yes!'

'Okay, then,' said Francesca, her voice rising with excitement. 'Stand by everyone for an emergency stop.'

Kate and Mario shouted together, 'Francesca, NO!'

'Now!' she yelled, slamming on the brakes. Kate was thrown violently forward. Mario was bathed in light from the following car as his body slewed against the dashboard and he thrust his hands forward just in time to stop his face smashing into the windscreen. The car's interior was filled with the scream of brakes and a klaxon blaring and for a moment Kate thought their pursuer was going to plough into the back of them smash her to pieces. Terror flooded through her body. Then the headlights fanned across the car and away to the left of them and, horn still blaring, the huge car swerved past them away down the hill and out of sight round the next sharp bend.

Mario was talking to Francesca in Italian, very rapid and angry Italian. Kate was shaking and drenched in sweat. She didn't have to be a linguist to get the gist of what he was saying.

Francesca sat with her hands on the steering wheel. She was panting. 'I knew what I was doing. We were perfectly safe.'

Mario, obviously, did not agree. 'Now I drive,' he told her. It was a statement, not a request. Francesca got out of the car and lit a cigarette and Mario did too and then they swapped places.

'I taught him a lesson, didn't I?' said Francesca as they drove away.

'Yes,' said Mario angrily. 'Very stupid lesson and Kate she

almost get killed. You act like crazy child, Francesca. This car it is not for toy.'

They drove the rest of the way smoking in silence while Kate's heart rate gradually returned to normal.

Dorabo was not a very big town, hardly more than a village with a couple of bars and a church. Kate crouched down to peer through the side windows of the car, trying to recognize the place they must have driven through that afternoon, but it looked closed up and mysterious, a nondescript Italian one-horse town that she would probably never see again. The shock of the near-collision had left her with a heightened sense of awareness. This town, this moment, suddenly seemed to be of vital importance in her life and she had to imprint every smallest detail on her memory.

Mario parked outside the bar. The Topolino was so close to the ground that Kate, tilting her head sideways for a better view, could still see only halfway up the entrance to the bar: several trousered legs and chairs and the bottom section of a fridge full of soft drinks.

Francesca twisted round and smiled at her. 'You okay, Kate? I'll get Hugo. I won't be long.'

She climbed out of the car. Mario shook out another cigarette from the packet. Kate had never seen him smoke like this before. She said, 'What was that guy playing at?'

He dragged on his cigarette and said, 'Francesca is crazy child. She think she has – hm – magic life and nothing can injure. Is bad accident coming, I know in my bones.'

Kate touched his shoulder, just where his hair curled down over the ribbed neck of his sweater. She'd been wanting to do it since leaving the Villa Beatrice. Such a casual gesture, and yet the shock of it sent a current charging up her arm. It was the same for him, she could tell. He reached up and put his hand over hers. Kate felt a giddying gust of desire, like nothing she had known before. As though she might faint with the power of it.

She said, 'You mustn't worry so much, Mario. Relax.'

'No, Kate, is important I must worry.'

'Why? You're not in love with her, are you?'

He removed his hand. 'You are all like children,' he said. He sounded irritated by the whole business.

'We're just having fun,' said Kate.

'Like stupid children.'

Kate felt as if she'd been slapped. 'Well, at least we know how to have a good time,' she said, and withdrew to the very back of the car.

Just then the passenger door swung open with a rush of cool air and the neck of an enormous wine bottle, like an elephant's trunk, was thrust into the car.

'God, poor Hugo,' Francesca was saying. 'He got a ride in a Mercedes and the driver just about raped him. Said he was a big shot in fish canning, as if that was some kind of excuse, can you believe it?'

'Hi, everyone,' said Hugo, piling in behind his bottle and nearly poking Kate's eye out with the cork. 'Thanks for the rescue. I thought I was going to have to walk.'

On the way back he told them of his mishaps. Kate was only half listening. Perversely, Mario's rejection had made him suddenly more attractive in her eyes. Which was odd, really, because she'd never made a habit of falling for difficult men.

Chapter 22

On the Terrace

A full scale row erupted between Mario and Francesca as soon as they got back to the Villa Beatrice. Kate assumed he was still angry about her dangerous driving and didn't bother trying to follow it, though she felt somehow satisfied that she wasn't the only person Mario had turned on. Hugo, who hated rows, disappeared into the party with his enormous wine bottle tucked under his arm like a lance and was welcomed with cheers. Kate was about to follow him when Francesca grabbed her arm.

'Stick up for me, Kate,' she said. 'Tell him he's not the boss of my life!'

'Can't you tell him yourself?' Kate was genuinely puzzled.

Mario said something to Francesca in Italian and she replied just as fast and just as angry. From all her *non vados* and *non voglios* Kate gathered he was trying to make her do something against her will.

Their argument must have been audible in the room where

the music was playing. David came into the hall. 'What's going on?' he asked Kate.

'Search me,' she said. David suddenly seemed remarkably attractive, with his black eyebrows and his sportsman's build, but most of all because he was familiar, and could be guaranteed not to tell her she was acting like a stupid child. 'We might as well leave them to it.'

David frowned. To Kate's annoyance he put a hand on Francesca's shoulder and said, 'Francesca, are you okay?'

She spun round. 'Tell him for me!' she said in English. 'Tell him he can't make me do this!'

'Do what?'

'Just tell him I'm through with whoring for my family!' There were tears of anger on her face. 'I won't do it any more. I won't!'

There was a stunned silence.

Then Mario asked, with genuine bewilderment on his face, 'Whoring? What is this?'

David put his arm round Francesca's waist and said to Mario, 'Maybe you should just leave her alone.'

'You not understand,' said Mario.

'I can see when someone's party is being spoiled for them.' He pulled Francesca to his side and Kate saw how she seemed to relax in his embrace. 'It's okay, sweetie. You don't have to do anything if you don't want to. Hey, know what? You look like you could use a dance.'

'A dance?' She echoed his words.

'That's right.' David's hand was caressing the nape of her neck, under her thick mane of hair. He looked across at Mario and smiled. 'It's party time, folks.'

'Francesca!' Mario was pleading with her. She said something crude in Italian, then laughed and went towards the *sala* with David.

Just before she got to the door she turned and said, in English, 'Just remember, Mario, you don't own me. No one does. No one's ever going to own me again.'

'That's right,' said David, kissing the top of her head. 'You tell him like it is.'

Then she and David vanished into the music and cigarette smoke of the party and Mario, watching them go, cursed loudly. Kate had never seen him like this, so full of rage and frustrated energy.

She was about to follow the others into the other room, but then she turned and said, 'What's all this about, Mario?'

He blinked, as though he'd forgotten she was there, he was so bound up in the power struggle with Francesca. He smiled bitterly, 'Francesca makes ruin of her life,' he said tersely.

'You don't think maybe you're exaggerating a bit?' asked Kate. She'd come here for a good time and now it all seemed to be getting a bit heavy. Mario needed to lighten up. She'd have been happy to show him how, but didn't want to risk a second rejection.

He didn't answer, merely shrugged and turned towards the front door.

'You're not going, are you?' said Kate, following him.

'I must make visit for her uncle,' he said.

'But what about the party?'

'Maybe later I return.'

'Wait. I don't understand. What's going on?'

They stood at the top of the steps and Mario lit cigarettes for both of them. His hand, Kate noticed as he held the lighter, was shaking.

She asked again, 'What were you arguing about? Why did she say that about people owning her?'

'Francesca she make big *esagerazione*.'

'She exaggerates?' Mario nodded and Kate went on, 'Was that why she talked about whoring for her family?'

'I do not know,' he said. 'What is this word whoring?'

'It's what prostitutes do. Selling sex for money.'

There was genuine shock on Mario's face at this translation. He said, '*Certo*, sometimes I think Francesca she is crazy woman.'

'She's my friend,' said Kate. 'I don't like to see her upset.'

'A real friend for Francesca would help her now. Not let her throw it all away.'

'Throw all what away?'

He looked intently at her for a moment, then took her arm and said, 'Come. I show you.'

They walked round the side of the house, their shoes crunching the small stones of the pathway, and came to a wide stone terrace overlooking the valley. Its pale marble balustrades were what you saw in that first view of the house from halfway up the drive. Here the sounds from the party were more muted, talk and laughter and 'Cathy's Clown' on the record player. There was a sense of the outdoors and the vastness of the Italian hinterland, distant hills and the huge canopy of sky, a scent of leaves and earth and woodsmoke. Far below them they could see the pale curve of the river in the valley, and as they watched a single headlight fanned over the river, then slowed as it crossed the narrow bridge.

'Is beautiful?' He turned to look at her.

'Very beautiful,' agreed Kate.

'It belong to Francesca's uncle.'

'And he's dying?'

'Yes.'

'Does he have children of his own?'

'No.'

'So who gets all this when he dies?'

There was silence. Mario dropped the butt of his cigarette and ground it under his heel.

She asked again, 'Francesca?'

'No one knows. Her uncle make the big secret.'

'But it might be Francesca?'

'She was always the – hm – favourite. Since long time.'

Kate had the sense that random fragments were beginning to form a coherent picture. Or if they didn't make the picture yet, that still, they would do. So many things about Francesca that she hadn't understood before. She said, 'Maybe the money's not so important to her as you think.'

He gestured with his hand, a gesture of impatience and dismissal. He said, 'She does not know. She think because she has – hm – good time in Florence with you and your friends, that she can make a different life for herself. But is a fantasy. She cannot be for always an *angelo del fango*.'

'But she can work. She can make a life for herself, same as the rest of us.'

'Francesca is not like the rest of you.'

'How can you be so sure? You haven't known her these last few weeks. She's changed while she's been with us in Florence. We've all changed a bit, but with Francesca it's gone really deep. As if she's discovering the person she really is. And anyway, why does it bother you so much whether she gets her uncle's money or not? What's in it for you?'

'I want the good life for Francesca.'

'Yes. Well. And so do I. But money isn't what makes the good life. What about her uncle? Has his money made him a happy man? The important thing is doing something you care about and being with people who love and respect you, that's all that matters in the end and—'

'*Basta!*' He interrupted her impatiently. 'Enough. This ideas is good for pop songs, not for real life. You have corrupt Francesca with this crazy talk.'

'Me? Corrupt Francesca? That's rich, coming from you. You're the one who's dragged her here against her will. All we want is for her to be herself and be happy. And she has been happy this last few weeks, you should have seen her. Then you'd know that I was right!'

There was a long silence. Mario turned to her and said, 'Kate, when you are angry, you are *molto bella*. You know what that means?'

It wasn't what she'd been expecting, but she refused to be thrown off course. She said, 'How come you're so involved in Francesca's life? Are you in love with her?'

This time the silence stretched out so long Kate thought he was offended at the question and wasn't going to answer at all. But finally he sighed, and said, 'In past I think yes, I love Francesca. But now . . .' He looked directly into her eyes and Kate felt a tremor, almost like fear, feather up the whole length of her spine. 'Now I am not so sure.'

She was holding her breath. Now, if ever, Mario would tell her everything: why Francesca had run away from her family, why she had been so desperate that night on the bridge, why this weekend had been so important, what the ties were that bound them. But there was something else trembling in the balance as they stood there on the terrace, some connection between Mario's uncertainty about his feelings for Francesca and the way he was looking at Kate right now.

She said, 'Let's not talk about Francesca any more.'

'You want we talk about you?'

'Or not talk at all.'

'No talk?'

'No.'

She hardly moved, and nor did he, just leaned a little towards her and she closed her eyes as their mouths drew together. His hands were on her shoulder blades and she let her body drift against his. She felt easy as thistledown, as though a breeze had blown them together and she would stay in his arms for ever.

His kiss grew stronger, hungrier, more insistent and she arched her spine towards him. She felt his desire increasing, like a force that's been kept in check too long. Her own desire was growing too, and alongside that there was a kind of triumph, a sense of obstacles overcome and the scent of victory, though victory over what or whom, she didn't know.

He drew back first. 'You like, Kate?' It was a teasing question.

'Maybe,' she said, the surface of her body vibrant with desire. 'Let's try again to make sure.'

He cupped her head in his hands, his fingers raking back her hair, and pulled her face towards his. Kate had never known that kissing could be like this, sensations so powerful it was like flying and drowning all at once. She wanted it to go on for ever and she wanted more . . . She could feel his excitement echoing hers, stronger than hers, his arousal pressing against her stomach. Surrender and power.

This time, she drew back, her lips swollen with kissing.

He was breathing heavily. He asked again, 'You like, Kate?'

Her whole body humming with desire, she never noticed the

harshness of his repeated question. 'Yes,' she said happily. 'I like very much.'

But this time when she moved forward to kiss him, he put his hands on either side of her face and held her away from him. She was startled by the strength of the two hands gripping her head and the dark anger in his eyes.

'Is what you like to do with your English boys?'

'What?'

'You like to fuck?'

'*What?*' Kate was so stunned by the change in him that for a moment it was all she could say.

He said, 'You want a Latin lover, Kate?'

She gasped. 'You bastard! How dare you!' There was a catch in her voice, hot tears of shock springing into her eyes.

Still his hands were holding her face, his eyes searching hungrily. He said, 'Is all a game for you, right? A stupid child's game?'

'What are you talking about?'

'You come here and you know nothing of Francesca's world, but you make big speeches and you help her to destroy her future. You think it is a game just like having fuck with stranger.'

Kate wrenched herself away and slapped him, hard. 'How dare you! You're the one who's got it all wrong, not me, you bloody pervert. What are you trying to prove anyway? I don't care about her uncle's money. All I care about is Francesca! Jesus! I can't believe you just did that!'

To her fury, Kate found she was weeping. Mario caught her by the wrist. She struggled, but his grip was too strong for her. 'Kate,' he said. 'Please—'

'Let go of me!' she yelled. 'Jesus, just because you're totally fucked up, you think everyone else is the same. Just let go of me, you creep!'

'Kate.' But he released her wrist. 'Maybe I am mistake, but—'

'Like hell you are!' she said, backing off.

'Kate!'

She turned, and ran back to the front of the house. She was shivering violently as she went back into the hall. Her heart was thumping with fury and the last remnants of arousal as she went back into the party and searched among the bottles strewn around the room for one with some left in the bottom. The huge room where the record player was seemed even larger now that one or two couples had disappeared. Francesca and David had vanished, so too Jenny and Aiden, but Larry was sitting sadly by the record player. He tried to engage Kate in a discussion of the Venetian contribution to the Renaissance but she snapped at him and he subsided into a rare silence. She was smoking a cigarette when Francesca found her.

'Where have you been?' asked Kate.

'I thought I'd better persuade Angelica to go to bed. She's got a room above the kitchen. Have you seen Mario?'

'No,' said Kate shortly. And if she never saw him again that was fine by her. 'Have you seen David?'

'No.'

They grinned at each other. The party was winding down. The wine had all been drunk and they'd listened to every record ten times over. Larry had fallen asleep by the record player. Dido was tucked up on a chaise longue, head to toe with an Irish mechanic called Fergus. Hugo was already fast asleep on a chair in the corner of the room, his empty wine bottle with the enormous neck propped up like a rifle against the wall.

'I'm pooped,' said Francesca.

'Me too. Pity we can't use the bedrooms.'

Francesca hesitated, then, 'There's cushions in the *camerino*.'

'What's that?'

'I'll show you.'

Francesca led her to a small room at the centre of the house. As far as Kate could tell by the light of the torch in Francesca's hand, it had no windows of any kind.

'Don't the lights work in here?'

'We don't need them.' Francesca stooped to gather up a couple of enormous cushions from the floor. There was no other furniture. 'You take those two,' she told Kate.

'What's it for?'

'My uncle used to keep his most valuable paintings in here. Now they're all up at his house. Hurry up. This room gives me the creeps.'

But Kate was too interested to hurry. By the light of the torch she could make out that it was an eight-sided room, panelled to about three feet, with spaces above the panels where paintings must have hung. 'Look,' she said, pushing the door behind her. 'If we shut the door, you'd never know where it was.'

'Stop it,' said Francesca, and there was real anxiety in her voice. 'I hate this room. Let's get out of here.'

They put the cushions on the floor in the room on the other side of the hall from the *sala* and lay down fully clothed. Francesca had found a blanket from somewhere which she pulled over them both.

'How did you get on with David?' asked Kate. 'I thought maybe you had something going between you.'

'Yes. Well. It didn't work out.'

'What's Mario's problem?' Kate wanted to know.

Francesca sighed. 'Where do you want me to start?'

'Is he in love with you?'

Francesca didn't answer right away. The silence stretched out so long Kate thought she must have fallen asleep. 'I don't know,' she said at last. 'He thinks he is, but . . .'

'But?'

'He wants to marry me,' said Francesca.

'Marry you?' Kate was horrified at the thought of anyone getting tied down so soon. 'God, what an idea!'

'Well, you have to marry someone,' said Francesca.

'Why?'

'I don't know, but you just do.'

'Maybe when you're thirty, or something.'

Francesca giggled. 'I think he's resigned to a long engagement.' She sounded happy as she said, 'Good night, Kate.'

'Good night, Francesca.'

They laughed, rolled over and were asleep within minutes.

Kate was woken just as it was getting light. Francesca was sitting up beside her; she was panting with fear. 'Go away,' she gasped. 'Leave me alone! I won't do it! No!'

Sleepily Kate reached up and patted her shoulder. 'Francesca, wake up. You're having a nightmare. Wake up, it's just a dream.'

It took a little while for Francesca's fears to subside. At last she let out a long breath and lay down next to Kate again.

'What was all that about?' asked Kate.

'Just a dream,' said Francesca. 'A bad dream.'

Chapter 23

Morning After

David woke with a fur-lined mouth and nausea in his guts. It was more than a straightforward hangover. He was depressed and angry, disgusted with the others and sick with himself. Last evening, he'd looked out of the window and seen Kate and Mario, first talking then kissing. He'd turned back into the room and bumped into Anna who seemed to be at a loose end too, and danced with her to stop himself from storming out onto the terrace and making an even bigger fool of himself than he had done already. He'd really thought he was getting somewhere with Francesca, but it turned out she'd just been using him to get her away from the argument with that creep Mario. After a couple of dances it was '*Arrivederci*, David,' and she was off to amuse herself with someone else. And thanks to her, he'd missed his chance with Kate as well. There was no doubt, from what he saw through the window, that the smoothie Italian doctor meant business.

He was still debating whether to march out and pick a fight

with Mario when he noticed that Anna was a very sexy dancer indeed, especially up close. She might look like she'd stepped straight out of a Victorian vision of Camelot, but she danced like a sensuous snake, writhing and coiling herself around him, in a way that suggested he might do well to try some kissing, which he did, as an experiment. She didn't seem to have strong feelings one way or the other about the kissing, but after a bit she leaned back and looked up at him in an appraising way, then said, 'There's a room at the back where we can be private.' She led him by the hand down a long corridor into a small room which looked like some kind of store, with boxes stacked up on one side and on the other a narrow green army camp bed with a couple of blankets.

It suddenly dawned on his wine-fuddled brain what was being offered. He moved forward to kiss her but she was already pulling her sweater off over her head, so he stooped down instead and picked a pale green sock from the floor. Its mate was not far away. 'Looks like someone's beaten us to it,' he said. When he stood up again, Anna was down to bra and pants. He'd never known it was possible for clothes to come off so quickly. He was standing there holding the pair of pale green socks when Anna unzipped his fly and put her hand inside his Y-fronts. After that, everything happened extremely fast, like a speeded-up version of a blue movie.

It had all been much too fast, David realized as soon as it was over. But when he mentioned this to Anna, she said that no, it was fine by her. Long hair falling in curtains over her face and shoulders, she was already pulling on her trousers.

'I mean,' he said, 'I thought we might try again. More slowly.'

Anna thought not. He observed that she was pulling on the pale green socks.

'Are those yours?' he asked.

She nodded.

David propped himself up on one elbow. He felt deflated in many different ways. 'Who was it the first time?' he asked.

She turned to look at him. 'Larry,' she said. Her face looked pinched and childlike, in a way he'd never noticed before.

'Larry? I thought he and Jenny—'

'She'd gone off with Aiden.'

'Jesus!' David leaned back so quickly he cracked his head on the wall. The pain and shock made him feel savage. 'Are you always the consolation prize?' he asked.

She was fully dressed. She looked down at her shoes and said quietly, 'I just keep looking for something.'

'I don't suppose you found it with me?'

'No.' Sadly. She gave him a little smile, a consolation prize for him too, then she turned and walked out of the room. He heard her shoes squeaking unevenly away down the corridor.

He groaned, rolled over and started to pull on his trousers. This had been all wrong, wrong, wrong, more wrong than he could have believed possible. Too fast, too furtive, too cold and heartless. But above all, Anna was the wrong person. Francesca would have been all right, but it was Kate he really wanted. Just how badly he'd wanted her, he didn't realize until he sat on the edge of the little camp bed and pulled up his trousers. It must be someone's fault that it had all gone so horribly wrong. Kate's? Maybe, but he preferred to put the blame on Mario. He felt sick with jealousy at the thought of Kate and Mario together, right now.

He was going to put on his shoes, but instead he rolled back onto the camp bed and fell into a gloomy sleep.

*

David emerged from the store room to find the morning world muffled and white. A shroud of mist had drifted up from the river during the night, so that when they threw back the shutters the rooms filled with eerie mist-light, making them seem larger, cooler, more impersonal. Their footsteps were dulled on the marble floors, voices and laughter were echoey and distorted.

No one had slept very much or very comfortably. David's little camp bed had been one of the choicer options. After all his anxieties about who they'd paired off with, he discovered that Kate and Francesca had spent the entire night together on a couple of flat cushions; Hugo had slept between two Louis Quinze chairs which slowly parted company leaving him suspended like a human hammock between them. He woke finally when the hammock broke. David was relieved to see that there was no sign of Mario anywhere.

The villa's hot water gave out after the first bath. The housekeeper told them triumphantly that it would take hours for the water to get hot again. Still, the Villa Beatrice was different. This was an adventure. Angelica's hostility only made them giggle. They stretched and yawned and warmed themselves with coffee and cigarettes.

And then they set out to explore.

When they arrived the previous afternoon they had noted in a haphazard sort of way that it was an interesting place, but the Villa Beatrice had been a stage-set for their party, hardly a real house at all. Now, in the chilly early morning mist-light, they saw that the house was solid and full of character, not a stage-set at all, and that it had its own very real magic. Cool, airy rooms opened onto a long terrace that overlooked the valley and the hills beyond. David was curious to know what kind of people it had been built for: wealthy merchants, perhaps, with fine clothes, or aristocrats with innumerable servants. Whoever the original occupants had been, they would have been as horrified as Angelica to see the place swarming with mud angels.

Nursing their cups of coffee and their hangovers they wandered from one huge room to another. The furniture was sparse but enormous, the kind of pieces that David had thought only museums and houses open to the public contained. Francesca was dismissive. 'Just the stuff that was too big to move up to La Rocca,' she said. 'My uncle has taken all the best bits with him.'

Jeremy, the antique dealer's son, tapped a gilt and marble console and said, 'What's left is hardly bargain basement, is it? Not an Ercol in sight.'

David was more interested in the pictures. It hadn't occurred to him before that ordinary people had paintings like these in their homes. Francesca's response was puzzling: she seemed to be enjoying their interest, but played down her uncle's collection. 'All this is fairly second-rate,' she said, waving a hand in the direction of a pair of sixteenth-century saints. 'The good paintings are up at La Rocca too.'

'But these are genuine, right?'

'Of course. Why would he want to have fakes?'

It obviously hadn't occurred to her that some people could only afford fakes. David read the little plaque at the bottom of a small portrait. 'Tiepolo?' he queried.

Francesca shrugged. 'It's not one of his best,' she said.

There was a snort of laughter from Dido, whom David knew would be making a mental note of this and filing it away under 'Idiosyncrasies of rich friends'.

At Kate's insistence they trooped into a small octagonal room with no windows. Apparently it was called the *camerino* and was where all the most valuable paintings had been hung when Francesca's uncle still lived full-time at Villa Beatrice. Francesca stood near the door.

'What were they?' asked Dido, running the edge of her finger along the line on the paint where a picture had been.

'A couple of Veroneses, a Raphael, a Piombino . . . I forget the rest.'

David let out a whistling breath. He didn't know which was more impressive, the ones that Francesca could remember, or the fact that she'd actually forgotten some of them.

'And look,' said Kate, 'if you shut the door, you can't see where it is.' She was about to demonstrate, but Francesca blocked her way.

'Don't,' she said. 'I can't bear this room when the door's shut. It's so claustrophobic.'

'Stand outside, then,' said Kate. 'I'll show them.'

Francesca shrugged and went out into the hallway. On an impulse, David followed. He felt more curious than ever about Francesca now that he was seeing her in the house which had obviously played such a large part in her life. The place posed more questions than it answered.

Once the door was shut, the voices of the others were muffled, hardly audible. Francesca was visibly tense. David lit them both cigarettes and said casually, 'I'm not too keen on small spaces either. That room's pretty creepy, isn't it? The sort of place Roman wives got walled up in as a penalty for being unfaithful.'

To his surprise, Francesca turned white as a sheet and pushed the door open. 'Come out, all of you! Come on out, that's enough! Come out I tell you!'

'What is it?' Alerted by the hysteria in her voice, they all tumbled out at once.

'I don't like you being in there,' said Francesca.

They looked baffled. 'Why not?' asked Dido.

'I just don't.' Francesca seemed close to tears.

'Bloody hell,' said Ross. 'I thought the house was on fire.'

They continued the tour.

Most of the pictures were in a long gallery at the back, where the shutters were kept permanently closed to protect them. Francesca opened one or two, letting in just enough of the opaque morning light to illuminate them properly. There were murmurs of appreciation.

'How did your uncle get them all? He must be fabulously rich.'

'Yes,' said Francesca simply, adding, 'But I think he got most of them fairly cheaply. He was one of the people in Italy who did well out of the war. If you didn't worry too much about which side you were on, there were plenty of bargains to be picked up. That's how he got this estate, I think. He's an unscrupulous old bastard, always was.' There was no affection in the way she spoke about her uncle, only disgust.

Dido had examined all the pictures in the room one by one. 'His taste is pretty morbid, isn't it?'

'What do you mean?'

'Well, everyone is being tortured or raped or having their throat cut. Not a happy angel or a still-life anywhere.'

As soon as Dido had pointed this theme out, it became a competition to see who could find the most gruesome picture.

'Here's some poor sod being barbecued,' said Aiden.

'That's St Lawrence,' said Francesca. 'And it's a gridiron, not a barbecue. He's the patron saint of Florence.'

'Doesn't look as if he's enjoying himself much.'

'What about these naked lovelies?' asked Hugo. 'They look like a troop of nudist girl guides.'

'Read the title.'

'Ah yes. "The Rape of the Sabine Women".'

'There's another rape in the big room,' said Jenny. 'I noticed it last night.'

'Ugh, here's a woman with what looks like two jellyfish on a plate,' said Kate. 'Only I've got a horrid feeling they're not jellyfish at all. They're her breasts.'

'That's St Agatha,' said Francesca.

'Gor-ree!' Anna squealed.

But it was the painting between the two windows in the middle room that eventually won the contest, in David's opinion. It showed a sort-of man stripped and naked and hanging upside down by his hairy legs. Several people were gathered round him and observing the proceedings with interest. One man held a knife.

'"The Flaying of Marsyas",' Dido read. 'Is he going to be whipped?'

'No,' said David. 'Flaying means skinning alive.'

'You're kidding!'

'He's right,' said Francesca. 'Marsyas was a satyr who dared to set himself up in competition with the gods, and flaying was his punishment. My uncle's got another version of it up at La Rocca. It's a wood carving, only about as big as my fist but very detailed. It shows Marsyas bent backwards over a hurdle and they've already begun to take his skin off. They've made an incision down his chest and they're peeling back the skin. It comes off quite easily, apparently, like peeling a tangerine.'

'And he's still alive while they do it?'

'To begin with, yes.'

There was silence.

Jenny said, 'At least this picture doesn't show it being done.'

'I think that makes it worse,' said Kate. 'Knowing what's about to happen. It gives me the creeps.' She looked round at the others and caught David's eye, before adding quietly, 'The moment when all the horror lies ahead.'

Chapter 24

Vespas

Towards noon the mist began to break up and sunlight shone through in patches. Aiden sat on the terrace, hunched over his guitar, and picked out a piece that sounded Spanish, and classical. He looked up gloomily when Larry and Jenny returned from a tour of the grounds. They reported that the garden was even better than the house itself, so David and a few of the others went out to explore.

It was a garden of contrasts, made more dramatic by the grey mist that gave way suddenly to bright shafts of sunshine. David's idea of a garden was profusion of flowers round a lawn: this one couldn't be more different. There were no flower beds or lawns, but a series of paths and terraces, some wide, some so narrow they had to walk in single file, which were defined by various kinds of hedging and ended in either a statue or an urn, or else in a vertiginous view over the surrounding countryside. On the neighbouring hills, the mist was peeling away in patches, prompting Anna to exclaim that nature was wreathed in chiffon scarves.

'That's the trouble with you, Anna,' said Dido. 'No one ever knows if you're sending yourself up or not.'

Anna's face got that hopeless look that David had first noticed after they'd made love, so he said, 'I'd love to see one of your poems one day, Anna.'

'Would you really?' She seemed surprised.

'Yes.'

'I only show them when they're good enough,' she said proudly, before adding, 'But none of them ever has been, yet.'

'When one is, then.'

'Okay.' She drifted away.

He felt there ought to be more connection between them, somehow. What had happened in the little box room might not have been the stuff of great romance, but *something* had taken place, for Christ's sake. But apparently not enough to make Anna treat him any differently than before.

He went off in search of Kate, finding her at the furthest end of the garden, where the dark columns of cypress gave way to scrub and little trees. She was standing with Francesca on the rim of a natural amphitheatre with views over the river.

'This is the most amazing place I've ever been in,' she was saying to Francesca. She turned to him. 'Don't you agree, David? You could have a proper outdoor theatre here, all it needs is some seats carved into the hillside and it's ready to use.'

Francesca laughed. 'Who would come here?'

'Local people?' asked Kate.

Francesca gestured with her arm towards the empty hills all around. 'You may have noticed, Kate, that we're a bit short on neighbours here.'

'Then you'd have to import people.' Kate wasn't giving up on her idea. 'Run some kind of summer school, maybe fill it with people who work in Florence and want to get away for a weekend.'

'Like you?'

'Yes, I'd come back here in a flash. And I bet David would too. How about it, David? Wouldn't you like to help build an outdoor theatre here?' He nodded, and she went on, 'It's criminal to let the Villa Beatrice just stand empty all the time. It ought to be full of people.'

Francesca thought for a moment, taking Kate's idea seriously at last, then said, 'Maybe you could help me, Kate. We'd make this an important place, wouldn't we? Make a total transformation.'

'Why not?' Kate grinned.

'It's a brilliant idea,' said David. Right then, standing on the edge of the Villa Beatrice's garden, his prospects when he went back to England seemed suffocatingly dull: he'd get his hair cut and learn the daily workings of the dry-cleaning trade. In time, inevitably, he'd make a decent living and probably settle down with a nice girl with shoulder-length hair pulled off her face in a velvet headband and at weekends he'd improve his golf and go down to his local . . . Did it have to be like that? Why couldn't he stay here and help Francesca build her dreams? He looked at Kate. Her eyes were shining with enthusiasm. He knew she hated the thought of going back to the kind of mind-numbing secretarial job her parents thought was appropriate as much as he did. Suppose the two of them simply stayed here? With Francesca? They'd find a way to make a different kind of future for themselves, after all.

'Do you think so, David?' Francesca was suddenly serious. 'It would be so amazing if we could make some good come out of – out of all the pain and horror and . . .'

'What pain?' asked David.

'It's—' Francesca seemed to be on the verge of confiding in them, but then she broke off abruptly. Mario was coming down the path to join them. David felt quick hate at the way this smooth Italian kept barging in at just the wrong moment. Francesca looked down and moved a pebble in a small arc with the toe of her shoe. '*Ciao*, Mario.'

'*Ciao tutti.*' He nodded a greeting to Francesca and David. He seemed to be avoiding Kate.

'Where have you been?' asked Francesca. 'We thought you'd left.'

It turned out he'd gone up to La Rocca at about ten the previous evening to pay his respects to Francesca's uncle and assure him that all was well at the Villa Beatrice. 'I told him all your friends were charming and thoroughly respectable,' he said. Kate said coolly that he had no right to slander them. On his return Angelica had ushered him in secret to one of the forbidden bedrooms. *Il dottore* must have a proper bed to sleep on. Unlike everyone else he looked rested and scrubbed, and he'd even had a shave. David thought how good it would be to see the smile wiped off his smarmy face. He hadn't felt that hostile to anyone in years.

It was gratifying to observe that Kate appeared to be none too fond of Mario either this morning. He wondered what had happened after their smooching on the terrace to make such a dramatic change.

Mario seemed to be trying to make up to her for some reason. He said, 'How you like the Italian garden?'

'It's beautiful.' She was avoiding his eye. 'We've been discussing how the Villa Beatrice might be used in the future.'

'In future?' he queried.

'That's right,' said Kate. 'So it can help people. Not everyone is obsessed with money, you know, Mario.'

He shrugged, then turned to Francesca. 'You see your uncle now?'

'If you like,' said Francesca. David got the impression her agreement took him by surprise. 'But Kate and David are coming with me. Is that okay with you two?'

David didn't have a clue what all this was about, only that Mario did not like the idea. It was enough to persuade him. 'Sure,' he said. 'I'm up for it.'

They began walking back towards the house. Mario fell in beside Francesca, Kate and David walked a little way behind. David said in a low voice, 'Where did you go, last night?'

'Nowhere much,' said Kate. 'What about you?'

'Oh, I just crashed.' She gave him an odd look and he wondered if she knew about Anna.

As they drew nearer to the villa they could hear a strange high-pitched noise coming from the gritty area of driveway at the front.

'What's that?' asked Kate. 'Sounds like two sewing machines having an argument.'

David groaned. 'Don't you start. You'll end up like Anna.'

'They've found the Vespas,' said Francesca, over her shoulder.

Rounding the corner of the house they came across Larry and Aiden bumping over the gravel on little scooters. Jenny was sitting on Aiden's black cloak on the step. Larry, thin legs sticking out at an angle, was declaiming sections of 'Hiawatha' as he travelled, his squeaky voice just audible above the high-pitched buzz of the Vespas. They came to a wobbly halt in front of the others.

'I've always wanted to have a go on one of these,' said Kate.

'Here, I'll show you how,' said Francesca, as Aiden obligingly got off.

'What about the Zio Toni?' asked Mario.

'Yes, yes, I haven't forgotten,' said Francesca impatiently. 'Why don't you go in and tell him I'm on my way? Then he can really get into the party spirit. Look' – she was explaining to Kate – 'this makes it go faster and this makes it stop. And that's all, really.'

'You will come soon?' Mario was persistent.

'I said I would, didn't I?'

Shaking his head with disapproval, Mario went up the steps. He stopped, turned back to look at Francesca, then went into the house. David felt obscurely satisfied as he watched Kate set off slowly. In his opinion Vespas were little more than glorified toys – he had a BSA at home – but if riding them annoyed Mario, then that was fine by him. Once Kate had completed a solo tour round the gravel circle in front of the house, she and Jenny did about three circuits side by side, their hair flying out behind them. As they grew more confident, they gathered speed and their shrieks grew louder. Drawn by the noise, most of the others had emerged from the house to sit on the steps and watch.

'They're just like ponies,' Anna observed. 'Why don't you do some races? A Vespa gymkhana!' To everyone's amazement, it turned Anna had had her pony with her at her Catholic boarding school. Until boys took centre stage in her life, she'd been pony mad.

She persuaded David and Aiden to be bollards so Kate and Jenny could weave back and forth. Then Aiden and David had a turn, racing up and down picking up twigs from one side of the driveway and putting them in a heap at the other. Everyone was laughing and cheering.

Suddenly Francesca ran forward and spoke to David. 'Quick. Mario's coming back. Let me climb on behind you.'

'Do you want me to take you up to your uncle's?'

'No way. This is much more fun. Let's race some more.'

'Anything you say.' David was more than happy to oblige, especially when Francesca clambered on behind and wrapped her arms round his waist. Mario was waving at Francesca from the top of the steps. He shouted at her in Italian. 'What does he want?' asked David.

'He's still banging on about my uncle.'

'Why is that so important?' asked David.

'It isn't. Let the old freak wait,' Francesca spoke into David's ear.

Dido had found a couple of old-fashioned brooms made from bundles of sticks. 'Why not try jousting?' she suggested.

'Brilliant,' said Aiden. 'Climb on behind and we'll charge them.'

But Dido turned out to be nervous of anything with two wheels, so Kate took one of the brooms and climbed on behind Aiden.

'Ready?'

'Ready.'

'Charge!'

The two little Vespas whizzed towards each other, brooms missing their targets by yards.

'Stop!' Mario tried to intercept their second bout and got whacked on the ankles by Francesca's broom for his pains.

'Watch out!' she yelled, but too late.

Mario was shouting to her in Italian as he retreated to a safe distance.

Kate said, 'I'm Audrey Hepburn in *Roman Holiday*. That makes you Gregory Peck, Aiden.'

'And we're *La Dolce Vita*!' shouted Francesca. '*Viva La Dolce Vita*!'

David was laughing. He hadn't enjoyed himself so much in ages, and Mario's disapproval was the icing on the cake.

They charged again. This time Kate's broom made contact with David's leg, almost toppling them over, but he managed to keep going. Francesca was urging him on, bucking backwards and forwards behind him so he had a job to keep the Vespa upright, and those watching from the steps were cheering and laughing.

All except Mario. 'What are you do?' he yelled. 'Are you go crazy?'

'Yes!' shouted Francesca. 'Everyone's mad except you, Mario. Isn't that right?'

The last of the mist had cleared away and the sun was beating down hotly now. Aiden and David stopped at opposite sides of the driveway and pulled off their sweaters. Kate and Francesca, perched behind them, steadied their brooms. The crowd shouted, 'One, two, three – GO!' and they hurled themselves at each other. This time both the brooms made contact. Kate's got David on the hip and Francesca was just too late whisking hers out of the way and a short twig glanced off the side of Aiden's head. A streak of blood appeared just below the yellow curtain of his hair. There were loud cheers from the crowd.

Mario ran towards Francesca and David. 'Stop!' he shouted. 'Stop before someone get injure!'

David turned to Francesca. 'You want to stop, *Dolce*?'

'No. Quick.'

Expertly, David spun the Vespa away from Mario and came to a halt beside Aiden and Kate. Francesca's arms were tight round his waist. He only wished it was a real bike between his

legs, not one of these tinny toys. Aiden wiped the blood from
his forehead and said, 'What now?'

Competition was sparking between them. They gunned
their engines. It wasn't a game any more. And David didn't feel
hungover any more either. His mind was clear and diamond
sharp. 'Let's have a proper race,' he said.

'Where to?' asked Aiden.

'Down to the main road.'

'Okay, down to the main road and back.'

'Broomsticks?'

'No broomsticks.'

'Chuck the broomsticks, girls.'

Kate and Francesca tossed the broomsticks to the side of the
driveway.

'Okay. Let's go.'

'On your marks, get set—'

'Go!'

They set off slowly, side by side. Behind them, David could
hear Mario shouting, 'Kate, Francesca, get off! These are Vespa,
not child toys.'

Francesca caught Kate's eye. 'Quick,' she urged David. 'Quick
before he stops us!'

A twist of the handle and the Vespa leapt away. Downhill, the
little machines were surprisingly responsive. They roared off
round the side of the building. Glancing back, David saw that
Mario had given up the chase and was watching, still yelling at
them to take care.

'He'll be sorry,' said Kate with a grin.

'*La Dolce Vita* for ever!' shouted Francesca into David's back.
'*Viva Roman Holiday!*'

Suddenly David knew that he wanted to win, he wanted to

win badly. He glanced across at Aiden. His yellow hair was blown back off his face, giving him an oddly naked look. He was concentrating intently. Good, he wanted to win too. That would make beating him all the more satisfying. Three-quarters of the way down the drive, they were wheel to wheel. David nudged his Vespa towards Aiden's, hoping to make him pull back.

'Woah!' shouted Kate. 'Foul!'

'What are you playing at?' roared Francesca. She threw her weight the other way, causing their Vespa to swerve towards the opposite verge.

'Careful,' said David through clenched teeth. There were places on the driveway, especially on the sharp bends, where the ground fell steeply away. He was concentrating with all his energy, certain he could keep them both safe and beat Aiden and Kate at the same time.

At the entrance to the Villa Beatrice, where the driveway met the road, he and Francesca were ahead by about ten meters, but they were slower on the turn and Kate and Aiden caught up with them and began to overtake. Side by side and much more slowly now they were going uphill, the Vespas struggled on. David cursed the little scooter for its lack of power, longing to be astride his own bike which would have roared up this hill with no problem,

Francesca's arms squeezed him more tightly. 'Isn't this great?' she shouted across to Kate.

'Brilliant!' yelled Kate. 'And we're going to beat you!'

'I don't care! I love the world!' She removed her arms from round David's waist and waved them in an expansive gesture that nearly made him lose his balance. 'I love everyone! I've never been so happy! I want to—'

The end of her sentence was drowned out by the noise of a car horn which seemed to be right behind them. 'Oh God, no!' Francesca's voice had dropped to a whisper, right in his ears. Her arms were clamped round his waist once more, as if she wanted to hide behind him.

'What?' David's question was lost in a second blaring of the horn. He and Aiden pulled to a halt on either side of the road and looked behind them. A large Mercedes, black and sleek as a hearse, was only yards away. It passed regally between the two Vespas. David could make out a man and a woman in the front, a third figure in the back. The car pulled to a halt about twenty feet further up the road. No one moved.

'Oh hell,' said Francesca. 'They weren't supposed to come till tomorrow.'

David turned round to look at her. All the fun had died on her face. 'Parents?' he asked.

She nodded.

Two short beeps on the horn summoned them forwards. David began to move but Francesca said, 'No, wait.' He stopped. Her hands around his waist were holding so tight his gut was hurting.

The front passenger door opened, a single high-heeled shoe emerged, then another and a pair of slim, stocking-clad legs. A tall, elegant, immaculately dressed woman stood on the road, facing them. The family resemblance only made the differences between them more noticeable. Where Francesca's face was vibrant with life, this woman's features were dull and cold. Beautiful, yes, but in the way that a china figurine is beautiful: impersonal and dead.

Francesca's mother didn't waste time on the others, but said simply, 'Francesca!' She didn't give the impression that she was pleased to see her daughter in the least. 'Francesca, *vieni qui*. Come here.'

Francesca released David and got down from the Vespa, but didn't move any closer. Her mother took a single step towards her. 'Christ, girl, look at the state you're in! What the hell do you think you're playing at?'

Francesca stood squarely in the middle of the road and raised her head high. 'You wouldn't understand, Mother. I'm enjoying myself. It's called fun. With my friends.'

'*Che stupida!*' said her mother dismissively. 'You look like a tramp. Get in the car at once. Zio Toni is expecting us for lunch.'

'I will eat with my friends.'

Her mother did not even glance at her friends. The implication was that they were beneath contempt. It was an impasse. David heard a man's voice talking Italian inside the car, then a rear door opened and a girl got out. David saw with a shock that she was a younger, plumper, plainer version of Francesca. Her hair was cut in a long bob and pulled back from her forehead in a satin ribbon and she had protruding teeth, but the pale green eyes and the fine cheekbones, all those were Francesca's too.

The girl glanced anxiously at her mother, then smiled at Francesca. '*Ciao*, 'Cesca,' she said, almost whispering.

David was watching Francesca. Her face was transformed, no longer defensive but bathed in tenderness. '*Ciao*, Simona,' she said.

The next moment the two girls had their arms around each other. David got the impression that Francesca was hardly aware of what was happening as her mother ushered them both into the back of the car and closed the door. The car drove off slowly.

'Wow,' said Aiden, admiringly. 'Nice work.'

'Did that woman remind anyone else of Cruella de Vil?' asked Kate.

When they got back to the Villa Beatrice there was no sign of Francesca or the black Mercedes and no one had seen them drive past. Uneasily, not at all sure what to do next, they joked among themselves that Francesca had been kidnapped by aliens.

Chapter 25

The Door

There was someone outside her door.

Kate had woken from a light sleep where she sat in the chair in the guest room at La Rocca. It was like waking from a nightmare, but in reverse. Usually, on becoming conscious, there's the relief that the bad feelings were just a dream, but this time the bad feelings were here, in the room, and very real. Someone was outside her door, and the room was filled with a sense of their dark presence.

Who was it?

She stood up, her limbs aching with fatigue and the discomfort of having dozed off in the chair, and walked to the door. She pulled her gown tight round her shoulders and waited. All she had to do was open it, but right now, that seemed an impossible task. It wasn't like her to be cowardly, but at this darkest hour of the night her courage had deserted her.

Her ears were straining for the smallest sound. Was that a floorboard creaking in the passageway? The press of bare feet on carpets? Was someone's hand reaching forward to turn the handle? For God's sake, she told herself angrily, just open the door. Summoning all her courage, she laid her palm on the smooth round of the knob and turned . . .

The door opened smoothly and she looked out. No one. But then, when she peered further out, she half saw, or imagined, or thought she saw, a shadow whisking round the corner at the end of the corridor.

She closed the door quickly. Had she imagined it? After just a few hours at La Rocca was she starting to come apart, so that she became a person who was frightened of shadows?

She went back to her chair, knowing it would be impossible to sleep again that night, waiting for the dawn. Her thoughts drifted back relentlessly to that final weekend. If only she had left when Francesca's parents had arrived. It had seemed such a small decision at the time. It wasn't fair that such trivial decisions should have such a mighty impact. There should have been some warning, some way of knowing what lay ahead. If she'd gone then, once the Vespa racing was over, she'd have forfeited the most romantic night of her life, but that would have been worth it if it meant Francesca survived. If Kate had gone with the others then her last memory of Francesca that weekend would have been her laughter and her fun as she careered down the driveway on the back of David's Vespa. Francesca enjoying herself, Francesca with not a care in the world.

Instead of which . . .

Chapter 26

Trespassers

The feeling of being trespassers grew worse. There was no sign of Francesca or her family, or, for that matter, of Mario. The exuberance of the Vespa racing had vanished. Kate wandered about with the others, uncertain what to do next, while Angelica talked fiercely to anyone who would listen and made violent sweeping gestures with her arms. Dido and Jenny came back from exploring the grounds and said they'd seen a house near the summit that looked like a medieval tower. Parked outside it was the hearse-like Mercedes, Mario's Topolino and another car no one had seen before.

Several people decided to hitch back to Florence right away. There was a rumour of another party near Santa Croce that night. Around three o'clock, a few minutes after the first batch trudged off down the drive to start hitching, the black Mercedes reappeared in front of the villa. There was only one occupant this time, Francesca's mother, who got out and briskly set about encouraging the others to return to Florence. Her guest-ejection technique was faultless. She was gracious, even friendly when necessary, but the message was as clear as if she'd handed them an ultimatum in writing. The party was over: it was time to go.

Angelica glowed with relief, her gold teeth glinting in a happy grin, now that the established order was being restored. She cleared the rooms briskly and soon the hallway was cluttered with piles of sleeping bags, rucksacks and coats.

Signora Bertoni continued to be courtesy itself: 'How do you propose to get back to Florence?' she asked in her husky, forty-Gauloises-a-day voice, which, with its strong American accent, would have been deeply attractive if she'd been saying anything halfway friendly. 'Can I order you a taxi? I do hope you've enjoyed your stay. Maybe you'll come back to the Villa Beatrice some day.' All spoken with a gracious smile, while *over my dead body* said her cold green eyes. She was like a mannequin, an efficient, ruthless mannequin.

Kate was in the hall with David. Jenny had already left with Larry, Dido had gone with Aiden. Hugo had somehow missed both groups and wanted to hitch back with her and David to avoid a repetition of the previous day's trauma. Two men and one girl was not an ideal hitching combination. Kate still hoped that Francesca would be coming back with them, that way they could go in two pairs.

'We can't go without Francesca,' she told Signora Bertoni when they were ready to leave. 'How will she get back to Florence?'

Signora Bertoni's mouth was a hard red line. 'My daughter's not going back to Florence, Kate. She's staying right here with her family.'

'Then tell me where she is. I can't go until we've said goodbye.'

'Francesca is busy,' said her mother, crimson mouth stretched to a too-perfect smile. 'I will tell her you said goodbye.'

Something made Kate set down her bag and say, 'I'd like to tell her myself.'

'It's not convenient.'

'Where is she?'

David was uneasy. He said, 'Kate, we ought to get going. It's always harder hitching in the dark.'

'I'm not going till I've seen Francesca.'

Signora Bertoni was no longer smiling. 'What makes you so sure she wants to see you? If she did, she would have come down herself.'

'All the same . . .'

'Come on, Kate,' said Hugo. 'We'll catch up with Francesca when we get back to Florence.'

'But . . .'

Kate was reluctant to admit defeat – Francesca had been edgy enough coming here with all her friends, so why would she suddenly agree to stay on alone? – but at the same time she didn't want to get stranded at the Villa Beatrice on her own. She wasn't going to risk hitching without a partner and she had no idea what other way there was of getting back to Florence. Rescue arrived in an unexpected guise. Mario came into the hallway and smiled at her as though they were old friends. Kate bristled. He said, 'Kate, is good I see you before you go. Francesca will be sad you do not say goodbye.'

'That's just what I was saying.'

'Unfortunately—' Signora Bertoni began.

Mario seemed to have grasped the situation in a glance. He said, 'I drive Kate to Florence later. Is not problem.'

Kate let out a sigh of relief. 'Thanks,' she said. She'd have to deal with the problems of a car drive with Mario when she got to it, and who knows, maybe Francesca would be going back to Florence with them. She didn't see how her parents could actually prevent her from going. Presumably, once she'd done her piece with her uncle, they'd all be happy again.

Right now, all that mattered was that Signora Bertoni was obliged to cede victory, though the glance she tossed in Mario's direction indicated she did not take kindly to being out-manoeuvred.

Kate was heading towards the door with Mario when David barred her way. 'Do you want me to stay as well?' he asked, his dark eyebrows gathered in a frown. 'I can wait for you if you like and we'll hitch back together.'

'Don't bother,' said Kate, hardly even noticing his inter-ruption, as she went past him and into the bright sunlight with Mario. 'I'll catch up with you both tonight at Santa Croce.'

David said something else, maybe goodbye, or maybe he repeated that he'd wait, or maybe it was Hugo who spoke. Kate wasn't paying attention. There was no reason for elaborate goodbyes or plans, no indication that anyone had just made a momentous decision. No way of knowing how these details would be picked over, like the last scraps of flesh clinging to a carcass, in the days to come. Just sunlight glinting off the windows of the Mercedes that squatted like a black toad in front of the house, and David and Hugo hefting their packs and preparing to set off down the driveway to the road. And Signora Bertoni giving Angelica instructions for the preparation of the rooms.

'We walk,' said Mario to Kate. 'La Rocca is not far.'

Kate didn't answer. Whatever his reasons for helping her out back there, it didn't mean she had to talk to him. All that mattered was seeing Francesca again. He owed her a proper apology anyway.

He said, 'You are angry, Kate?'

'You bet I am.'

They walked in silence. But when she saw La Rocca for the first time, she forgot all about being angry. Zio Toni's home was like the enchanted castle in a fairy tale, a strong square tower covered in creepers, the bare summit of the hill rising up against the blue sky behind it. And there, on a paved area beside the tower where a vine was just beginning to grow out over the trellis, sat the two sisters from the fairy story, both alike with their long brown hair and green eyes, the older sister beautiful like the morning, the younger plump and plain with her sticky-out teeth, clearly enchanted by what she was hearing.

'Kate! I was just talking about you!' Francesca's greeting was so enthusiastic it was as if they hadn't seen each other for days. She jumped up and put her arms round Kate, then pulled out a chair for her. She seemed almost feverish in her excitement. 'I want Simona to meet all my friends.'

'Hi, Simona,' said Kate.

'Hello,' said Simona shyly.

Though she was only a few months or so younger than Kate, Simona still had the air of childhood. Partly it was the clothes. Her wardrobe must be chosen for her by the formidable Signora Bertoni. She was dressed in a plaid skirt that came to her knees, a cream twinset and neat black court shoes. But the difference went deeper than just clothes. Simona had the soft, slightly boneless look of a girl who has so far only tried to please others, not yet dared to imagine what she might want for herself. Beside her, Francesca, in her borrowed man's shirt and her worn jeans, with her hair looped back over her ears, looked lean and bold and feral.

'Kate's the one I was telling you about,' said Francesca. 'But I want you to meet the others too, David and Jenny and Aiden and—'

'They've gone,' said Kate.

'What? Gone where?'

'Back to Florence.'

'But they can't! The party's not over till tomorrow.'

'We didn't know your parents were going to show up today, though. That changed things, obviously.'

Francesca looked as though someone had just punched all the air out of her. 'But that's not fair! They weren't supposed to come till tomorrow. It's not my fault they changed their plans.'

'Well, it's too late now. Everyone's gone except me. Mario said he'd give me a lift later.'

'Mario?'

'Yes.' Kate looked round, but Mario was nowhere to be seen.

'My mother threw them out, right?'

'She kind of made it obvious we weren't flavour of the month.'

Francesca was scowling, hunched over and furious. 'Damn her,' she said. Then she brightened. 'I've been telling Simona about what it's like in Florence, the work we're doing in the Baptistery, how we live and everything.'

Simona smiled shyly at Kate. 'It sounds great,' she said. In an odd way, she reminded Kate of how Francesca had been when she first showed up in Florence: the contrast between them illustrated how much Francesca had changed since joining the mud angels.

'Oh, Simona, you'd love it,' said Francesca, her enthusiasm

reviving. 'I know you would. Just come for a few days and see.'

'Mamma would never allow it.'

'So? Come anyway.'

Simona didn't answer, but her eyes spoke for her, green eyes shining with a hopeless longing.

Francesca said, 'Just try, Simi. We'd take care of you. And it's the chance of a lifetime.'

'But Mamma would never—'

Right on cue there was the crunch of tyres on gravel and the Mercedes came to a halt. Signora Bertoni got out of the car and came towards them. Her crimson smile was back in place. Kate could see how one might learn to dread that smile.

'Good, you've had a chance to say goodbye, Kate. I expect Mario will be wanting to leave soon. Where is he, Francesca?'

Francesca made a pretence of looking all around. 'I don't see him, Mamma,' she said. 'Do you see him, Kate?' Kate didn't answer. 'No, Kate doesn't see him either. No one sees him, Mamma.' She made the sentences sound like phrases from an early reading book.

Signora Bertoni pursed her lips in irritation, then said, 'Simona, Zio Toni will be waking from his nap now. Go and see if he's ready for his afternoon tisane.'

Simona started to rise from her chair, but Francesca caught her by the arm, forcing her to stay where she was. She said, 'Zio Toni has servants to bring him his tea.'

'I know, honey. But he prefers to see Simona.'

'So do I. And we just happen to be in the middle of a conversation.'

'Which can surely wait.'

'No, as a matter of fact, it can't.'

Signora Bertoni sighed, then spoke tersely to Simona in Italian. This time she was giving orders. Simona stood up.

Francesca said, 'Simona, don't go. She's not the boss of your life, you know.'

'Francesca, stay out of this,' said her mother.

'Why? She's my sister!'

'Then start acting like a sister and stop leading her astray.'

'What makes you think—?'

'Mamma, 'Cesca, please don't . . . ' Simona's plump cheeks had gone very red and she was on the verge of tears.

'Oh, Simi, I'm sorry!' Francesca jumped up and put her arm across her sister's hunched shoulders.

'Sorry?' Signora Bertoni was contemptuous. 'Maybe if you thought before you interfered, young lady. Simona, go to your uncle right now.'

'*Non è necessario.*' The voice came out of the shadows near the house. 'The mountain is coming to Mohammed.' His English was grammatically correct, but still heavily accented.

A man, made older than his years by illness, walked slowly towards them. He was leaning on Mario's arm. Stooped and obviously in pain, he was regarding them all intently. His eyes were still clear and bright, though his face appeared to be dying round them, skin so desiccated it already had the pallor of a corpse. Mario helped him into a chair. A middle-aged man with an amiable, handsome face was hovering behind them. Kate guessed he must be Francesca's father.

Signora Bertoni was all solicitude. 'Are you comfortable there, Zio Toni? Do you want me to fetch you another rug?' There was no warmth in her questions. 'Simona was just going to get you your tisane, weren't you, honey?'

He waved her away irritably. 'Stop fussing, woman. Lucia

will bring it. Simona can stay here with me.' He looked keenly at Francesca, who met his gaze defiantly for a moment, then looked away. His attention lighted on Kate. 'And who are you, young lady?'

'Kate Holland.' She held out her hand. There was something about his gaze that made her uneasy, but she was determined to be polite. 'I'm a friend of Francesca's. We've been working together in Florence.'

He took her hand and held it for a moment, still sizing her up. Kate was aware that the Bertonis were all watching anxiously, as if his response to any visitor were of vital importance. Kate didn't share their anxiety, since she was soon to leave and would probably never return. But more importantly, Zio Toni reminded her of her own grandfather, a man who liked to think he ruled his family with a rod of iron but whom she'd been able to wrap round her little finger ever since she learned to talk. The only difference was that this man was near death. All these people fussing round him because they wanted his money – Kate felt sorry for him.

'You are one of these so-called *angeli dell'alluvione*?' Still he held her hand.

She grinned. 'That's what they call us. Among other things.'

Francesca's father shook her hand formally. '*Piacere*,' he said. He was smiling, but it was the permanent, meaningless smile of a man whose only role in the family is to be nice.

Zio Toni was looking her up and down slowly, a cool assessment by a man who, in his time, had been a connoisseur of many kinds of beauty. He said, 'You are a good-looking girl.' Francesca's father nodded his agreement, as the old man continued, 'You should dress like a woman, not a workman.'

Kate felt a tremor of unease. It was weird being subjected to such an openly sexual stare from a man who was so clearly past all sexual activity. She said firmly, 'Smart clothes wouldn't last a minute with the work I'm doing.'

'Here? In this house, Kate Holland, you are my guest.'

'Not for much longer, I'm afraid,' she told him cheerfully.

'Kate has to get back to Florence,' Signora Bertoni said. 'She and Mario were just leaving.'

'Mamma, stop getting rid of my friends!' said Francesca. 'Besides, I'm going too, don't you forget.' She turned to Simona. 'Come with us, Simona. Just for the weekend. Just for a day. You'll never regret it, I promise.'

'Francesca, stop this or you'll go straight to your room!' said her mother.

Francesca flushed. For a moment she seemed lost for words. Then she said coldly, 'And which room would that be, Mother?'

Kate was appalled at the way her friend had been spoken to, as if she were still a child. She said firmly, 'You don't need to worry, Signora Bertoni. If Simona came to Florence we'd take good care of her and she'd have a great time.' Just as she'd decided that Zio Toni was a poor old man, isolated by his wealth even when he was dying, she'd come to the conclusion that Signora Bertoni was a battleaxe who needed to be divested of her power. She appealed to Zio Toni for support. 'You trust us, don't you? You know Francesca and I would make sure Simona didn't come to any harm. And a chance to help with the restoration of Florence, even for a couple of days – she'll remember it all her life.'

'Just you stay out of this, young lady—' Signora Bertoni began, but the old man held up his hand, commanding silence.

He was staring at Kate. His eyes were twinkling and his pale lips hovered into a smile. 'You have very definite opinions, Kate Holland,' he said.

'Thank you,' she said, meeting his eyes, though her instinct was to look away. 'I'll take that as a compliment.'

He nodded briskly, then said decisively. 'There is a solution to this problem. You and Francesca wish to return to Florence with Simona. Their mother wants them to remain here. Let us postpone the decision for twenty-four hours. Why don't you stay here also, Kate Holland? Just for a night. Tomorrow –' he flicked a quick glance towards Francesca's mother – 'tomorrow there are some family matters to be attended to, and after that . . . who knows?'

Signora Bertoni intervened. 'Unfortunately, Zio Toni, Kate is getting a lift back with Mario and—'

'Dottore Bassano,' the old man turned to Mario. 'Does your busy schedule permit you to stay for a night more?'

'Yes, of course, *signore*, but—'

'Then it is settled. There will be no more arguments. You will stay, Kate Holland?'

'Yes,' she said. There was no way she'd abandon Francesca now, and besides, she was curious to see more of her strange family. 'I'll stay.'

'*Bene, bene.* That's good,' said Francesca's father. Signora Bertoni looked sick with rage, but there was nothing she could do.

'Come,' said Francesca eagerly, 'I'll show you your room, and we can tell Simona about Florence. Oh, I'm so glad you're staying, Kate!'

Chapter 27

Mother Love

Annette Bertoni took care never to lose her temper. Years back, when she was still cute little Annie-Belle Harper, doing occasional modelling jobs and waiting tables in the cocktail lounge in Manhattan, she'd learned that to get what you want you stay sweet and pretty and wait your chance. Any loss of control, anger most of all, is messy and counterproductive and therefore must be avoided. Her capacity for rage frightened her: when she'd learned the truth about her husband, she would have happily killed him if there'd been a weapon to hand.

But on this occasion she felt justified in letting rip. The tensions of the last weeks and months, the scheming and hoping and manoeuvring, the frustrations and the sleepless nights and the wretched powerlessness that drove her half out of her mind, all that had taken its toll. It was good to lash out. Let her wrath be both a warning and the punishment he deserved.

She kept her voice low. This conversation was for their ears only. He stood there in silence while she drew on her extensive repertoire of Italian abuse. 'You son of a whore, after all I've done for you! It's all your fault! You refused to tell us where she was hiding out and now look what has happened! We should have brought her home right away, but no, you thought you knew what was best. And now you're doing it again! How dare you take that girl's side when you knew I wanted to get rid of her! I could kill you for this!'

Mario stood his ground. 'Francesca would have been distressed if all her friends had left without saying goodbye.'

'Excuse me, since when did you know better than I do what's right for my daughter?'

'She's changed, Annette. I've been watching her, these past weeks, and I tell you, she's not the same girl who came back from the States before Christmas.'

'Damn right she's not, and more's the pity! If I'd known what was going on, I'd never have allowed her to stay with that rabble. You were supposed to report back to me and you let me down.'

'I thought it was for the best. Even you must agree that Francesca is stronger, happier, than ever before. The improvement is all due to friends like Kate.'

'Seems a strange way for you to talk. Doesn't it bother you, knowing your girl is carrying on with people like that?'

'To begin with, yes, it did. But . . . I like to see her happy, Annette.'

'Happy? What nonsense. Francesca will lose all respect for you, and I don't blame her. Mario, I want that English girl out of here. She's dangerous.'

To Annette's fury, Mario actually laughed. 'Dangerous?' He walked over to the window. From the grounds outside the small sitting room in which they were talking, came the sound of girls' voices, talking and laughing. That kind of easy banter among friends that Annette had never known. People had never been drawn to her. They'd admired her, but never liked her. Respect was what she wanted, it was what she had to have. 'Kate's not dangerous,' he said in a low voice, and she saw how his face warmed as his gaze lingered on the three girls. 'She's hardly more than a child herself.'

'You don't know what you're talking about,' snapped Annette. 'She's got you under her thumb same as Francesca. Well, I intend to make damn sure Simona doesn't go the same way!'

'Has it ever occurred to you, Annette, that you might not have any choice? Simona is nearly eighteen. You can't keep her a child for ever.'

'Now you sound like Francesca. What's got into you, Mario?'

'Nothing. Francesca has to have a chance to spread her wings before she settles down. Simona too. It's like the song says, Annette, the times are changing. I used to see things your way, but now – well – I'm sorry, but I think you're wrong.'

'How dare you! Who are you to judge what is right and wrong? Unlike you, Mario, I do not have the luxury of thinking only of Francesca. I must consider the interests of the whole family. I thought you of all people understood that. Zio Toni does not have long to live and we have to safeguard the future.'

'You mean, his money? But what if Francesca doesn't want it? What if even Simona would be better off without it?'

'I can't believe I'm hearing this.' To calm herself, Annette fished in her bag for a packet of cigarettes and lit one, inhaling deeply. She did not offer one to Mario. After a few moments she said coolly, 'Listen to me, Mario. This isn't some game we're playing here. I'm not after the money so the girls can buy a few fancy dresses and go to finishing school and have parties. I'm talking survival, Mario. Staying afloat. I've been hanging on by my fingernails for so long I've forgotten what it's like any other way. You think your family have debts because they paid for you to go through medical school? Well, think of a number and add a few zeros and you might come close. If Zio Toni doesn't come through with the money then this family is finished. Kaput. Wiped out. Totally.'

'You'd manage somehow, Annette. You always do.'

'You're not listening. It will be the end. My useless husband will probably kill himself, if I don't get there first and do the job for him. We *have* to get the money. If Francesca won't play ball, then Simona must do it. Otherwise we have no chance.'

Mario didn't answer right away. He went back to the window and looked out at the girls. Their laughter was free and infectious. At length he turned and said to her, 'I regret you've got into this mess, Annette, but it's not the girls' fault. You know I hope to marry Francesca eventually, but in the meantime, if she wants to see a bit of the world, then I'll help her any way I can.'

'You'll lose her.'

'It's a risk I have to take.'

'No.' The contradiction was made with such certainty that Mario flinched. He controlled himself and remained motionless as Annette crossed the room and stood in front of him. She raised her right hand and touched the rim of his collar, where his hair curled over. 'You need a haircut, Mario. You'll be as bad as the *capelloni* soon.'

'Annette, don't.'

'I'll do as I please, young man.' She gripped the back of his neck, holding him in position as she touched his mouth with her fingertips.

Instinctively he turned away, then reached up and wiped his mouth with the back of his hand.

'Don't you like it any more?' He didn't answer. She went on, smiling now, 'I guess Francesca would be kind of upset if she discovered, eh? Is that what's worrying you?'

'You know damn well it would kill her.'

'Oh really? Maybe now you're the one who's exaggerating, Mario. I admit she's always been a sensitive child, one of those girls who takes things hard, but still, I don't suppose it would actually *kill* her to know that her fiancé – not official, of course, but all the same – that her beloved fiancé had been keeping Mamma amused while the little girl was in the States.'

'You make it sound like a real affair but . . . it was only a couple of times.'

'Three. I remember each occasion so vividly, don't you?' Mario was silent, staring at her. She continued easily, 'I sure hope she never does find out about what happened. She wouldn't like it, would she? It might even bring on a relapse.'

'A relapse?' He looked at her incredulously. 'It would destroy her.'

'So. We just have to make sure she never finds out.'

'What are you saying? You think I would tell her?'

Annette stubbed out her cigarette. All trace of anger gone, she was smiling now. 'Oh, I'm sure *you'd* never tell her, Mario.'

'Then . . . no, I don't believe it.' He met her gaze for a few moments, her hard, challenging stare, then turned away and walked across the room, putting as much distance between them as he could, before looking back and saying in a low voice, 'Not even you . . . you'd never tell her.'

'I might do. If I was pushed hard enough.'

'But . . . are you jealous?'

It was the wrong thing to ask. She was hissing with rage as she said, 'Me? Jealous of my daughter? Never! I always thought my daughter could do better than a shrink from a dirt-poor village. I only went along with it for Francesca's sake. Nothing would give me more pleasure than to tell her every sordid detail if I have to.'

'Then I'll deny it. She'll never believe you.'

'No?' She smiled, regaining her composure. 'But I kept your little notes, Mario.'

'You did?' He plunged his hands into his hair. 'That's disgusting. It's blackmail!'

'I prefer to call it a bargain,' she said. 'A business deal.'

'But . . . you know what it would do to her. I can't believe you'd hurt your own child that way.'

'No?' She looked at him in triumph. 'Perhaps you're right. Maybe I wouldn't. But you'll never know, will you, because you daren't put it to the test. Because you know I *might*, if I had reason enough.'

'But your own daughter . . .'

'No need to sound so shocked, *mio caro dottore*. As I said already, unlike you I have the whole family to consider, not just one person. So?'

'She must never know.'

'Excellent. Then you will do as I say.'

He nodded bleakly. 'What do you want?'

'Sit down,' she said, 'and I'll explain.' After a brief hesitation he went to sit on the edge of a straight-backed chair. 'We will close ranks,' she said, suddenly businesslike. 'We have to get rid of this English girl, send her back to Florence tonight. Break the

connection. I don't want Francesca to have any more dealings
with those foreigners. She will stay here. Alone, she's never been
able to stand up to me.'

'Not many people can,' said Mario quietly. Louder, he said,
'But Zio Toni has invited Kate to stay. If I can't persuade her to
leave, what then?'

'I'm sure you'll find a way. But if she refuses – then you must
help me do whatever is necessary to keep my daughters on side.
Francesca's still in love with you, you know. I know my
daughter. She's acting up now, but she's never really cared for
anyone else. And as for Simona, she regards you as an older
brother – she's probably a little bit in love with you too. A few
words from you and I'm sure both girls will be easier to handle.'

'Is that all?' Mario stood up.

She ignored the sarcasm of his question. 'For the time being.
You can be sure I'll let you know if there is anything else.'

Mario had his hand on the door. He turned, his face white
with suppressed rage, and said, 'I wish to God I'd never had
anything to do with the Bertoni family.'

Annette laughed. She had sat down in a blue velvet chair and
was lighting herself another cigarette. '*Mio caro*,' she said, 'I
know just how you feel. I've wished the selfsame thing every
single day of my married life.'

Mario went out by a back door and walked quickly up a track
that led away from La Rocca, striding up the hillside until he
could go no further. He couldn't stand to see anybody, least of
all Francesca. He didn't think he'd ever be able to face Francesca
again. Regret wasn't a strong enough word for what he felt right
now. If he could have turned the clock back . . . but he knew
Annette Bertoni would never let him off the hook.

When he could climb no higher, he sat down on a rock and stared unseeing at the wide expanse of hills and woods all around. He was struggling to identify the moment when he'd made the fatal decision to become Annette's lover, but it was impossible. When he first encountered her, at a fund-raising evening for a medical charity he supported, he'd been desperate to find out where Francesca had been sent, to find some way of contacting her. It was only natural he should try to court favour with Francesca's mother, since she obviously held the reins of power in the family. And Signora Bertoni had been willing to be courted. As she'd told Mario, Francesca was vulnerable: even though she could see Mario's feelings for her daughter were sincere, she still needed to find out for herself if he was someone she could trust.

Trust. The memory of the word, how she had dangled it in front of him, made Mario feel ill. But at the time, it had seemed like a reasonable request, so he'd agreed to all her suggestions that they meet. He even learned to look forward to them: she could be good company, witty and urbane and interested in his work and his studies. One day he had met her for lunch as usual in one of her favourite restaurants and told her that for the sake of her reputation they would have to cease their meetings: already there were rumours that he was her lover. To his amazement she'd laughed at the notion and he realized that, far from being shocked, she was pleased people thought she had such an attentive young lover.

She had invited him back to the apartment. There were some things of Francesca's she wanted him to see. Her husband was out. Mario knew by now of her disappointment in her husband – the husband who'd flattered her with expensive presents and promises of wealth but who, when they got back to Italy, had turned out to be poor as a church mouse. He'd learned to see Filippo through her eyes and to despise him too. Mario was flattered by the confidences of this attractive and obviously unhappy woman. He went back to her flat at that hour in the afternoon when the servants were out and the city seemed half asleep in the heat.

She had shown him a poem Francesca had written when she was fifteen, a poem full of thoughts of death and despair. Why couldn't she have brought it to their meeting at the restaurant? He grew nervous and made some joking reference to the ridiculousness of the gossip that they were lovers.

It had been a mistake, he realized as soon as he said it. 'Ridiculous?' she asked, the question husky and plaintive. 'Do you really find me so unattractive?'

Of course not, on the contrary, she was extremely attractive. Mario struggled to repair the damage. She was the most attractive of women . . . and it was true. He'd never been alone in the company of anyone so sophisticated and elegant. But still she was not reassured. He'd been thrown off balance by her sudden shift to vulnerability. He put his arms round her to comfort her. To demonstrate just how attractive she was, he'd kissed her. And somewhere between the kissing and the reassurance the moment when he could have drawn back passed without him noticing it, and was gone for ever.

Three times, she said. He'd said two. He didn't count the final time, after he'd happened to notice a letter from the clinic where Francesca'd been sent and memorized its address. He'd been appalled to learn Francesca had been sent to a private clinic, not the college he'd been told about. Why? He didn't believe Annette's account of Francesca's violence against her uncle, that she'd poured boiling water on his leg. He thought they were making it up, horrified that even now it was possible for parents to incarcerate their inconvenient children. His final encounter with Annette had been brief, without any pretence of tenderness. He'd been intending to tell her it was the last time, but perhaps she'd sensed what he was about to say and she'd got there first. Saving face. From then on there'd been no more lunches, but he was careful to remain courteous and friendly: he'd known it would be a mistake to make an enemy of Annette Bertoni. But he'd never imagined the lengths to which she was prepared to go.

Well, now he knew. He was furious with himself for having been so gullible. Had she seduced him because she was attracted to him, simply, or had she set the trap so she could use it against him one day if she wanted to? He wondered how he dared to call himself a psychiatrist when he was so easily fooled by human nature, but his schizophrenics and depressives were plain sailing compared to the Bertonis.

He had lost Francesca. After that hideous meeting with Annette just now there was no going back to the illusion that one day he and Francesca could make a life together away from her family. Her mother's threats, the blackmail, his terrible sense of powerlessness, would always come between him and Francesca. He'd waited three years while she was in America and would have waited another three if necessary, but it was only now, when he knew he was condemned to walk away for ever, that he recognized how strongly he had loved her.

Desperately, he tried to work out how to get round Annette's threats. He thought that if she ever dared to tell Francesca about their liaison he would simply deny it, brazen it out and say the woman was fantasizing. It would be his word against her mother's – if Francesca cared for him, which deep down he still believed she did, then surely she would believe him rather than the mother she detested? But . . . but . . . a life together founded on a lie? What kind of a life would that be? Sooner or later the truth was sure to come out, as it always did, and then what? A marriage with poison at its heart was a lingering death. He'd never be able to endure such a thing.

But supposing he were to take back the initiative and tell Francesca about the affair himself? If he confessed, she'd be horrified and angry for a while, and desperately hurt, but if she cared for him – again, that *if* – she would be reconciled in time. Perhaps. Alternatively, she might hate and despise him for ever; his pride could not endure the thought of that. Better by far to sever all links while she still thought well of him, perhaps even loved him the same way as he loved her. There was no guarantee that Annette would act on her threat, so why divulge a secret that was better left a secret for ever?

He knew his only real option was to walk away, hard though that was. So long as he remained within reach of the Bertonis, he was doomed to remain a pawn in whatever game Annette chose to play. And the worst part was knowing that he had brought this misery on himself.

It didn't stop there. He had always thought Francesca exaggerated her need to escape from her family; now he saw clearly that her only chance of finding happiness was away from their embrace. He was the one person who could have taken her away from them and he was powerless to help her.

One last task Annette had set him and it could not have been closer to his heart. He was to see that Kate returned to Florence that afternoon, which meant he was to leave also. Leave, and, if he had his way, never come back. There was an ache in his heart at the prospect of never seeing Francesca again. She had been his first and truest love. He could not believe he'd ever care for anyone as he cared for her, but she came at too high a price.

He stood up and began walking down the mountainside to look for Kate.

The moment he was gone from the room, Annette's composure vanished. She leaned her head back against the chair and closed her eyes. She was quivering like a leaf, shaking so much that when she tried to put the cigarette to her lips, ash tumbled down the front of her blouse. My God, what must he think of her? No need to ask the question, you only had to look in his eyes to see the depths of his contempt. And she had so craved his good opinion. Time was, they had been allies as well as lovers. Oh, she wasn't under any illusions. She had always known he didn't care for her the way he cared for Francesca, but even so . . . he had admired her and desired her and she'd revelled in that.

All gone. Irrevocably gone. But it was a small price to pay. What kind of mother would resort to blackmail and threaten to destroy her own child? Simple: a desperate mother. A mother who'd teetered on the edge of the abyss for so long she'd forgotten what it was like not to wake every night in the small hours in a cold sweat of terror at what the future might bring. A mother who'd lied and cheated and schemed for years to keep her family afloat. And anyway, she knew Mario would never dare to call her bluff.

He believed her threat, just as she'd known he would. He was innocent and idealistic, so he believed people less scrupulous than himself to be capable of anything, even the destruction of their own child. Because surely Francesca's fragile equilibrium would be utterly destroyed if she knew of their affair. Mario wasn't to know how much she cherished her wayward daughter, in spite of everything. She'd learned to play the part of unfeeling termagant with consummate skill. Sometimes she even came close to deceiving herself.

This was not how her life had meant to turn out. When the good-looking and easy-going young Filippo Bertoni came into the cocktail lounge with his handmade suits and his wallet bulging with dollars she'd thought she'd found the wealthy husband of her dreams. It was only later, after the wedding and the trip back to Italy, that she'd discovered it had all been a facade, a sham, a six-month spree on his father's inheritance and it was all used up. Not that lack of money stopped him spending. The first words of Italian she learned were about interest rates and deferred payments and credit. If it hadn't been for Zio Toni . . .

He'd always had a soft spot for Francesca, and no wonder: she'd been a child like a little angel. He'd paid for her to be educated at home because they thought she was too sensitive for school. Annette had learned to plump up the expenses for Francesca and get by on the surplus. And he'd dropped hints about his money: he'd always said it would be a shame to break the estate up, that the pictures and the land should stay together. Hints, but nothing definite. Annette had grown mean-spirited as a starving dog, disaster only kept at bay with casual scraps of hope.

And now the old crook was dying. The doctors said it was a matter of weeks, not months. No one knew how much he was worth, but the estate and the art collection alone were worth a fortune. Several fortunes. Annette had already borrowed vast sums at extortionate rates of interest on the expectation of inheriting his money. But recently, Zio Toni had let her know he was displeased with the way Francesca was turning out, and no wonder. In his odd way, the old man had forgiven her that incident with the boiling water – had even said that she was a girl after his own heart and knew about inflicting pain. It was the way she turned her back on them, disappeared to God knows where, which had caused the problems. And all the time she'd been in Florence with those deadbeats. But she always had been wayward and hard to handle. Not like Simona. Thank God her younger daughter had always been pliable. All her hopes now were pinned on Simona. She had to replace Francesca in her uncle's affections and inherit the fortune for her family.

Otherwise they had no future. No future at all.

Chapter 28

Disguises

By early evening, the Villa Beatrice had been transformed. Angelica had swept away every last trace of the party. Where there had been empty wine bottles and damp rings on the marble surfaces, now there were jugs of spring flowers. Rugs that had been rolled up were back on the floors, shutters were flung wide to let in the light, fires blazed a welcome in all the main rooms, even in the hallway. The stink of cigarette smoke and socks, and the winter-long smells of damp and neglect, had been chased away by polish and fresh air. Kate was so amazed by the change that she was prepared to credit Angelica with magical housekeeping abilities until Francesca informed her that two women from the nearby farm were always on hand to help out at short notice. Angelica herself was busy in the kitchen, and if the pungent aromas drifting into the hallway were any indication, they were in for a treat that evening.

Kate relished every detail. She'd stayed in comfortable houses before now, but never one as palatial as the Villa Beatrice. The previous night the bedrooms had been firmly off-limits and she'd made do with a cushion on the floor, but this evening she had a room to herself, crisply laundered white sheets and fleecy towels and a bottle of San Pelegrino on the table beside her bed. When Zio Toni issued his surprise invitation she thought he meant she was to stay with him at La Rocca, but it turned out that accommodation in the converted tower was limited and since his illness took hold he'd insisted on eating his meals alone, so guests were always put up at the Villa Beatrice. She'd been told they'd be returning to La Rocca for a drink before their dinner at Villa Beatrice and she was looking forward to the guided tour of the art collection she'd heard so much about.

But in the meantime, there was plenty to keep her occupied at the Villa Beatrice. Mario, for instance. She couldn't make him out. The previous evening he'd come on strong and then been gratuitously rude. Then he'd come to her aid when she was being stonewalled by Signora Bertoni. And now here he'd come knocking at the open door of her bedroom. 'Kate, I must talk with you.'

'Oh, really?' She stared at him coldly.

'Can I come in?'

'I suppose so.'

He came in and closed the door carefully behind him. Every gesture was bristling with tension. 'I think maybe I go back to Florence,' he said.

'Good,' said Kate. 'Goodbye then.'

'I want for you come with me.'

'You must be joking!'

'Is not joke. Is better not to stay here, with this family.'

'Is Francesca coming too?'

'No, she must stay with her family.'

'I'm not leaving Francesca,' said Kate. 'And you must be mad if you think I'd go anywhere with you after last night.'

'I apologize,' he said. 'I say bad thing, but is not important.' He made a dismissive gesture with his hand. 'But going, going now, that is important. There is much family trouble here. We must go to Florence together.'

'What kind of family trouble?' Kate wanted to know.

'Is their business, not for us. We do not belong with this family.'

Kate stared at him. To her amazement, he seemed perfectly sincere. She was baffled. 'I don't understand you, Mario. You were so fired up about Francesca coming here this weekend, I can't believe you're just going to abandon her now.'

'Is not abandon. Is for her own good.'

'That's what you say, but unless you tell me why, I'm afraid I don't believe you. I'm staying right here with Francesca just as long as she wants me to.'

Mario swore in Italian. 'You are foolish child,' he said bitterly. 'You do not understand what you do. Come back to Florence with me – it is best for Francesca.'

'Sorry, Dr Bassano, but I don't see it that way. Now, will you get out of my room, please? I'm going to take a shower.'

He moved towards the door, obviously deeply unhappy with her decision. The weirdest part of it, thought Kate, was that he really did seem to be sincere. To her amazement, he said that if she wasn't leaving the Villa Beatrice, then he intended to stay there too. She started to argue with him, but discovered he could be as stubborn as she was. Unless she left with him, he was going to stay put. If she hadn't still been so suspicious of his motives, she'd have been flattered. As it was, confusion was her strongest emotion.

Once she'd showered and put on her jeans and her rumpled

shirt, she went down to the hall where she found Francesca and Simona arguing in Italian with their father. Or rather Francesca was arguing all on her own while Simona watched miserably and he occasionally spoke in a quiet, conciliatory voice. Mario was nowhere to be seen. It was the first time Kate had had a chance to study Signor Bertoni. Medium height, brown haired and with a kindly, contented face, he looked a lot younger than his wife, more like an older brother to the two girls than a father. She felt embarrassed at gatecrashing what sounded like a full-on family row, and she was about to move silently up the stairs, when Francesca spotted her.

'Kate,' she said in English. 'You'll never guess, now Pappa is trying to make us wear skirts at dinner – knee-length *skirts*! Can you believe it?'

'I'm sorry,' said Kate, smiling angelically, since she figured this was another male member of Francesca's family likely to be susceptible to young women, 'but I've only brought jeans with me.'

'That doesn't matter,' said Signor Bertoni, 'either my wife or Simona would be happy to lend you what is necessary. You must all be about the same size.'

The idea of borrowing clothes from Francesca's mother was distinctly alarming, and Kate would rather dress in brown-paper bags than the kind of clothes Simona was wearing. 'Oh, for God's sake, Pappa,' exclaimed Francesca. 'You can't make us look like frumps.'

'What is a frump?'

'An old woman who wears horrible clothes.'

'Neither of you would ever look a frump,' he said charmingly. 'Can't you just do this small thing for me, 'Cesca? It will mean so much to your mother—'

'No—' Francesca began.

But Simona burst out, 'Please 'Cesca, just this once. I can't bear it when everyone is arguing all the time. You know how Mamma will go on, it'll spoil the whole evening if you stay in those dirty trousers. Why do you have to upset her on purpose? It's just clothes, for goodness' sake. It doesn't really matter what you wear, that's what you've always told me.'

'Yes, but . . .' Francesca's arguments died away. It seemed she was a match for any amount of opposition from her parents, but found it impossible to resist an appeal from Simona.

All three retreated to the bedroom Simona and Francesca were sharing and went through the clothes she had brought with her. Kate couldn't see what Francesca had made such a fuss about. As far as she was concerned, Simona's clothes might just as well have come out of a dressing-up box, they were so far removed from anything she'd normally wear. Simona was more than happy to treat the whole business as a joke. Kate was particularly taken with a bottle-green dress with tucks across the bosom which tied at the back. 'It's a *frock*!' she exclaimed in delight. 'I haven't worn a *frock* since I was nine!'

Simona giggled. 'Mamma made me buy it last winter. It makes me feel like a cabbage!'

'And look like one, too,' said Francesca. 'Poor Simi, why don't you try on some of our clothes? Then you can see what it feels like to be a mud angel.'

'Don't you mind?' asked Simona shyly, but it was obvious she was longing to put on the forbidden garments. Kate and Francesca dug out their shabbiest things.

'Look, here's a shirt I got off Aiden,' said Francesca. 'It still smells of him – ugh!'

Kate laughed, remembering the fastidious girl with the

patent-leather handbag and shoes they'd first seen on the bridge over the Arno.

'And here's some really cheesy jeans,' she said. 'They haven't been washed in a month.'

Simona was scandalized, and enjoying every moment. 'The nuns tell us it's a sin to wear trousers that do up at the front,' she said, her eyes shining. 'In fact they're not really very keen on trousers at all.'

'Quite right too,' said Francesca. 'All that chafing will give you bad thoughts. Go on, put them on – you won't go straight to hell, you know.'

Kate and Simona paraded up and down in front of the mirror, Kate in the green dress. 'Hello, cabbage,' giggled Simona.

Kate said, 'My, what very *front-opening* jeans you're wearing. They look very sexy on you!'

In the end, no one wore the cabbage dress. Simona had brought two twinsets with her as well as the one she was wearing, so they all wore sensible A-line skirts with twinsets. Kate's was green and Francesca's was pale blue.

'Now we're all dressed the same,' said Kate, 'we look like a backing group. What shall we call ourselves? The singing cabbages? Twinset and pearls?'

She was acting up to Simona, who gave the impression she'd never met anyone so sophisticated and amusing. Basking in the unexpected hero-worship, it was some time before she realized that Francesca did not seem to find their clothes funny at all. Far from it. As soon as she was clad in the pale blue twinset and the brown A-line skirt, she fell silent and seemed to shrink.

'What's the matter with you?' Kate asked as they were walking up to La Rocca. 'It's only for one evening.'

'You don't understand,' said Francesca.

'Of course I don't if you won't explain.'

'I can't.' Francesca spoke in a small voice, like a child's. 'I just can't.'

'Well, at least your *zio* will approve,' said Kate as they approached the house.

'That only makes it worse.'

'Honestly, Francesca, you do make heavy weather of them all.' She caught sight of Zio Toni standing by the window and watching out for them and she flashed him a smile. 'I mean, I know your mother's a bit of a battleaxe, but your family aren't that bad. Simona's all right when she's not dressed like a cabbage, and your father's perfectly nice, and as for your uncle, I think he's a dear old man.'

Francesca didn't respond, only stared at Kate with misery in her eyes.

Chapter 29

The Price

Alone in his room, Umberto Bertoni doubled over in pain, the worst he'd ever known. There had always been pain in his life, from his step-father's brutality and the first beatings given by the good fathers to drive out the sin from the priest's unwanted bastard, to the arthritis that had blighted the last decade – but never pain like this. Pain like a white-hot blade scything through his guts, like vermin tearing him to pieces from within, like a foretaste of the torments of hell that lay in wait for him, soon, so very soon. But this agony would pass. He knew it would. Sweat pouring from his face as he rode the waves of pain, he waited for it to ease. No morphine, not yet. There was still work to be done before the night's forgetting.

With tormenting slowness, the pain released its grip. As soon as it was possible, he forced himself to breathe normally, wiped his face with a lawn handkerchief, waited for the trembling to die down.

Even the worst agony passes in the end; he'd learned that

much in a life dominated one way and another by pain. But terror? Ah, terror's a different matter entirely. Terror never goes. On the contrary, with each day that passed, his terror grew.

He was dying. No need of doctors to confirm what his body told him hour by hour. It was not death he feared. If death was simply a matter of shucking off a rotten body that had become both prison and skilled torturer, then he would have welcomed it with open arms and laughing. It was the prospect of what came after death that turned his bowels to water: all those images from childhood that he'd never quite shaken off, those hungry fires and the everlasting torment of the damned.

He'd spent his life in defiance of God. He'd grown rich and powerful to prove to his early keepers that he was stronger and cleverer than they ever imagined, and he'd never missed a chance to spit in the face of the Almighty. He hated God with a passion, but he'd never ceased to believe in Him. Right now, he'd forfeit everything he'd ever owned to know that the journey into death would be no more than a light going out: darkness and nothingness for ever. But he wasn't going to get off so easily.

There was sure to be some special punishment waiting for him. But why him? Was he truly so much more evil than others? Wasn't everyone capable of terrible deeds if temptation came their way? God knows – and God did know, he was sure of it – he'd watched enough people turn from innocence to corruption and on each occasion he'd revelled in the change. Watching others fall from grace was the best way he knew to keep the terror at bay.

And now the terror was back, worse than ever. Well, if he was wicked beyond redemption, then it was only because he was human. Others were just as bad. He could prove it easily.

The lawn handkerchief was a sodden ball in his hand and he threw it down in disgust and rang the silver handbell that stood on the table next to his chair. A young man with a broad, smiling face came in at once.

'Brandy, Dino.'

The young man poured him a glass and set it in his hand. He drank it down quickly, and let out a sigh of relief.

'Now, tidy me.'

Without a word the young man wiped his face with a scented towel, combed back his hair and straightened his clothes. He stooped to pick up the crumpled handkerchief and straightened a pot of white jasmine, then stood, waiting for further orders.

'Fetch the ivory box.'

Surprised, but always obedient, Dino went to a low table at the side of the room and picked up an elaborately carved box, about the size of a book, and set it under the single lamp on the table beside the old man.

'I'm cold.'

His servant crossed the room and closed the window, fetched a cashmere shawl from the ottoman and laid it across his shoulders. Then he held up a hand mirror for inspection.

Umberto Bertoni nodded. He was ready. 'Tell her to come in.'

A few seconds after Dino left the room, the door opened once again and Annette walked in. She was wearing a sheath dress of shimmering blue silk, her hair swept back in a chignon, diamonds on her ears and throat. A fine-looking woman, he'd always thought, and far too good for that useless nephew of his. Tense, though. Strung out like a thin wire, ready to snap. Well, he'd find out soon enough.

'Zio Toni, how are you?' She addressed him in Italian. 'Is there anything I can do? You look tired.'

He gestured for her to sit down. 'Dear Annette, you're more beautiful than ever this evening.'

'Thank you.' She touched her earrings with a nervous gesture as she took her seat on an upright chair and crossed her legs. Diamonds. He wondered where they'd come from: a grateful admirer, probably. There'd been several of those, he knew.

'I hope you have everything you want at Beatrice,' he said.

'Yes. Angelica is very good.'

'Excellent. And the girls are well?'

'Yes, thank you, but I fear that Francesca's friend is a bad influence.'

'I rather agree.' He was silent for a moment, thinking. The English girl had shown no fear when she smiled at him and he didn't like that. There'd even been pity in her gaze and he liked that even less. 'I think he's a dear old man.' Her words had floated up to his open window on the evening air. *A dear old man.* That was unforgivable. Never in his life before had a good-looking young woman treated him with such contempt, like a doddering old fool, a nobody. He said slowly, 'Maybe you should find a way to get rid of her.'

'God knows, Zio Toni, I've tried. Luckily she has to go back to Florence tomorrow. Before she goes I intend to break the hold she has over Francesca.'

'How?'

'I have one or two ideas, but haven't yet decided.'

'Maybe it won't be necessary.' She started to speak, but he interrupted her, 'Enough. I have something to show you, Annette.'

'Yes?' Always so eager to please.

'In this box. Here.' He dipped his hand into his pocket and pulled out a small key suspended on silk thread.

Her fingertips were caressing the carved lid of the box. '*Zio*, it's exquisite,' she breathed. 'You always have such beautiful things.'

He smiled. The fool. Had she even bothered to look at what the carvings depicted? 'Thank you, my dear. Now, unlock it for me. I want you to see what's inside.'

Still smiling, like a child with a Christmas present, Annette fitted the key in the lock and turned it. She pushed back the lid. Inside there was something wrapped in a scrap of faded silk. She raised her eyes questioningly and he nodded at her to go on. She lifted the silk out and let it fall back over her hand, revealing half a dozen small photographs; two or three were old, sepia and curled, the most recent was a faded polaroid. She smiled nervously before laying them out in a fan on the little table that stood between their chairs. And still she smiled, prepared to be delighted by whatever she saw.

Gradually, as she absorbed the contents of the photographs, her smile died away. Disbelief, horror, revulsion . . . it was gratifying for him to observe the emotions that passed over her face.

She pulled back her hand as though there was acid on the silk. 'Where did you get hold of them?' she asked. She was fighting the urge to retch. 'They're disgusting!'

'Why, Annette, I might not be much of a photographer, but all the same . . .'

'You mean . . . *you* took them?'

'I did.' His smile hinted at a modest pride in his achievement.

'But . . . who are they?'

'You want their names? That recent one was a youth called Guido, the girl was Beata, but those early boys and girls . . . it was wartime. If I ever knew their names, I've forgotten them now.'

'But . . . ' Rapidly she glanced at the photographs and just as quickly looked away again. Her breathing was light and shallow. 'Why – why do you keep photographs of *corpses?*'

'Souvenirs,' he said softly. 'My rogues' gallery. The road to success. And its fruits. Each one tells a story. Do you want to hear them?'

'No.' She was looking at the floor, unable to meet his eyes any more. There were more questions, but he knew she would never dare to ask them.

'Take another look at the one on the left,' he told her gently, and saw her eyes flicker towards it, nervous as a snake. 'I took it at Villa Beatrice, in the *camerino*. That's where he died. We closed the door and he couldn't find the way out. Doesn't he look peaceful? As though he'd just fallen asleep. Chloroform is such a kindly death, I've always thought.'

'Why?' she whispered.

'The stupid boy got in my way. He stood between me and the purchase of this house,' he told her. 'His brothers had agreed, but without his signature we were powerless. And as you probably know, I do not like to be thwarted. There are others, but these are my favourites. Do you want to see the rest?'

'No. Don't show me any more. They make me sick.'

'Strange,' he paused, watching her closely, then said quietly, 'That's exactly what Francesca said.'

'Jesus!' Horror-stricken, Annette was on her feet at once. 'You showed these pictures to her, too? When? When did you show her?'

'Calm down, calm down. It was years ago. I forget the exact

date, but it must have been before she went to America. I was still living at the Villa Beatrice, so it was five years ago or more. It was a wet afternoon, we were both somewhat at a loose end. I thought my little photographs might amuse her, but unfortunately her reaction was similar to yours. Perhaps stronger.'

Annette was staring at him, her face taut with shock. 'She never told me.'

'Of course not. It is easy to make children keep silence.'

'Why did you do it?'

'Why? Because I like to share my pleasures. Francesca understands.'

'So *that's* why she attacked you!'

He chuckled. 'The boiling water, yes. It was a good response. She has learned the value of pain. I appreciated that.'

'Jesus, no wonder . . .' Annette was silent for a moment as a new horror occurred to her. She took a step towards him. 'Zio Toni, if you ever laid a hand on either of my girls—'

'Annette, please.' He interrupted her briskly. 'What do you take me for? A monster? Those girls are my own flesh and blood. I'd never harm them.'

'What?' Her laughter was a bark of disbelief. 'Never harm—? How can you say that? After what you've done to my poor Francesca? You knew how sensitive she was, and you showed her these? My God, you're sick!'

He chuckled, genuine amusement lighting up his face. '*Mia cara*,' he said. 'Consider what you're saying. I'm not sick, I'm dying.' His laughter continued until he was seized by a spasm of coughing.

While he was recovering she paced across to the window, then back again. She stood over him. 'Why did you show me those?' she asked. 'Why put such a weapon in my hand? Surely you know I can take them to the police. With evidence like this, I could see you ruined.'

'Annette, please, show a little intelligence. We both know you'll never do that. I'll be dead and buried long before the police even start their investigations and all you'd have to show for your loyalty would be the scandal. Very likely the estate would be forfeited along with my reputation.' He observed the way her expression altered at the word 'estate'. He continued, 'When I'm dead you will quite naturally move swiftly to protect the reputation of your beloved husband's family and make sure these beauties are all destroyed, and the others which are in the ebony box over there. Five photographs here and seven in the other box. Twelve in all. But thirteen has always been my lucky number. Now, sit down and pay attention.'

She sank down into the chair. 'Why have you shown them to me? I don't understand.'

He didn't answer right away, but fussed with the arrangement of his cashmere shawl. Half an hour ago, Annette would have leapt up to do it for him, but now he knew she could not bear to touch him. He could sense the revulsion emanating from her in waves. Good. The strongest reactions were always the most gratifying.

After a while he said, 'You are desperate for my estate to go to your family when I die.'

After so many years of circling round each other, it was shocking to have the statement made so baldly. Annette winced. 'It is *your* family too,' she said.

He went on, 'You've wanted it for a long time. I thought first you should know the price that was paid for it.'

She ran the tip of her tongue over her lower lip. 'You mean the young man who didn't want to sell?'

'Him, and others. A bastard like me who comes from nowhere doesn't get to where I am today without sacrifice, as you of all people know well. The trick is to make sure that others make the sacrifice for you.' He tapped the nearest photograph with the tip of his index finger and said, 'It's not always easy, being ruthless. It costs, you know. This was the price I paid. Are you prepared to pay it too, I wonder?'

She said, 'You must promise me you will never show these to Simona.'

'I have not the slightest intention of showing these to Simona. Where would be the pleasure in that? But you have not answered my question.'

'I'm sorry. What . . .?'

'Are you prepared to pay the price?'

'I – I don't understand.'

'You want the Villa Beatrice estate, but how badly do you want it? Do you want it as much as I did? Would you, for instance, be prepared to kill for it?'

'Kill?' Her eyes darkened. He remained silent. After a few moments she asked in a low voice, 'What are you talking about? Kill who?'

'I thought perhaps the troublesome English girl.'

'Kate? Francesca's friend? But what does she have to do with the Villa Beatrice?'

'Nothing whatsoever, and there's the beauty of it. She is simply irritating, and . . . expendable. Look on this project, my dear Annette, as a test, a dying man's whim. After all, I did not get hold of this glorious estate by simply being charming and well-connected, so why should my heirs be let off so easily?

Even you must see there's no justice in that. I know you desire this for your girls, but are your desires as strong as mine were? Strong enough to make you kill?'

'Kill?' She echoed the word dreamily.

'Yes, kill.'

She stared at him for a moment, then shook her head in disbelief. 'Zio Toni, stop this madness! What do you expect me to do? Strangle her with my own hands? Find a gun? A knife? Do you want me to take pictures?' She was almost laughing.

'Calm down, Annette. You're getting hysterical. I thought you had more sense than that. No one is suggesting you actually do the deed yourself, unless of course you want to. You may prefer just to give the order. Dino has already shown promise. He's not too bright, but it's always good to have a blunt instrument to hand. An accident is usually easiest to cover up, a car crash perhaps, some unforeseen tragedy. I understand they were fooling around on Vespas earlier today – what an opportunity that would have been. But never mind, something else will occur. Now, please sit down, so we may continue.'

'I won't—'

'Sit,' he commanded in a voice he seldom used, and she sat at once. 'That's better. Now, let me explain the full situation. Tomorrow the notary comes to make the final amendments to my will. I doubt very much if I'll survive long enough to change my mind again. For some time, I have been uncertain how to leave the bulk of my estate. As you know, for years I planned to make Francesca my heir, but since she has decided to join these mud people—'

'They are working for Florence,' said Annette.

He waved his hand, silencing her. 'Francesca has turned her

back on me. When she attacked me, I could forgive her, but now she has gone her own way . . . She is no longer part of the equation. That leaves my half-sister's child Dario, whom I must say I've always found a rather contemptible specimen, or your dear Simona. Now, which is it to be? It's not as if you even like the English girl.'

Annette touched the side of her cheek, then smiled suddenly. 'Zio Toni, for a moment I thought you were serious! What a horrible kind of joke this is!'

'I've never been more serious.'

The smile faded from her face and she stood up slowly. 'You really want . . . And if I say no?'

'Then the notary will be instructed accordingly. Who knows, Dario may even end up surprising everyone and showing himself a worthy heir.'

'This is monstrous. You know I could never do such a—'

'Wait, Annette. Don't make your decision right away. This has been a surprise for you and you need time to think it over.'

'On the contrary, Zio Toni—'

'I repeat, I don't want to know your decision yet. Come and see me in the morning. Maybe you'll already have some good news for me. And believe me, Dino is a treasure, discreet and altogether most obliging.'

She bowed her head. Already she looked like an old woman. 'Is that all?' she asked.

'Yes.' He settled back in his chair, more comfortable than he'd been in a long time. She was a good-looking woman and she wore her suffering well. Pain and beauty, beauty and pain, just as it had been all his life. 'Tell Dino to come in. I will see you again in the morning. Before the notary arrives. Sleep well, Annette.'

She didn't answer, but left the room slowly, feeling her way with her hands, like a blind woman.

Umberto Bertoni was still smiling when Dino came in with his evening dose of morphine. It was good to know that at least one person was going to sleep worse than him tonight.

Chapter 30

Sleepless

Francesca had never looked so beautiful. She was wearing proper clothes again, which helped, in Mario's opinion, but more than that, it was the happiness she had discovered with the mud angels that made her radiant, even here, at this house she loathed. All her gestures, that used to be so tight and hunched, were now becoming expansive, generous. Reflecting her true self. It made her more desirable than ever. Mario knew he should have left as soon as he'd spoken to Kate, but now it was too late. Just one last evening in Francesca's company – he could not tear himself away.

She found him on the terrace. He was smoking a cigarette and looking out into the twilight. 'So that's where you've escaped to,' she said, in Italian. 'I wondered where you were.'

'I thought you were with Simona,' he said.

'Oh, Kate's telling her all about Florence.' She slipped her arm through his and gave it a squeeze. Mario's nerves were so strung out he thought he might snap. She said, 'It's wonderful to see Simona again.'

'You saw her at Christmas.'

'But that was different. *I* was different then. I guess I was still wounded from the clinic, from all the things people said about me. But now I'm getting stronger, Mario, I know I am, and I can see a future. That changes everything.'

'Yes,' he said bitterly, 'it's good to have hopes.'

She turned. 'What's the matter?'

'Nothing.'

He knew she didn't believe him. She said, 'I guess I owe you an apology. You've been so patient through all this and I know . . . well, it can't have been easy for you, but I knew you understood . . .'

'I'm glad to see you so happy,' he said wretchedly. And he meant it, every word – so why did it come out sounding stiff and insincere?

'But you're angry with me, and I can't say I blame you. I don't quite know how to say this but . . . it's only because I felt so sure . . . I mean, about you and me and . . . well, the future. Even when I was with Kate and the others in Florence, it was like you were . . . inside me.' She flushed, then said, 'Well, beside me, maybe. Just like you were when I was banged up in that hellhole they sent me to. If I hadn't known that you were there, that you believed in me . . . well, I would have gone mad, for sure. They could have locked me up and thrown away the key. I suppose what I'm trying to say, Mario, is that I owe all this to you. I – I –'

'Hush,' said Mario quickly. 'Don't say any more.'

'But I must. It's important. We've got to get Simona away from here. She has to come back to Florence with me and Kate tomorrow.'

'You know your parents will never permit it.'

'Mario, Simona is nearly eighteen. They can't keep her a child for ever. And look how happy she is with Kate! Even if she came for a couple of days, just to see what our life is like and meet the others, it would make all the difference. Here she's a prisoner.'

'Not a prisoner.'

'You don't know, Mario. They want her to be "nice" to our uncle. Did you see how my mother kept pushing her at him just now? Ugh, it made me sick to watch them. That's how it used to be for me: "Why don't you go and see if Zio Toni wants some company, Francesca? Show him that dance you learned. Sing for him. Make him laugh." And now they're doing it to Simona, but I won't let him get her. The only way I can protect her is to bring her back to Florence with me and Kate. But I'll need your help. Please, Mario, just this once, trust that I know what I'm doing.'

'Francesca, don't ask me . . .'

'Why not?'

'It's not right for me to interfere in your family.'

'You don't understand. It's not . . .' She hesitated. 'I never told you . . . I couldn't talk about it before. But I won't let my uncle get hold of Simona like he did me. I'll kill him before that happens.'

'Francesca, what are you saying? Your uncle is an old man. He's dying. How can he hurt Simona?'

'He's got . . . photographs.' Her voice was hardly more than a whisper.

Mario almost laughed. '*Mia cara*, what harm can photographs do to your sister?'

'It's serious, Mario. It's . . . the reason I attacked him, because he showed me, wanted to make me a part of it . . . and it was . . . horrible.'

'Francesca, this doesn't make sense. Why didn't you tell me before?'

'I didn't tell anyone. I . . . couldn't. They were so . . . bad.' Her voice had become small, like a child's. 'Corpses. He's got photographs of corpses. And he says he killed them. He tried to tell me how . . . they died. And . . . some of them were just children.'

'My God.' For a moment Mario was too shocked to say anything else. He remembered the young girl he'd first found weeping on the park bench in Padua. She'd been so vulnerable and innocent, so troubled. In spite of his professional experience, he found it impossible to imagine that a member of her family would have deliberately hurt her. And if it were true, if her uncle really had committed terrible crimes and then recorded them with a camera . . . the possibility was too horrible to contemplate. Mario knew from his work the power of fantasy. Most probably her uncle had made up those stories to frighten her.

'Did you believe him?'

'I didn't know what to believe. He said some of them died here. In the *camerino*. It was disgusting, but the worst part was the way he told me. As if he thought I wanted to know. As if I was part of it.'

There was no doubt Francesca had been powerfully affected by her uncle's actions, and no wonder. 'Oh, my poor darling.' Mario had his arms around her, could feel her warmth pressed against him and the beating of her heart. 'Don't worry, my Francesca. We'll think of something.' His love for her was combined with a fierce rage against her family. There had to be a way to get free of it.

He kissed her, tenderly, and after a moment she responded,

kissing him as she hadn't kissed him since that night when her
father found them in his little room. That had changed, too.
These weren't the kisses of the sheltered unworldly girl he'd first
loved in Padua, but the kisses of someone experienced. At first
he found it exciting, this newborn woman in his arms, then
arousal gave way to doubt.

He drew back. 'Where did you learn to kiss like that?'

'Like what?' she asked dreamily.

'With the tongue. Like a whore. Like the foreign girls.'

She stepped back and looked at him directly. 'In Florence,'
she said simply. 'I have fooled around with some of the boys.
But only kissing. Never more than that.'

He didn't want to believe her. Inside the house, he could hear
Annette's voice, calling them in to supper. This whole family
brought him nothing but pain, Francesca included. All he
wanted was to break free of them. Maybe she had made up that
story about her uncle to win his sympathy. How could he know
if she was telling the truth about the photographs? About those
boys in Florence? How would he ever be able to trust her? And
when she found out about him and Annette . . .

'How can I believe you?' he asked coldly.

'Because it's the truth. Why would I lie to you?'

'I can think of several reasons,' he said, steeling himself to
ignore the way her expression changed from bewilderment to
hurt. 'You want me to help you. Isn't that why you're making
up to me now? So I'll go along with your plans and help you get
Simona to Florence? You're using me, just like everyone else in
your family.'

'Using you? What are you talking about?'

Annette had appeared at the far end of the terrace. 'Since
you're still here, you may as well join us in the dining room,' she

said acidly. Mario almost welcomed the interruption of her harsh voice. It made his task so much easier.

'Oh, you know what I'm talking about, Francesca,' he said.

'But—' She broke off. 'Damn. There's my mother. Mario, we'll talk again. I don't know what's got into you, but . . . you've got it all wrong.'

He watched her as she hurried across the terrace towards the house. He felt as though he was falling into endless dark, the void of a world without Francesca in it. The worst part was that she didn't realize this was more than a lovers' tiff. She was so confident of his love for her – and why shouldn't she be, after all? – that she had no idea that when he left tomorrow, it would be for the last time.

Numb with misery, he followed her into the house.

At dinner in the frescoed dining room, he was seated next to Francesca. She did not address a single word to him through the whole meal, but then, she hardly spoke at all. By contrast, Kate, who sat opposite, seemed to be enjoying every moment. If he hadn't been so caught up in his own misery, he'd have been full of admiration. For once she was appropriately dressed: a green twinset which highlighted her strong colouring and a coral necklace she must have borrowed from Simona. She wasn't beautiful in the way that Francesca was, but she radiated vitality and good humour.

Not only did she look good, she knew exactly the right note to strike with everyone. Sensing the tensions in the family, she was doing her best to make the evening a success. With Francesca's father she was flirtatious just enough to flatter him but not enough for anyone, not even Annette, to take offence. Towards Annette she was respectful, but fearless also and when she disagreed she did not hesitate to say so, which was a combination Annette was not at all used to. She was warm, almost tender with Francesca: aware that her friend was unhappy and doing her best to cajole her into a better mood. Simona clearly adored her already. It was hard to believe the two girls were only months apart in age since Kate seemed so much older, but Kate was never patronizing towards Simona.

But it was her manner towards Zio Toni when they'd been up at La Rocca for a drink that had most impressed him. Mario had become accustomed to the way Signor Bertoni was simultaneously cosseted and kept at arm's length by all those who were supposed to be closest to him, so it was almost shocking to see Kate treat him like what he was: an old man who was dying a slow and painful death. She alone expected nothing from him and by her compassion the self-interest of the others was exposed.

Mario didn't bother analyzing her manner towards him: she must think he was crazy – to have insulted her the previous evening and tried to make her leave with him twenty-four hours later. The actions of a mad man – well, that wasn't so far from the truth.

About halfway through the meal, just as the veal was being cleared away and salad and cheese passed around, Dino came down from La Rocca with a message for Annette: Zio Toni wanted to speak with her urgently. She stood up and left at once. No question of keeping the golden goose waiting. Mario was sickened by the speed of her response.

When the meal was over, the girls made their excuses and escaped upstairs, while Francesca's father suggested they retreat to the *sala* and enjoy some brandy and a cigar. For a while they discussed Signor Bertoni's favourite topics, cars and women, until Mario could bear it no longer and excused himself. He put on an overcoat against the chilly night and went out into the garden, following the cypress walk until he reached the point where the ground fell away in a precipice beyond the balustrade. For a minute he toyed with the idea of throwing himself over, but only for a minute: you needed to have a taste for melodrama to pursue such solutions and he'd seen enough botched attempts at suicide to know the crude ways are never the best. If he ever did decide to make an end, he'd do it quietly and efficiently, with the right combination of pills, a proper doctor's death. Besides, filled with self-loathing though he was that night, he did not yet hate life itself.

But oh, Francesca . . .

He must have groaned aloud. A man's voice in the darkness said, 'Who is it?' and then came the sound of a shotgun being readied for firing.

'*Il dottore*,' Mario called out swiftly.

'*Ah, dottore, buona sera*. Good evening, doctor.' A figure emerged from the cypress walk. He was carrying a shotgun and had a couple of dogs at his heels, but behind the torch Mario could not see his face. 'Lucky I recognized you,' said the stranger, his voice heavily accented with the local dialect. 'Or you might have been shot!' And he laughed uproariously at this possibility.

Mario knew him from his voice: Angelica's son Dino who had been employed at the Villa Beatrice since he was a child. Of limited intelligence, he had the countryman's love of killing things, but otherwise Mario reckoned he was fairly harmless.

They talked for a while in the darkness. Apparently there'd been reports of a lone wolf in the neighbourhood recently:

some chickens had gone missing. 'I thought that was you!' Dino still seemed to think Mario's near escape was highly entertaining. 'Better bring a torch next time or else –' he waved the gun and grinned – 'boom boom!' And he roared with laughter again.

Mario pretended to laugh too. 'I'll stay here a while longer, Dino. Take care you don't shoot me.'

It was a great joke. Dino was still laughing as he set off into the darkness, his dogs at his heels. Mario remained where he was, smoking and staring into the night. Remembering the weeks when he and Francesca had fallen in love, he cursed the day he'd allowed himself to be snared by her mother. Looking back at the house, he saw the downstairs lights being extinguished, one by one, then the lights on the first floor, until only two were left, those in the hall and on the landing. They must have left them on for him. Unless, of course, they thought he'd already gone to bed and had locked up for the night. In which case, he'd have the perfect excuse for driving back to Lucca right away.

He felt in his pockets and cursed. He had emptied his pockets when he changed into his suit for the evening. The keys to his car were on the chest of drawers in his room.

Aware now of the bitter cold, he walked back to the house. The front door was barred and bolted, as was the door at the back that led into the passageway beside the kitchen. Then he noticed lamplight shining through the large windows of the sitting room. Thank God, someone was still up. He walked quickly along the side of the house and looked in.

Kate was standing in the middle of the room with her back to him. She was wearing a borrowed man's dressing gown of dark silk that came to just below her knees, and her feet were bare. In front of her stood Annette, still wearing that blue cocktail dress. She had her hands on Kate's neck.

Mario rapped loudly on the glass. Annette looked over Kate's shoulder towards the window. Her eyes were huge as if she'd seen a ghost and she dropped her hands. Kate turned, recognized him at once, and crossed the room quickly, pushing up the window to let him in. As she did so, the cord tying her dressing gown loosened, revealing the smooth, pale flesh between her breasts, almost to her navel. Under the man's silk dressing gown she was naked.

'Thank you,' he said as he climbed over the sill. 'I wasn't looking forward to spending the night in the shed.'

'It's lucky for you no one can sleep tonight. What have you been doing?' Kate smiled as she pulled the dressing gown more tightly round her waist and reknotted the cord.

'I'm sorry if I gave you a fright,' he said to Annette, who had turned away and was lighting a cigarette.

Still with her back to them, she said in a low voice, 'I assumed you'd gone to bed already.'

'I must have lost track of the time.'

'You should be more careful in future.'

'Yes. I'll try.'

Kate said, 'You look frozen. I'm sure no one would mind if I poured you a brandy, would they, Signora Bertoni?' She walked over to the side table where the bottles, hidden away by Angelica the previous evening, were now set out on a silver tray. Mario observed the way the dark silk shifted over her buttocks and hips as she moved.

'I think it's black coffee I need,' he said.

'Then you'll have to make it yourself,' Annette told him. 'Angelica went to bed an hour ago.'

'Mm, coffee,' said Kate. 'What a brilliant idea. Do you want some too, Signora Bertoni?'

Annette was watching them both as they moved towards the door. 'No. I'm going to bed.' They said good night to her and heard her footsteps going slowly up the stairs.

The kitchen was immaculate, everything scrubbed and polished, china and cutlery already laid out on the counter for the morning. They hunted down coffee and a pot and worked out how to light the stove, the practical activity breaking down some of the barriers between them. When at last the kitchen began to fill with a rich aroma, Kate said, 'I can't make Francesca's mother out.'

'Don't try,' he said, with feeling.

'No, seriously. I know it sounds crazy, but I was really glad when you turned up at the window like that, even though it scared us half out of our wits.'

'Glad?'

Kate nodded. 'Relieved. She's been acting weird all evening. When I came down she was sitting in that room, just smoking and staring into space. She didn't even notice me at first, but then she was all over me, so friendly you'd think I was her long-lost best friend or something. Except you could tell it was phoney.'

'What is phoney?' He had not come across the word before.

'False. Like she was pretending. She kept asking me all sorts of questions about my family, what I was going to do, how I'd got to know Francesca and everything.'

'You are friend of Francesca. It's natural she is curious for you.'

'Yes, I suppose so . . .' Kate stared at the coffee pot, not seeing it at all. 'But it's just . . .'

Mario waited. If he had his way he'd never have to think or talk about Annette ever again. But something had clearly made Kate uneasy and he was glad of any distraction from his own thoughts.

At length she said, 'You're right, mothers always want to know about their kids' friends, but it wasn't that. It was . . . she kept going on about the way I looked, my clothes . . .'

'She is traditional, Kate. Old-fashioned. She does not understand your world of jeans and miniskirts.'

'Yes, I understand that but . . . she wouldn't let up. And . . . she wanted to talk about jewellery too, this coral necklace of Simona's.' She fingered the stones at her throat. 'That I should try putting earrings with it. And . . . it was like it was all just an excuse to . . . to touch me.' She looked up at him and laughed in her embarrassment. It was the first time he'd seen her so unsure. 'You must think I'm nuts. Like I'm saying she's a lesbian or something.'

'Kate.' He smiled. 'You are very attractive, but even so . . .'

'I know. Don't tell Francesca I said that.'

'When I see through the window—'

'Yes,' said Kate, still fiddling with the necklace. 'She said she had a choker that would suit me. Pearls or diamonds or something like that. She thought it might fit . . . She was so creepy about it . . . Oh, I can't explain.' She gave up. 'Let's have the coffee.'

'You want in here?'

'No,' said Kate. 'My feet are freezing on this floor. At least there are rugs in the sitting room.'

They put the coffee on a tray and carried it back through the silent house to the sitting room. The fire had died down, all but a blackened log that was still smouldering. Mario put another log on and poked a few sparks into life. Kate poured the coffee, then sat on the pale leather sofa, tucking her feet up beside her and rubbing them to get warm.

'Your poor foots,' he said, sitting beside her. 'They are too cold.'

'Yes.' She wiggled her toes at him. 'My foots are frozen.'

He smiled and took one of her feet between his hands and began massaging gently, just above the toes. 'Is change from hand,' he said, almost to himself and began singing softly, '*Che gelido piedino, se lo lasci riscaldar . . .*'

'I know that tune,' she said.

'I think so. Is *La Bohème*, most famous opera of all. Mimi's hand is cold and Rodolfo make it warm again. You know.'

'No. I've never seen an opera.'

'Is because you are ignorant English girl.'

'Now the other one.'

'This one is not finish.'

'But it's freezing!'

'Must wait.'

He was concentrating on the task, working the ball of his thumb in steady circular movements over her foot, and as he did so he felt a slight lessening of his own ache of grief at all he'd lost that day. It was what made him a good doctor, the relief of forgetting himself in reaching out to heal another's pain. The friction of flesh on flesh was soothing, helping him to forget, and Kate had beautiful feet, a bit grubby, it was true, but strong and supple.

'Now the other,' he said, laying the first one on his knee and turning his attention to the second.

Kate didn't answer, but allowed him to pick up her foot and massage it back to warmth as he had the first.

'Is finish,' he said eventually, and looked at her. She was lying back on the cushions at the end of the sofa, her breathing was shallow and rapid, and her eyes were huge. He had never seen anyone look so desirable as she did then. He wanted to hold her, just hold her, and escape from his solitary grief. 'Ah, Kate . . .' he breathed and without thinking what he was doing, he leaned over to kiss her.

'Oh no, not a second time.' She swung her legs round and sat up very straight. 'No more of your games, Mr *Dottore* Bassano.'

'Kate, I am apologize.'

'Drink your coffee.'

'Okay.' He reached across and slid the neck of the silk dressing gown back onto her shoulder. She was sitting very still. He said, 'Whose this is?'

'It's an old one of Francesca's father's.'

'Is good for you.' He rubbed a tiny piece of fabric between his thumb and forefinger, then touched the edge of her neck, just below her ear. She did not move away. Slowly, the silk began to slither off her shoulder again.

Mario turned and picked up his coffee. Kate turned to him. 'What is it you want, Mario?'

He sighed. 'I do not know.'

'Well, you ought to bloody well work it out. I mean, you keep on doing this to me. One moment you come on strong and the next moment – either you are rude or – or nothing.' Her voice was angry but he noticed that the tip of her nose had turned pink, as though she might be on the verge of tears.

He thought for a few moments, then set down his cup and said, 'What I want, Kate, right now, more than anything else, I want to hold. Just hold, nothing more.'

'Why?'

'Is what I want, that's all.'

She turned, to see if he was sincere this time. Whatever she saw on his face must have convinced her, because she said, 'Then hold me, Mario,' and slipped into his arms.

They made adjustments, then stretched out next to each other on the sofa, Mario on the outside braced to stop himself from falling. He breathed in the scent of her hair, relished the soft warmth of her body against his. After a while Kate said they should switch off the light in case anyone came downstairs and found them, and he put another log on the fire at the same time. Then they stretched out again and after a while, when she had not spoken for some time, he thought she must have fallen asleep. He began to stroke her hair, very gently, not wanting to wake her, then let his fingers trail along the silk surface of her robe, her shoulders and her upper arm.

Her voice came softly in the darkness. 'Mario?'

'Am I disturb you?'

She wriggled round between him and the back of the sofa so that her face was less than an inch from his. He leaned forward a fraction to kiss her, but she put her hand up between their mouths.

'You do not want?'

'What about Francesca? I've never figured out what's going on between you. I won't do anything that would hurt her.'

He was silent for a while, then he said slowly, 'For a long time, I love Francesca. But now is finish. Finish for ever.'

'Are you sad about that?'

'Yes. Very sad.'

'And is she sad too?'

'No. I think Francesca she finish with me when she go to Florence and become mud angel like you.'

He could sense Kate smiling in the dark as she reached out to kiss him. 'Oh, those wicked mud angels. Don't be sad, Mario.'

After a long time of kissing he began to caress her breasts, her thighs, her stomach. His desire for her was almost strong enough to make him forget all about Francesca and her family, and that was all he asked. It was Kate who asked, 'Shall we do it, Mario?'

'Do it?'

'Make love, properly.'

He said, 'You are too young, I cannot make love with you.'

'Oh, you don't need to worry about that,' she said. 'I've done it before. I'm on the pill.'

'*Certo?*' He was surprised, didn't understand these foreigners at all. But the final barrier between them was melting away and he could think of no reason not to complete what his body had been aching to do for what seemed like an age – since he took her cold foot between his hands, maybe for a long time before that. 'You want, Kate?'

'Yes, I want.'

She was slick with desire as he entered her. It was like nothing he'd experienced before, all the tension and heartache of the day released in the thrust and pulse of their two bodies moving together. He heard her gasps of pleasure and then he lost himself and roared out in grief and satisfaction and finally let go.

When it was over he lit cigarettes for them both and sat on the end of the sofa, looking at the soft red glow from the dying fire. At length he asked quietly, 'Kate, why you lie to me?'

'Lie?'

'It was first time for you.'

'No, not really,' she said. 'I've done it before, but never . . . like that.'

'How is it different now?'

She hesitated. 'I guess I never really saw what all the fuss was about before.'

He pulled her close, feeling a great gratitude towards this girl who had given herself to him just when his life seemed most hopeless. It made him feel there might be a life beyond the Bertoni family after all.

He said, 'Is late now. We go to bed.'

She pulled her dressing gown round her for the last time and they walked up the stairs together. They padded quietly past the door of Francesca and Simona's room and the one opposite theirs behind which Annette and her husband were sleeping. Kate's and his room were opposite each other at the far end of the corridor.

'This is my room,' he said in a whisper.

'I know. You've got a double bed.'

'Kate, my dearest Kate . . . ' He put his arms round her and kissed her, intending it to be a kiss of farewell, then picked her up in his arms and carried her into his room and laid her gently on the bed.

Chapter 31

By Heart

Afterwards, before she'd learned the trick of blanking that final weekend from her mind, Kate sometimes wondered if she and Mario had known they would only have a single night together. It seemed as if a whole courtship had been packed into those few hours, hours too precious to waste in sleep. They learned a hundred different things about each other, secrets of touch and taste and dreams, and the endless lovers' pleasure in talking about nothing at all. If Kate had imagined having sex with Mario she'd have expected him to be the experienced older man, initiating her into pleasures she'd not known before. But when they made love for the second time, just before dawn, they were two travellers, exploring new territory together.

'Is soon morning,' he said, as they lay back against the pillows, her head in the crook of his shoulder. 'Now you must go.'

'Yes, I know.' But she didn't move. 'What happens next, Mario?'

'In the morning we say goodbye to the Bertonis,' he told her, 'and I take you to Florence.'

'Will you be sad to leave them?'

He only hesitated for a moment before saying, 'No, Kate, I think now maybe I will be happy. Very happy to go. You make me happy.'

By the time the sky was beginning to turn pale and she reluctantly tiptoed back to her own room and her neatly made bed, Kate felt as though not just her world, but that she herself had been turned upside down. She was no longer the same Kate Holland who had turned up at the Villa Beatrice two days before. She was in love, properly in love, for the first time in her life.

She thought it would be impossible to sleep, that she'd just get under the covers so the bed looked as though it had been slept in, but when she came to the sun was high in the sky and the air was full of the discordant clanging of bells from villages far and near. It was her first Sunday morning in the Italian countryside, bells out of sync and out of tune and yet harmonious. She got out of bed and flung back the window and drank in the scents and sounds of the morning. The mist was thinning already, a few trails following the line of the river, and the sun was warm against her face. She'd never known it was possible to be so happy.

When she heard the bathroom door open and close for a second time, she pulled on her borrowed silk dressing gown and went out into the corridor. Mario was there, about to go into the bathroom. Never was a man so attractive to her eyes as Mario in his striped pyjamas and leather slippers, with a towel over his arm and a sponge bag in his hand.

'*Ciao*, Mario. Did you sleep well?'

'*Ciao*, Kate,' he said softly. 'I did not sleep so much, I don't know why.' But when she padded over to put her arms round him, he held her away and whispered, 'Are you crazy, Kate? Suppose we are see?'

'Then Signora Bertoni will think I'm a fallen woman and will drive me out into the snow,' she teased. 'But that's okay by me. I don't care about her.'

'Signora Bertoni is not problem. But – hm – Francesca . . .'

'So? You said this was nothing to do with her.'

'Yes, but Francesca is a nervous temperament. This place is not good for her and she is jealous for her friends. We tell her later, in Florence, maybe. Is better this way.'

'If you say so,' Kate agreed reluctantly. 'But I'm not very good at secrets.'

'I know.' At last his eyes mellowed into a smile. 'You are wonderful without secret. Is why I love you.'

It was the only time he said the words. Hardly the most romantic scenario, standing in the corridor in the morning chill, fending her off with a sponge bag and towel. Afterwards Kate wondered if he'd really said those words, or if she'd imagined them.

'When can we be together again?' she asked him.

'Soon. We will leave and I drive you to Firenze.'

'What about Francesca?'

'I think she will not leave her family while Simona is here. She love her sister too much.'

Kate felt a guilty pleasure that she'd be leaving alone with Mario. But Francesca was busy with Simona, and not interested in Mario any more, she was sure of it. And right now, Kate didn't want anything to come between them, even for a short time.

*

She was convinced when she went downstairs that her jubila-
tion was so intense it must be shining from every pore, and
they'd all want to know the reason, but she was wrong. That
Sunday morning everyone at the Villa Beatrice was so caught
up in their own private dramas she would have needed to
sprout wings and fly into the dining room before any alteration
was noticed. Apart from Signor Bertoni, who seemed armour-
plated against all the emotional currents that eddied round
him, only the painted nymphs and gods cavorting on the
dining-room walls were unaffected.

Francesca and Simona, outwardly demure in their twinsets
and straight skirts, were fizzing with suppressed excitement.
Simona's was the nervous kind, like someone about to go on a
terrifying fairground ride for the first time, but Francesca had
been transformed overnight from the miserable creature who
sat hunched and silent through supper. She radiated energy,
laughing and joking and teasing Simona with affection, until
Signora Bertoni gestured for them to be quieter.

'Girls, girls,' she said, lighting another cigarette. 'Less noise,
please. My head . . .'

'Do you have a migraine, Mamma?' asked Francesca, sweet
as pie.

'Yes. I did not sleep . . .' She put her fingers to her forehead
with a weary gesture. Her face was grey and haggard, dark
circles round her eyes as she sipped black coffee and refused to
eat.

The windows were open and a cool breeze that smelt of
spring was gently shifting the curtains. Down in the valley a
cock crowed.

'You should have stayed in bed, Mamma,' said Francesca,

with a solicitude that should have instantly aroused suspicion. 'Simona and I would have brought you breakfast on a tray.'

Signora Bertoni didn't reply. Her forehead was deeply furrowed and she rested her head on her hand, occasionally tugging at the side of her cheek as she gazed with her pale eyes almost dreamily towards Kate.

If she hadn't been so full of the glow of loving Mario, Kate might have felt uneasy at the way Signora Bertoni was staring at her. She remembered the feel of her thin hands against her throat the night before when she'd talked about that necklace. And she had no idea why Francesca and Simona were so nervily excited. This whole family was absorbed in some secret, intricate dance which made her more impatient than ever to get away from the Villa Beatrice. She said, 'Signora Bertoni, Mario and I will be driving back to Florence this morning. It's been very kind of you to have me stay.'

Signora Bertoni's frown deepened. 'So soon?'

'Yes.' Kate wondered why the woman bothered pretending to mind.

'What time are you leaving?' asked Francesca.

Kate caught Mario's eye. He nodded imperceptibly and she said, 'Right after breakfast,' and had to suppress her telltale smile of joy. The future had never been so full of possibilities.

He was waiting for her in the hall when she came downstairs with her pack. It felt deliciously comfortable to be in her own clothes again: her well-worn denim shirt and jeans. Simona's green twinset and sensible skirt had been folded and left on the bed.

'I'm sorry I took so long,' she said to him. 'I couldn't find my plaid shirt anywhere, but never mind.'

Mario touched her sleeve gently. 'You should have proper woman clothes,' he said. 'Now we go.'

'Francesca and Simona are coming down in a minute. And I have to say thank you to Francesca's mother. Do you know where she is?'

'Right here,' came a voice from behind her as Signora Bertoni emerged from the dining room. She looked stooped and old; her make-up, always so carefully applied, seemed to belong on a different face altogether. 'Are you really leaving, Kate?' she asked. 'Well, that's a shame . . . I hate to see you go.' She was frowning as she spoke, still tugging at the skin on the side of her face in that nervous gesture. 'I thought maybe I could show you round the place a bit . . . there's such a lot you haven't seen yet. And we've hardly had a chance to get to know each other. But you're going now . . . well, maybe that's all for the best. Maybe it will all work out after all. I really don't know . . .'

Kate stared at her. Francesca's mother appeared to be un-ravelling in front of her eyes. She said, 'Are you okay, Signora Bertoni?'

The older woman stretched her magenta lips back into what was more a grimace than a smile. 'Why, how very thoughtful you are, Kate Holland.' She frowned and looked away, plucking a thread of cotton off her sleeve. 'Well, I guess that's just how it is,' she said, more to herself than anyone else. 'I'll go talk to Zio Toni. He'll see sense, maybe. He's not such a bad man. And he's fond of Simona. That's it, I'll take her with me. She's a cute child in her way. So you see, there's a chance, there's always a chance.' She looked at Kate again, raking her face with eyes that were small pits of misery. 'Off you go then, Kate, before . . . before . . .' Her voice trailed into silence.

Kate glanced at Mario. He was a doctor and would know if it was all right to leave Signora Bertoni like this, but he was looking at the woman with an odd little smile on his face. 'That's right, Annette,' he said and it was the first time Kate had heard him call Francesca's mother by her Christian name. 'Kate and I are leaving now. Is last time for us at Villa Beatrice.'

There was a commotion upstairs, the sound of doors banging and footsteps pounding along the landing. 'Wait!' yelled Francesca. 'Wait for us!' She had Simona by the wrist and was carrying two small packs as the sisters hurtled down the stairs together.

Kate, seeing how Simona was dressed, said, 'My plaid shirt!'

Signora Bertoni turned to them with horror. 'What's going on? What do you think you're doing dressed like that?'

Francesca regarded her mother in triumph. 'We're going with Mario and Kate,' she said.

'Don't be ridiculous,' snapped Signora Bertoni. In an instant her abstracted mood had vanished and she was bristling for a fight. 'I never heard anything so outrageous in my life. Get right back upstairs and change, both of you!'

'No, Mamma! I told you, we're leaving. We're going to Florence and you can't stop us.'

'We'll just see about that. Simona, come here right now!'

Francesca kept hold of her sister's hand. 'Don't pay any attention, Simona. She can't force you.' But Simona's eyes widened with terror as Signora Bertoni strode towards her and grabbed her by the arm.

'You go, then, Francesca,' said her mother. 'Get out of this house and never come back, but Simona stays right here.'

'No!'

'Simona, go change at once. We're going up to see Zio Toni.'

'No!' yelled Francesca. 'I won't let you!'

Jagged with rage, Signora Bertoni let go of Simona, raised her hand and struck her elder daughter hard across the face with the flat of her palm. Francesca's head swung away from the blow. 'And how –' She struck her again – 'just *how* are you going to stop me?'

'Mamma, stop it!' Simona wailed as Francesca reeled backwards. 'Stop it, stop it, *stop it*! You're always blaming her, but I'm the one who wants to go.'

Kate had run to Francesca's side and put her arms round her. Livid red bars were already striping her cheeks and she was panting with shock. 'It's okay, Francesca,' said Kate. 'You're coming with us.'

'Simona . . .' she gasped.

'Of course,' said Kate. 'Simona comes too.'

Mario had been watching in horror. He spoke to Signora Bertoni in Italian and reached out to take Simona gently by the hand. She put herself behind him, a protecting shield. Now four were ranged against one: Signora Bertoni fell back as though beaten. Safe behind Mario, Simona was weeping quietly.

'Are you sure you want to come with us?' Kate asked her gently.

She nodded. 'Quite sure.'

'Then let's go.'

They picked up their bags in silence. Kate still had her arm round Francesca and Simona was leaning on Mario as they headed towards the door. Just as they stepped out into the fresh air, Signora Bertoni's voice came after them: 'Simona, I won't let you go.'

'You can't stop her, Mamma,' said Francesca, her voice almost tender now that her mother had been defeated.

'Who will take care of my baby?' asked Signora Bertoni in anguish. 'She's just a child.'

'She's a woman, Mamma,' said Francesca. 'I'll look after her. And so will my friends.'

Signora Bertoni followed them out into the sunshine. Suddenly her voice was sharp as a razor. 'And which friends would those be, Francesca?'

'Mario and Kate,' she answered calmly. 'And the others you haven't met. Believe me, Mamma, Simona will be fine with us.'

'Oh really?' Something in the way Signora Bertoni asked the question made Kate turn to look at her and what she saw there, some spark of hope and triumph, made her suddenly fearful. 'Just tell me one thing, Francesca,' the woman said, each word diamond precise, 'does Mario fuck all these so-called friends of yours, or is it just Kate?'

'Mamma, don't be disgusting,' said Francesca. She was shaking, but nothing was going to stop her now. 'Come on, let's get out of here before she comes up with any more lies. I can't stand much more of this.'

'Disgusting, am I? Why don't you ask them?'

'There's no need. I know they wouldn't . . .' Francesca looked from Kate to Mario and back again. Slowly the smile faded from her face and she withdrew the arm that Kate had been holding. 'But . . . Kate, tell me she's lying,' she said in a low voice.

'Francesca, please, Mario said that you and he were finished—'

'Oh!' Francesca doubled over in pain as though she'd been punched in the stomach, a far worse blow than any her mother had delivered. 'No,' she was gasping. 'No, no!'

'God, Francesca, I'm so sorry, but I never meant . . .' Kate moved towards her.

'Stay away from me!' said Francesca, and Kate hung back helplessly. Simona escaped from Mario and went across to comfort her sister. Now Signora Bertoni had both her daughters beside her and she stood in front of them.

'Get out of here!' she said to Kate. 'Get out of here, both of you.'

'No,' said Kate. 'I'm not leaving like this. Francesca, please, you have to listen to me.' Francesca turned away from her with a sob of grief and rage.

Simona said, 'Francesca, please, let's go.'

'Simona, no!' said Signora Bertoni.

Mario said quietly, 'Come, Kate. Is better we leave now.'

'But how can we? We can't just walk away. We can't—'

'Listen to me, young lady,' said Signora Bertoni to Kate as she stood like a guardsman over her two daughters, 'you're lucky I didn't do it last night, but I swear to God, if you don't get into that car right now and drive away from here and never come back, I'll kill you with my own bare hands!'

For a moment Kate almost believed her threat, there was such hatred on her face.

'We go now,' said Mario, guiding her down the steps to his little car. 'Before worse things—'

'But we *can't!*'

Almost roughly, he pushed her into the car. 'This is a bad place,' he said, glancing back towards the house. 'Bad place for us.'

Just as he'd got into the driver's seat and switched on the ignition, there was a scream from the house. Simona had broken away from her mother and was running down the steps towards them.

'Mario, wait!' yelled Kate.

'No!' he said and the Topolino sped off down the drive, its tyres churning through the dry surface of the road, so that when Kate twisted round to see what was happening behind them, all she could make out were anonymous shapes moving eerily through a column of white dust.

Chapter 32

Departures

The criss-cross pattern of noises made a fine-meshed net, raising her out of the deep well of nothingness into which she'd fallen. Closest sounds first: the crackle of starched cotton as hands turned her in the bed, squeak of shoes on linoleum; unknown voices raised to cough or call out, '*Sorella*! *Sorella*!' in a sea of words she couldn't understand at all; and then the murmur of talk she recognized from some other, distant place, David and Jenny and Dido, their conversation weaving through the air above her head, English-speaking voices that must assume she couldn't hear as they whispered among themselves about an accident and about Francesca. '*Poor Francesca*', as they called her. But she must be still dreaming after all. It couldn't be real. They were talking as though Francesca were dead.

Her head hurt.

No, no. Not Francesca. Not dead, not dead. Please God, don't let it be true.

She slid back into the dark.

Next time she surfaced there was another voice – a voice from England – was she home again? It was her mother's voice, calm but out of place in this murmuring sea of Italian. 'It's all right, Katie. We'll soon have you well again.'

'Mum?'

'Yes, dear. I'm right here.'

The most familiar face, out of focus but smiling at the edge of sight, was looking down at her. 'Mum, what's happened to Francesca?'

'You rest now, dear. It's all going to be all right.'

'But Francesca—'

'Hush, now. Don't fret.'

So it must be true. Kate struggled to emerge from the blackness and the pain. 'What's happened? Where am I?'

'You were in an accident, Katie, and now you're in hospital, but you're going to make a full recovery. They say you'll be out again in a few days.'

'But . . . Francesca . . . and Mario . . . where's Mario? I want to see him. I must . . .' But iron hooks of pain dragged her back into unconsciousness before she heard the answer, if there even was one.

The next time a sound detached itself from the hubbub of conversation all around her it was one that made her want to shrink back into the pillows. 'Kate, honey, can you hear me? Kate?'

She didn't want to hear, but she could. She opened her eyes. Dressed all in black, right down to the black gloves held in her hands and the black hat with a veil rolled back to show her chalk-white face, Signora Bertoni was seated on a chair beside her bed. Kate's mother and a nurse were standing behind, their faces anguished. 'It's so kind of you to come,' said Mrs Holland, 'at a time like this. So terrible for you.'

Now Kate saw that the Signora's eyes were small dark holes, red-rimmed from weeping. For the first time, her own tears welled up and trickled down her cheeks.

'Are you in pain, Kate?'

Slowly Kate rolled her head from side to side. No, no pain to compare with the pain of losing a daughter. 'What happened?' she whispered.

'Don't you know?' asked the signora.

'They won't tell me.'

'You must remember.'

'No.'

'Think, Kate. Try to remember.'

Kate's mother said, 'It's hard for her, Signora Bertoni. She doesn't remember the accident at all.'

'Really?' Signora Bertoni smiled and said, 'Then I'll tell her. The girl needs to know.' And her voice sounded almost tender, as though softened by grief. 'Tell me, Kate. Don't you remember anything at all?'

'No.'

'Not even the argument? When you and Mario were leaving?'

'Yes.' Kate closed her eyes in pain as the memories came back. 'I remember the fight. And I remember you slapping Francesca. And . . .'

'That's right. Francesca and I had an . . . an argument. And you all went outside. Can you remember what happened after that?'

'Yes.' Kate's voice was stronger as the memories came back. 'You said you'd kill me.'

'Signora Bertoni.' It was Kate's mother speaking. 'I think she's still delirious.'

Signora Bertoni held up her gloves, silencing Mrs Holland. 'Of course,' she said, 'I understand perfectly. And then, Kate?'

'Then I got in the car with Mario.'

'And then?'

'We drove away.'

'Yes?'

'And . . . and . . . I can't remember any more. What happened? What happened to Francesca? How did she die?'

'There was an accident, honey. Francesca tried to follow you on one of the Vespas, but she was upset, her judgement wasn't too good. We think she was trying to overtake the car, to make you stop, but she must have lost control. She went into a tree beside the road and fell off. Mario swerved to avoid her and that was when you hit your head. Lucky it wasn't worse for you. Mario reckons Francesca must have been killed instantly.'

'Oh my God . . .'

Kate's mother put her hand on Signora Bertoni's shoulder. 'If there's anything we can ever do . . .'

'No. Nothing. And there's nothing more to be said, is there, Kate? Except goodbye.' She leaned forward and the scent of her face powder was pungent as she kissed Kate on the left cheek. 'Goodbye, Kate. Get well soon.' And then, when she stooped to kiss her other cheek, she said in a voice so low that only Kate could hear. 'Just remember one thing, Kate honey, you're to blame. Francesca's death was all your fault. If you hadn't interfered in our private family business, none of this would have happened. Francesca would be alive right now. I guess that will be on your conscience for the rest of your life, won't it, honey?'

She straightened up and smiled.

'Thank you so much for coming,' said Mrs Holland. 'It's very kind . . .'

'Not at all.' Signora Bertoni was pulling on her black gloves. 'It was the least I could do.'

'Say goodbye, Kate.'

'No! No, it's not true!'

Mrs Holland tried to comfort her daughter, then exchanged a few words with Signora Bertoni. Kate heard their absurdly polite conversation but she couldn't speak. Where was Mario? She needed him, needed him to wash away the poison Signora Bertoni had dripped into her brain. What had happened to him? Why didn't he come? Couldn't he hear her? Hysteria was building up inside her, a huge tide of misery and rage and denial. She screamed out for Mario, pushing her mother and everyone else away, convinced that he had been killed too and no one had the courage to tell her, and eventually the nurses had to administer sedatives to plunge her back into welcome oblivion.

David came the next day. He had a bunch of carnations in his broad fist and he looked wretched. The Bertonis had been adamant they didn't want any of Francesca's foreign friends to go to the funeral, that it was going to be a private family event.

'It feels all wrong,' he said miserably. 'Why won't they let us say goodbye to her? It's almost as if they blame us for what happened.'

'Maybe they do,' whispered Kate.

'But that's crazy.'

'Isn't it just?' said Kate. 'But so much easier than blaming themselves. God, I wish there was some way we could get

Simona away from them, it's what Francesca would have wanted us to do, I know it is. Remember when we met her, when she was standing on that bridge? She pretended it wasn't true, but I *know* she was thinking about suicide then. While she was with us she learned what it's like to be happy – that's what they can't forgive us for, because she was free and happy for the first time in her life.'

'You sound very sure about this, Kate.'

'There's nothing to do in here, except think.'

'But why didn't her parents want her to be happy?'

'It's her mother,' said Kate slowly. 'She's . . . she's weird and . . .' She broke off, unable to find the words.

'Well, you can understand if she's acting strangely now, losing her daughter and all . . . Still . . .' He was silent for a while, looking at his hands. Then he said, 'I'm going back to England the day after tomorrow.'

'I thought you were planning to stay till the end of April.'

'I know, but . . . it's not the same any more. Not since Francesca died – and now you're going. There doesn't seem any point in staying. Jenny's gone already, so has Aiden. Dido's leaving at the end of the week.'

Of course. The carefree world of the mud angels had been shattered for ever. There was no point in staying in Florence any longer.

'I've got your address,' he said. 'I'll get in touch in a week or so. Dido and the others are talking about organizing a reunion in London in the summer. Maybe we could—'

She interrupted him. 'No, don't write to me, David. Or phone. Maybe I'll get in touch with you some time, when all this has faded.' But she knew she wouldn't and he must have guessed it too.

'Not even a card?'

'I need to get away from all of this. Everyone who had anything to do with it.'

He nodded. 'It must be worse for you, because you were there. You saw it happen.'

'But I can't remember.'

'Dido thinks you blanked it out, because the memory was so horrific.'

'Maybe. There's no way of knowing. Her mother said she died instantly, but I keep worrying that Mario told her that, just to make it easier for her.'

'Of course it was instant!' David had been staring at his hands. Now he looked up at Kate in disbelief, then quickly looked away again. 'Oh my God,' he said. 'No one's told you, have they?'

'Told me what?'

'How she died.'

'Her Vespa came off the road and she was killed. Isn't that what happened?'

'Yes, but . . .'

'But what? What aren't you telling me? David, I *have* to know!'

He hung his head and said in a low, almost inaudible voice, 'Apparently Francesca was flung off the bike but it wasn't the fall that killed her.'

'So . . . what did?'

'The Vespa fell on top of her. The windscreen caught her throat. It cut right through to the bone. That's how she died. Quick, yes. Like a guillotine.'

Kate thought she was going to be sick. 'I can't believe it. How do you know? Did Mario tell you?'

'Mario? No one's seen him since the Villa Beatrice. But it's true all right, we heard it from Hugo, who got the news from the consul.'

'Oh God . . . ' Kate lay back on the pillows, tears rolling down her face.

'Kate, I'm so sorry. I thought you knew.'

She wiped her eyes. 'I don't know why it makes it so much worse, but it does.'

'Yes, I know.'

'To think of her . . . mutilated like that. She was so . . . so beautiful . . . and . . . I loved her.'

'Yes.'

After a while, Kate said quietly, 'Will you do something for me, David?' He nodded. 'Will you take these flowers –' she took up the carnations he'd brought her and handed them back to him – 'and go to the bridge where we first talked to her? And throw them into the river. Say a prayer from us, or something. You'll know what to do. It can be our goodbye.'

Another day passed and still there was no sign of Mario. The doctors were pleased with her progress and Kate's mother began making preparations for their homeward journey. 'You'll start feeling yourself again once you're home,' she said, worrying now more about the damage to Kate's mind than to her body. 'You'll be able to put all this behind you.'

'I can't go yet,' said Kate. Why hadn't Mario been to see her? It didn't make sense. She couldn't shake off the idea that he had been maimed or even killed in the accident and no one would tell her the truth. Her longing for Mario was a raw hunger, an ache deep in the pit of her stomach. She went over and over the night they spent together, every word and gesture and caress. If it had meant to him even a tenth of what she'd felt, how could he stay away from her now? 'I'm not going till I've seen Mario,' she said.

The resulting argument left both Kate and her mother exhausted and with aching heads. But Mrs Holland had observed a new steeliness in her daughter, so she made enquiries.

'He's coming in tomorrow morning,' Mrs Holland said when she returned to the ward the next day. 'He's going to be taking time off specially. And after that we're catching the three o'clock train, no matter what. I've been to that room of yours and got all your things packed and ready.'

'Okay, Mum.'

But Kate didn't believe in the reality of the three o'clock train back to England. She still clung to the idea that once she saw Mario a more generous future was sure to open up.

It felt strange to be back in her own clothes after the shapeless hospital gowns she'd been wearing for nearly a week. Her head hardly hurt at all any more but the back of her neck was stiff and her legs felt as if the bones had turned to water. She had that convalescent feebleness which made her feel as though a small thing would be enough to make her cry.

Visiting hours were strict, but Mario, being a doctor, was permitted to come in after the morning rounds. He was wearing a rumpled suit and there were dark shadows under his eyes. The nuns fussed over '*il dottore*' and brought him a chair.

'Hello, Kate.' He pulled the metal chair further away from her bed and sat down.

'Hello, Mario.' The words came out more as a sob of relief. Such love was welling up inside her, it seemed as if nothing else mattered, not even Francesca's death, so long as they had each other.

He avoided her eye. Something was wrong: Kate felt a chill of fear as he asked coolly, 'You go to England tomorrow?'

'This afternoon.'

'Is good you go home. Better for you.' His manner was all wrong. Kate had waited nearly a week to see him, but this cold, distant man was not the person she'd been yearning for. How could someone change so much in just a few days?

'Why didn't you come earlier? I was afraid you'd been injured too and no one would tell me.'

'I am very busy man, Kate.' His voice was reproachful, as though she had no right to make any demands on him. 'Is not possible to make visit before.'

A whole week? And not a moment when he could have visited? Kate didn't believe him, and the knowledge that Mario was lying made her heart ache with a new kind of pain. She shivered. His hair, she noticed, was cut very short, as it had been when she met him first.

'What is it, Mario? What's happened?'

He must have thought she was referring to Francesca. He sighed, more a groan than a sigh, and said, 'Is terrible. Big tragedy for the family. Terrible, terrible.'

Of course, she told herself, relief flooding through her body, that must be the reason why he hadn't been in to see her until now: it was only natural that the Bertonis and their tragedy had taken up all his time. Francesca's grieving relatives needed his support much more than she did.

'How are the family?'

He made a gesture with his hands as though to say, what did she expect? He said, 'Is hard, very hard. They are brave people but . . . to lose a daughter. And in such a way . . .'

'Have they had the funeral?'

'Yesterday. It was most beautiful funeral. So many flowers.'

'Signora Bertoni didn't want any of Francesca's friends to go.'

He shrugged. 'Is bad time for family. You must try to understand . . .'

'I do try, but it's hard. Did you know Francesca's mother came to visit me?'

'Yes, she said you remember nothing. Is true?'

'I remember the fight in the hallway, Francesca's mother hitting her and everyone yelling and screaming. Then I remember us going down to the car and driving away, but after that, no. I don't remember a thing.'

'Is better that way. Is terrible thing to see. I am a doctor, I see many bad things, but nothing so bad as how she die . . . the pictures never go out from my mind.'

'Francesca's mother said . . .' Kate hesitated, but she had to unburden herself to someone, and who else would ever understand? 'She said that it was my fault, all of it.'

He raised his head, looking directly at her for the first time. 'Is not true, Kate,' he told her gently.

'I know, but . . .'

'She saw her daughter's death. I think maybe that make her go a little bit crazy. Is terrible thing for mother to see. And poor Simona too.'

'Simona saw?'

'*Certo*. She was on Vespa also. She see everything.'

'But I thought it was just Francesca and . . .' Kate's head was beginning to thump, the pain of forgetting and that black cloud where memory should be. 'Mario, tell me what happened.'

'You know already.'

'All I know is that Francesca was thrown off the Vespa, and it fell on top of her, cutting through her . . . through her . . .' Kate couldn't finish the sentence. 'No one said Simona was there too. You have to tell me,' she said.

'Why you want to know?'

'I don't *want* to but . . . I *have* to. Or else it's going to haunt me for ever.' Even as she said those last words she thought, what was she saying? This horror was never going to go away. 'Please, Mario, tell me what happened.'

'Okay. I tell you and then I go. You are well now and you are going home to England. With your family – that is best. And Francesca she is dead, dead for always.' He closed his eyes in pain, then opened them again and said, 'You and I, we drive in the Topolino, but Francesca and Simona, they come after us. And then Signora Bertoni follows in the Mercedes, but I do not see the Mercedes until after. Francesca tries to overtake, but there is not room enough on the road, so I pull to the right, like so, to make space, that is why the Topolino goes into the ditch and you have injury to your head. But is no help. The Vespa hit my car in back, Francesca and Simona fall off, Vespa come down on Francesca. Is very quick. Is over when Signora Bertoni see.'

'Was Simona hurt too?'

'Simona? Poor Simona . . .' An expression of real grief shadowed his face, then he said briskly, 'Not in her body, just bruises, no broken bones, but she see . . . everything.'

'Oh God, that's so terrible. Poor Simona. Is there anything I can do?'

He didn't answer right away. Then he said quietly, 'Yes, Kate, is one thing you can do which help all Francesca's family.'

'Yes, tell me. Anything.'

He rose to his feet and looked down at her, his face impassive. 'Go back to England, Kate. Don't come back here, not ever. Stay away from this family. Always.'

It was like a blow to the stomach. 'Why? What have I done? It sounds like you blame me too!'

'Is better this way.'

'And what about you, Mario? Don't you want to see me again either?'

'No. Is finish for us.'

She said, 'We didn't kill her, Mario. It wasn't our fault she died.'

He shrugged. 'I know, but . . . I go now,' he said.

'Wait, Mario, please wait. There's just one more thing I need to know . . . that last night . . . at the Villa Beatrice . . . even if we never see each other again . . . I need to know . . . that it meant something to you as well.' She could hear the pleading in her voice but she was powerless to stop it.

'Is because it was special time for you, but for me . . .' He sighed. 'For me, I regret, Kate, it was . . . nothing.'

She didn't believe him. She said, 'Don't lie to me, Mario, please. I can bear it if we never see each other again. I'll have to, somehow. But I can't bear it if you lie to me. I thought you loved me, just a bit and—'

'No, Kate. Was just big dream. I am not man for love you.'

He turned, as though he was intending to walk away without another word.

'Mario, stop! Won't you even say goodbye?'

He had his back to her. She saw his hands clench and unclench, his shoulders loosen. He turned again and stooped, took her hand and raised it to his lips.

'Goodbye, my lovely Kate.' His voice was breaking. 'Be well soon and be happy with your life.'

His face was shining with tears and with something else besides, something that looked to Kate almost like love.

'Goodbye, Mario.'

He held her hand a moment longer, then nodded briefly as he set it back in her lap. Quickly he turned from her and walked out of the ward without a backward glance.

PART III

Chapter 33

Flood

By the summer of 1967 Florence was welcoming tourists again. Most of the major roads were repaired, the galleries and museums opened their doors once again, shops were rebuilt on the Ponte Vecchio. Some evidence of the devastation remained, but as a curiosity for visitors, no longer a barrier. Even today, in places, you can see the black tideline where the filthy floodwater reached up to twenty feet on the night of the fourth of November, 1966.

The ravaged crucifix by Cimabue became a permanent symbol of all that could never be repaired. Several reputations were ruined also. In the aftermath of the flood it was discovered that eight hours before the Arno burst its banks, water was released from the hydroelectric dam near Montevarchi. In order to protect their generating equipment, the duty officer had acted according to the letter of his responsibilities, but at the time it was widely believed that this contributed to the flood. Now, it is generally agreed that his actions had little effect on the severity of the flood.

Similarly, it emerged that the Prefect of Florence had ample warning that a disastrous flood was approaching. He chose not to warn the city's inhabitants or to make the emergency services ready, so that two weeks after the flood half the fire stations were still underwater and inoperable. His inaction was widely criticized. In his defence he pointed out that if he'd issued a warning there could have been widespread panic and that citizens fleeing the city in cars would have been at far greater risk from the rising waters than those who remained in their homes. The minimal loss of life supports this claim.

There were even a few beneficiaries. Some prisoners escaped from Le Murate during the first impact of the flood. Most were recaptured, but a few remained at large indefinitely. Those less fortunate were terrified of being drowned in their cells. The reassurance of bystanders was hardly encouraging as doctors and prison officials informed them they were 'reasonably safe'. The following day, when the prisoners were again panicking, police fired to quell the riot, bringing a new note of horror to a city that was already described as resembling a hallucination.

The greatest impact, for good and ill, was on Florence's standing in the world. The unprecedented response of the international community to the disaster confirmed once and for all that the city's reputation was unique. Its position as the epitome of all that is most civilized in western culture was unassailable. The downside was a massive increase in tourism. From now on Florence would become virtually a museum city, overrun with visitors the year round.

As with cities, so too with people and families. After the tragedy at the Villa Beatrice that March morning, Kate and her friends from Florence and the Bertoni family all went their separate ways and picked up the patterns of their lives. In time the scars and hurts became all but invisible to outsiders. Kate went on to university, then trained as a conservator. She married twice, had two children. Like the other volunteers from around the world, she filled her days with activity in the way that passes for normal in our world where every individual and family hides their secret vaults of pain. Sometimes the passing of the years is enough to heal these secret wounds; occasionally they fester and grow unobserved until some trigger occurs which causes them to erupt into the light with devastating power.

Chapter 34

Gala

Already by ten o'clock it was obvious it was going to be a hot day. A steady stream of cars had been making their way up the twisting drive to the Villa Beatrice since soon after nine, as visitors arrived to celebrate the success of the Fondazione's tenth season. Kate couldn't help being impressed.

'Sit here, where I can see you.'

Simona, looking effortlessly elegant in a grey silk jacket with enormous white polka dots and a pencil slim skirt, showed Kate to a seat with a reserved sign on it in the front row. Already the gilt room at the Villa Beatrice was filling up with the great and the good from as far away as Rome and Milan, who were arriving to support, or simply to be associated with, the work of the Fondazione.

For once, Kate would have preferred to be sitting at the back. With the coming of daylight the fears that had kept her awake through most of the night had receded and at breakfast she'd accepted Simona's explanation that Dino must have acted from myopic idiocy when he fired at her on the mountain. Looking around at the crowds of respectable people who had turned up in their expensive cars and at the enthusiastic young students who'd been participating in this year's summer programme, Kate felt ashamed of her paranoid anxieties during the night. The events of the previous evening, that sensation of being a moving target she'd experienced in her flight from the summit, seemed like a bad dream. There was no reason for her to be afraid. David was driving up from Rome and had promised to be here by noon, and anyway, this huge room with its exquisitely gilded plasterwork on ceiling and walls hardly looked like the kind of place where danger would lurk. A soothing murmur of voices filled the hall as people drifted in and found a place to sit. It wasn't yet eleven in the morning but already the air was warm with the last of the summer's heat.

Simona had been cornered by one of the Fondazione's administrators, who was insisting she welcome a white-haired man who looked as though he considered his presence at the Villa Beatrice's gala day its ultimate accolade. As soon as she could, Simona escaped and came back to perch on the chair beside Kate's.

'This is going to be so boring for you!' she commiserated. 'Nothing but pompous speeches for the entire morning – promise you won't give up on me and run away!' Simona kept her tone light, but she was in deadly earnest all the same. 'As soon as this is over we'll have lots of time to be together. I want to talk to you so much!'

Not half as much as I want to talk to you, thought Kate.

She was frustrated by the way Simona kept going on about talking, then squandered any time they had together in trivia. As a result, Kate was still no closer to knowing why this visit was so vital to Simona, nor why she'd chosen to use altered paintings to lure her there rather than send some kind of ordinary invitation. It couldn't be that hard to persuade old friends to visit a place as stunning as the Villa Beatrice and La Rocca.

'Now I have to abandon you,' said Simona. 'The business is about to start. Ah, good, here is Mario. He will take care of you.'

Mario walked in briskly and greeted first Simona and then Kate with a kiss on both cheeks before he sat down in the chair that Simona had just vacated. Dressed in a pale linen suit, he was every inch the successful and still handsome doctor. Kate would have given a lot to know exactly what his role was in the Fondazione, and how he and Simona were linked. She wondered if she'd ever find out.

Simona went up the two steps to the dais at the front of the hall and took her place behind the microphone between a man and a woman.

'*Buon giorno*, Kate,' said Mario. 'Are you all right? I hear Dino was up to his tricks again last night. I am sorry – it must have been terrifying for you.'

His choice of words was faultless. So it must have been his manner of delivery, or some incongruity between speech and gesture, that set Kate immediately on her guard. The thought flickered into her mind that it could just possibly have been Mario firing at her. After all, he was the one who'd told her she'd have done better to stay away and he'd 'left' the house just before she began her descent from La Guardia. She dismissed the idea.

'Yes,' she told him. 'I was bloody scared. If that's how Dino usually carries on, then the sooner you get rid of him the better.'

He looked at her intently for a moment or two, then said coolly, 'If I had my way the imbecile would have gone years ago. Unfortunately I am not in charge of the staff at La Rocca.'

'No?' Kate was stung. 'You were very accurate yesterday when you said it would have been better if I'd stayed away.'

Mario looked baffled for a moment, then he laughed, a glimpse of a young man she'd known years before. He patted her arm and, still smiling, said in a low voice, 'Yes, I did warn you, but I wasn't expecting the danger to be as real as that.'

Kate was prevented from replying by the start of the ceremonies. The young woman on the dais stood up and came forward to tap the microphone. Conversation dropped to a murmur, then died away completely as the first of the speeches began – in Italian, of course. Kate was finding it hard to concentrate. The sleepless night had left her feeling as though her head was stuffed with sand. The sense of unreality was increasing. It was hard to believe that the successful middle-aged doctor sitting next to her had once turned her world upside-down.

She couldn't remember many details of that last weekend at the Villa Beatrice. So much had been overshadowed by Francesca's death. But the legacy of those days had coloured her life for years. Falling in love with Mario had been so effortlessly simple: for a few brief hours the world had been transformed into a place of magic, rainbow colours and endless possibilities. When it ended and she came back to England, she had been devastated, of course, both by Francesca's death and by losing Mario. But she had believed those who bombarded her with platitudes about time healing and there being plenty more fish in the sea. She'd expected the 'in love' experience to be repeated, even if she had to wait years.

But it never was, not in the way she remembered it and hoped for, and gradually she came to believe that what she'd felt for Mario had been an illusion all along. She settled for the 'reality' of a decent marriage with a man she'd never really been in love with, but whom she liked and respected. Though not enough, it turned out. And as for the second marriage . . . well, she'd been older, and wiser, and expected less. Maybe she'd even expected too little.

As speech after speech congratulating the Fondazione on its contribution to the arts and opportunities for young people washed over her head, Kate was intensely aware of the man sitting beside her, Dr Mario Bassano, the same man but altogether different from the man she'd loved all those years before.

When Simona stood up there was a huge round of applause and some cheering from the students. She smiled, waited for the applause to die down, then began to speak. Hesitant at first, she grew in confidence, borne along by her passion for the Fondazione and the lives that were changed there. Already, it seemed, after only ten years in operation, several gifted children from poor families who had benefited from its programmes were making their mark in the world of art and music.

Kate was impressed. Francesca's little sister with the buck teeth and the cabbage-green dress was now a mature woman who had used her wealth in a creative and generous manner and was rightly honoured for it. A lump rose to her throat as she thought how proud Francesca would have been, proud and pleased by all that was being achieved in her name.

Simona paused, then looked down directly at Kate and said in English, 'Today I want to welcome a very special visitor to the Villa Beatrice, Kate Holland from London, who has established a brilliant international reputation for her work in the conservation of early oil paintings on canvas. Kate was the dearest friend of my sister Francesca, and for that reason alone she will always be a welcome guest at the Fondazione. But there's another, more important reason, which perhaps even she has forgotten, why I am especially pleased that she is able to be with us to share this special day.'

There was a murmur as Simona's words were translated in low voices by those who understood to neighbours who didn't, and people craned their necks to get a look at the foreigner in the front row who was being singled out for attention. Kate was uneasy; she had no idea what Simona was building up to. Was she being set up for some kind of trick? If Simona's intention was benign, then why hadn't she given some warning? She wasn't alone in being uneasy. Beside her, Mario was suddenly all attention, sitting forward in his seat, his face taut with anxiety.

Simona was smiling, now, talking directly to her. She said, 'I have never spoken of this until today. In the past I've often felt a fraud when people praised me for the work I've done here at Villa Beatrice. Yes, a fraud, I cannot take the credit myself.'

Kate was suddenly aware of Mario. Sweat was pouring off his face and he wasn't just sitting forward in his chair, he was coiled like an animal about to pounce. Her first thought was that he was ill, then she realized that he was reacting to what Simona was saying – or what he was afraid she might say.

Simona continued, 'No one has known until now where the idea for the Fondazione was born, but today I can tell you. In the weeks before her death, my sister Francesca and Kate were working together in Florence with the *angeli dell'alluvione* whom we've all heard of, and it was Kate who gave the idea to my sister just before she died – "Why not turn this place into a

centre for the arts so it can be enjoyed by many many people?"
– and Francesca in her turn told me. It took a long time, but
the idea never entirely left me. From such a casual, throwaway
remark do great enterprises grow. And I am glad that today at
last, Kate, we can offer you our thanks.'

Kate's anxiety switched to acute embarrassment as there was
a burst of applause and she scanned her memory in vain to trace
this conversation. As the clapping died down and the white-
haired man took the podium and began praising Simona in
lavish terms, Kate glanced at Mario. No longer the wealthy and
successful doctor, revered by all who came into contact with
him, he looked beaten and old. He had slumped back in his
seat, his face grey with exhaustion.

Mario had recovered by the time the speeches ended and lavish
bouquets had been handed out to half a dozen women who
worked for the Fondazione. The most spectacular bouquet, an
arrangement of orchids and foliage, was reserved for Simona.

As soon as the last speech was finished she stepped down
from the podium and made straight for Kate.

'How did you like my speech?' She seemed as excited as a
child at Christmas. 'Were you surprised?'

'Yes, but I don't remember—'

Simona took her by the arm. 'That doesn't matter,' she said
firmly. 'Because I remember everything.'

A buffet lunch had been laid out in the frescoed dining room.
The dancing nymphs with their garlands and their diaphanous
clothes looked down on a crowd of about a hundred people, all
eating and talking in loud voices. Kate, momentarily abandoned
since Simona had been whisked off to talk to a deputy from
Rome and Mario was nowhere to be seen, found herself remem-

bering the party when they had hitchhiked up from Florence. What music had they listened to? The Beach Boys? The Stones? Looking around at all the guests and the laden tables and the uniformed staff, she thought it was hardly surprising they'd had trouble creating a festive atmosphere back in 1967. There'd been too few of them to make any impression on a space like this.

'Still here? I thought you'd have quit after last night.'

Kate turned abruptly. She hadn't seen Simona's mother in the gilded hall that morning but she'd recognize that rasping smoker's voice anywhere. Annette Bertoni, leaning heavily on an ebony cane, looked painfully thin under her butter-yellow suit and hat. Her wispy hair was streaked silver and blonde and her make-up was immaculate; the overwhelming impression she gave was one of frailty and courage.

'You heard about it, then?'

Annette nodded. She seemed to have forgotten her outburst of the previous evening and her manner towards Kate today was much more benign. Even so, Kate could never forget that this was the woman who had blamed her for Francesca's death. The injustice of her accusation only made it ten times worse.

The old woman raised her glass in a white-gloved hand and sipped her wine, then said, 'Dino's always been a fool.' Her voice was harsh with contempt. 'And a terrible shot – lucky for you, eh?' She laughed.

Kate shivered. Changing the subject, she said, 'You must be so proud of Simona and all she's done here.'

Annette's wizened little face peered up at her. She appeared genuinely puzzled by this suggestion. 'Proud? What in the name of all that's holy have I got to be proud about?'

Kate gestured round the room, packed with all the patrons and artists and dignitaries who'd gathered to celebrate Simona's achievement. 'The Fondazione,' she said. 'All this.' And when Annette showed no sign of having the first idea what she was talking about, she added, 'I wonder what Zio Toni would make of the way Simona has used his fortune.'

'Who?'

'Zio Toni. Wasn't that the name of Simona's uncle?'

Annette didn't reply. The flesh on her face darkened and she was having difficulty breathing. Then she said with quiet certainty, 'That man's in hell. Where he belongs. I hope he rots there for ever –' the volume was rising as her invective got under way and one or two people turned to look at her – 'whatever that evil bastard is suffering right now, it's less than he deserves . . . And you too, I hope you die and go to hell for what you did to me!'

More heads were turning as Annette's rant gathered momentum. Kate looked about her in desperation. 'Stop it,' she said, 'You're talking nonsense.'

She caught sight of Mario making his way through the throng towards them. 'Annette,' said Mario in a low voice, taking her by the arm. '*Andiamo.* We go now?'

She looked up at him, her old eyes filmed and unseeing. 'Take your hands off me!' she yelled. 'Who are you anyway?' In spite of her crazy accusations, Kate felt a strange pity for her. Even after all these years, the memory of her daughter's death was unbearable.

'It's me. Mario. You must not tire yourself, Annette.' Holding her firmly by the arm, he gestured with his head to a figure standing at the edge of the room. Smiling as always, Dino moved silently through the crowd. Kate stepped out of his path, but he did not notice her. He was looking only at Annette. She had been bristling with confused anger, ready to do battle with

Mario or anyone else who stood in her way, but as soon as Dino
came into her line of vision, she relaxed, breathed a sigh of relief
and said something in Italian. She took his arm and together
they walked away through the crowd.

'What was all that about?' Kate asked Mario.

He said, 'You must have said something to upset her.'

'All I said was that she must be proud of Simona's achieve-
ments. And I wondered what Zio Toni would have made of it
all. Not exactly dynamite.'

Mario made a gesture of exasperation. 'Let me give you a
word of advice. Do not speak to Annette again. And never
mention the girls' uncle.'

'Why on earth not? I mean—'

'Just don't say his name, okay? And it's a good idea not to
mention Francesca either.'

'I don't understand . . .'

'My point exactly,' said Mario and, turning on his heel, he
walked away. Kate had the impression he'd opted to quit the
conversation before his temper got the better of him.

'Hang on a minute,' she said angrily, starting to follow him,
'You can't just—'

'Kate, believe me. I can do what I want.'

Kate was about to argue with him when she saw David
approaching through the crowds. Thank the Lord, she thought,
surprised by the strength of her relief and pleasure at the sight
of his familiar black-browed face. Someone who doesn't talk in
riddles all the time.

Chapter 35

Wolfbait

'So what's been going on?'

The maid who'd brought David's bags up the stairs had just closed the door behind her and he and Kate were alone in the palatial bedroom where she'd spent her sleepless night. He was looking about him, taking in the generous proportions of the room and the beautiful old furniture, then he walked over to a window cut into the deep walls and leaned on the sill, breathing in the clean late-summer air. On the long drive leading down to the road he could see a steady stream of cars, rear windows glinting in the afternoon light, as the gala-day guests headed home.

'Someone tried to shoot me,' said Kate. 'Yesterday evening.'

'With a camera?'

'A gun.'

'You're kidding.'

'No.' Kate sighed and flopped down on the edge of the bed. 'I only wish I was.'

'Really shoot?' David was having problems getting his head around this idea. Over a hundred guests had just spent the whole day praising the work of the Fondazione and it was hard to reconcile that with the idea of anyone wanting to shoot at Kate. He pulled off his jacket and threw it over a chair. 'Are you sure?'

She nodded. 'Everyone says it was an accident because the idiot nightwatchman mistook me for a wild boar or a wolf or something but—'

'A wolf? You?' David was on the verge of laughing with disbelief, but then, seeing the expression on Kate's face, he said, 'You'd better tell me exactly what happened.'

As briefly as she could, Kate recounted the events of the previous evening: her walk up to La Guardia with Simona and Mario, Simona's fall, how she said she'd walk down later on her own. And then the realization that she wasn't alone on the mountainside, and those gunshots, hitting the hillside close by not once but twice. David tried to take in what she was saying, but it just didn't add up.

'You're sure it wasn't an accident?' he asked.

'How can it have been? I mean, you can see how he might have made one mistake, but I called out after the first shot and the bastard fired again.'

'Are you sure you called out? Maybe you just think you did. After all, it's easy to misjudge in a situation like that.'

'I *know* I did. It was something daft like, "Hey, watch what you're doing!" – something really original like that.'

'You think it might have been deliberate then?'

'Well, if it wasn't an accident . . .' Kate pondered. 'No,' she said eventually, 'it doesn't make sense. Why would anyone want to shoot at me? It must have been the

nightwatchman like Simona said – and maybe he's deaf as
well as half-blind.'

David considered this. But it was obvious Kate had been
deeply shaken, and he knew she wasn't the kind of person to let
her imagination run away with her. It seemed unlikely, but: 'Is
it possible someone was trying to warn you off?'

'Why would Dino want to warn me off?'

'Maybe it wasn't this Dino character after all.'

Kate stared at him for a moment, then shook her head.
'David, you're way off your script.' She smiled wryly. 'You're
supposed to tell me there's nothing to worry about, that it was
all an accident and I'm absolutely safe here.'

'I always thought the bodyguard's job was to evaluate risk.'
He moved across the room to stand in front of her.

'This bodyguard's just supposed to be reassuring.'

He leaned over her. 'This bodyguard has other things on his
mind. He's missed you.'

There was a long silence, then Kate said slowly, 'Good. I've
missed you too, David.'

Kate lay back on the pillows. The bed was covered with a
faded silk spread bearing a Japanese design which must have
been eighteenth century. Kate knew she ought to remove it
first, but she didn't have the energy. 'God, I've never been so
tired,' she said.

'Don't go to sleep on me, Kate, not yet. Have you found out
who sent the paintings?'

'Simona.'

'Why?'

'No idea.'

'Have you asked her?'

'Of course. She keeps saying she wants to talk to me, but

whenever we get the chance she just fritters it away.' Kate rolled onto her side and closed her eyes. 'She'd better spit it out soon, because I plan on leaving first thing tomorrow.'

'From what I've seen of Simona so far, she seems just as highly-strung as her sister ever was,' said David. Kate didn't respond. 'Kate?'

No reply.

Leaving her to catch up on some sleep, David went into a bathroom so vast and cavernous he half expected to see stalactites hanging down from the ceiling. While he showered away the dust and sweat of his drive up from Rome, he reviewed the previous twenty-four hours. His visit to his daughter had gone all right until the final evening, when, over enormous bowls of *pasta alle vongole* in a Trastevere restaurant, she suddenly dredged up a whole slew of old resentments and grievances, dating back to her first pony which had been, apparently, not competition material. By the time he'd walked her back to her shared apartment he was so baffled by her outburst he half thought she must have grown up in someone else's family, not his. There then followed a tearful (on her part) farewell. It had been a huge relief that morning to pick up his hire car and drive north. The Fondazione's gala day at the Villa Beatrice provided the perfect excuse for an early start, allowing no time for either more reproaches or more tears.

He'd spent the first two hours of his journey angrily chewing over the ingratitude of daughters and paid no attention at all to his surroundings – he could have been driving on the dark side of the moon and he wouldn't have noticed. But then, once he'd turned off the motorway and started the slow ascent into the hills, he realized he was travelling through a beautiful and wild part of Italy he'd forgotten about entirely. He must have hitched

that way when he came out from Florence to the party. It
amazed him that the landscape had made so little impression
on him the first time he saw it, and he began wondering what
it would be like to make a home here.

It was his automatic response to any new place. David had
reached that stage when a fresh start in an entirely new location
seemed like the best way to fend off approaching age. Several of
his contemporaries had already taken early retirement and their
horizons had narrowed to golf and gardens – he wasn't ready for
that. A new life entirely, a new culture, new horizons and new
friends and a new language to become fluent in – now that was
the sort of challenge he'd enjoy.

The Bertoni estate, with the classical elegance of the Villa
Beatrice and La Rocca's ancient beauty, was just the kind of
place to fuel fantasies of a new beginning. There was a grandeur
to Simona's world that was definitely inspiring. The drama of
the altered paintings, and now this talk of shooting, was almost
a bonus. He didn't for a moment think anyone had shot at Kate
deliberately, but it was interesting to speculate, just as he'd
enjoyed speculating on the reasons why the paintings had been
sent in the first place. Whatever else could be said about the
present situation, it wasn't humdrum. He pulled on a towelling
robe and went into the bedroom.

Kate was sitting bolt upright on the half-canopied bed,
looking about her in alarm. She looked tousled and infinitely
desirable.

'Have you ever thought of living in Italy?' he asked her.

'What?' She looked bewildered. 'I thought you'd gone.'

'No. But I thought you'd prefer a clean bodyguard.'

Kate had only fallen asleep for a few minutes, but the dreams
seemed to have lasted for hours – dreams of pursuit and terror.

She said, 'David, I want to get away from this place. It gives me the creeps.'

'Don't worry,' he told her. 'We're going in the morning.'

'I want to go now.'

He sat down on the edge of the bed and put his arm around her. 'Kate, please. I've only just got here. And I'm your body-guard, remember?' He smiled. 'It'll be all right. Nothing bad can possibly happen to you while I'm here.'

Chapter 36

Bodyguard

Mario and David were both trying too hard; it was obvious they didn't like each other any more now than they had done in 1967. The only difference was they were making more vigorous efforts to mask their antipathy. David asked Mario about his role in setting up the Fondazione, which was obviously substantial. Mario explained that Simona had the vision and the courage, and had supervised the day-to-day building and design while leaving bureaucracy and finance to Mario. 'Right from the start,' he explained, 'Simona concentrated on the Fondazione itself, while I dealt with the outer world.'

Simona didn't argue with that, which left Kate wondering if his tasks had included lying to her about the price her paintings and other treasures had been sold for. After all, the two paintings that had arrived at her studio were seriously undervalued, which was especially worrying because Simona herself had seemed to be ignorant of their true worth. It wouldn't have mattered so much if Simona hadn't told Kate that most of the capital costs of the Fondazione had been paid for by the sale of items from her uncle's collection. 'I sold a Cranach to pay for the swimming pool,' she had told Kate when they walked down to the Villa Beatrice that morning, and not for nothing was the purpose-built practice block called Casa Veronese. If Simona intended selling any more of her work, then she had to be properly advised how to get the best price for them. Kate needed to talk to her about this, but once again, it was impossible to get a moment to talk to her alone.

The four of them had come out to eat at a restaurant halfway up another hill, about a twenty-minute drive from La Rocca. Simona said she needed a change of scene but Kate thought it more likely she wanted to avoid having yet another meal sabotaged by her crazy mother, which was fine by Kate. The restaurant itself was small and welcoming, but its food, though good, was not a patch on the meal Simona's own cook had prepared the night before.

All evening, Simona had been on edge and distracted. She'd repeated that she was eager to talk to Kate when they were walking together up the steps to the restaurant, but whenever Kate spoke to her she hardly seemed to be listening. She must be tired after the gala day, Kate thought. The morning's speeches and the long buffet lunch had been followed by a concert by students which continued long past five o'clock and everyone wanted a piece of Simona's attention. The last of the guests had only just departed before they set out for the restaurant.

By the time their main course arrived, it was Mario's turn to show courteous interest in his guest. Having discovered that asking David about his career to date was not a fruitful line of enquiry – 'Dry cleaning, that must have been interesting,' Kate actually heard him say – Mario hit on David's future plans as a

more promising topic, and David responded by making that
morning's fantasy of setting up home in the Italian hinterland
sound like a fixed intention.

'In that case,' said Mario, apparently delighted to be of
help, 'I know just the place for you. It belongs to a friend
of mine whose husband died recently and she's eager to sell.
They were planning to renovate it, but have only got as far as
making a beautiful property look like a building site, so it will
sell for much less than its real value.' And he went on to
describe a place that was potentially idyllic, with fine views
and old stone walls. 'I can take you to see it tomorrow, if you
like,' said Mario.

Kate could see that David was tempted. Already he was
imagining a new life among whispering cypresses and ancient
terraces. She said quickly, 'Sorry, Mario, but we're leaving
tomorrow.'

'Oh, you can't go so soon.' Simona, who was sitting next to
her, seemed to snap out of her reverie. 'We've hardly had any
chance to talk yet.'

And whose fault is that? Kate wanted to ask. But all she said
was, 'We can talk whenever you want, Simona.'

Mario looked anxious, but he still seemed determined to be
helpful. He said, 'If I show David my friend's house in the
morning, you can still leave tomorrow if you want to. Would
you like me to arrange it?'

'Why not?' said David.

'Great,' said Simona. 'That means Kate and I will have the
morning together.'

Kate felt uneasy at the prospect of being left behind at La
Rocca with Simona and her mother. There was security in
David's company. If he was determined to go house-hunting

with Mario, then she would go too. 'If you really want to see it,' she said, 'I'll come as well.'

Simona was disappointed, but, 'We'll all go,' she said.

'Excellent,' said Mario.

'What's the house called?' asked David.

Mario laughed. 'Not a very original name, I'm afraid – Bella Vista. But that can always be changed by the new owner.'

'Isn't changing names unlucky?' asked Kate.

'Only the names of boats,' said David. 'It's all right with houses.'

'Have you ever thought of changing your name, Kate?' Simona asked her, and when Kate said that no, she'd never given it much thought so she supposed she must have always been quite happy with her name, Simona looked baffled. 'I *hate* my name,' she said. 'I've always wanted to change it.'

'Then why don't you?' Kate asked.

Mario was sitting opposite Simona. Now he reached across the table, took her hand in his and said gently, 'But you have a beautiful name, Simona. It suits you so well.' He smiled and, still holding her hand, he recited: '"What's in a name? That which we call a rose by any other name would smell as sweet," Simona Bertoni.'

Simona snatched her hand away. Suddenly she was shaking with rage that seemed to have sprung from nowhere, out of all proportion. 'Damn you, Mario Bassano! God damn you to hell!'

His eyes darkened and he leaned back in his chair. '*Piano, mia cara,*' he said quietly. 'Easy does it. Don't repeat the Florida mistake.'

This time she recoiled as though she'd been hit. 'Why do you have to bring that up?' she whispered.

'Sometimes shock tactics work best,' he said.

'Florida?' David asked.

Mario raised his eyebrow and looked at Simona, as if daring her to explain. Kate wished David hadn't asked; she had a feeling he was playing directly into Mario's hands, and whatever was going on, it made her extremely uncomfortable, the way watching the powerless baited by those stronger is always painful. But why did she think of Simona as powerless? Puzzled, she said, 'David, leave it. It's none of our business.'

Simona jutted her chin in the air. 'Oh, but I'm sure you'd be amused by the story.' Her voice was sharpened by pain. 'It was really extremely entertaining. Mario and I were staying in a hotel in Florida and I tried to kill him, that's all. Isn't that hilarious?' No one spoke. She said in a low voice, 'And oh God, oh God, oh God, how I wish I'd succeeded!'

'That must be why you tried again in Guatemala,' said Mario coolly.

'Was that the second or the third time?' asked Simona. 'It was all so long ago the details get muddled sometimes.'

'No, the third time was in Mysore.'

'That's right. I remember now. All that meditation obviously didn't produce the right results, eh?' Simona seemed to be struggling to pretend it was all a macabre joke.

David sloshed some more wine in his glass and turned to Mario. 'Really kill?' he asked. 'As in ending up dead?'

'Oh yes, they were serious attempts. Simona has never been one to do anything by halves, have you, Simona? If the knives in these foreign hotels were sharper, I wouldn't be here today to tell the tale. I'd show you the scars, only the other diners would not appreciate the exhibition.'

Simona was shaking. 'The worst scars don't show on the outside,' she said in a voice so low that only Kate could hear.

David looked across at Simona as though she'd taken the day off from a travelling freak show and asked lightly, 'Any particular reason for the homicidal streak, Simona, or were you just having a bad hair day?'

'Stop it, David! Stop being so bloody insensitive,' Kate intervened angrily. She was sickened by the way the two men were taking pleasure in winding Simona up. She couldn't understand why David had suddenly turned against their hostess. 'This is none of our business, and anyway, I don't find it the least bit amusing.' As soon as she had finished speaking she knew her outburst had only reinforced the bonds between the two men. They exchanged a furtive all-women-are-irrational smile.

David said tightly, 'Then perhaps you'd like to choose a more suitable topic for us to discuss, Kate.' Clearly, he was furious at being reprimanded in public.

Mario said, 'You're right, Kate. Simona and I should not wash our dirty linen in public. Isn't that so, Simona?'

Simona looked at him. She raised the back of her hand to her eyes, like someone brushing away imaginary cobwebs, and said heavily, 'You know, Mario, you pollute the air with your poisons. It gets hard even to breathe around you.'

The smile faded from his face and he shrugged. 'I am sorry if you find my company uncongenial,' and to Kate's amazement there was real hurt behind his words. Somewhere in the last few seconds, Simona had gained the upper hand. Kate had no idea what had tipped the balance of power between them, but she knew more surely than ever that she and David were spectators in a drama that had a long and convoluted history.

Not surprisingly, conversation during the rest of the meal was strained. When the waiter asked if anyone wanted dessert or coffee, they all quickly said they'd had enough, each one of them equally eager to bring the evening to an end. They hardly talked at all on the journey back to La Rocca where Mario dropped them off. Simona went straight into the house without inviting him in.

As soon as Mario had driven off in the darkness down the winding drive, Simona relaxed. They were standing in the hall, under the modern abstract painting of angels that Simona had pointed out to Kate the day before. This evening, under artificial light, the grey veils of paint seemed more ghostly and mysterious than ever. 'How about a drink?' she said to Kate. She had shaken off her fatigue and was suddenly all energy. Standing there, Kate realized she was in no mood for the 'conversation' Simona had been building up to all this time. After her sleepless night and the tensions of the day, she was shattered. Besides, there'd been too many hints of her mental fragility. The 'homicidal streak' that Mario and David had discussed so mockingly at supper might have been an exaggeration, but the woman was clearly unstable. Yet in spite of everything, over the past twenty-four hours Kate had grown fond of her. Partly that was loyalty to Francesca's memory, partly admiration at the achievement of the Fondazione. She promised herself that in the morning she would talk to Simona seriously about the undervalued paintings; perhaps, after all, this practical assistance was the best she could offer.

'I'm all in,' she told her. 'Let's talk in the morning.'

'Are you sure?' Simona looked disappointed.

David said, 'I wouldn't mind a nightcap, if you want someone to keep you company.'

Kate looked at him in surprise. What was he playing at? But Simona merely gestured in the direction of the main drawing room. 'Help yourself,' she said, then yawned ostentatiously. 'You'll find everything you want in there. I think I'll turn in as well, Kate. These gala days always take it out of me.'

She followed Kate up to the first floor, leaving David alone in the hall. At the top of the stairs their ways parted, since Simona's room was at the opposite end of the house from Kate's, but Simona followed her to her door. Kate noticed that Simona's footsteps were kitten quiet on the thick rugs.

'Do you have everything you need, Kate?'

'Yes, thank you.' It could have been Simona standing outside her door the previous night. She knew there had been someone. Why had David chosen to stay below? Was he angry because she'd told him off in the restaurant? She wished he was up here with her, because she realized she didn't trust Simona – didn't trust her at all.

'Are you sure?' Simona was spinning this out for as long as she could.

'Quite sure. And now I really am tired, Simona, I'm going to bed.'

'Yes, of course.' But somehow, when Kate went into her bedroom, Simona had slipped in beside her. She looked about her as if it were a place they were both visiting for the first time. 'This is a fine room, isn't it?'

'It's great. And now—'

'I love this Sisley, don't you? Mario wanted me to sell it a few years ago, we needed the money for something, I can't remember what it was, but I couldn't bear to part with it. It's the light that makes it so dramatic.'

'Yes.' Kate was about to start undressing, but with Simona

still standing there, she felt inhibited. Heavy footsteps sounded on the landing and David came into the room. He swayed slightly, his dark brows ferocious as he glowered at Simona.

She said, 'Oh well, I'd better be going to bed. Goodnight.'

'Goodnight,' said Kate as Simona hurried from the room. David said nothing until the door was closed behind her.

'Fucking rude,' he said thickly.

'What is?'

'Asking you to have a drink with her, then saying she was going to bed so she didn't have to stay and talk to me. Fucking bloody rude.'

'David, you're drunk.'

'So what if I'm bloody drunk? I can't stand bad manners. Just because she's got this place and all those bloody bigwigs telling her how amazing she is doesn't mean she can get away with treating me like dirt.'

'For God's sake, David. If I remember rightly, you were doing your best to wind her up back there in the restaurant. Christ only knows what's going on in this place, but the last thing Simona needs is someone making fun of her.'

Their argument escalated from there into a bitter, pointless row. It was the first real one they'd had. Kate had always hated rows. Exhausted as she was, all she could think about as she fell into a deep and troubled sleep was that in the morning she could escape this place for ever.

Chapter 37

Francesca

It was precisely the scenario Kate had wanted to avoid.

'Didn't David tell you?' said Simona. 'He and Mario left for Bella Vista ten minutes ago.'

'But we were all supposed to go!' said Kate.

'He said you'd changed your mind,' Simona told her, 'so I thought I'd stay back and keep you company.'

'Hell.' Kate was appalled. The memory of her first night at La Rocca was still too fresh in her mind for her to relish being left there with Simona, Annette Bertoni and the mysterious Dino. She'd been relying on David. Needless to say, he hadn't told her he was going off alone with Mario. Either this was his way of punishing her for their unresolved row last night, or maybe he just preferred not having her along.

Simona looked delighted with the way things had turned out. She was sitting on the terrace overlooking the valley, a huge cup of coffee cradled in her hands. The sky was milky white and the air was sultry. Kate crossed over and sat on the balustrade and looked down at the curve of the river far below: it seemed a cruel irony that the place she least wanted to be right now was one of the most spectacular places she'd ever been in. All the same, her immediate instinct was to phone for a taxi and leave at once.

'If I'd have known you were so keen to see the property,' said Simona sweetly, 'I'd have made them wait.'

Kate didn't believe her. She wouldn't have been surprised if Simona had planned the whole thing. Just the thought was enough to increase her discomfort. She came to a decision. She could tell Simona about the undervalued paintings just as easily in a letter. 'Look, Simona, would you order me a taxi, please? There must be someone locally who would drive me to Florence.'

'But what about David?'

'He can follow when he wants.'

'What's the hurry?' Simona looked baffled.

'That's my business. Look, I don't want to be rude, Simona, but I'd like to leave right away.'

'You can't!' Simona had come to stand beside her. 'We haven't had a chance to talk yet.'

'We can talk while I'm waiting for my taxi.'

'But that won't be enough time.'

'For Christ's sake, Simona!' Kate had run out of patience. 'If there's something you want to say to me, then either say it now or put it in a letter.'

'Kate, you musn't go!'

'I've made up my mind.'

Simona caught hold of her sleeve, but Kate shook her off roughly and went back towards the French doors that led into the house. Just as she was about to step into the gloom of the house, there was a cry. 'I *won't* let you go!'

She turned. Horrified, she said, 'Christ, Simona, what the hell are you playing at?'

'This is for real, Kate.' Simona spoke in a low, sure voice. She had climbed up onto the parapet and was outlined against the white haze of the sky. 'The moment you walk through that door, I promise you, I'll jump.' Kate's heart plummeted with dread. An image of Francesca on the bridge over the Arno flashed into her mind.

'Stop being such a bloody fool.'

'I mean it, Kate. If you go now, I've got nothing to lose.'

'Why? For God's sake, Simona, what's all this about?'

'I promise I'll tell you, but you must stay here at least until they come back. Please, Kate, just a little longer.'

'Get down then and we can talk about it.'

'You have to promise first.'

For a moment, Kate was tempted to walk away and wash her hands of Simona and her whole crazy family. Look what had happened when she fell for Francesca's game all those years ago. Ten to one, if she had the courage to call Simona's bluff, she would climb down and try some less dramatic means of persuasion. But there was always the chance she meant it, and it was a chance Kate didn't dare to take.

'Okay,' she agreed reluctantly. 'I'll stay until they get back.'

'Promise?'

'I promise. Now, for God's sake, get down.'

Simona smiled. She spread her arms out like wings, raised her shoulders and tilted her face towards the sun, then stood without moving for a couple of seconds, poised like a bird about to take flight. Kate had stopped breathing, terrified of what was coming. Simona turned and sprang lightly down onto the terrace.

'You bloody fool!' Kate shouted at her. 'You could have been killed.'

'I had to make you stay.'

'Well, here I am.' Kate was shaking. 'You want to talk to me? Well then, talk. I'm listening.'

'But not here. Let's go somewhere we won't be overheard.'

'Oh no, that wasn't part of the deal. We're staying here until David and Mario get back and then I'm leaving, no matter what crazy stunts you pull. So if there's anything you want to say to me, I suggest you say it right now.'

'How can we talk if you're angry?'

'That's your problem, not mine.'

'Oh, Kate, I didn't mean to give you a fright.'

This statement was so blatantly untrue, Kate didn't even bother giving her an answer. She sat down on the edge of a wicker chair and stared at Simona without saying a word. If Simona wanted to talk, then let her talk. So far as Kate was concerned she was just passing the time till David and Mario returned, and she could leave.

Simona sighed, then sat down on a chair facing Kate's, reached out to pick up her coffee cup, then set it down again. Frowning, she gazed across at Kate and said, 'Did you ever go to the circus when you were a child?'

'What?' Simona's ability to come out with the unexpected never ceased to amaze her. 'Simona, for God's sake, why don't you just come to the point?'

'I remember the first time I went,' Simona ignored her question. 'It was when we were living in the States so I must have been about six or seven. There were tigers and elephants, but the thing I remember most was the trapeze act. Right up at the top of the tent, those girls in their spangly costumes had white plumes in their hair just like circus ponies. There were two little platforms and swings hanging from the middle and those men with the huge arms who hung upside down by their legs and held on to the girls so strongly as they swung back and forth under the big top, and then right at the furthest point of the arc the men released them and they flew like birds, beautiful white birds – they didn't have safety ropes in those days – those girls just flew and then right at the last minute when you thought they were going to go too far and they'd fall and be killed, just in time, the other men caught them. It was all timing, of course, timing and trust. I learned then that you can't let go and fly unless you've got a catcher waiting on the other side, a catcher you can trust absolutely.'

She paused. She was watching Kate to see how she reacted to this, her eyes like green lamps, waiting. Kate didn't speak.

Simona said, 'You're my catcher, Kate. I can't fly unless you're there for me.'

There was silence. Kate was still fuming at the way Simona had bludgeoned her into agreeing to stay, and had no intention of making this easy for her, but all the same, curiosity was eroding her anger.

'So here you both are.' Annette's voice broke the silence. Kate and Simona turned almost guiltily towards the doorway as Annette Bertoni emerged onto the terrace on the arm of the ever-smiling Dino. She was wearing a dress of pale flowered crêpe, her legs and arms poking out like brittle twigs. Even though walking was obviously difficult for her, she wore precariously heeled sandals. Kate was impressed by her determination to look elegant and feminine in spite of every obstacle of old age.

'Good morning, Mamma,' said Simona, as Dino helped her mother into a chair.

'Good morning dear. And Kate.' She threw Kate a smile.
'How was your meal last night?'

'Fine, thank you,' said Kate.

Annette nodded. She seemed perfectly lucid this morning.
'Did you try the *cinghiale*, Kate? Giulio is famous for his wild
boar.'

'I had the veal.'

'Ah yes, a good choice.' Annette had settled in her chair and
was fanning herself with her magazine. 'The *cinghiale* is too
heavy for this thundery weather.' She turned to Simona. 'Dino
is going into town this morning to pick up my watch. Do you
want him to get anything for you?'

'No. I'll go in myself later.'

Annette spoke to Dino in Italian, and when she was finished,
he nodded in silent acknowledgement and then left without a
word. A moment later the maid came out with a cup of hot
chocolate for Annette.

Simona said, 'Will you be all right here on your own,
Mamma? Kate and I thought we'd go down to the river.'

'Are you going to swim?'

'We might do. It would be refreshing.'

'I'll probably have a nap,' said Annette. 'You two go off and
enjoy yourselves.'

Kate couldn't work out what was odd about this exchange,
until she realized that for once Simona and Annette were
talking to each other like members of an ordinary family. At La
Rocca, she had learned to expect the unusual at all times.

Simona stood up and Kate followed suit, but when they had
both gone into the house she said, 'I told you already, Simona,
I'm not going down to the river.'

'Why not? We can talk down there without being disturbed.'

'Because I'm leaving as soon as David gets back. There must be somewhere in this house we can talk in private.'

'Yes, but it's so stuffy up here and I thought you'd like to see the river.' Now Simona was looking hurt, as though Kate had rejected some gift.

Kate was on the verge of a retort when the phone rang. While Simona answered it, she went to the front door and watched as Dino climbed into a dark grey Mercedes and drove off slowly away from the house. He was still smiling, even as he drove. As the car disappeared from sight, Kate felt a slight easing of tension. Hardly surprising, she thought wryly: after all, he was the man who'd mistaken her for a rogue wolf and fired at her.

'That was Mario,' said Simona as she put down the phone. She seemed nervous. 'He says they've seen Bella Vista but there's a couple of other places he thought David would like to see.'

'What is he, an estate agent?'

'He just likes to be helpful. They'll be back at lunchtime.'

Briefly, Kate wondered if this whole thing was being set up just to keep her at La Rocca, but then she reminded herself that however paranoid she was, there was no way David was a part of the Bertoni intrigues. And Dino had gone. And it was hot and humid. 'Okay,' she said grudgingly, 'you win. Let's go down to the river, but you'll have to lend me a swimsuit. I could use a swim.'

Ten minutes later, Simona drove in her open-top car almost to the bottom of the drive. They parked, then cut through the scrub until they reached the public road, crossed it and followed a path down to a shingle beach. Trees came down to the water on both sides. 'My sister and I used to come down here when we were teenagers,' said Simona. 'It was the only chance we had to get away from everyone. It's completely private.'

'Doesn't anyone else come here to swim?'

'This is still our land, so they're not supposed to. The students at the Fondazione always use the pool near the villa, but I guess local people do come here sometimes. Yes, look.' She stooped and picked up a beer can and a crumpled cigarette packet. 'What pigs people are.'

The beer can and the cigarette packet were the only signs of life. Apart from the occasional car passing unseen along the road above them, there was nothing but sparse birdsong and the swiftly moving river – no houses, apart from La Rocca and the Villa Beatrice, for miles around. Both sides of the river were densely wooded. It was beautiful, but also, Kate thought, claustrophobic.

They were standing side by side looking across the river when Simona said quietly, 'She always seems very close to me here. That's why I wanted you to come.'

Kate shivered. Some spirit in this secret spot made her uneasy. She slipped off her shoes, went to sit on a boulder a little distance away and dipped her feet in the water. It was icy cold and the ripples made her feet look pale and distorted.

Simona followed and crouched down close by. She said, 'I came down here a lot when I was planning the Fondazione. For years I'd been wondering what to do with my uncle's money – I wanted to use it in a way she would have approved of. I haven't said this to anyone before, but you were her friend, Kate, so you'll understand. She's been by my side through the whole enterprise. I could never have achieved what I did without her help.'

'Why do you have to put yourself down?' asked Kate. 'The

Fondazione was your idea and you had the courage and the vision to set it up. No one else did that.'

'But I couldn't have done it on my own.'

'Well, I expect Mario was a help. But the whole thing was your baby.'

'Was it?' Simona picked up a small pebble and threw it into the river. 'I'm not so sure about that. Sometimes it feels as though, when my sister died, a part of me died too and a part of her became me. Or some of me became her. As though our spirits merged and instead of being two people we're now one.'

Kate looked at her to see if she was joking. Her heart sank: Simona was totally sincere. She sighed and said, 'Simona, that's not how it happens.'

'How can you be sure? I know that when she died I stopped being just me, just a single person, and became me and her together. That's why I named the Fondazione after her, so both our names would have equal prominence.'

'But that's not right, Simona. You were the one with the idea and you put it into practice. You should take the credit for what you've achieved.'

'But why shouldn't she have some of the credit too?'

Kate didn't answer. Simona was so determined to cling onto the fantasy of her omnipresent sister, trying to reconnect her with reality was an impossible task. She said, 'I'm going in for a swim.'

'I've brought you a swimsuit.'

'Don't bother.'

Kate found she was reluctant to borrow anything belonging to Simona and besides, this patch of river was completely private. She stripped quickly down to her pants and walked into the water. The pebbles were painful underfoot and as soon as the water was over her knees she crouched down and let the water carry her. It was cold, fast-moving and deliciously refreshing. She plunged her head under the surface but as soon as she emerged, Simona was in the water beside her.

'Stay on this side,' Simona warned. 'The current is fastest under those trees. We can swim upstream to the corner and then let the river carry us back down.' As Kate began to swim with slow, steady strokes, Simona swam alongside her and said, 'You remember what Francesca was like, Kate. She was always such an idealist, not like me.' The current was strong enough to make their progress upstream very slow. Simona stayed close. 'All I was interested in was clothes and boys and having a good time, not that I had a clue how to do it. She wanted to help people; that's why she went to Florence. She didn't care about the dirt and the hardship.'

Kate would have preferred to swim in silence, but this was too much. 'So?' she protested. 'Francesca wasn't the only one, you know. Hundreds of people went to help out after the flood.'

'But it was different for her,' insisted Simona. 'You saw what the Villa Beatrice was like. And our childhood wasn't like other people's. We never even went to school. No one ever expected us to do any kind of work, let alone working in mud and filth and all the rest of it. All our family ever thought about was money and keeping up appearances, but Francesca wasn't like them. She had ideals!'

Kate realized that Simona's teenage hero-worship for Francesca had been frozen by the tragedy of her early death. Had she lived, Simona would no doubt have come to see her as she was. Instead, the cult of the blessed Saint Francesca was invincible.

'It wasn't such a big deal, Simona,' she said. It was still hard to make any headway against the current, but slowly they were moving away from the shingle beach where they'd left their clothes. 'Everyone has ideals when they're twenty. Just because she'd had a privileged upbringing, that didn't make her any different from everyone else.' They had reached the bend in the river where the water was so shallow Kate grazed her knees on the pebbles and came to a halt, sitting half submerged as she turned to Simona and said crossly, 'If Francesca told you it was all heroic self-sacrifice in the Arno mud, then that was just bollocks. She was having the time of her life, same as everyone else.'

'Are you telling me she didn't care?' demanded Simona angrily. 'Because that's just not true! She did care, she cared passionately! She wasn't greedy and selfish and—'

'Well, she wasn't bloody Mother Teresa either. Sure she cared about what had happened, everyone did, but she had fun too.' Simona looked as if she was about to protest again, so Kate went on quickly, 'And if you really want to know the truth, half the time she was a right royal pain in the butt.'

Simona gasped. 'What do you mean?'

Kate hesitated. She'd never meant to put Francesca down, but what the hell, if Simona was burdened with some crushing posthumous inferiority complex, then maybe Kate was doing her a favour by injecting a dose of reality into her memories. 'Oh, I don't know,' she said vaguely. 'It was little things mostly. She just had trouble fitting in with everyone else. She took it all too seriously. I guess it was her upbringing, I don't know.'

'But she was your friend!' Simona sounded horrified at the criticism.

'Yes, I know, and I loved her. But in the real world, Simona, even your closest friends aren't perfect.'

Something about the way Simona was looking at her made

Kate uneasy. 'I'm swimming back,' she said, launching herself into the deeper part of the water.

'Did you really love her?' Simona splashed in after her.

'Of course I bloody did!'

It must have been an instinct to escape from Simona's crazed questions that made Kate go out into the centre of the river where the current was strongest.

'Watch out!' yelled Simona. 'Stay over this side!'

'I'm fine!' shouted Kate, savouring the tug of the river as it bore her downstream. The next moment, as the current caught her, she realized she was far from fine. She struck out strongly for the bank where she'd left her clothes, but the river spun her past.

'Kate!' Simona's voice was following her. 'Swim to the other side and catch the branch! I'm coming too!'

Kate was being carried along by the water and almost missed it, but just in time she saw the low branch up ahead and caught hold of it, nearly wrenching her arms out of their sockets as the water tried to carry her further downstream.

'Now work your way towards the shore!' yelled Simona.

Kate did what she was told and within moments she was in the gloomy shadows where the water was dark and tranquil. Simona had flung herself into the current after Kate, but with the confidence of long practice she caught hold of the over-hanging branch easily and handed herself along to join Kate in the shadows.

'Now what?' asked Kate. Her teeth were chattering.

'Did you really love her?'

'I already told you, didn't I?' said Kate angrily. The shock of losing control in the river had left her feeling raw and exposed.

'Even though she was a pain in the butt?' asked Simona, her eyes shining.

'Oh, for Christ's sake, all my best friends are pains in the butt. Do you mind telling me how we get back to the other side?'

'It was a good time, wasn't it?'

'Yes. It was magic.'

Simona had worked her way very close to her in the gloom under the overhanging tree. Her hair was plastered against her skull and her skin was glistening with water, making her look sleek and glossy as an otter, her long eyes accentuated in the dappled light. She said, 'It's true, isn't it, Kate? You remember it too. Those weeks in Florence were the best weeks of my life.'

'You mean Francesca's life,' corrected Kate automatically, and then the realization hit her with such force that she nearly let go of the branch. She stopped speaking.

And stared.

The woman's face so close to her own in the dappled light, the woman with the features of Simona, so similar to Francesca's and yet so subtly different, blurred over. In the fuzzy gloom of half-seeing, Simona's remembered face dissolved and reformed. Now it was Francesca's eyes staring back at her, Francesca's mouth drawn back in that hesitant smile. Older by many years, but aged as only Francesca could have aged.

'The best weeks of *my* life,' the woman said again.

Kate's limbs went numb with shock. This time she let go of the branch and would have floated back into the current if the other woman hadn't caught her by the arm. 'Careful, Kate,' she said in a voice that had never been Simona's. 'Drowning's all right, but it's not like the real thing.'

Kate struggled back to grab onto the branch. 'Francesca?' The question came out as barely more than a croak.

She nodded. 'You do recognize me, don't you, Kate?' And

then, when Kate didn't answer, her eyes darkened and she said urgently, 'Tell me you know it's me! Please, just say you know who I am!'

'Jesus!' breathed Kate, too winded to say anything more.

'Please, Kate.' The woman's words were choked with sobs. 'I've held on to this so long it's driven me halfway to crazy and back, but if *you* believe me . . . just say my name. Please.'

Kate was clinging on to the branch as if her life depended on it. Suddenly that few feet of smooth bark seemed like the only sure thing in the world. She blinked and tried to return to the reality she'd been living in until a minute ago, but it was impossible. That world had vanished, raced away in the strong current of the river. There was only one person she'd ever known who looked and sounded like the woman in the water beside her.

'Yes,' she said. 'You're Francesca.' Her teeth were chattering. 'Oh my God, I don't believe it!' And then, seeing the other woman's horrified expression she said quickly, 'But I do believe you. It's okay, Francesca, deep down I think perhaps I've known all along.'

What was she saying? She tried to cling onto the familiar and asked in a shaking voice, 'Now, Francesca, would you please tell me how we get back to our clothes?'

Chapter 38

Future Perfect

By the time they'd looked over Bella Vista and were headed towards a converted school house in a nearby village, David and Mario were discovering they enjoyed each other's company after all. They were in no rush to return to La Rocca, so they stopped for a leisurely drink in the village square.

The beer was cool and refreshing. David, sitting at a table in the shade, watched two old ladies with aprons tied round their enormous hips, loaves of freshly baked bread poking out of their baskets, who were catching up on the day's gossip. An old man walked slowly down the street with his grandson, stopping to exchange a few words with everyone they passed. There was a sense of rhythm and dignity to the lives he was glimpsing, and to an outsider like David it seemed a rich and satisfying life. A future was forming itself in his mind, a future in which he created beauty from old stones and terraced walks, where he was greeted daily by the local shopkeepers, ate in the shade of a well-grown vine and gained a reputation for lavish hospitality with his daughters and friends.

He drank his beer, then said, 'You could make a damn good life in a place like this.'

'Yes.' Mario looked around at the activity of the square. He narrowed his eyes, trying to see what David saw, then said quietly, 'I envy you, David.'

'Why?'

'Because you have the chance to make a new start when most people are thinking about retirement and growing old.'

'Would you like to start afresh somewhere else? What could be better than the life you have?'

Mario didn't answer right away. He was looking thoughtful, then he grinned suddenly and said, 'Canada. If I could choose, I would go to live in Canada.'

'Are you out of your mind?' David assumed he was joking. 'Have you any idea what the climate's like there? And what on earth has Canada got over a place like this?'

Mario shrugged. 'A new beginning,' he said.

'But . . .' David was temporarily lost for words.

'Do you think Kate would like to live here too?'

'We'd have to ask her.'

'You're right. No point trying to guess what women want. There is another place you might like to see, but it's quite a way from here,' said Mario. 'If you're serious, we could have lunch there too.'

'I don't know. We told them we'd get back by noon.' David was already feeling bad about leaving Kate in the lurch so long after she'd made it clear she didn't want to be there on her own. He'd been angry about the row, but knew he had to take some of the blame for it himself. He always said things he regretted after too many drinks.

'We'd be back by three,' said Mario. 'Plenty of time for you and Kate to get back to Florence by evening.'

'Okay then,' said David. After all, where was the harm? And he really was beginning to think he might to settle in a place like this.

'You know,' said Mario as they began walking back to the car, 'I envy you because of Kate, too. It's not often you get a second chance with someone.'

David nodded; 'Kate's pretty special. I hope I don't blow it this time. What about you and Simona?' he asked. He liked knowing how people fitted together and he'd been puzzled by their obvious closeness. Even their antagonism was like the antagonism of a long-married couple.

'We are . . . it is hard to explain. I was married but . . . Simona has always been the most important person for me . . .' Mario hesitated. Their discussion was moving beyond the usual conventions of acquaintances and into territory he'd never yet discussed with anyone.

'She doesn't feel the same way?'

Mario paused, his hand on the roof of his car. He said quietly, 'Years back, I did her an injury,' he said. 'I think, the way she looks at it, I betrayed her. What happened has tied us together, so that neither of us could ever really break free, but also it put a barrier between us. That barrier has never gone away.'

David assumed he was talking about sexual infidelity. He said, 'Hell, Mario, no one's perfect. Even Simona can't hold a grudge for ever.' Though in David's opinion Simona was a neurotic lady and the only real question in his mind was why Mario had stuck by her for so long.

'Your door's not locked,' said Mario, opening his car. 'A non-existent crime rate is another advantage of these sleepy little villages.' When they were both seated and Mario had switched on the ignition, he asked casually, 'So what was your real reason for coming here with Kate?'

'Didn't she tell you?' asked David, without thinking. 'Simona sent her some pictures to be restored. They arrived via a Florentine dealer, so in theory they were anonymous. But Simona had added coded messages to each one. Ingenious, in their way – or devious, depending on how you look at it. Anyway, Kate realized where they must be coming from, so she decided to come over and find out what was going on.' While he was talking, David felt a twinge of unease, remembering Kate had told him not to mention this to anyone. He dismissed his anxiety – there couldn't be any harm in Mario knowing.

'What kind of messages?' Mario still had his hand on the ignition.

Something in his tone made David wary of further indiscretion. He said vaguely, 'Oh, I can't remember the details now. I don't suppose they meant anything.'

Mario glanced at his watch. 'David, I apologize. I have run out of time. I just remembered a junior colleague is phoning me at one o'clock about a patient who's due to be discharged. We will have to drive back to La Rocca at once.'

Chapter 39

By the River

'Why?' asked Kate as they emerged from the river onto the shingle bank where they'd left their clothes. 'And what happened to Simona?'

'She was killed in the accident,' said Francesca, helping Kate to her feet and giving her a towel. Now that she'd taken the plunge, she wanted to pour her story out, and not stop for breath until every last word was spoken; she wanted to shout it to the heavens and paint it in gold letters on the sky, but she could tell that Kate was still dazed with the shock of first hearing. It was vital to tread carefully so as not to overwhelm her precious audience. Her catcher.

'Why the pretence?' asked Kate, pulling the towel over her bare shoulders. She sat, shivering and baffled, looking out over the river. 'I don't understand.'

'Because of my uncle's inheritance, of course. It turned out he'd left everything to Simona. He gave up on me when I went to Florence after the flood. It was so weird: he didn't mind when

I attacked him – in some creepy kind of way, he seemed to think that brought us closer together – but he couldn't bear it when I started to make a life away from my family. By the terms of his will, if anything happened to Simona, my cousin Dario would have inherited the lot.' She paused, then corrected herself. '*When* Simona died, my cousin Dario *should* have inherited the lot. The Fondazione has been created on the most almighty fraud, but at least I've had the satisfaction of knowing I put the money to better use than Dario would've done. On his twenty-first birthday, I made my parents settle a part of my uncle's fortune on him – a small Rubens' worth,' she added with a smile, 'but he blew the lot in about five years. Most of it on drugs. I've been keeping him in rehab ever since.'

'But your uncle must have realized it was Simona – '

Francesca shook her head. 'No one knew how much he'd taken in, because he had a stroke when he heard about the accident. My mother had to tell him and . . . it was too much for him. The old bastard must have had a heart after all. He hung on for several weeks, but he never really recovered.'

'It seems impossible,' said Kate, shaking her head in disbelief. 'How on earth did you get away with it?'

'More easily than you'd think. People see what they want to see – or, sometimes, what they're paid to see – just as you have done over the past few days.'

'But I hadn't seen you in years.'

Francesca hesitated. She was so desperate for Kate to understand the whole story, it was hard to know where to begin. She said, 'Imagine how it must have been in that first week, Kate, the week when you were in hospital. Everyone was stunned by the news: not just of the accident, but my uncle's stroke all in the same day. After a double tragedy like that, people just wanted to be supportive – and when my parents said they needed to be left alone to grieve in private, my guess is their acquaintances were relieved to have an excuse to stay away. That kind of huge disaster frightens people. No one ever thought it was odd. My parents didn't have any real friends and they had always tried to stop me and Simona from mixing too.' She frowned, then said carefully, 'I've spent years trying to figure it all out, Kate. They say families with secrets put up a barrier between themselves and the outside world. Our secret had always been our poverty and debts: our well-heeled facade was totally fake. It was feast or famine, depending on whether my uncle chose to foot the bill or not. That's why we never even went to school but had a succession of useless tutors at home. And because I'd been in America for three years, it was a long time since anyone had seen me and Simona together. Apart from you.'

'So that's why we weren't wanted at the funeral.'

'The funeral, yes.' Francesca was silent for a few moments, then she said quietly, 'I went to my own funeral. Can you imagine what that's like? Seeing all those people weeping for me, seeing my own coffin covered in flowers. Seeing everything through that thick black veil, so convenient for the deception. For years it seemed as though I only ever saw the world through a black veil.'

'Oh, Francesca . . . But you were taking such a risk – how could you know you'd get away with it?'

Kate turned to look at her for the first time since they'd come out of the water. Her arms were covered in goose-bumps, and she looked troubled. Francesca realized she'd omitted to explain the most important fact of all. 'Oh, Kate,' she said, 'I never *wanted* to become Simona! I didn't give a shit about the money, surely you remember that.'

'Then why go along with it?'

'Because I never had any choice! When Simona was killed –
and in such a horrific way – well, I guess I must have lost the
plot for a while. I kept seeing the accident: you were in Mario's
car, your head was covered in blood and I thought maybe you'd
been killed . . . and Simona's head . . .' Her heart was pounding
and there was an acid taste in her mouth as the sequence reeled
through her mind.

'It's okay, Francesca. It's okay.' Kate reached over and put her
hand on her arm. 'It's over.'

Francesca was shaking. She said in a low voice, 'But it's never
over, Kate, never. I keep seeing it again and again, wondering
what I should have done that was different. How I might have
saved Simona.' She was silent for a few moments, thinking.
'Well, maybe I couldn't have stopped the accident. But people
get over tragedies in time, even one like that. For me the
nightmare never ended because I lost control of my life. I even
lost control of who I was. If only I'd stayed calm . . .'

'You can't blame yourself, Francesca. Not after what you'd
been through.'

'You can't blame yourself, Francesca. Not after what you'd
just been through.'

'Yes, I know, that's what people always say, but, oh God,
Kate, I *should* have been stronger! I'm so ashamed, even now,
but the truth is it was a *relief* when they sedated me. I thought
when I came round everything would be okay again, but it
wasn't. It was worse. They told me Simona was dead and you'd
gone back to England and Mario was going to take me to
America so I could get well again. It was all such a fog. Now of
course I realize that it was because of the tranquillizers I was
taking – doctors used to dish them out for just about everything

back then – so I couldn't think straight. I must have signed things – they told me there were a few things Simona should have put her signature on before she died, so I signed her name. They said it was just to make it all "tidy", and I was such a zombie I did whatever they wanted. It wasn't until Mario and I were in the hotel in Florida that I discovered I'd travelled with the "wrong" passport. That was when he told me what they'd done.'

'So Mario was in it too?'

'Oh yes. Mario was involved right from the beginning.'

'Why?'

'The worst part was he kept saying he'd done it for my sake. This terrible wrong had been done to me and he tried to make out I should be *grateful*! He said I needed the money, that I'd never be able to get by without it. He said I shouldn't complain about losing my name because with my uncle's wealth I had the chance to be whoever I wanted. Names don't matter. He claimed he'd done it for my whole family, because my parents would have gone under if my cousin had got the money. And I think maybe he believed it, too.'

'Is that when you tried to kill him?'

'Yes, in that crummy hotel in Florida – God, how I hated that place. I don't know if I really wanted him dead. It was more that I wanted him to hurt the way I was hurting. I don't think he ever understood what it's like to have to spend your whole life pretending to be someone else. If just *once* he'd acknowledged the price I had to pay, then it might have been different. But he didn't. He made a joke of it. "What's in a name?" he said, "A rose smells just as sweet . . . " But it's not true, Kate. A name can be your whole world. He's never understood that. Never.'

'God,' said Kate. 'You must really hate him.'

'Hate him?' Francesca's eyes were swimming with tears. 'Oh, Kate, if only it was that simple. Mario's the only man I've ever loved. I think he used to feel the same about me, but because of everything that happened it never worked out for us. So we've never been able to part and we've never been together properly . . . just torment. For both of us.'

'So how did you survive?'

Francesca laughed bitterly. 'I didn't really, not for years. I stayed away from Italy, and of course that suited everyone just fine. They spun all sorts of stories about what the crazy heiress was up to abroad, but I never found out about that until I came home again. My parents ran the Beatrice estate and sent me money. So I travelled. I even got married once. I was in New Mexico and we'd been living together for six months. He was the kindest, gentlest man you ever knew. His name was Paul Denver. Just an ordinary guy – and I tried to be his ordinary wife, Fran Denver. I told him Fran was my nick-name, even though it said Simona on my passport. For a while, I was almost happy with Paul. But then he started asking questions, wanting to know more about me. And I couldn't tell him, so one day I just left and set off on my travels again.' She fell silent, bumping up against the impossibility of ever explaining to Kate what those empty years had been like when 'Francesca' no longer existed and 'Simona' felt like a death sentence – sometimes it was only under an assumed name that she felt she had a chance of being herself. She slid Kate a sideways glance and said, 'I took on other names, sometimes, just to see what they felt like. A few times, Kate, I pretended to be you.'

'Me?' Kate looked shocked.

'Yes, if you go through the records of one of the ashrams in Poona, you'll discover that a Kate Holland made several visits.'

'Why did you choose my name?'

'Because you were always so confident, Kate, so sure of who you were and your place in the world. All that time when I was floundering around, I thought: *Kate* would have known how to handle this, Kate would never let other people take over her life and wreck it. Sometimes I felt as though I was dissolving, becoming a non person, but you were always . . . *solid.* At least, that's how I remembered you.'

'But the last time you saw me, I was leaving with Mario. Weren't you angry about that?'

'Not really, I envied you. I wished I had the courage to grab what I wanted and head off for freedom. But I couldn't even hang on to my own name.'

'God, Francesca. That's so dreadful.'

'Yes.' Francesca felt a kind of calm spreading through her body. It was all she had wanted, all these years. Not pity or sympathy. Just someone who recognized who she was and accepted what she'd been through. It didn't seem such a lot to ask, yet it had taken her half a lifetime to find it. Half naked and sitting on the riverbank in the afternoon sun, she dared to hope her life might one day make a kind of sense, after all.

'But I still don't understand,' said Kate. 'If you thought I could have helped, why didn't you come and find me back then? Why wait until now?'

Why? Francesca remembered the despair of those rootless days. 'That was the whole trouble, Kate. You were the one person I couldn't reach.'

'Why on earth not? You know I would have helped you,

Francesca. If it was so impossible for you to carry on as Simona, why didn't you just tell the truth?'

'My God, you think I didn't want to? I imagined it a thousand times, but Mario had developed very sensitive antennae and he always guessed when I've been planning to come clean. He always found a way to persuade me not to. There would have been a huge scandal – well, I could have survived that. But there'd have been a court case too, because of the money, and my parents would probably have ended up in prison. That's what Mario kept telling me, and I think he was right. And they'd already suffered so much, with Simona's death and everything – how could I inflict that on them too?'

'But it was *their* fault, not yours. Why should you pay the price of their mistakes?'

'I know, but, oh, Kate, it's easy to see it clearly now, but it's different when you're in the middle of it and it's your own family who would have to pay. From my point of view they'd wrecked my life, but according to their way of looking at things, they'd done the best for me they could. I had the wealth they'd always thought was so important. And it's not easy to shop your parents. I did go to see our family lawyer once, but Mario had got to him first.'

'You mean the lawyer was corrupt as well?'

'No, I don't think so. It was more subtle than that. My mother told people I was mentally unstable and had these occasional psychotic outbursts – of course, the fact that I'd attacked Mario and my uncle, and spent those years in the clinic before Florence, meant the odds were stacked against me. Mario did the same thing last night when we were at the restaurant, do you remember? I mean, who would *you* trust? A crazy heiress who keeps changing her story or the parents who've been running the show and their friend the well-respected doctor?'

Kate turned slowly. She said, 'I trust you, Francesca.'

There was a long silence. Francesca let the words enfold her, like the circles of sound from an ancient bell. *I trust you, Francesca.* Then she whispered, 'Thank you, Kate.'

'Francesca,' Kate said the word again.

Francesca sat quietly. Her spirit began to inhabit the name that had been waiting for her all these years.

Then she frowned. There was still so much more to get out in the open. Now she'd started, she felt as though she wouldn't stop until the last lie had been exposed. She said, 'The worst part of living a lie is that to make it work you have to believe it yourself. Once I got the idea for the Fondazione and saw a way to make some good come out of all the horrors, I came back here. To achieve what I wanted, I had to forget about Francesca and become Simona. It's what Mario had been telling me to do all along.'

'Jesus. That must have been hard.'

'Yes it was.'

After a while, Kate asked, 'So why are you telling me now? What's changed?'

'In some ways, it's a question of what *hasn't* changed. However hard I tried, I could never really shake off the feeling of being an imposter. It was like that story about the emperor's new clothes. Sooner or later, I'd be found out. Every time I stood up to make a speech, like yesterday, I'd be waiting for a member of the audience to yell out that I was a fraud. Even when I answered the phone, I always expected someone to ask for Francesca, not Simona. For years I've had a recurring nightmare where I'm stabbing my reflection in the mirror, only instead of being glass, the mirror is made of flesh, and real blood comes out. But I kept going until my father died. That was when I sent you the first picture.'

'"Truth is the Daughter of Time?"'

'That's right. I wasn't very clear exactly what I wanted from you. I guess I was trying to reach you, see what would happen next. Because something had to give. I knew I couldn't live the lie for ever, but I'd always tried to protect my father – sometimes he seemed to be as much a victim of my mother's schemes as I was. Once he was dead, I felt more free to act. And you've seen what's happened to my mother – no court would find her fit to plead the way she is now.'

'And you?'

'When my father was dying, he still called me Simona. It terrified me, the idea that I too might die and no one would mourn for Francesca, not this time, they'd be grieving for someone who never existed. It's one thing to live a lie, but to contemplate dying, with the lie still in place – can you imagine what that feels like?'

'No. I can't.' Kate grinned ruefully. 'I guess I must be solid, after all.'

Francesca stood up and went to the edge of the river. She reached up her arms and spread them wide. She wanted to embrace the universe. 'I've imagined this feeling for so long. What it's like to be me, Francesca. No more pretending.'

'And what does it feel like?'

Francesca turned. She saw Kate looking up at her, seeing Francesca. 'Better than I ever imagined,' she said. She began to pick up her clothes.

A little later, when they'd dressed and were walking slowly along the path that led away from the river, Kate asked, 'I still don't understand why you chose me.'

'Do you mind?'

'No, I'm flattered, but all the same . . .'

'It's odd?' asked Francesca anxiously.

'I suppose so.'

'Well, in a way, I don't think it was the real you I wanted. I'd built up a picture of an imaginary Kate Holland in my mind, kind of halfway between how you used to be and an idealized person, the sort of mother I wished I'd had, or the perfect friend and confessor. That's why it's taken me two days to pluck up the courage to tell you – I guess I had to get to know the real Kate a bit before I knew if I could trust you.'

'But why me? There must have been other people you could have told.'

Francesca walked ahead in silence before she answered. They emerged from the scrubby undergrowth to the place on the driveway where the car was parked. She said, 'You were my only link to the person I was starting to be in Florence, the person I might have become if I'd made it back to Florence the day Simona was killed. You know that poem about the road less travelled?'

'Robert Frost? Of course. "Two roads diverged in a wood and I—"'

'"I took the one less travelled by." Well, that's true of my life and I hope to God no one else has ever had to travel the road I've been on. When I was with you and the others I was just setting out on the road I knew I wanted to travel on for the rest of my life. I thought I had found a way to be different from the person my parents were trying to turn me into. After Simona died I lost all that, I forfeited even my own name. Until now.'

They got into the car and flung their wet towels in the back.

'So what happens now?' asked Kate.

'That depends.' Suddenly she felt afraid. 'You will help me, won't you, Kate?'

'Yes. I'll help you.'

She let out a sigh of relief. 'The first thing I have to do is go away for a few days, somewhere Mario can't find me. From there I can work out a proper plan.'

'Why is it so important to get away from Mario?'

'He'll do anything he can to stop me, because he will lose everything if I go public – his status, his reputation, his wealth – everything. He might even end up in gaol.'

'But you were implicated too. People may not believe you didn't know what you were signing after Simona died. Aren't you worried about that?'

Francesca almost laughed. 'Believe me, Kate, I've given this a lot of thought, but no prison cell could be worse than the lies I've been trapped in all these years.'

'Are you sure, Francesca? Why risk everything now?'

'I have to, Kate. Surely you understand that.'

'I guess I do.'

She sounded doubtful and Francesca wondered if someone as straightforward as Kate could ever realize why it was so vital she live out the rest of her days as her true self. Kate must find it impossible to imagine what it was like to live a lie. There was another dream that had haunted her for years. She was in a house, neither La Rocca nor the Villa Beatrice but some place that contained the atmosphere of both houses: she was wearing a mask, a beautiful mask, a bit like Deception in the first painting she'd sent to Kate. And when the time came to remove it, she couldn't, because the mask had stuck to her skin. Or else her skin had grown into the mask. She was trapped, and the fake flesh was growing over her eyes . . .

She shuddered. Later there would be time to talk to Kate about these things. For now, it was enough that Kate believed in her and was prepared to help her achieve her goal. 'Mario mustn't guess what I'm up to,' said Francesca, firing up the engine and turning the car round so they could head back to La Rocca. 'God knows what he'd do to save his skin.'

Chapter 40

Gathering

Thunder was close. High white clouds blotted out the sun, but the air was still oppressively hot. Scarcely aware of his passenger, Mario drove swiftly along the narrow roads through the hills, his only thought to get back to La Rocca before it was too late.

Apartment 89, Torrens Heights was the flat he'd bought for himself in Montreal. He'd always known that so long as there was a chance her parents might be prosecuted for fraud, Simona, as he had trained himself always to think of her, would remain silent. But since her father's death his own security was less certain and he'd laid elaborate plans for his escape, should escape ever become necessary.

In Canada, Dr Mario Bassano would no longer exist. The flat – which Mario himself had not yet seen – had been bought in the name of Dr Guido Neroni, a man fortunate enough to have various bank accounts in the country which contained sufficient funds for him to live comfortably until it was safe to access his assets in Switzerland. Gaining the necessary documentation for his new life – including the CV of a doctor who had died tragically young – had been complex and time-consuming, but it was all now in place.

But at a price. Mario had realized some years before that his salary, though good, was nowhere near enough to finance a whole new life. He needed capital. The solution to his problems presented itself when he met Luigi Rinaldi, a Milan art dealer who was not too fussy about the provenance of the works he sold. Signor Rinaldi was invited to value some of the paintings at La Rocca when Simona was raising money to pay for the Fondazione. He was scrupulously accurate – except for half a dozen works whose current value he grossly underestimated. A private sale was arranged for two of them. His clients got a bargain while both Mario and he split the difference; Simona was none the wiser. This excellent arrangement was repeated with two more paintings three years later.

It was highly unfortunate that Simona must have decided that the final pair, being of limited value, would serve as a way of contacting Kate Holland, with the result that the time may well have arrived for him to put his escape plan into action.

From time to time in recent months he'd found himself looking forward to starting again as Dr Neroni. There was much in his present existence that had been compromised; sometimes he thought he'd stopped liking Mario Bassano altogether. The new doctor was not about to make the mistakes of the old one. Dr Neroni would probably confine himself to private practice. Mario had no doubt that he would be able to build up a fine reputation in a new country. He was good at his work and always popular with patients. He even had a scheme for establishing a school devoted to the therapeutic techniques he'd developed over the years – all he needed was a clean slate, a chance to start afresh. If ever Simona decided to destroy everything they'd achieved together over these past years, then Dr Mario Bassano would be out of the country and starting his new life within twenty-four hours. All that was necessary for the success of his plan was sufficient warning. There must be no surprises.

A lorry, an impossibly slow lorry, was blocking his way on a long, winding hill. Mario rode its bumper for half a mile or so, then leaned on the horn and cursed.

'What's the hurry?' asked David.

The lorry changed down into first in a cloud of dust and slowed to a crawl. Mario swung out to the left on a right-hand turn but there was no room to overtake. He jammed the flat of his palm on the horn then pulled out further as the road straightened. His foot was hard down on the accelerator when a windscreen glared in the dust cloud ahead and he just had time to swerve back in behind the lorry. A pickup truck rattled down the hill past him.

'Jesus!' exclaimed David. 'Are you trying to get us both killed?'

Mario didn't answer. Sweat was pouring off his face. Getting past the damned lorry had become the most important task of his life. Simona had got Kate to come to the Villa Beatrice and had lied to him about it. She must have been planning this for months, and now that it might be necessary for Dr Guido Neroni to start his existence, Mario knew with absolute certainty that he would hate it. A fresh start in a cold North American city would be for him grey nothingness, all the people and places he loved left far behind. At best he might be able to eke out a half-life among strangers in an unfamiliar landscape, an exile not just from his country and home but from his very self. He had to act now, to prevent the destruction of everything that made his life worth living.

White-faced, he cursed the pigheaded driver whose crap lorry was threatening his entire future, then, pulling out again, he saw his chance, changed down into second, pressed on the accelerator and roared past. He swerved back in front of the lorry just in time to avoid smashing into an elderly man on a Vespa who was so shaken by his narrow escape that he pulled off the road altogether and stopped.

'Christ!' David had been transfixed by the sight of the old fellow swerving onto the rough ground. 'What's got into you?'

Mario eased up a fraction, then said with exaggerated calm, 'I'm worried about Simona.'

'So getting us both killed is going to help Simona?'

'I think Kate may be in danger, also.'

'Kate? What kind of danger?'

'I should have explained to you before,' said Mario with a sigh. 'I should have warned you, but I had not realized how bad the situation was until you told me about the pictures.'

David ran his fingers through his hair. 'What the hell do the pictures have to do with anything?'

'Simona is a sick woman, David. Ever since Francesca died she has been – well, let us be generous and call it fragile. She was there, remember. She witnessed her sister being killed. The accident was not how people think – not how Simona thinks she remembers it. I have worked long and hard to protect her from her nightmares and my efforts have been rewarded. In spite of everything, Simona's made a good life and she deserves to be proud of what she has done with the Fondazione.'

'But?'

'I hate having to say this, David, and I'm only telling you

because I think she may have got to Kate. Ever since the accident, Simona has suffered from delusions. Not all the time – they come and go and for months, years even, she can appear perfectly rational and sane. But then something happens to trigger off a relapse – something like you and Kate showing up at La Rocca – and she enters a fantasy world. And in that parallel world she believes herself to be the innocent victim of massive injustice. She is under a compulsion to destroy the people who, according to her deluded view of the situation, have done her these terrible wrongs.'

'And that includes you?'

'Oh yes.' Mario smiled grimly. 'I am the number-one culprit.'

'Is that why she tried to attack you?'

'She tried to *murder* me, David. Not once, but three times. I've always managed to cover it up, and now when the subject comes up, I make light of it, for her sake, but they were serious attempts, believe me. She becomes like a wild animal.'

'Jesus.' David was thoughtful. Then, 'But why would she want to have a go at Kate?'

'Because Kate was there when Francesca died. Like her mother, I think Simona still blames her for her sister's death, which is totally unfair, of course, but when Simona gets into one of her psychotic states, fairness doesn't enter the picture.'

'I still don't see why she should blame Kate, just because she was there.'

'It was more than just being there. As always, there is a grain of truth to feed Simona's delusions. Let's say that if Kate hadn't been there, Francesca would most likely still be alive today.'

'I don't understand,' said David.

'It's complicated,' said Mario, slowing down for the narrow bridge over the river. 'Later I can explain, when the danger is past and we have more time. But those pictures . . . If she has gone to such lengths to lure Kate back to Villa Beatrice, then it may well be that she is planning some kind of revenge for what she still sees as Kate's part in her sister's death.'

'Jesus,' said David again.

They turned the car off the road and began the winding ascent to the Villa Beatrice and La Rocca.

'If my suspicions are correct,' said Mario grimly, 'then we should never have left them alone together this morning. Kate is in real danger. I only hope we are in time.'

Chapter 41

Beginnings

'Kate, I don't know if I can go through with this.'

Francesca sat on the edge of her bed, a small overnight case open beside her. Apart from a knitted silk top, it was empty.

'Why not?'

'It's all . . . too big.' Francesca gestured hopelessly. The exultation she'd known beside the river had vanished and she felt sick and empty. 'I'm . . . I'm frightened, Kate. So many other people are going to get hurt, and all because of me.'

Kate stood in front of her, her feet rooted in the land of ordinary people, so solid and sensible and so horribly far away. 'So what's the alternative?' asked Kate. 'Carrying on as before, is that what you want? Living the rest of your life as someone else?'

'I can't go back to that. But . . .' Francesca shook her head.

'But what?'

'I . . . I haven't told you everything.' She was whispering now, not sure if it was ever going to be possible to get the words out.

'It was different down there, in the open air. But when I come back to this place, where my uncle lived, it all changes . . .'

'Why, Francesca?' Kate knelt down in front of her so their eyes were level. 'Your uncle is dead. This is your home now.'

'But . . .' Francesca twisted her head, unable to look into Kate's eyes. 'Do you remember the *camerino*?' She was aware that Kate nodded. Bile was rising in her throat as she forced herself to say, 'Kate, oh, Kate, he *killed* people. He had photographs of their bodies. He . . . he enjoyed looking at them and he made me look at them too. He said I was special, that I was like him and I'd understand . . . it was . . . horrible.'

'Oh my God,' Kate breathed, her face ashen. 'You poor baby.'

She reached out to put her arms round her, but Francesca drew back. 'No, don't touch me.'

'Why not?'

Francesca shook her head.

She said, 'When I got the idea for the Fondazione, the first thing I did was have the *camerino* pulled down. Now most people don't even know it existed.'

'You did the right thing,' said Kate. 'You made something positive and strong come out of it all. You ought to be proud.'

Francesca was silent for a few moments, gripping Kate's hands tightly, then she raised her head and said, 'Thank you, Kate.' A burden was shifting from her heart. Not the whole burden, that was never going to be entirely gone, but enough. Feeling stronger again she said, 'It would kill me to go back to how things were, and I'm tired of paying the price for others.'

'Okay,' said Kate, getting on her feet again. 'Let's pack. Why don't you come and stay with me in London for a bit? There's plenty of room in my flat.'

'Thanks, but it wouldn't work. If we disappear together, that's the first place they'd look. And there's so much to do.' Suddenly furious with herself, Francesca stood up and began throwing things into her suitcase. 'God, I'm so useless. I should have worked this out years ago. All I've ever thought about is telling you. Now I don't know what to do next. Do you think I ought to tell the police, or get a lawyer? And what kind of lawyer do I want? Maybe it would just be easiest to make an announcement in the paper or—'

'All that matters right now is getting you away from here. Damn!' Kate had crossed to the window and was looking down on the driveway as Mario's car crunched to a halt on the gravel. 'They're back.'

For a moment Francesca was frozen with fear. But it was old fears, the fears of a woman who'd been forced to make a false life in order to protect others. As her terror ebbed, she drew herself up to her full height and said firmly, 'Well, I guess we're going to have to fake it, Kate, just till lunch is over. Mario will go home after that. He usually spends Saturday afternoon with his daughters.'

'He can't stop you from leaving if you want to.' Kate still hadn't understood the complexity of it all. 'Why don't you just tell him we've decided to go off on our own for a couple of days – or even just for lunch? Mario doesn't have the right to tell you what to do.'

Francesca took her suitcase off the bed and shoved it out of sight. It was impossible to explain that Mario had been her closest ally as well as her gaoler: breaking free was going to be the hardest thing she'd ever done. She said, 'I know, Kate, but just for now, let's go down and pretend nothing has happened.'

'If you're sure that's what you want.'

'Quite sure. Oh, Kate!' Impetuously Francesca flung her arms round her friend and hugged her. 'One more hour, maybe two, and then I'll be *free!*'

Francesca stepped back. She was resolute, all her earlier fears vanishing as she set her sights on the new life ahead. Now it was Kate who was lagging behind. She said, 'Is that why you and Simona followed us when Mario and I were leaving? Because you wanted to come back to Florence with me?'

'Of course.' Francesca was surprised by the question. 'Why else would we have come after you?'

'I thought perhaps you were trying to stop me from going off with Mario.'

'You can't force people to care for you. I knew that even then. I was angry with you, but . . .' She smiled again. Now that she had decided to break free, nothing was going to dampen her spirits for long. 'It was all so complicated. Even though I was shocked and unhappy, there was a part of me that recognized you were doing me a favour by removing him from my life. I loved Mario, in a way I've always loved him, but I could never be my own person while I was with him – and no one is worth sacrificing your own self for.'

Kate said quietly, 'Thank you, Francesca. It means a lot to know that.'

'Simona never got away,' said Francesca. 'Maybe it sounds corny, but I owe it to her memory to make something decent out of the rest of my life. This time, we have to succeed.'

They went out of the bedroom. Men's voices were rising up from the drawing room where drinks were laid out before lunch.

'Okay,' said Francesca as she paused at the top of the stairs. 'This next couple of hours will be the last lie. Do you think we can fake it, Kate?'

'Of course,' said Kate. 'But you have to carry on looking like Simona, just a bit longer.'

'Sure,' said Francesca, starting down the stairs.

But already she'd forgotten the trick of how being Simona was done.

Chapter 42

Under the Angels

The scent of home-cooked minestrone was rising from the kitchen as Francesca and Kate started down the stairs. It seemed extraordinary that such an everyday activity as lunch could still take place when her whole world had been turned round. Francesca stepped carefully; from now on she musn't put a foot wrong.

'Ah, there you are. I wondered where you'd got to.' Mario emerged from the drawing room, a drink in his hand, as they came down the stairs. He was smiling, but his eyes were wary.

'We didn't realize you were back so soon,' said Kate. 'How did the house-hunting go? Did you see anything you liked?'

David had come to stand beside Mario. He was watching her closely. Francesca recognized the look in his eye: she'd seen it so many times before on the faces of new aquaintances, old friends. It meant Mario had got to him and told her she was mad – oh, he had a hundred ways of wrapping it up and making it sound like a judicious, reluctant, medical opinion –

so that whatever she said or did would be perceived through the filter of her supposed madness. He said casually, too casually, 'Oh, none of the places we saw were quite right. But there's an old schoolhouse I'd like to check out some time. Did you have a good morning?'

'Fine,' said Kate. 'We went down to the river and swam. The water was freezing, but very refreshing – perfect for this hot weather.'

'You should try it, David.' Francesca knew her voice sounded wooden. It was so hard to act naturally when the person you were talking to thought you were crazy.

'I'd love to,' he said. 'But unfortunately Kate and I have to leave after lunch.'

Kate touched her lightly on the shoulder. 'Some other time, maybe,' said Francesca.

Kate's brief gesture of support had been a mistake. Mario was suspicious. He knew her too well and was sensitive to all her moods; he must know that a fundamental shift had taken place inside her. However hard she tried to look like the old Simona, she felt her new self insisting that everyone take notice. Mario forced himself to smile, that old, calculating smile, then said, 'You both look . . . as if the swim has done you good. Ah, Annette.'

Signora Bertoni had her arm through Dino's as she walked in slowly from the terrace. She was concentrating too much on the task of walking in her delicate sandals to give any attention to the group watching her from the hall. Now that she was on the verge of breaking free, Francesca was able to recognize that her mother was a frail old woman whose mental faculties were slipping away, rather than the tormentor who had ruled her life for so many years.

'*Buon giorno*, Mamma,' said Francesca, every nerve taut with the effort of appearing normal. 'Now you are here we can begin lunch.'

She and Kate had reached the bottom of the stairs. Francesca resisted the temptation to stay close to Kate, and slipped her arm through David's. 'I want to hear all about the places you saw,' she said as they moved towards the dining room. 'Just think, we may end up neighbours. Wouldn't that be great?'

Kate and Mario followed. Once they were in the dining room, its windows open to let in the September warmth, Francesca went to stand behind her chair at the head of the table. David moved to her right. Mario walked round behind her and said softly, so that only she could hear, 'Francesca, what's going on?'

She jumped, as though she'd been touched with a cattle prod, then drew in a deep breath and said quietly, 'Don't you mean Simona?'

His hand closed round her upper arm, forcing her to turn towards him. 'Simona, of course. How foolish of me.'

She was thinking fast. With that sixth sense that never let him down, Mario must have guessed everything. She had to get away from La Rocca before he thought of a way to stop her. She didn't know what he would come up with, but he was resourceful, and had always found a means of blocking her escape in the past.

She looked across at Kate. 'Kate,' she said coolly. 'Where's that necklace you were wearing when we went down to the river?'

Kate's hand flew up to her throat. There was no necklace, but thank the Lord she obviously understood the significance of what Francesca was saying. 'I – I must have left it by the river,' she said.

'That's just what I was afraid of,' said Francesca. 'I'm sorry, but you'll have to start lunch without us. Kate and I need to go back and look for it. We'll only be five minutes.'

She began to move into the hall, but Mario blocked her way. 'Can't it wait till later?' he asked. 'No one except us ever goes down to the river. Kate's necklace will be quite safe.'

'All the same,' said Francesca. 'I'd be easier in my mind . . .'

'What's so important?' he asked.

Kate said firmly, 'It's a pearl necklace that belonged to my mother. I'd hate anything to happen to it.'

David was looking baffled. He said, 'I don't remember ever seeing you in pearls, Kate.'

'A pearl necklace,' said Mario. 'No wonder Kate is concerned. I tell you what, Kate, I'll drive you down myself.'

'No,' said Francesca. 'I'm going.'

'There's no need to trouble—' began Mario, his voice like steel.

'I tell you, Mario, I – will – *go*!' she blazed. She felt the last vestiges of Simona falling away from her as she squared up to him. There was a long silence, a silence that seemed to stretch endlessly, no one speaking, and then, more quietly, she repeated, 'It's no good, Mario. I'm going,' and this time her words carried a different meaning altogether.

'Going?' His face was blank.

'Yes, going.' Dear God, the relief of speaking plain. She turned briskly to Kate. 'Will you get my things for me, Kate? My passport's in my bag. There's no point in staying any longer.'

'Passport?' asked David.

'Simona, for God's sake, consider what you're doing!' Mario caught hold of her arms but she shook herself free.

'Francesca!' she yelled. 'It's Francesca, remember! From now on everybody gets to call me by my real name!'

'What the hell?' asked David. Francesca saw him move towards the doorway, as though intending to stop her by force. 'Is this the delusions you were telling me about, Mario?'

'David, stay out of this,' said Kate.

'You don't understand,' he said urgently. 'She's not right in the head and she's bloody dangerous. This whole business has just been a way to get you here, so she can trap you.'

Francesca gripped the back of the chair. If Kate believed what David was saying about her now . . . 'Kate, please. Don't listen to him.'

Kate smiled, that generous smile Francesca had waited half a lifetime to see. 'It's okay, Francesca. He just can't see the whole picture yet, that's all.'

Mario ignored them both. 'Don't do this to us,' he pleaded with Francesca. 'Don't throw everything away just for a *name*. Christ, Simona, what's the point? Just think for a moment, please, think before you act.'

She laughed. Did he really imagine this was just a spur-of-the-moment whim? 'Think? *Think?* I've had a whole lifetime to think this through and now I've made up my mind. There's no way I'm turning back now and there's nothing you can do to stop me. So don't even try.'

Mario rounded on Kate, his face contorted with fury. 'You're to blame for this, Kate! She was fine till you showed up.'

'Don't blame Kate. She's helping me, sure, but unlike poor old Simona, who you've kept wrapped round your little finger all these years, *Francesca* Bertoni is going to make her own decisions.'

'Will someone please tell me what's going on,' said David helplessly. No one even glanced in his direction.

Annette was standing behind her chair, still leaning on Dino's arm. Her head was tilted and she was sniffing the air, like an animal that scents danger. Now she said sharply, 'Simona, what's all this carry-on?'

'I'm not Simona,' she said firmly. 'You know I'm not and I'm through pretending. I'm sorry, Mamma, but I couldn't wait any longer. No one going to blame you. It's too late for that.'

'Not Simona?' Her mother was looking around in anguish. 'Not Simona? Then where's my baby? What have you done with her?'

'She died, Mamma, you know she did. She died in the accident. I've just pretended to be her, like you always wanted, but I can't do it any longer. I'm Francesca.'

'Francesca? But Francesca died . . . in that accident . . . when Kate . . .' Francesca watched, horrified, while her mother's eyes flickered round the table, then finally lit on Kate. Annette seemed to shrink visibly as she said, 'Dino, help me please. It's getting kind of hard to stand.' You poor thing, thought Francesca, you're just a pathetic old woman.

'Of course, Mamma. This has been a shock for you.' Francesca took hold of her mother's other arm and together she and Dino guided her to a chair.

'Simona—' began Mario.

She flared up again. 'Damn you, Mario! From now on I only answer to Francesca!'

'Francesca?' Annette looked up at her in bewilderment. 'What's going on? Are we going to be ruined, Mario?' She was fiddling with the drawstring of her beaded bag. Then she said plaintively, 'Damnation, I've brought the wrong bag with me. Go get the other one, Dino, the one with the dragon embroidered on it. It's in my drawer. Well, go on then, don't just stand there.'

'He doesn't understand you, Mamma.' Francesca repeated her mother's instructions in Italian. A faint look of comprehension spread across his placid face, the only time Kate had ever seen any expression there at all.

'Yes, yes,' said Annette petulantly, adding further orders in Italian. Dino left the dining room and his heavy footsteps could be heard as he went up the stairs.

'I'll fetch our bags too,' said Kate.

'You're going?' asked David. But Kate followed Dino without bothering to explain.

Mario was talking to her now in Italian. '*Mia cara*, please. I don't understand why you have to destroy everything we have built up together.'

'Because it was all built on lies, Mario, don't you understand that? And I can't live a life of lies any longer. I want everyone to know the truth about me, about my family, no matter what.' She turned to Kate who had reappeared in the doorway. 'Shall we go?'

'Where's Dino?' demanded Annette. 'Where's my bag?'

'He's coming, Mamma.' Francesca tried to speak gently, but she was unable to keep the excitement out of her voice. 'I'm going away for a few days, but I'll be back again soon, I promise.'

'I don't want you. I want Dino.'

'And what do you think you're going to do now?' asked Mario, standing stiffly in front of the door. 'What do you plan to do with this great truth of yours?'

'I'll tell you when I've made up my mind.'

'When you get back?' He laughed bitterly. 'I won't be here.'

'Well, then . . .'

'Please, *mia cara*.' He was pleading with her. 'Don't do this thing.'

'I have to.'

'I won't let you.'

'You can't stop me.'

'No? My dearest love.' Suddenly his voice ached with tenderness. 'How will you manage without me?'

Francesca felt herself falter. It had been her Achilles heel all through: according to this version of her story she was a frail and damaged person who could never survive without him. Kate spoke up: 'Francesca will manage just fine! She doesn't need you any more, Mario.'

He turned on her in a fury. 'She will, eh? And what makes you such an expert all of a sudden?' He snatched Francesca's case from her hand and said, 'I'm not letting you go! Okay, then, you want the truth? You really want the truth?'

'Stop it, Mario,' said Kate. 'Francesca's coming with me.'

'You want the truth?' he demanded again. Francesca stared at him. 'You're tired of lies and you want everyone to know what really happened? Are you sure?'

Francesca felt a kind of paralysis creeping through her limbs. Then she nodded slowly.

Mario hesitated. 'Please, don't make me do this.'

Francesca said, 'Hand me back my case, Mario. We're leaving.'

He turned on her. 'Oh no, it's not that easy! You think you can walk away, just like that? My God, I've spent my whole life protecting you from the truth and now this is all the thanks I get.'

'Forget it Mario, I don't need that kind of protection any more.'

'No? So how come you've been telling yourself lies all this time?'

'I haven't . . .'

'You were there, *mia cara*, you know what really happened.'

'But—'

'You were there when Simona was killed. You saw the whole thing.'

Francesca faltered. She said, 'But you told me—'

'I told you what you wanted to hear. That Simona had died in an accident. Well, it wasn't an accident. It was deliberate.'

'What are you talking about?'

'Ask your mother,' said Mario. 'She can tell you. She was there too.'

'Mamma?' whispered Francesca.

Her mother seemed to have shrunk into herself. She looked like a hunted animal as she fumbled with her two little bags, the beaded one and the silk one with the embroidered dragon that Dino had just brought down.

'Why d'you think she went so crazy after Simona died?' asked Mario contemptuously. 'Wouldn't any woman go mad when she'd been responsible for the death of her own daughter?'

'Stop it, Mario!' Francesca felt suddenly cold. 'Don't say those things! You can't stop me from leaving, no matter what you tell me.'

'I thought you wanted the truth!' he said in triumph.

'It's madness. Why would my mother have wanted to kill Simona?'

'Oh, that part was unintentional. She was trying to kill Kate.'

'Kill me?' asked Kate.

'Yes. Poor Simona just got in the way.'

Francesca was shaking with horror as Kate turned to her and said, 'Francesca, don't listen to him. He's only saying this to upset you and stop you from leaving. Let's go before he comes out with any more crazy lies.'

'It's the truth,' said Mario. 'Ask her.'

They all looked at Annette. She was sitting on the chair, the two bags in her lap, tears streaming down her face. 'He said it was the price,' she muttered helplessly.

'I don't believe you,' said Kate stubbornly.

'Why the hell would anyone want to kill Kate?' asked David.

'That's all I ever got out of her,' said Mario. ' "He said it was the price." God knows what she meant by it. Maybe she was just mad at Kate for stealing both her daughters. Maybe there was another reason.'

Suddenly Francesca felt as though she was going to faint. Kate went to put her arms round her. Leaning on her, Francesca murmured, 'Mamma was in the Mercedes . . .'

'You see,' said Mario cruelly, 'you do remember after all.'

'So how did Simona die?' asked David.

Mario was watching Francesca as he began to speak. 'Well, then I'll tell you, since suddenly the truth is what we want. When Kate and I left in the Topolino, Francesca and Simona were following right on the Vespa. One Vespa. Francesca, you were sitting on the back. You tried to overtake. God knows why, I've often wondered. It was that part when the ground falls away steeply to the left. One misjudgement and you'd have gone over the edge. I pulled over hard, and that's when Kate was thrown forward, and hit her head. She was out cold. I stopped the car and Francesca, you and Simona pulled up a little way ahead. You must have heard the crash. You started coming back. All I could think of was getting Kate to a hospital. But then Annette drove up behind us in the Mercedes and smashed into the back of my Topolino. I thought it was an accident, but when she reversed her car and smashed into the Top a second time, I realized she was ramming my car deliberately. It had begun to roll. Simona was hysterical. She ran forward to try to stop her mother doing it again. And I think, maybe the third time it happened, Annette wanted to stop, but she must have been confused and her foot hit the accelerator instead of the brake. I know she was screaming when her car ran into Simona. Simona was thrown up in the air and when she came down she fell across the windscreen of the Vespa. That was what almost severed her head from her body. You saw it all, Francesca. You were screaming, screaming, screaming, until I put you under. By the time you came round, I'd prepared a kinder version of events for you to take with you into your life. And you know what? You never questioned my version, not once. So that, Francesca, is the precious truth I've carried for you all these years and protected you from. Now, tell me, is that really what you want the world to remember your family for, now and for ever?'

His question was calm, almost matter of fact. He seemed drained of all emotion. Francesca didn't answer. For the first time since it happened, with absolute and brutal clarity, she was reliving every moment of her sister's tragedy.

'Jesus,' said David.

Mario sighed. 'Because, if you still want the truth to be known, I won't stand in your way. I thought I was doing the best for you back then, the best for us both, but maybe I got it wrong. I know it came between us. Just tell me what you want, 'Cesca. I'll still help you if I can.'

Francesca let out a sob. It was the first time he'd called her that since the horrors began. Suddenly she was afraid of losing him, not because she might not survive without him, but, on the contrary, because she was concerned for his survival in a world without her. 'But what will you do?' she asked.

'Oh, I can vanish easily, if I have a bit of warning. I'm sure you'll not grudge me that.' He smiled wearily. 'There's no need to worry about me.'

'And my mother?' She gestured towards Annette.

'Simona's death was closed and forgotten long ago. And as for the fraud, well – no one can touch her now. Just look at her. Don't you think she's suffered the torments of the damned every day since it happened?'

They all looked at the old woman who was muttering incoherently to herself and plucking at the neck of her embroidered bag. 'Oh, Mamma!' Francesca was torn between disgust and pity. 'Why did you do it?'

'Do what?' asked Annette. 'We were only lovers for a short time. He adored me – they all did – but I got rid of him before you came back.'

'What lover? Mamma. what are you talking about?'

'Mario,' said the old woman. 'He and I were—'

'Stop it, Annette,' said Mario sharply. 'You're making this up. Don't listen to her, Francesca.'

'Don't worry, I won't. God, what a crazy idea. As if you and she could possibly . . . She's just trying to shift the attention away from what she's done. Ugh.' For a moment Francesca thought she was going to be sick. 'You killed her, Mamma. It was your doing.'

'What's going on?' said the old woman, looking round in confusion. 'It's all that woman's fault, all of it. When she came before, I lost my baby girl, and now she's here and you're talking about leaving. It's all her doing. ' Suddenly she looked directly at Kate, her harsh voice stronger than Francesca had heard it in years. 'But you're not getting away with it a second time. Oh no. Not this time.'

'Mamma.' Francesca started to move towards her mother to reassure her that she'd still be cared for, no matter what.

Then she stopped.

And stared.

Her mother, her poor, confused old mother, had removed something from her embroidered bag. Something small and smooth and made of mother-of-pearl and ivory. She was holding it between her two hands. Hands like little claws covered in rings. Hands so frail she could barely lift a fork to her mouth, but now those hands were holding something level with the centre of her chest and pointing it directly at Kate. A gun.

Francesca recognized the gun. It had always been a kind of joke in the family, the elegant little lady's pistol with its mother-of-pearl inlay, which Annette had been given by Signora Bertoni senior when she first arrived in Italy. 'You never know who you can trust,' her mother-in-law was supposed to have told her. 'If you're travelling without your husband, you must always take this with you.' Where had she hidden it all this time? Why had Francesca not known about it?

Mario said with quiet authority, 'Annette, put that thing away right now.'

She ignored him. 'Kate Holland,' she said in her harsh old smoker's voice, 'you should've kept away. I warned you, didn't I? I warned you twice, but you never listened. And now you're going to pay the price. *Il prezzo*. Just like I did.'

'Mamma, no!'

The first shot sounded like a child's firework. Francesca saw Kate jerk backwards, her eyes widen with surprise as her hand flew up to her shoulder. Then, slowly, slowly, she began to fall. David was at her side in time to catch her. Gasping, she collapsed in his arms.

'The fucking bitch!' she panted. 'What the—'

Francesca's mother made a small tutting sound, as though displeased with her aim, and she held the gun more tightly, still pointing it towards Kate.

'Stop!' Francesca lunged forward, but Mario was ahead of her. His body was almost on top of Annette's when the second shot went off and he grunted and fell backwards, sliding awkwardly onto the polished marble floor. 'Mario!' Francesca fell on her knees beside him. She hesitated only for a moment before putting her arms round him and cradling him. He put his hand over hers, gripping it with all his strength. It was years since they'd held each other so close.

A small red flower had appeared on his chest, right over the heart. ''Cesca,' he began.

'Hush, now. It's all right. I'll take care of you.'

Kate was slumped in a dining chair, watching intently. Angelica and Dino were standing in the doorway, mesmerized by the scene, still awaiting orders. It was David who crossed the room and eased the little gun from Annette's hand, opened the cylinder and shook out the four remaining bullets, then flung it down in disgust.

Francesca was cradling Mario's head. His head suddenly lolled uselessly against her arm. 'Quick!' she shouted in sudden panic to all those people who were watching and doing nothing. 'Get help! Call a doctor! For God's sake, why don't you *do* something!'

Mario smiled up at her. His face had gone a strange bluish colour and his eyes were dull. He said, 'You forget, *mia cara*, I am a doctor.' Francesca's tears were spilling down on his face as he went on, quieter now, 'I always loved you, 'Cesca, only you. You know that, don't you?'

'Yes,' she said softly through her tears. 'Yes, Mario, my dearest heart. I've always known.'

'You were right – about the lie – it was wrong – it came between us – stopped us loving – thought it was best.' His voice was fading to a whisper. 'Sorry, 'Cesca. Forgive me.' The voice had faded to nothing.

She rocked him tenderly, tried to press the warmth of her body into his, feed him with her spirit, but he was dead before he had a chance to hear her absolution.

Later, when the ambulance came, and the police cars, men in uniform with oxygen and bandages and papers to be filled in, Kate and Francesca were sitting on a bench at the side of the house. Annette had been helped into a police car by the ever-smiling Dino – only this time his smile was a rictus of pain on his face. Francesca watched her mother's departure from a safe-distance; maybe one day she'd find it in her heart to feel compassion for the old woman, but not yet. Right now she was numb with horror.

The police car vanished behind the trees and the dust settled slowly. Flocks of black swifts were swooping round the tower, noisy as ever and completely unaffected by the dramas that had been played out below. Kate's arm was in a sling. Distant thunder was still rumbling through the white sky and a few random drops of rain were falling.

'They still want you to go to the hospital,' said Francesca. She was pale and drained, sitting limp as a rag doll on the bench.

'My shoulder's okay. It just aches a bit,' said Kate calmly. 'I'm staying here with you, just until things get settled.'

'Are you sure?'

'Yes. So long as you meant what you said about Dino going.'

'Of course he's going. And his mother. It *was* him shooting at you that night. He says my mother told him just to give you a fright, but he's such a bad shot . . . you could have been killed.' She shuddered. 'What about David?'

They looked across at him. He was talking to a policeman, gesturing with his arms.

Kate said, 'I think this has been more of a shock for him than for anyone. He never had any idea. But . . . well, he's sorry that he got it all so wrong. He says he wants to stay for a while as well, if that's okay by you. I think he wants to make up.'

Francesca looked at Kate carefully. She wondered whether David wanted to make up to Kate more than to her. She was glad for them, of course, that they still had the chance to put right the mistakes of the past. Whereas she and Mario . . .

She forced herself to say briskly, 'Of course he can stay. So long as he doesn't think I'm crazy.'

'No one thinks you're crazy any more.'

Francesca smiled. 'Thank you, Kate.'

'It's my pleasure.'

'Some pleasure.' They both began to laugh weakly, a kind of hysteria building up.

'What happens now?' asked Kate, pulling herself together. 'Do you think you'll lose the Fondazione? Will you be prosecuted for the fraud?'

'God only knows. All I know is that it will be happening to the real me. It still feels like a miracle.'

David was walking towards them, accompanied by a tubby man with a grandiose moustache and an anxious expression.

'Kate, I've tried to keep them away, but they keep asking questions. Do you mind?'

'Of course not,' said Francesca. She wondered how long it would be before David felt comfortable about speaking to her directly. She knew that she could wait, however long it took.

'Signora Bertoni.' The tubby policeman stabbed at his clipboard with the tip of his biro. 'I regret to trouble you but I'm afraid you've made a mistake here. I asked for your own name, not your sister's. See here, where it says . . .'

Francesca was instantly serious. Her heart was pounding. There was still time to go back to the old lies. Now that she had made her point, would it be better just to let matters rest? She thought of all the upheaval, the publicity, the danger for the Fondazione.

Kate gripped her by the hand.

She drew in a deep breath and came to a decision. 'Leave it as it is,' Francesca told him quietly. 'Tomorrow I will answer all your questions, but just for this evening, you'll have to take my word for it. My sister Simona died a long time ago. Believe me, *signore*, because it is very important to get the facts right in your report.' She hesitated, then said firmly, 'My name is Francesca Bertoni.'